It Ends with Knight

"Nena Knight can cover Orphan X's six o'clock any day! Stolen from her village in Ghana, Knight reinvents herself as an elite assassin capable of all orders of badassery. One of thrillerdom's rising stars, Yasmin Angoe paints Knight with nuance, strength, and grace. These books burn hot and read fast."

—Gregg Hurwitz, *New York Times* bestselling author of the Orphan X series

"*It Ends with Knight* finishes this trilogy every bit as heart pounding, soul-searching, and explosive as it started. Nena Knight now takes her place alongside crime fiction's most unforgettable heroines."

—Rachel Howzell Hall, *New York Times* bestselling author of *We Lie Here* and *These Toxic Things*

"Yasmin Angoe returns with both barrels blazing in *It Ends with Knight*. Nena Knight is such a well-crafted character, and Angoe's writing is an absolute joy. You need some pretty strong writer mojo to get readers to root for an assassin, and Angoe pulls it off. I truly hope *It Ends with Knight* is not the end of this wonderful series."

—Tracy Clark, bestselling author and winner of the Sue Grafton Memorial Award

They Come at Knight

"There's nothing ho hum about Nena Knight, the killer at the heart of Yasmin Angoe's *They Come at Knight* . . . In one blistering action scene after another, we get to see how good Nena is at what she does."
—*New York Times Book Review*

"A second round of action-packed, high-casualty intrigue for professional assassin Nena Knight. A lethal tale of an all-but-superhero whose author promises that 'in this story, there are no heroes.'"
—*Kirkus Reviews*

"This action-packed novel drives toward an explosive conclusion. Determined to survive devastating loss and mete out justice, Nena is a heroine readers will embrace."
—*Publishers Weekly*

Her Name Is Knight

"This stunning debut . . . deftly balances action, interpersonal relationships, issues of trauma, and profound human questions in an unforgettable novel."
—*Library Journal* (starred review)

"A parable of reclaiming personal and tribal identity by seizing power at all costs."
—*Kirkus Reviews*

"Angoe expertly builds tension by shifting between her lead's past and present lives. Thriller fans will cheer Aninyeh every step of the way."
—*Publishers Weekly*

"An action-packed thriller you can lose yourself in."

—*PopSugar*

"Memorable characters, drama, heart-pounding danger . . . this suspenseful novel has it all."

—*Woman's World*

"A crackerjack story with truly memorable characters. I can't wait to see what Yasmin Angoe comes up with next."

—David Baldacci, #1 *New York Times* bestselling author

"Yasmin Angoe's debut novel, *Her Name Is Knight*, is an amazing, action-packed international thriller full of suspense, danger, and even romance. It's like a *John Wick* prequel except John is a beautiful African woman with a particular set of skills."

—S. A. Cosby, *New York Times* bestselling author of *Razorblade Tears*

"It's hard to believe that *Her Name Is Knight* is Yasmin Angoe's debut novel. This dual-timeline story about a highly trained Miami-based assassin who learns to reclaim her power after having her entire life ripped from her as a teenager in Ghana is equal parts love story, social commentary, and action thriller. Nena Knight will stay with you long after you've read the last word, and this is a must-read for fans of Lee Child and S. A. Cosby. I found myself crying in one chapter and cheering in the next. I couldn't put it down!"

—Kellye Garrett, Anthony, Agatha, and Lefty Award–winning author

"This was a book I couldn't put down. Yasmin Angoe does a brilliant job of inviting you into a world of espionage and revenge while giving her characters depth and backstory that pull the reader in even more. This story has depth, excitement, and heartbreaking loss all intertwined into an awesome debut. The spy thriller genre has a new name to look out for!"

—Matthew Farrell, bestselling author of *Don't Ever Forget*

"This brave and profoundly gorgeous thriller takes readers to places they've never been, to challenges they've never faced, and to judgments that leave the strongest in tears. *Her Name Is Knight* is a stunning and important debut, and Yasmin Angoe is a fantastic new talent."

—Hank Phillippi Ryan, *USA Today* bestselling author of *Her Perfect Life*

"*Her Name Is Knight* is a roundhouse kick of a novel—intense, evocative, and loaded with character and international intrigue. Nena Knight is a protagonist for the ages and one readers will not soon forget. *Her Name Is Knight* isn't just thrills and action, either—the book lingers with you long after you've finished. More, please."

—Alex Segura, acclaimed author of *Star Wars Poe Dameron: Free Fall, Secret Identity,* and *Blackout*

IT
ENDS
WITH
KNIGHT

OTHER TITLES BY YASMIN ANGOE

They Come at Knight

Her Name Is Knight

IT
ENDS
WITH
KNIGHT

YASMIN ANGOE

Published by Thomas & Mercer, Seattle

www.apub.com

Amazon, the Amazon logo, and Thomas & Mercer are trademarks of Amazon.com, Inc., or its affiliates.

ISBN-13: 9781662508288 (hardcover)
ISBN-13: 9781662508295 (paperback)
ISBN-13: 9781662508301 (digital)

Front cover design by Regina Wamba
Back cover design by Ray Lundgren

Cover image: © Mikael Damkier, © yurok, © Diana Indiana, © Beauty Stock, © RESTOCK images / Shutterstock; © Nikol Bartzoka / Trunk Archive

Printed in the United States of America
First edition

To all of my family—by birth, the ones I found, and the ones who found me.

BEFORE

My first sanctioned American dispatch comes soon after I have settled into my new home in my quaint little neighborhood of Citrus Grove in Miami. Though my older sister, Elin, lives not too far away, in an exquisite high-rise condo in the upscale area of Coconut, and our parents would prefer I reside with her now that she and I have moved here from England, I prefer the simplicity of Citrus Grove and the people who make the place a home.

Some weeks prior, Witt, my mentor and the head of the Dispatch team of the African Tribal Council, sent me intel on a broker set to arrive in Charleston, South Carolina, of all locations. Charleston is apparently a place of great import and export, and the broker is no longer an asset to the family by whom he is employed. He is about to sell valuable assets of theirs to competitors, ones who are not within the Tribe, so Witt has received dispatch orders, and I am to execute them.

I land at Charleston International in the afternoon and take a shuttle to the French Quarter Inn, where the mark will stay. He is due to arrive later that evening, if my intel is correct (and it normally is), and my plan is to be in the lobby to find out what room he will be assigned when he arrives.

Charleston is reminiscent of New Orleans. It is small and quaint. I learn it is full of old slave plantations and was a bustling port for the slave trade. It even has a marketplace in the center of downtown where the slaves were sold to the highest bidder. Now the market has been transformed to an open-air flea market. I decide to stay on a bit longer after my mission to tour this city that has been around since the start of this country and holds so much history. I am from the world from which the enslaved who ended up here were stolen. I am from where their last memories of Africa were of the doors closing behind them, and to be in a place where so many of my fellow Africans ended up weighs heavily on my soul. I know what it means to be stolen, to be ripped from all you once knew. I know something of their pain, and their fear. I should like very much to walk the grounds of one of the plantations that surround this city, imagining what life used to be like for them. Of how they suffered. And of how I have suffered as well.

But first, the job I must complete.

The hotel is beautiful. I check in quickly, keeping my sunglasses on in my attempt to be as invisible as possible. I do not cause any fuss, not like the woman before me, who complains that her room doesn't have the best view of the city. She is obnoxious and loud, and dispatching her would be a bonus to the world. There is no reason to be rude to the people who work behind those desks. I am sure there is more money in one of my accounts than this woman has in all the world, this Bethany Davidson (her name and room number lock into my memory . . . for just in case), and yet I would never presume to think it gives me any right to mistreat or look down on others. What if I paid Bethany Davidson a visit later to remind her of such? Would that be so bad? She has caused quite a scene, and the concierge, a young Black girl with almond-shaped eyes glistening with water that threatens to fall as she endures the tirade, looks up at me like the weight of the world is on her shoulders. We are worlds apart, the girl and I, and yet we are unified in this moment of trauma, at being subjected to unprovoked harassment because of class. I do not cause any fuss, not like the White woman before me, who complains. Because of . . . whatever.

Her feelings are my own. When people treat you horribly, you wear it like a second skin. Never comes off and makes you question if you did something to deserve it in the first place. I offer the girl—Cynthia, her tag reads—kindness.

"I will take the room with the worst view," I say. I am not there for the view anyway.

Cynthia's eyes blink rapidly at me to rid themselves of their building tears.

"Ma'am?" Cynthia asks, trying to collect herself so she can continue providing the top-notch service that the French Quarter Inn is known for, or so their website tells me.

I break out into a grin. I am in character, and when in character, an occasional smile is required so that I am not off-putting. Being a Black woman who doesn't smile is something people seem to remember, as outrageous as it sounds. One shouldn't be forced to smile if not inclined to do so. But I want no one to remember me here, and for that to happen, I must assimilate as best I can.

Cynthia finally gets it and lets out a relieved laugh that actually moves me a bit. Making this young girl smile is a stark difference from the dark nature of my trip. And from that little bit of levity, I am upgraded to a suite even my sister Elin would find acceptable to her bougie nature. Better than Bethany's; I check her room later, as she showers, to lift the hundreds she has in her purse to gift to Cynthia—for her troubles, of course. Consider that my Robin Hood act of kindness for the year. I won't do that again.

When the mark arrives, I am in the lobby, sitting in one of the overstuffed chairs with a magazine and a cup of tea. I am close enough to hear the exchange at the counter and which room the mark will be in. He comes alone, as I knew he would. He is working in secret, so he will not want to let his employer know his whereabouts by traveling with his usual entourage.

It is not my intention to engage him. I want to make quick work of his demise so I can enjoy the rest of my mini vacation, as I have decided this to be.

"Where is a good bar around here?" the mark asks the new concierge at the counter. "I want to go get a drink."

"We have a bar on-site, sir, or we can bring a drink to your room?"

The mark shakes his glistening bald head. "No, I would like to go to a bar. See the sights a bit and grab some dinner before my meeting tomorrow." The concierge obliges, asking him what he is in the mood to eat.

"Seafood, I think," the mark says.

"Maybe try Hyman's. They are out of this world."

Hyman's it shall be.

———

I work alone, with neither Witt nor Elin in my ear providing overwatch as I run through my mission. There is no one to check in with, no team members to provide support or cover or to be my wingmen. Only me. It is both unsettling and exciting, and I wonder if this is what a baby bird feels like when it is ousted from the nest.

With my travel clothes changed to workout clothes—tight yoga pants, formfitting black hoodie, sneakers, hat, an earbud for my music, and honey-colored wig with hazel contacts—I am ready to take my run around the city. The mark should be dining at the same time.

The inn is on Church Street and the restaurant on Meeting. It is only a block and a half away, near the historic Charleston City Market, where the slaves were sold. While he gorges on surf and turf, drinks cognac, and flirts with the young college girls who work at the busy seafood restaurant, I get my exercise in and take the lay of the land.

The landscape of Charleston provides good cover. The buildings are densely packed and aged. There are plenty of alleyways and nooks and crannies to do what is needed without many eyes on you. I calculate any possible direction the mark may take. He will walk because he will want to take in the night air after so much eating and drinking. Plus, a two-minute cab ride back to the inn is just plain lazy.

I run, a form of exercise I do not particularly enjoy, and stop to stretch, checking for my mark. I can see him at his table signing the check and downing the last of his drink. I sit at the bench and stretch my legs some more. My music blares in my ear as I twist my neck left and right.

The mark says his goodbyes to the greeter and steps through the door the valet has opened for him into the cool night air. He rubs his hands together, checks his phone, then slips it back into the pocket of his pants. He turns right, away from me, and begins walking. He is taking the long way back to the hotel, probably wanting to see some sights before he heads in for the night. According to intel, he has a huge day tomorrow. One that will make him millions and cost the Tribe at least triple that in money, commodities, and respect.

He walks nearly out of my sight before I lift myself off the bench, stretch once more, and begin jogging slowly after him. His gait is unhurried, and he is well within my sight in a matter of seconds. There are people on the street—couples strolling hand in hand; giggling students from the College of Charleston, according to their hoodies; families on vacation, enjoying this fall evening. But the time is rather late, about ten o'clock, so the street isn't as busy as it was an hour ago.

We pass closed boutiques and other businesses. A horse and carriage strolls by with a couple snuggling in the passenger seat. We approach Market Street, passing a side street, and my pace hastens. I break into a light run so the soles of my feet do not alert the mark before I am ready. He slows at the dark alley, and I hesitate, thinking he is on to me.

My right hand slips into the wide front pouch of my hoodie, where my gun with attached silencer rests. The bass from a hip-hop song thumps in one ear, but not so loudly that I am not keenly aware of what goes on around me with my other ear, where there is no earbud.

My hand grips the gun, pushing it through until its barrel just barely clears the other side of the pocket. The mark slows to a stop. He makes a quick sweep of his surroundings but doesn't look behind him, where I still approach, but at a reduced pace.

I am just upon him, ready for the possibility that he has made me and will try to attack me from within the alley. I could stop and turn and take him down at the inn, but I like the inn and don't want any commotion there or with Cynthia, who has that cash I took for her. No added heat will be needed there when Bethany starts screaming about her money. I should have thought about that before I stole from the repugnant to give to the kind, my own decreed punishment for Bethany Davidson's misbehavior. With her, I am my own Council.

The mark steps into the alley, and just as I am about to pass it—to see if he awaits me, if I will have to engage or will have to abort, a failure—I hear him muttering, followed by light spatter. It is the sound of liquid hitting pavement. I hear a groan and realize with disdain that the mark is relieving himself. I swallow my disgust like a bad pill and push the barrel of my gun out farther from the pocket of my hoodie.

The hit will have to be precise because I am moving. I cannot stop, because if there are cameras I have missed—and there may be—I do not want them to see the jogging woman stop and pull out a gun. Maybe she can slow because she heard a noise that happened to be a business-man being assaulted, but she doesn't stop. What woman jogging alone would?

His back is to me. His legs are apart, and a steady stream of urine vacates him through a cloud of smokelike vapor in the cool air. He grumbles, groaning his pleasure at the release. That coupled with the liquor has dulled his senses. Perhaps because it is not in his nature to be aware of danger, not like his security would have been, he does not look around. Maybe because he, like Bethany, thinks he is so entitled and important that no one would dare screw with him. That is how the high and mighty typically are.

I switch my hands, deciding at the last moment to use the hand closest to him and the alley rather than shoot from the hoodie. I am not sure I can take a clean shot while moving, and I have to ensure he is dead. I fumble with the gun in my pocket and with my iPod, making it appear as if I am changing music.

My right hand tightens around the grip, and I slow down just enough that I can aim and shoot as I pass, catching a whiff of pungent odor as he finishes and shakes himself off. I quickly let off two to the back of his head—the kill window so short and with not a second to spare for an error—and clear the rest of the alley's opening, jogging at my same measured pace down the street. I slip the weapon back in the pocket, like any normal twenty-year-old would, before his body hits the ground in his puddle of urine. It is a good hit.

The next day I follow my plans to visit the hauntingly beautiful plantations that once boomed with cotton and tobacco. I stroll past merchant tables overflowing with handmade wares at the marketplace that was once the location of a burgeoning nightmare for people who look like me.

Though I did not come to America as the enslaved people did long ago, I know personally what it means to be one. The connection I feel in this place is humbling. I cannot help but think about the stolen who were sold on these streets I freely walk on now. I accept a handwoven flower crafted from straw from one of the young boys bobbing in and out of the mass of visitors. His eyes widen when I give him a twenty for his two-dollar flower.

This city is like me, with its old-world feel: the cobblestone paths and tight streets, the gnarled sprawling oak trees reaching toward the sea just beyond them, are all a facade masking an ugly history behind a beautiful, picturesque surface. Yes, this city is *exactly* like me.

I squint at the brilliant, hot sun. I stretch my arm up toward it and fan my fingers to block the rays hitting my eye. A young couple with their double stroller and two babies walks past. They smile and say good afternoon and ask me how I am doing. It takes me a moment to realize they are speaking to me. They would be different if they knew of the life I took last night. Charleston is very much like me. Its outsides perfectly confine the deadly monster within.

I mimic their smiles and regurgitate their greetings back to them. I remember Elin's notes and even compliment their little bald babies, though one has all its toes in its heavily drooling mouth, and that visual is most unappealing. Its sibling is more hygienically sound and stretches a hand to me. I nod at it, turn on my heel, and take my leave.

Then my phone vibrates in my back pocket. I pull it out to read a message I had been trepidatiously waiting for all day.

WITT: Well done on number one, E. I think you'll do just fine.

His words are Christmas, and the world of worry that I had failed him and wasted the countless hours he spent training me lifts off my shoulders. His words are confirmation of what I feared I could never achieve in Dispatch and in life . . . in my *after*.

That I, Nena Knight, once known as Aninyeh Asym of N'nkakuwe, will be just fine.

1

Nena Knight was not okay.

But right now, there was only the body.

His body.

The casket was all Nena stared at, knowing he was inside it. Her teacher. Her mentor. Her family.

Witt.

In there by her hand.

That night three months ago, standing at the bottom of the cliff as Witt—Nena's mentor and teacher, and someone she'd considered closer than family—waited for Nena to retire him, to deliver a death decree as the ultimate punishment for his betrayal of the Tribe. Of her father. And of her. No, Nena was not all right at all, and she wondered if she would be truly okay ever again.

She had meted out that punishment. Killed him. Forced yet again to kill someone she cared about. Every night, Nena thought about what she had done and about how she was put in this situation over and over again, the one where she had to take the lives of people she had trusted or cared about. She thought about how death had seemed to follow her wherever she went since she was young, only fourteen, and in her now extinct village of N'nkakuwe.

Nena drew in a deep breath, pulling herself out of the dark reverie she'd plunged into, and pulled her eyes up, catching the furtive glances of funeral goers as they studied her, curiosity and superstition in their eyes. When they saw she'd caught them, they'd avert their gazes, as if being in her line of vision would bring about their sudden deaths. Nena wasn't surprised by any of this. She often thought the same about herself—that she was cursed, a bringer of death, and not even loved ones were safe around her.

Since Nena had returned alone to the mayhem at the charity dinner in Ghana where her father, Noble, was nearly assassinated, she'd received nothing but that look—the one that accused her of killing their most trusted Tribe member, the one who'd ensured everyone's safety, who'd gone from foot soldier to head of Network operations and Dispatch and was the most loyal Tribe member there'd ever been.

In the end, Witt had not been loyal. And that was something none of these people attending his funeral, grieving him, looking at her like some pariah, would ever know. Because to tell them of the depths of Witt's betrayal would upend everything the Tribe believed. It would undermine the loyalty and trust they had built—that their most loyal member would turn on them and facilitate an insurrection.

"I am prepared to tell them," Nena had said when she'd told Noble what happened at the bottom of the cliff when Witt and his minion Mariam had revealed that they'd been working together to destabilize the Tribe and put in a new regime of mercenaries.

She and her father had sat side by side, just the two of them at the breakfast table in the hotel suite where they stayed under heavy guard after the dinner. Noble's arm nestled in a sling, a result of Mariam's attempt to assassinate him as he gave a speech. They were lucky the shot hadn't been more serious. It was a good thing Nena had come in time to distract the shooter. But still, with the high-caliber rifle used, Noble had been very lucky. So, maybe her juju wasn't bad all the time.

Noble had looked disheveled, nothing like the normally gregarious Tribe leader everyone expected to see. Since learning of Witt's betrayal, he'd become more subdued, more reticent. His closest friend and confidant had attempted to overthrow him and was dead.

"We can tell the Tribe what Witt has done. Perhaps they should know. Perhaps we shouldn't always protect them from the realities of what we do."

They could do that, tell everyone everything just to exonerate Nena. But to what avail? So, Nena said no. They should remain silent. They should say Witt was killed as they went after Mariam. They should lay him to rest as he'd want in his Rwandan tradition and keep his legacy intact, despite what he'd done. Because in the end, Witt's intentions for the Tribe had been pure—to ensure all its members were cared for—though his means to that end had not been. Nena could forgive him that. And Noble should as well.

"You know how people are. Superstitions and fear. And if you say nothing, they will spin their stories and cast you as the villain, or a witch, or whatever fairy-tale monster that scares them."

There are no heroes.

It was the last thing Nena had said when Mariam had accused her of trying to be one, before Nena put one in her head. There were plenty of villains. And whatever Witt had been in the end, Nena would never take from Witt what was rightfully his. His good name, or his legacy.

It was custom for the deceased to be held for an extended time while the family planned the funeral. Oftentimes, it was to get everyone who was abroad back in country so they could lay their loved one to rest. Witt didn't have any family that Nena knew of. He'd never spoken of children, a significant other, or siblings, or even of his upbringing. Nena had searched all over to make sure that what had happened with Goon's family—how they'd fallen through the cracks, and no one saw to them when Goon died—wouldn't happen to Witt's family. She had found no one. And so, Witt's funeral rested on the Knights' shoulders, which they took as a badge of honor, with Noble preparing and dressing the body for burial, as was custom. Witt had been their good friend, their family, despite how things had turned out in the end.

Nena focused on the casket and away from the accusatory or curious stares. On the regal traditional cloth spread over the smooth cherrywood in the small cemetery outside the Rwandan town of Witt's childhood as the pastor said his words. Witt's final rest would be where he began, though his village was likely vastly different than he'd remembered. Its name was one of the sparse pieces of personal history he'd shared.

"How could this have happened?" came a whispered question from two women in the row behind Nena.

Nena stiffened. Next to her, Elin sat, her face obscured behind huge black sunglasses and her mouth setting into a grim line. Nena was in tune with her sister's movements and moods. Her years of training had taught her how to study tells people didn't even know they had. And so Nena could sense the shift in Elin.

"Happened when trying to apprehend the person who tried to kill Noble Knight" was the second woman's response, which was not much of a whisper, either intentionally or not.

"Who's taking over for him?"

There was silence, but Nena could practically feel the second woman pointing at her back. It felt as sharp as a knife. Nena inched her hand toward Elin's arm, suspecting what would come next and needing to head it off before anything happened to ruin the ceremony. Nena's fingers curled around Elin's arm.

Woman One clucked her tongue. "Hmm," she said. "Wasn't she there, too, when he died?"

"Ennhh," the second affirmed.

Nena's squeeze came as Elin was about to turn and cut in on the conversation behind them, which was meant for Nena to hear, and give them a piece of her mind. Nena kept a firm hand, the gesture begging Elin to be still, remain silent, please. For her.

The fight bubbling up behind Elin's lips was not worth having on the day they bid Witt farewell and safe journey to his final place.

Not when there would be so many more on the horizon . . .

2

In the same year, Nena Knight had celebrated both a death and a life. Six months after they laid Witt to rest, life, Nena supposed, went on. At least she could get behind this particular life event: her nephew's extravagant outdooring, hosted by the Knights. It was a full-scale affair held in the lavish Leeds Castle in Kent. Go big or go bigger. The castle was decorated to the hilt and teemed with enough attendees to make up a small country gathered in celebration of the first grandson of Noble and Delphine Knight.

And for him, they were throwing an outdooring as only Ghanaian-born Delphine knew how. It was the official presentation, a naming ceremony or baptism, of the child, where a blessing would be received, his name would be offered to the world, and everyone could celebrate his little life and all he would come to be. It was a coming out, so to speak, for the child and parents after they'd stayed shuttered in the house for as long as the elders made them.

For Elin Knight, firstborn of Noble and Delphine, it had been six months before Delphine declared Asym would be old enough at eight months to be officially presented to the world. According to their mother, Asym was now strong enough to withstand any germs or ill will or bad juju anyone might have toward him or toward the adults in his family, which, of course, would affect him. Plus, the eight months allowed Delphine this one extravagance: to plan a party befitting not just a king but a Knight.

Nena swelled with pride and unbelievable love for this little brown, chunky boy who bore the name of her natural father, Michael Asym, and all the history of Nena's N'nkakuwean people. He was her brother Ofori's son, and that was a memory full of some sweet but a lot of sour. However, Asym also had Knight blood coursing through him. He was the grandson of a village chieftain and the High Council of the African Tribal Council. In their world, Michael Asym Knight was royalty, and the fierceness Nena felt to protect him and her sister, their legacies, and everyone in her circle knew no bounds.

Cortland Baxter, Nena's significant other, grasped Nena's hand as they walked slowly behind his daughter, Georgia, who, even at the ripe old age of nearly seventeen, twirled in her yellow-and-green gown made especially for her with the authentic African Kente cloth. She was a regal tribal princess, taking Nena back to the ceremonial days in N'nkakuwe. Her face tilted toward the tunnel of lights that enveloped the three of them as they made their way through the half-circle canopy of bulbs. They flickered in timed stages, in hues of green, blue, pink, purple. Georgia was in heaven, having never seen anything like this up close and personal.

She giggled and broke off to touch the sides of the shimmering tunnel, her fingers fanning out and trailing down. Her mood was a far cry from that of the temperamental or apathetic teen she could sometimes be—nothing seemed to impress her these days. Beyond the tunnel of lights, leading toward the castle where the party was in full force, lay a sprawling maze made up entirely of lights. Delphine and Noble had spared no expense. Now if only Asym was old enough to remember this glorious thing. Nena guessed pictures would have to do.

Cort gave Nena's hand a reassuring squeeze. She looked down at it, then at him, admiring how he looked in his tux and the swath of deep-yellow cloth draped over his shoulder and torso like a sash, complementing Georgia's dress. Nena's long flowing dress of the same coloring, made of African print, dazzled brightly with multicolored shapes dotted throughout.

The dress was a one-shoulder number with a knot tie at the top. The rest of the family also wore the same cloth in a variety of designs. Noble, like the chieftain he was, wore his cloth draped over his right shoulder and arm as well as a thick gold-and-diamond family-crested link chain beneath his jacket lapels.

Rich, colorful tribal cloths flown in from both Ghana and Senegal, the home countries of Delphine, Nena, and Noble. Exotic palms and greenery laced around golden-backed chairs and round tabletops adorned with fine pure-white linen and vibrantly colored exotic plants, crystalline vases filled with clear liquid and some sort of light that shone brilliantly from within. Ceilings covered in an intricate weave of sparkling lights. It was breathtaking.

Not to mention the seemingly endless table laden with every African delicacy one could think of, and some one might not. The smells of spiced stews like kontomire laden with roasted meats of goat and beef filled the air. The piles of fluffy white rice and boiled cocoyam. Pans of golden-fried ripe plantains, whole fried fish to go with kenkey and the pepper shito. Mounds of cakes and bofrot and meat pies, as well as English and American delicacies for those whose palates weren't ready for the level of spice Ghanaians delivered. If one could imagine it, the dish was there.

"The spread is like the United Nations," Cort joked when they first saw the rows of food.

Nena spied Keigel, her best friend and leader of the Miami gang who'd, interestingly enough, adopted her. Not usually having an occasion to be so formal, Keigel was dressed in a tux that showcased his bright and energetic character. He'd opted to have the jacket made entirely of the same yellow cloth, his hair tied back in a golden rope. He was busy taking selfies for his crew back home, chronicling his journey into how the other half lived, especially since his Miami folks didn't quite believe the wild adventures he'd had abroad with Nena and her family last year, when they'd spent Christmas in Ghana.

Keigel ceased his self-promulgation, grinned lasciviously at her as if they shared some little secret, and mouthed, "*Coming to America . . .*" He held up two fingers. "*Two.*"

Nena knew that was coming. And she knew she'd never hear the end of it either. The movie was Keigel's bible on Africa, apparently, and it wasn't a fight she felt worth having at this point.

This palatial estate was not their family home because Noble would *never* hold a party there, where people would be in their most sacred, intimate space, the place where they weren't the Knights of the Tribe but just a dad with bad jokes, a mom who couldn't cook, and two daughters . . . oh, and a grandkid. This venue still felt comfortable, even in its decadence, adorned in African regality.

Nena broke from Cort, making a beeline for Elin, who happily entertained a group of eligible bachelors. Their mother watched hawkishly from Noble's side, where he also held a group of very important people in rapture with his Tribe sales pitch. He was working on securing a big invite to a highly sought-after American summit of high-tech corporate owners. Delphine studied which of those men, any single man in the building, could be the right match for Elin.

Elin laughed loudly, lightly touching the arm of one of her potential suitors while holding the rest in dazzlement, as if she'd cast a spell on them. But when she noticed her younger sister had quietly approached and was standing unassumingly behind them, she became all-business, charging through the group midspeech, making them part like the Red Sea, and taking Nena's hand to lead her away.

"Thank you for the save, little sis."

Nena was midthirties and little nothing, but she'd always be so to Elin.

The group of men watched them leaving, the spell not yet dissipated.

"Didn't look like you were the one that needed saving."

Elin cackled. "Sis, you don't even know. Mum has decided I'm finding a husband tonight. Who the hell wants to settle down when Mum's had me on lockdown since the baby popped out?"

Truth. Traditional Ghanaian (and likely most African) beliefs were that no one outside the family and close, close extended family could see the baby until months in. And the mother was housebound for nearly as long. Such was the case that Elin Knight, head of financial for the Tribe, who would assume her father's position on the Council whenever he stepped down, was still victim to the old traditions and beliefs of her Ghanaian mother.

"Mum's just excited to be throwing a party after the year we've had."

"I'm just glad she's no longer making me walk around with cloth tied so tight around my stomach I couldn't breathe. Worse than shapewear. 'To get rid of the baby belly,' she says. Bollocks." Elin sucked her teeth.

It was mostly amusing to observe Elin and their mother going at it. Delphine chasing behind her eldest with this and that concoction for Elin to try. Elin begging Nena to deliver her from Delphine's motherly clutches.

"You're Dispatch," Elin had whispered on the phone during a particular moment of distress. "Abeg, rescue me from this crazy woman. Send a team!"

Nena did not. Opting, like their father, to remain happily out of that drama.

But despite all this beauty and its recall to their homeland of tradition and culture, Nena was well aware of the curious looks and hushed musings about where the Tribe was going, about how they'd enforce their laws with no one to helm Network operations and Dispatch. Who would train the teams? Recruit new members? Ensure the safety and stability of the Tribe?

Even after nearly a year since Witt had been gone, still they whispered and spun tales about how he had died. Who would be Witt's successor?

Her? Was *she* even ready?

She was not.

However, she would fake it until she made it, or until Noble found someone worthy of the task, because that was her mission. And ready or not, she accepted it.

3

She strode down the blue-and-white hospital corridor with purpose, AirPods tucked in her ears, bopping her head slightly to an imaginary beat for the four nurses dotting about the nurses' station. They were so engrossed in preparing for the start of what would be a busy day of recovery patients who'd undergone outpatient services, they barely looked up.

Still, she sent them an airy wave as she passed by their station, pushing her cart loaded with linens, blankets, socks with the rubberized soles, and cleaning supplies at the very bottom, just in case one happened to look up. They wouldn't. According to her maroon top and khakis, she was with Environmental Services and thus didn't warrant that much attention, especially at the start of the day.

Not getting any attention was just what she wanted.

Even though this was a solo job, she would never be alone. Network was always right there, an eye in the sky to provide cover when needed and a way out if trouble hit.

Nena remembered the one time when Network had not been there.

Couldn't think about that day now. There was a job to do, a dispatch to perform.

She counted off the rooms as she went by. First one was occupied, the tan curtain behind the glass sliding door pulled for patient privacy.

Second and third rooms not, their curtains open, ready to receive their next patients.

Through her comms, the Network operative provided an update. "The nurse has done her final check. Shouldn't be another for four hours, but the doctors will likely visit before that time is up."

Four-hour rounds, depending on how many recovering patients and how great the patient's need. There were only three right now, and it was still early, so the nurses would be in no hurry to get to their sleeping patients if all remained quiet, though they knew it wouldn't.

Four hours seemed like an eternity. If all was successful, she'd need only five minutes.

Nena ran through the plan: Leave cart on the outside of the room, right outside the sliding glass door, to obstruct anyone who attempted to come in. Get in. Go to the IV, where fluids and medicine were being dispensed. Operative confirms the mark's ID. Then Dispatch gives the go for the mark. Get out before the medication hits and the monitoring devices alert the nurses that something is amiss with their patient.

"Why housekeeping?" Nena was asked during the logistics meeting. "Why not go in as a nurse?"

"Because the nurses know the members of their team," Nena had responded. "They'll notice a new face."

"The simplest way is always the better way," Witt had once told Nena. She'd learned throughout the years that he was absolutely right. Simple lies were easy to remember. Simple planning was easiest to execute and left opportunity for modification, should any be needed.

There was pushback. "They might know housekeeping too."

"Less likely than a nurse. Plus, nurses are assigned specific patients. If a new one attempts to enter a patient's room they're not assigned to, it could raise suspicion. Housekeeping always has people coming and going."

Not for the first time, Nena wondered whether if Witt had said the cover was Environmental Services, his people—now her people, she supposed—would have questioned him as they'd just done her. Likely not. But she continued with her run-through as if they hadn't fazed her.

Environmental Services it was.

The cart slowed upon approaching the sliding glass door.

"The nurses are otherwise engaged," Network said.

"And the doctor?"

"Not in yet. Still early," Network said. "But be quick."

Five minutes was what Nena had planned for. In and out. No extra steps, no pauses.

She wheeled the cart until it was right outside the door and pulled the sliding glass door open enough to slip her body through, positioning the cart so it was in front of the door. A fail-safe in case one of the nurses, or someone else, decided to check the patient again, though the Network operative tracking the monitors would alert her to anyone coming near the room.

She closed the door behind her with a muted thud. Once inside, she made sure the curtain obscured any view from the outside. She assessed the room.

"Watch your time."

The mark's form was beneath the white knitted blankets and asleep. Hadn't noticed he was no longer alone, the narcotics the nurse had administered doing their job. The monitor reflected a jagged line of heartbeats, strong and steady. The IV bag was full. The blood pressure cuff made a suction sound as it took its readings. All would kick out to the nurses' station for the nurses to read there.

From her pocket, she pulled out the syringe and stepped to the man so she could see him clearly. He was snoring slightly, and she leaned over a bit to get his face fully in her line of vision.

"Confirming," Network said. One second later. "You're a go."

Only a second for facial recognition to confirm the face she peered down at was a match. The doctor who'd performed intolerable acts on his patients back home in Uganda. Who'd left a long string of traumatized victims in his wake from his disgusting deeds, forcing patients who couldn't afford his services to pay in ways that humiliated and degraded them, then absconding to New Jersey to live a comfortable life and tend to his own health needs—this one a gallbladder surgery—by doctors unlike him. If only he'd lived by the same Hippocratic oath to do no harm, hadn't left victims dead or scraping their lives back together, then perhaps the Tribe wouldn't have had to chase him across continents for his dispatch.

With one hand she flipped the cover from the needle's tip. With the other, she pulled back the blanket at his side, exposing his arm where the IV line was attached, tape wrapped around his elbow to hold it into place. She inserted the syringe's tip into the port of the catheter and pushed atropine into the open line to his vein.

She'd replaced the needle's top, pulled the blanket back exactly as she had found it, and was at the door when the monitor's beeps began accelerating. She pushed her cart out of the way and shut the door—careful to keep her face from the cameras she knew were there, just as she'd done when she arrived—and wheeled the cart around the other side of the U-shaped hall so she wouldn't double back past the side of the nurses' station she'd passed earlier.

Because she didn't need them remembering her now. They were too busy grouping at the monitor as it screeched wildly that one of their patients was in serious trouble. She heard the rushed, alarmed tone of the nurse calling for a doctor. She was already down the hall and heading toward the elevator doors, opened wide (thank you, Network), and was pressing *G* when she heard feet pounding away from her toward the mark's room as the blaring *beep, beep, beep, beep* became one long *beeeeeeeeeep*.

No stops. No slowdowns.

Indicating his heart had beat so furiously he'd gone into cardiac arrest, and they weren't going to be able to pull a crash cart around in time to charge his already taxed heart enough to start up again.

Next trip he'd be making was with Patient Transport. Right down to the morgue.

On her way out, she dropped the used syringe and the gloves she'd worn the entire time in a red hazardous-materials container, the irony of what she'd done with that syringe not lost on her.

The main doors of the hospital closed behind her as she—sans the wig, the nonprescription glasses, the maroon shirt, all discarded at various locations on her way down—turned right at the street corner, heading toward the bus stop per the plan.

She slipped her hands in the pockets of her khakis and said in a deceptively carefree voice, "That's all, folks."

4

It was amusing. Femi completed each job with a new sign-off to let them know the deed was done. Nena adjusted the skinny headset, watching the video feeds on multiple screens for the results of Femi's dispatch and listening to the doctors call the mark's TOD. She pulled the headset down a little when she felt a hand fall on her shoulder. One of Network's operatives congratulating Nena on conducting another successful job. She hadn't conducted anything, she wanted to say. All she'd done was sit back and watch. All Nena needed was a bowl of popcorn, extra butter.

Nena swallowed the melancholic pill at being on this end of a dispatch. She reminded herself to remain in the present and not think about how much she wanted to be the one in the hospital room instead of miles away in their Jersey satellite office.

Another successful job. It was said as if conducting dispatches successfully were an anomaly for her. Nena turned from the monitors to face the owner of the hand, Billy, a high-level Network operative who'd worked with Witt and Nena for many years and was still having trouble adjusting to the fact that Nena was here, overseeing jobs instead of being on them, and Witt was not.

Well, she missed Witt too.

Fact was, missing Witt was the reason Nena hadn't grabbed Billy's hand from her shoulder and twisted it until the bones in his wrist snapped. Missing Witt was the *only* reason she gave any of them a reprieve. How much longer a grace period she'd allow them, she wasn't sure. It had been a year since Witt died—three months since she had stepped into his role as head of Dispatch and Network. A year of dealing with the side comments, the side quips, the insults masked in niceties. Months of Billy talking down to her as if she were an idiot. Yeah, this had been just about long enough.

"You're becoming good at this director business," Billy said, patronizing her.

He drawled on, but Nena found his mohawk tapered cut and frosted ends more interesting than the man. Wasn't high. She wondered if it could be called a low hawk.

He surmised, "You must have studied Witt closely."

Talking like she was an underling was one thing. Insinuating that she ended up here due to a nefarious reason was entirely another. Plus, Billy was doing this in front of other Network personnel, a choice. Evers had been the one on tech and was currently closing out all their surveilled areas: the hospital, the street, transit, all the places they needed to see to conduct their mission.

For a second, Nena wished Elin were here for one of her cutting comebacks. Unlike Elin, Nena was never great at quips, often unable to think of something to say until later. When she was alone, she'd think of many things to say to Billy's arrogant face. It would be too late because the moment had passed.

All Nena did was stare at him with no words, keeping her face as unreadable as a blank page. Her capacity to wait was immense, and she stayed like that until the mohawk bobbed when Billy broke eye contact, clearing his throat. His outstretched hand hovered in the air between them, and when she didn't respond, he slowly retracted the offending hand until it was tucked safely behind his back.

Several more beats passed, his discomfort amplifying. She'd stay there all night if she had to because she wouldn't be the one to leave first.

Actually, she couldn't stay all night. Nena had a plane to catch. But to drive home her point, she just might have to miss it. Billy swallowed, shifting his weight to his other foot.

He cleared his throat. "Evers, we good there?"

Evers turned to him. "All good, Boss."

Nena sniffed. Goon, from her first team, used to call Witt "Boss," back when she'd been in training. Witt had hated the title, while Billy delighted in it.

Evers twisted around toward her, giving her a tiny nod. "Well done. Witt would agree." He said it low so only she could hear.

"And Femi?" Nena asked.

"Is on the bus heading toward the station. She'll take the train into the city."

Billy was known for his apathetic attitude toward his colleagues, and this was something that Sierra, Nena's former team member, had accused Nena of after their mission at General Konate's Kenyan outpost had failed. Sierra had said Nena didn't care enough about their six-person Dispatch team to even know their real names. Nena had known the names of every Dispatch team she led. She had cared for them in her way, but in the field, there was no room for sentiment, and Sierra couldn't understand that.

Always learning from past mistakes, Nena had abandoned the military code names they'd been using. She took a page from Sierra's book, had learned to know her people as people. In multimember jobs, they numbered off, the team lead being One, and so on. One-operative missions like this required no names at all, and in Nena's mind she called them what she would if they were here with her now.

That was Sierra's final lesson to Nena. Perhaps if Nena had been more thoughtful and treated her team more as people, individuals, rather than as robotic operatives, then Sierra wouldn't have felt she had no other recourse but to turn on the Tribe. And maybe Nena wouldn't have had to kill her.

Billy ran his hand over his collarbone, rubbing a red mark into his reddish-brown skin. Maybe he was allergic to the abrasive cologne of his that was stinking up the room. Nena forced her nose not to twitch, though she sensed a sneeze coming on. Billy coughed.

"Please put together current profiles of all active Dispatch members." She watched as his eyes widened.

"That's nearly a hundred."

His words were triggering, and Nena was suddenly months back, boots on the ground with her team, calling out instructions. Then calling for help. Then calling her team members' names as she heard their last moments of life, bullets and fire raining down on their heads like it was Armageddon. A horde of bloodthirsty militia led by a crazed general ahead of Nena's team with Network at their backs—

Not Network. Network hadn't been there. Network had been infiltrated, incapacitated. Network had gone dark, and Nena had lost her entire team, except Sierra, in that ambushed outpost mission.

Then, at Mariam's safehouse in Gabon, Sierra and a very much alive Alpha, who'd been Nena's former second-in-command and who Nena had watched die, revealed they were double agents and had formed an alliance with Mariam, the woman intent on destroying the Tribe because the Council decreed her brother Goon—from Nena's first team—be permanently retired. And then Nena learned about the part Witt played in the coup against the Tribe . . .

It was a long, sordid story. One Nena still didn't understand and wished she could forget, though she never would.

And she could never forget what it was like to be out there in the field, like Femi was now, enforcing edicts from the Council. Nena was here, fooling with the likes of Billy and some utterly ridiculous power play that only he had the game controller to because Nena didn't play any games.

Nena made the calculations in her mind. One hundred, less her team of six. *Ninety-four.*

"Ninety-four, to be exact," she replied.

"But you requested a data pull only a few months ago. Nothing's likely changed since then." His eyebrows creased, and aggravation flooded his face. "I'm sure there's a better use of my and an analyst's time than to pull data we just pulled for you not six months ago."

Billy glanced to Evers. Evers remained glued to the multiple screens before him. Tracking their operative on the ground. Or avoiding being drawn into whatever this was that Billy thought he was trying to do with Nena.

When would Billy learn? That was the talk around the proverbial watercooler.

Nena asked, "There have been missions since then, yes?"

"Of course there were," he stammered.

She leveled a gaze at him that would have made him combust where he stood if she'd had eyes like Superman. "Then put together current profiles of all ninety-four active Dispatch members."

His mouth dropped ever so slightly, hand back to rubbing his collarbone raw.

Then, she added, "You, Billy. Not a data analyst."

He stood there a couple of beats too long, staring at her with a face swirled in emotion. For Witt's second, he sure didn't hold his emotions well. He sure inserted his opinion too much. He sure thought himself better than she. And she knew why. It was because he was a man. And he thought this job was man's work. He thought wrong.

"You should get started on it," she said. "I expect the profiles delivered to me before end of day tomorrow."

He blustered, "But, but there's . . . that's a lot of . . ." He blew out a breath. "What if I can't pull them all together that fast?" It came out as a whine.

"You are Network," she said, turning her back on him, as the conversation was very much over. "Figure it out."

5

Only when Billy was gone did it feel like the operations room had air. Nena would have to do something about him, and soon.

Beside her, Evers worked his screens. "You did well. Witt would approve," he said without looking.

She bit her lip, inclining her head in thanks, though whether he saw it, she didn't know.

"Headed home."

"Roger that," Evers said, already deep into whatever was up next on his to-do list.

She made ready to leave, stopping suddenly when realization struck.

"Thank you, Evers," she said.

Maybe it was the tone of her voice or the way she was entirely focused on the young Network operative that made his agile fingers halt over the keyboard in midair. He pushed himself away from the desk with his palms, turning to give her his full attention. His eyes looked luminous behind his thick, wide-rimmed glasses. He couldn't have been more than in his early twenties and yet was so very serious about his computers and his work. This time awe replaced his typically dry personality.

"You're welcome, ma'am." It was as if he'd never been thanked before.

Nena flinched involuntarily. She didn't like the sound of that at all. "Nena," she said. "Please."

Evers might have fallen on the floor if he hadn't already been seated. "N-nena." As if he were committing a crime by addressing her so informally.

Nena headed through the doorway. The two of them might work out all right.

———

In the car on the way to the airport, Nena allowed herself to reflect on the events of earlier and wondered if she'd treated Billy poorly. Had she cut him down in front of his subordinate in her attempt to establish herself as the boss? Yes. But should she have done it? Would Witt had done the same? Or had she allowed Billy to get under her skin, letting her insecurity peek through her cracked armor?

Cut the bullshit, Nena, Elin would tell her. *His ass deserved it, and more.* Cort and her mother would agree, only much more nicely.

Noble would bellow, *Dissension in the ranks? Retire them!*

The thing was, retirement was what had gotten them all in this mess in the first place. Noble's death decree, spewed from a place of anger when it had no place. The decision had ignited a spark that fueled a raging fire in Witt. Noble's emotionally charged decision was the fissure of his and Witt's unbreakable brotherhood and loyalty. It was the beginning of Witt's end and ultimately his own retirement. One handled by Nena's unwilling hands.

Retirement was the final act for dereliction of duty to the Tribe.

Goon hadn't abandoned his duty. He had just needed to use the restroom during a mission, and that had put a teenage Nena in danger.

Witt's death had left an indelible mark on Noble and Nena—on the Tribe as a whole. Everything they thought they had known, they had not. With as much as Nena had been through, one would think she would be a pro at this. But deceit and betrayal never got easier, no matter how many times she faced them.

Facing deception and betrayal seemed to be Nena's lot in life.

Noble had made the wrong choice and not only lost a valuable Tribe member but had caused another to lose faith in him, and that loss of faith had cost them Nena's team, the lives of some Network operatives, and the lives of innocent bystanders during the attack in Gabon, where Nena had been taken captive. A discussion the two of them would have to have if she was going to continue to head up Dispatch.

Until someone else. Someone else, she prayed.

Witt's face materialized in her vision, wavering as if heat were rising from the ground. *You, Nena.*

Keigel would say she needed to stop blaming herself because everyone made their choices and had to live with them. *Or die because of them,* she thought grimly.

6

Though Nena arrived late from the airport that night, her night owl neighbor was still out on the porch of his house, three up from her own. Keigel was her closest confidant and right hand, and the abrasive Miami native had become a younger brother to her. Instantly, she felt settled in his normalcy. Nena pulled her Jeep into the garage, and the door closed behind her. She lingered in the seat a moment longer than usual, trying to decide what it was she wanted to do, what she was feeling she should begin with.

She'd battled conflicting feelings since she'd left Network's Jersey satellite office and flown back home, hating that no matter how hard she tried to brush off the judgments she'd been receiving from people like Billy or from some members of the Council and within the Tribe, she cared about what they thought, especially if it was that she was doing a poor job as pseudo–Dispatch director.

Nena decided she wasn't yet ready for the solitude of her home with only her thoughts to keep her company. Her thoughts were what she was trying to get away from. So, Nena left her Jeep; put her bags on the floor of her kitchen, where the garage door was located; made a stop by the hidden security vault in her office, which doubled as a guest room in her quaint two-bedroom abode; and went out the front door to walk the three houses up to Keigel's.

His crew wasn't watching the perimeter. Nena wasn't sure if that was a good idea or not, with Keigel pretty much running the trade on the streets of their side of the city. Even though Keigel took more of a back seat to any hands-on action, especially after establishing a successful and growing co-op with other heads of local gangs, he still had to remain vigilant. When Nena shared her thoughts, he shrugged her off like she was some nagging older sister. Perhaps she was, and from their history together, he should listen.

"Let me tell you what you need to stop doing," Keigel said, taking a slow inhale of his blunt.

As usual, Keigel offered Nena a toke, and as usual, Nena declined with a raised eyebrow and pursed lips that asked if he'd forgotten whom he was dealing with.

"My bad." He laughed out a thick waft of smoke, making her nose twitch. "One day you might surprise me and partake of God's green. It'll help you chill out."

Nena got comfortable in the plastic chair beside his. She doubted she could ever be that chill. "What is it that I need to stop doing?" There was a growing list of what Keigel thought Nena should stop doing.

"Doubting yourself about running both Dispatch and Network, and giving a shit about what those assholes think about you running it."

Yes, these were definitely items on the list. Nena leaned back, settling in.

"They're just jealous, you know. And worried about what changes you'll make, whether you'll call them on whatever shit they've been doing this last year or not."

"They don't say anything aloud. But I can sense they question why I'm there." She hesitated. "And how I got there."

"Which is why they're assholes. Look at who your family is," Keigel said. "I'm not trying to be funny or anything, but everyone already knew you were set to head up whatever you wanted, you and Elin. So now it's happened, earlier than everyone expected, but so what? Shit happens."

The *shit* with Witt wasn't supposed to happen.

"They liked Witt more." She hated that she sounded like a child, but the words slipped out before she'd had a chance to rein them in.

"I don't know that anyone can like a guy like Witt," Keigel joked. "Fear him, maybe."

I liked him. Nena's heart twisted.

"Real talk, that's how it is whenever a new order takes over. When your pops retires and Elin heads up High Council and half of the family biz, people will bitch about that too." He blew out a thick plume above them, and they watched it dissolve. "But you'll show them you know what you're doing, and you'll add your own flavor to it."

She looked down at her knees. Did she even have a flavor? Her flavor had always been to run missions, not head them.

"I had to do it when I took over the crew. I had to show them I deserved the top spot and that no one could fuck with me. You gotta do that too. It's a rite of passage." He said that proudly, his chest even puffing out a bit.

Nena shook her head.

She took a deep breath, deciding that Keigel was the only person she could be completely honest with about this. Cort was too straight and narrow. Noble had no tolerance for betrayal.

From her back pocket, she pulled out a rectangular object. It was an envelope, unopened and bent from her sitting on it. She handed it to Keigel, who mashed the rest of his blunt in the ashtray before flipping the envelope over in his hands to read the writing on the front of it.

Nena

He looked up at her curiously. "Love letter from Cort?"

She pulled a face. "Not from Cort. Not a love letter, either, I suppose."

Keigel's raised brow and impatient face. "Okay?"

"It came by courier many months ago, maybe a month or so after Witt's death."

Understanding dawned on Keigel, and he looked down at the envelope from Witt again with a mixture of reverence and foreboding. He glanced back up and saw she wore his same expression. Between them was nothing short of a bomb.

"Why haven't you opened it?"

For a lot of reasons. Fear of what was in there. Concern that the pages secured in that thick envelope held secrets she didn't want to know about. But most of all, trepidation that when she opened the envelope and read its contents, it would mean the final end of Witt. There would be nothing more. No anticipation that somehow, he was still alive, even though she'd shot him, and she was an expert shot.

"It's unfair, Keigel." She just needed to be out with it. "All of it. It's just . . . unfair." It was as if everything from the past couple of years that she'd bottled up inside was about to explode. She'd fought so hard to keep it under wraps, fought so she wouldn't crumble under the intense pressure and scrutiny and all the eyes watching, leaving her so very angry. All the things she'd been forced to do because of other people's choices. The lives that had been lost on her watch. It was not fair, and in this moment, Nena couldn't hold in her deepest feelings one second longer.

Silent tears as hot as lava slipped down her face, and she turned away a little, ashamed they'd come and that she was putting Keigel in the awkward position of seeing her like this.

"I'm sorry."

"Aw, girl, don't be," he said. "If anyone deserves to vent, it's you. You never say shit, and you've been through the most. You have a right to be pissed about everything."

She did, didn't she? And she was pissed. Very much so.

"I know what I do for a living, and I make no apologies for it. I know it all comes with the territory," she said. "But the betrayals . . . from my brother, from my own Dispatch team members—Alpha and Sierra . . . from Witt." Her voice came out strangled, and indeed, it felt like uttering Witt's name was cutting off her air. Fresh tears trickled down, which angered her even more.

"They forced me to do something I never imagined I would have to do in taking their lives. And now I question everyone's intentions— except yours, of course," she corrected when a hurt look marred Keigel's face. Then she froze, raising one eyebrow questioningly. "Right?"

Keigel's lips quirked, and his own eyebrow mimicked hers. He gave an exaggerated shrug, his response easing the momentary tension Nena's words had caused.

He indicated for her to continue.

"You sure?" She double-checked. "Shall I hold your hand to show you I care?"

He twisted his lips again, and he twirled a finger in the air to move it along.

"Because of them, I second-guess who's for real and who might be a snake beneath their smiles. They made me carry a weight I thought was finally lifting after Ofori. But that weight has since compounded with the deaths of three people I trusted with my life and the lives of my family and the future of the Tribe."

"I get it," Keigel said. He left it at that, knowing nothing else needed to be said. All Nena needed from him was to listen. Nothing could help Nena when she spoke the truth. He let her speak because it was truly the first time she'd done so, the first real sign of vulnerability she'd allowed him to see in the years he'd known her.

What Nena had given Keigel in this moment was a gift, something Nena wouldn't recognize she'd done. The man who'd become as much a brother as the ones she'd lost when she was a child.

After a while, Keigel circled back. "What about his letter?"

Thinking of Witt's letter was like a gut punch.

"Not ready to read what he has to say."

"Okay then." He handed it back to her, and she stuffed it in her pocket.

"One more thing."

She gave him a cautious look.

"Please don't add me to that kill list. I enjoy my life." He broke out into a grin, showing all his brilliant-white teeth. "A lot."

The sudden switch in topic, having to shift her mind from the intensity of a second ago to . . . now, left Nena momentarily stunned.

"What did I say?" he asked innocently as he watched her get up. "Too soon? Don't leave."

The eternal jokester. She appreciated Keigel's levity and his instinctual ability to tell when it was time to pull her back from the edge of the bottomless void of grief and guilt and anger that hung around Nena's neck like an anvil. She wasn't going to admit it to Keigel that night. And she wasn't going to tell him that even though she knew he was joking, hearing the words spoken out loud was a straight shot through her. There was no levity in that feeling.

Nena shook her head. It was too soon, but Keigel had meant well. She left her savior and tormentor with a single wave goodbye.

Only Keigel, she thought ruefully.

Because if anyone else had made a comment such as that . . .

7

Back in her sanctuary and alone with her thoughts, Nena let them all rush in. Why did her father have so much faith in her ability? What had she ever done to deserve his unflinching faith? Or her mother's? Or Elin's? Or even Georgia's and Keigel's? All of them saw something in Nena that she still had trouble seeing in herself. Despite all she'd done and who she'd become. In spite of surviving a past that could have—should have—destroyed her, Nena still doubted herself.

Nena nestled a cup of tea in her palm before heading to her office. Several items awaited her in her inbox, but she was looking for the profiles from Billy and the intel from Evers. She didn't allow herself any celebration that Billy had done what she'd asked without delay. He was probably fuming, and when he next heard from her, he might quit on the spot. She might not be thinking clearly herself if she actually went through with the plan already brewing, like the cup of tea she'd made, in her mind.

She held off on opening Billy's and Evers's messages. It had been several days since she'd last checked on her charge, and Nena wanted to make sure all was well. She accessed the dark web, never going through Network systems since she didn't want a trail that someone could pick up and disclose to anyone in the Tribe, least of all her father.

When she was in, Nena accessed the computer system of a Mali hospice in the main city using her false log-in credentials. If anyone checked, which they wouldn't because there were already too many patients and not enough time, they may have noticed several log-ons from a Nurse Victoria Ogembe. Nurse Ogembe saw multiple patients, ensuring their comfort before they journeyed on to their final resting place.

Victoria's job was to ensure their final days were spent in comfort and with everything they could possibly need. Victoria was real and not only an employee of Eternal Days Hospice of Mali but a paid employee of Nena's as well. Victoria had even had the pleasure of meeting Nena when Nena made a private trip in country once she'd eventually located the whereabouts of a Ms. Gladys Edeson after a months-long search.

Gladys was mostly incoherent, in the last throes of Alzheimer's, with failing lungs—an effect of years of working in a factory, inhaling carcinogens that ate away at her from the inside. She was a tiny woman with a pillow of white hair that Victoria made sure was always coiffed, as if Ms. Gladys would be receiving guests. She used to have guests more often. Her daughter frequented the hospice as often as she could, in between work travels. But in the last year, those visits had waned and then stopped entirely. The payments had stopped as well.

Gladys had been transferred from the luxury hospice to a state-run facility. One that was not able to provide the same level of care, not that they didn't try. Too many patients and too few resources and staff. Gladys was more bones with soft paper-like skin stretched over them. She slept mostly, thanks to the cocktail of medication that eased her pain and managed her illnesses.

The older woman had moments of lucidity, when her vacant eyes cleared and sharpened. She'd look around the nicely furnished room that Nena had had refurbished, along with funding upgrades to the whole facility. Gladys barely recognized the room Nena took care to make comfortable for her, especially making sure her bed faced the window so she could have the warming sunlight on her face. It was during one of those lucid moments that she called for her children. She found neither there, but she was not alone.

Gladys struggled to sit up in her bed and felt the back of it begin to rise on its own. She glanced around wildly, the bed's unwilled movement unnerving her, until her gaze landed on the woman clad in all black, observing her. In a blink, it seemed as if the woman she'd never seen before had materialized next to the hospital bed like a spirit, with remote in hand, pressing the button to elevate her to a sitting position.

The young stranger's voice was like a low wave, lapping against the shore, melodic and soothing. Sounded like a lovely girl, like her daughter, who'd been gone too long, and her son, who'd been gone even longer.

"Would you care for some water?" the woman in black asked.

Gladys nodded, thanking the stranger, accepting the cool cup of water she was offered. She took a couple of small sips, swallowing hard.

Her eyes roamed the room expectantly, dimming when she didn't find who she was looking for. "Have you seen my children? I am ready to go home now. I am feeling better."

Nena knew she wasn't better. Ms. Gladys would never get better. There was no more home. There were no more children. Not anymore.

"My boy and my girl?"

Nena patted the woman's delicate hand lightly, feeling the veins and bones beneath the papery skin. She thought about her own mother, in the final days, when her mama was ill. Nena wished she'd had the same chance as this to sit with her and hold her hand, but with Nena's mother there had been no notice. Sick one day, gone the next.

Nena watched the woman intently. Nena's mind held all the answers, which presented themselves, pressed on the backs of her lips. She would tell this woman what became of her children and how she had a hand in both ends, one purposeful, one not. But just as soon as the clarity had come upon Ms. Gladys, the cloud of confusion descended, and the woman's face smoothed from concerned to content.

"Marcel still needs to fix our window. It won't close well." Ms. Gladys blinked, her eyebrows bunching in a frown as she toggled the line of knowing and forgetting. "No, that's not right. Marcel is . . . I don't know what's happened to Marcel."

Nena looked away. This was how Ms. Gladys would leave the earth, never knowing what had happened to her son, what had happened to Goon. Perhaps that was for the best.

"Has Mariam returned yet? She's due any day now from her new job. Highly classified. From"—Ms. Gladys lowered her voice—"from the government. Like my Marcel. They are very important, my children."

Nena nodded in agreement. She wasn't going to say otherwise.

Ms. Gladys smiled, wide and happy, her face awash in a bliss Nena envied. To be left with only the good memories, and never know the bad, was a gift. Nena would hold back the curse.

"My Mariam and my Marcel. You three would get along very well. I'll introduce you when they come home from work. You are a good girl."

Ms. Gladys had fallen asleep after that, and Nena hadn't visited again, leaving instructions for Victoria to provide her everything she needed. Nena paid all her expenses and would pay for the burial when the time came, which wouldn't be much longer. It was the least Nena could do for Marcel . . . for Goon.

And even for Mariam, who died as the consequence of her brother's unjust retirement. Goon's death had poisoned and ultimately turned her in a domino effect of death, destruction, and revenge.

Had it not been for Noble's rash decision, made from emotions rather than from logic, things would have turned out differently.

Nena wouldn't be here alone and trying to upright all the fallen dominos.

She wouldn't have had to go to her secret locked drawer that held the Olay and Hugo Boss—memories of her first parents. Items she had nearly stolen, back when she was fifteen, one cold night from a small French convenience store before Delphine Knight stepped in like a lifeline, offering that fifteen-year-old girl a choice that would forever change the course of Nena's life.

She wouldn't have had to pull out the lightly wrinkled envelope that lay nestled between those two most cherished keepsakes.

And Nena wouldn't have in her possession Witt's final words, words that had been delivered much too soon.

8

The following day, Nena gripped her blade in one hand, the tip pointed down and behind her in a readied position. Her other palm was out, ready to deflect any assault coming in from her front. She made eye contact, her hips moving in sync as she crouched lower to the ground for balance and better leverage. Her eyes followed the motions of her adversary, calculating their next move.

The blade came at her from the angle opposite to the one she held. With her free hand she batted it away and lunged with hers, connecting the tip to the soft underside of her mark's jawline. They jerked their head back as it nearly connected, swiftly bringing their arm up and around Nena's weapon hand and twisting themselves into her so their back was to Nena to push her away.

She raised her knee, connecting it with their side in two hard jabs, and they instinctively curved their torso the opposite way to save their side, forgetting her knife was the bigger threat. She used her free hand to pull her second blade from its housing at her back and tapped the blade's tip on her mark's exposed neck; beneath their breastbone, where she'd find the heart; on their temple; on their stomach. Then, Nena released them.

Georgia wrenched away, spinning around to face Nena. She gritted her teeth. Her light-brown eyes, looking too much like her father's, flashed in frustration and annoyance. Little beads of sweat dotted her forehead as she panted loudly. She watched Nena, who studied her without the slightest indication that she had rolled out of bed, much less run a combat maneuver.

Wordlessly, Nena pulled herself up to her full height, slid the second rubber blade back in its temporary housing, and flexed the wrist Georgia had twisted when attempting to free the knife. Her wrist sent a sting of pain in protest. Nena was pleased Georgia had been forceful, had actually hurt her a bit. It meant the girl was learning. But . . . there had been too many mistakes. And Georgia was mad that Nena had shown her only a fraction of how many mistakes she had made in their role-play.

Georgia put her hand on her hip, not wanting to look at Nena. She focused her attention on the ceiling, her face hard and lips tightening into a thin line as background sounds of fists against punching bags and grunts from practice matches taking place in the ring filtered through the air. No one paid attention to the woman and the girl running through what looked like self-defense practice on the mats in the back room, which was reserved only for them.

Nena offered, "You're still learning." It was a feeling Nena knew very well, the same she'd had every time she missed a step during her own training or had to tap out because she couldn't overcome her opponent. It was a painful embarrassment she'd suffered over and over again until one day she wasn't the one stunned on the ground, wondering what misstep she'd made.

"We've been training forever."

"And we'll continue to do so," Nena said. "Forever. Training never ends. Plus, this is new to you, so relax."

Georgia gave Nena a little side-eye. "The pot calling the kettle."

Nena was still learning that dealing with teenagers was a whole other set of skills she had not yet mastered. She chose to ignore Georgia and refocus them on what mattered the most, which was getting this move down.

For months now, Nena and Georgia had been training at the nondescript gym that sometimes served as a local boxing ring in the warehouse section of the Miami port. They'd been going there since they'd first met, not long after Georgia was attacked by a rogue trio of local gang members, the Royal Flushes. That night, after Nena had taken care of the three—two down and one left to tell the tale—Nena had seen a need in Georgia she recognized in herself, a need to protect herself from bullies like the Flushes and Sasha, the girl who'd put gum in Georgia's hair at school and "mean girled" Georgia ever since. Since Nena didn't touch kids (not even to scare them a little like Georgia wanted), Georgia begged Nena to teach her hand-to-hand combat techniques, and Nena acquiesced, much to Cort's discomfort. She understood the importance of feeling safe and secure. But still, after months of lessons, Nena had to ask.

"Why do you still want to learn this? Do you really think you'll ever need it? Not with your father around." *Or me,* Nena wanted to add, but didn't.

Georgia offered a sullen look, drawing away from Nena in a manner indicating she wasn't cool with where their conversation might be headed.

"He wasn't around when those gang guys attacked me," Georgia returned, sounding defensive and betrayed, as if she thought Nena was no longer on her side. "You were. And he wasn't there when that guy Paul kidnapped me either."

Cort hadn't been there the night Georgia had been attacked outside of Jake's burger joint by the Royal Flushes. And Cort hadn't seen how swiftly Georgia used a technique Nena taught her to get away from Paul when he was holding a gun to her head. Cort seemed to sometimes forget that Georgia was the daughter of an ex-cop and district attorney. She needed the training more than Cort thought because cop kids were more apt to find themselves in situations where they'd have to protect or extricate themselves.

Nena couldn't give up the fight that easily. "Perhaps you're right, but things are different now. You don't have to learn this. You won't do as I do."

Or become as I have, Nena nearly added, but didn't. Nena wasn't ashamed of her line of work or the reasons why she did it. But she didn't want Georgia to have to face the same life-and-death choices Nena had been faced with.

Nena drilled down. "But why do you really want to learn?" It was important that whatever Georgia's reason, it wasn't because she underestimated the repercussions of what she knew.

Georgia's answer was a shrug. Nena disliked when she did that. Georgia needed to use her words.

"Why did you want to learn to fight?" Georgia asked.

Nena disliked answering a question with a question even more than sullen-teen shrugs of disinterest and passive-aggressiveness, but she answered anyway.

"My reasons differ from yours. My situation was different."

They stood in silence for longer than Nena cared to. When it looked like Georgia wasn't going to volunteer anything, Nena continued. "Before I began my training, my father asked what I wanted to do, what would make me feel better than how I had been feeling."

Georgia's disinterest morphed into the opposite, and she lifted her eyes up to meet Nena's.

"When I began training, I had survived situations that stripped me of my sense of self and safety. I felt powerless and untethered from reality."

"Like a balloon when someone accidentally lets one go."

Nena nodded. "Learning to do what I do was about survival. It was literal life or death for me."

"It's about survival for me too," Georgia said. "I have to learn to protect myself."

"You can do that without having to learn how to fight or handle weapons."

"I don't plan on using either." Georgia played with her toy knife. "I just like knowing it's there. For just in case something else pops off."

Nena scrutinized Georgia closely, trying to determine whether Georgia meant what she said or was trying to pull a fast one. "And when I'm teaching you these techniques that could kill someone, the responsibility lies solely on you. Heavy is the crown, Georgia, okay? You use what you learn wisely. And just because you know how to fight or handle a weapon doesn't mean you don't remain on guard and use your knowledge only in extreme cases and if there is no other recourse."

Georgia nodded, looking perplexed. "Sure, Nena."

Nena fell silent, considering Georgia, who busied herself with an imaginary stone or hole in the blue gym mat they'd been working on.

"Okay then. Tell me, what was your mistake?"

Georgia expelled an audible breath, dropping her shoulders in defeat or teen angst. Nena couldn't decide which. Likely both.

Georgia mumbled, "Turned my back."

Nena cocked her head. "What was that?" She couldn't stand the mumbling.

Georgia looked Nena firmly in the eye and said, "I turned my back and lost sight of the free hand. I made myself vulnerable."

"Your movements were also too slow," Nena added. "In hand to hand, close proximity like that, you cannot give your opponent a chance to think and recalibrate. You must remain on the offensive, your moves already precalculated and rapid fire, to unsettle and immobilize them."

"By immobilize you mean kill?"

Nena blinked. That's right. This wasn't Dispatch training, so while she absolutely meant kill, here was another story. "By immobilize I mean immobilize. You won't be killing." She emphasized the last point with a severe look. She didn't plan for Georgia to ever make it up to that level.

Georgia's smile was crooked. Flipping her own rubber blade and catching it, she looked as pleased with herself as if she'd been practicing, like it was the wild, wild West or something.

"You never know," she said.

Not if Nena had anything to do with it. Or Cort for that matter. It was bad enough that Cort thought Nena was going too deep with the training. He didn't think Georgia needed the type of training Nena had undergone, even though Georgia had said she wanted it. And, getting to the age where she'd soon be off to university and away from her father, Georgia was older than Nena had been when she started her training with Witt.

Nena's eyebrow quirked as she slid back into position. "Again."

9

ELIN: Video meet w/ D in 30

A meeting with their father now? Nena frowned, glancing at the clock panel reading 5:30 p.m. She'd had no alerts from Network that something had transpired. What was so important her father would call a meeting now?

NENA: Can it wait? Taking G home

ELIN: D says important. Run her home ltr.

They were already running more behind than she would have liked on a school night. Nena frowned as she glanced at the stoplight at the intersection, making sure it was still red. She checked Georgia in the passenger seat of Nena's Audi, where Georgia was too engrossed in some YouTube video on her phone, earbuds firmly in place, to notice.

What now? Nena thought. The Jersey mission had been only two days prior. This was supposed to be her downtime.

Nena let out a sharp breath, pressing down a little too hard on the gas when the light turned. She dropped her phone into the cup holder, pretending not to notice when Georgia looked up and then at her, startled by the sudden jolt. Georgia had been around Nena long enough. Her eyes quickly swept in front of them, to the side, and then behind before she finally returned facing forward and settled back in her seat. Nena wasn't sure if she was proud of the girl's attentiveness or ashamed that sweeping scenes was the seventeen-year-old's go-to.

"Can you let your father know we need to make a run to my flat, please? We'll be at yours a little later," Nena said, eyes on the road, doing her own sweep, but for traffic changes.

"Yep." She scrolled through a list of videos to watch next.

"Make sure you let him know." The girl didn't move. "Right now, Georgia."

Georgia shot her the annoyed-teenager look as she dramatically plucked one of the earbuds from her ear. The one that made Nena want to rethink that whole "don't hurt kids" rule she had. Georgia waved the phone in the air. "Doing it. See, here's the message right here." Her voice went up at the end, her mood going from zero to ten in half a second. It was enough to give Nena whiplash.

"Why are you so on edge, Georgia?" Nena asked, mystified. "Is something wrong?"

Could it have been their earlier training? Georgia had been laser focused on taking Nena down. And she'd been so angry with every little mistake she'd made, not realizing that reaching half Nena's level took months, if not years, to achieve.

Georgia shot her a look, one that held so many things Nena couldn't decipher in the quick seconds during which she could turn her eyes from the road. She thought she saw Georgia's eyes welling up, but the girl turned away too fast and popped her earbuds back in. The moment—if there had been one—was gone.

Nena deflated. She was failing miserably at this part of her life too. Couldn't lead Dispatch and Network well enough. Couldn't manage a kid. Nena had been the top team member during Dispatch missions. Her success rates—for kills, extractions, or securing assets or intel—were nothing to play with. She could surveil and plan a mission down to the millisecond, plus contingency plans. Had conducted and then led countless missions around the world, removing the corrupted within the Tribe's society. She'd been taken prisoner under fire and had still come out of it. She'd handled the depths of depravity and outmaneuvered high-class dignitaries.

And yet she just couldn't win with a moody teenager.

———

Keigel was out handling his own business, so Georgia was forced to post up in the backyard with a strong warning from Nena to not snoop around. That elicited a teeth-grinding eye roll, which Nena wisely opted not to address at the moment. She needed to get to the meeting, but she had every intention of correcting that disrespect at the next opportunity. Nena went into her office, closing the door behind her. The room was soundproof. The monitors were on so she could keep an eye on Georgia's movements while getting through this meeting about the most recent thing to go wrong in the Tribe's journey to African self-sufficiency.

Her dad was deciding which cigar he was about to partake in. Elin was saying her goodbyes to baby Asym as he squealed in the arms of his grandmother. Delphine and Noble were on babysitting duty while Elin was away in New York on business. Nena tried to imagine Noble changing diapers. She couldn't.

"Suppertime?" Nena asked as their father selected a cigar from his cedar box and closed its top.

"You know how Mum is with him. Anything he wants he gets. Even if it means he'll be off his schedule."

"True, there's really no use arguing with her," Nena agreed. She finally had to ask. "Dad, do you change his nappies?"

She held her breath. Elin raised an eyebrow, her reach for a dark wine bottle halted in midair.

"Are you mad, child? I didn't even change Elin's."

Elin held up her hand. "Please. Let's leave me out of it."

"It's a terrifying ordeal, really. Thank the Lord for your mother or else you'd have run bare." He cut the tip of his cigar and pulled out his gold lighter with *N. K.* emblazoned on it, one tip of the *N* and *K* making up two red-tipped tribal spears that, if extended, would cross one another in an *X*.

Elin poured her drink. "Let's not discuss my bum either."

"I'm just speaking facts, is all. Now, let's get on with it, shall we?"

He placed his cigar in the ashtray and read through the single sheet of paper, ready to get to the business at hand.

"Elin, this hotel you've convinced me the Tribe needs is your top priority. I want the sale and turnover from the previous owners to be quick and without any hiccups. Spare no expense to make this happen."

Nena caught Elin trying horribly to keep her lips from upturning. "Spare no expense" was rarely in Noble Knight's vocabulary.

"And Nena will have Network get the facility up to our security standards. Above them, actually."

There were no standards above theirs. The Tribe's security was of the highest level, from the companies that supplied the highest governments in the world.

Nena nodded, checking the clock. Cort returned home by six. Georgia had school the next day. The Baxters liked to have dinner together as much as possible, so Georgia couldn't be late for that.

Noble paused, back to reading his paper before setting it down. Now came the true topic. Nena could tell from the way her father's vibe became more serious and his tone graver. The hotel was fun talk. Now came the work.

"Tanzania," he told them.

Currently the top priority of the Tribe, though it had been something Elin and Noble had been working on along with acquiring the hotel in New York. Nena thought things had been going fairly smoothly, but from the grimness on Noble's face, there must have been a downturn.

"At first, brokering the deal between the miners and the government had been going well for the sale of tanzanite and structuring the mining reform," he began. "However, a local group—I don't want to call them a gang because they are not really—but they are run by a man named Judah—"

Nena repeated the name to herself, tucking it in as Noble continued.

"—who has been making negotiations difficult. He is spokesperson for the villagers."

Nena asked, "What kind of difficulties?"

"Ah, convincing the elders and miners not to sign. Demanding more aggressive mining reform and full disclosure between the Tanzanian government and the private buyers. It's not bad what he's asking. But I fear he's not well versed in the ways of business, and he may, unwittingly or not, cause more harm than good. Councilman Tegete is running point between the miners and the government. We'd have miners set to come to the table with what they want, and then they would back out because Judah says the deal's no good. Very small, annoying things."

"And now?" Elin asked, brushing a piece of flyaway hair from her face, her bracelets catching the light.

"Now more are opting out. Said they prefer Judah to speak for them because he knows how politicians work. Because Judah has grown up in the villages, has gone to university and returned to his village, he is their golden boy. But he is an idealist. He has many aspirations for his people of rural Tanzania and wants them to keep the rights and profits from the mines on their lands."

"Doesn't sound different than what the Tribe works toward." Nena took note of the incoming intel from Network.

Elin snickered. "He sounds like you, actually, Dad, back when you were young."

Elin was lucky they were miles apart. The glower their father gave her had less impact on the screen.

"Judah has the ear of the village chieftains, the people, and the attention of the government, be it good or bad. We need Judah fully on board, but he won't listen to anyone there. He trusts no one, so we need someone he can connect with." Noble's words dropped off, his silence loaded with meaning.

Nena straightened, registering her father's uncomfortableness, her dismay growing. A slow smile slid across her sister's face.

"No way," Elin whooped out loud. "Please, please tell me you're about to say what I hope you're about to say. I'll be totally chuffed. For real, mate, say it."

He wouldn't. They wouldn't expect Nena to . . .

"Dad," Nena said. "You don't mean for me to be a honeypot."

Her dad plucked at the computer, looking down at it from over his glasses, his focus on doing what anyone with basic knowledge of tech could do. Send attached files.

"Is what?" Noble frowned, his keystrokes paused. He peered at them in the video with narrowed eyes.

Elin was in full laughter now, a glass of merlot sloshing around precariously. Behind her New York was turning from dusk to dark.

"Oh, Dad, you know. You're sending Nena to seduce the mate and flip him to our side."

Nena shook her head in a silent plea, hoping her father understood and corrected himself, while Elin's smile only grew wider and wider as she enjoyed her uptight sister's discomfort. Immensely. The files populated Nena's screen, but she couldn't even look at them. She was frozen in place, praying her father wouldn't instruct her to do the thing she couldn't bear to do.

Elin sang, "Whatever would the good former DA Cortland Baxter think about that?" She batted her eyes.

Noble was taking way too long to answer. In fact, he seemed to be mulling it over, which only enhanced Nena's fear. Forget hostile teenagers. This was worse. Having to play at seduction was infinitely more terrifying. Nena would take twenty sullen Georgias ten times over.

"Hadn't thought of that," Noble mused, sounding like he was actually considering it. They'd both gone mad—both Elin and their father. Where was Delphine to bring sense into this mess?

After much too long, Noble said, "That's not what will get through to this man. He'd see through the ruse. I just need you to get a feel of him, see what he's about, ensure Councilman Tegete remains safe, and most of all, ensure those miners agree to the new mining reform the country is trying to create so they can finally have a process in place that doesn't take advantage of the people."

Seemed simple enough. Nena's body released the tension building between her shoulder blades.

"You know it's the Tribe's belief of a One Africa. When one eats, we all eat. We all succeed off the spoils of our land. Has Africa not sacrificed enough with centuries of theft, defilement, treachery, slavery, colonization? It is our time, am I wrong?"

He wasn't wrong. But what their father refused to see was that not every person from Africa believed this and that they'd need more work to get there. And what their father shouldn't do but continued to do was to take it personally. That was Noble's Achilles' heel.

His daughters remained silent, having heard variations of this speech since they were young.

When he paused for a breath, Nena tried redirecting them back to the matter at hand. "How do you want this Judah handled?" she asked. "Dispatch?"

He shook his head. "We're not there yet. I hope it doesn't come to that, if I'm being honest."

Nena and Elin both looked away at something more interesting in their respective rooms.

"What? I am not quick to dispatch," Noble said defensively, catching their response.

He wasn't. Anymore. However, there was one person whose dispatch had come without the same thought and consideration as all the others'. Nena wasn't going to bring that dispatch up now, even though she thought about it—and him—every day. Even though his sister had come after the Tribe for revenge, and Noble's most loyal friend, Witt, had been disenfranchised, and now Nena felt it her duty to care for Goon's mother in hospice as some sort of recompense.

Noble started over. "We are not there entirely for Judah. This deal is number one. And we have many players seeking to have their way with it. We are there to broker this deal between the miners in the villages and the government. We're there to ensure the miners get a better-than-fair deal under this new reform for the tanzanite and whatever else is mined on their lands and that they are well represented when the government deals with outside players, who are already eager to own these resources . . . as they have always historically done."

"Surveillance then?" Nena scanned the text from Evers informing her the intel was waiting in her inbox.

Noble nodded, stretching as he stood. He plucked his nearly forgotten cigar from the ashtray and scooped the lighter from the center table's top. "Yes, I think so. For now. I don't want to come in there and disrupt their order of things. Judah is the big man there, but for now just see what he's about. Ensure Councilman Tegete's efforts in his home country are not undermined. Surveillance with the option to intervene if it comes to it, but let's hope it doesn't."

Elin asked, "Who are they? The outside players you mentioned?"

Nena rifled through the intel, already coordinating logistics with Evers. She flipped through photos of the main players. Councilman Tegete she already knew. He'd always been so nice to her. Was the kindest, gentlest of them all. Then there was Prime Minister Samwell Asogi, who looked magnanimous enough. He had cheerful eyes and a gregarious smile that seemed welcoming. Didn't really mean much. Next was the minister of mining, Farida Odemba. She looked . . . formidable. Her photo was unsmiling, but Nena knew why. Whereas Asogi was a man and could afford to smile and look like the Black Santa Claus, Odemba was a woman, and many women in power were made to feel that smiling made them look soft and would undercut their authority. Judah was as Noble described. Serious, strong, unpretentious, and wearing a sports jersey. His expression was shrewd. He'd see behind any ruse.

Elin read off the profile. "Frances Dubin, from the great state of Montana, owner and CEO of DubiCorp, a private securities firm. Short stint in the marines. Was in Iraq and Afghanistan. Served in Desert Storm. Then had a private security firm that assisted the military when he left, and he became rich off that. Later he established Dubin Investments International when he married."

"Dubin and I go way back. Over twenty years and have been competitors for that amount of time. He's always hated the strides I've made in the industry. He's tried hard to make it so that the business world didn't take me seriously. Until they did."

Listening to Elin and their father, Nena was getting a bad feeling that her father really meant for her to take on a political-type role rather than surveillance. He wanted her to be in the room making deals happen, and that wasn't her. That had never been her; that was Elin. Nena vocalized the point.

"I think it's time, Nena," Elin said softly when Nena had finished. "Plus, there is Asym and the hotel. It's the perfect time for you to step in for me."

Nena wished they were meeting in person rather than on video so their father could feel how much of a mistake he was making in using her.

"Dad, come with. I can't compel people to sign deals. At least not in *that* way. I am the wrong one for this job."

Noble smiled, picked up his cigar, and relit it. "Which is precisely why you are the perfect one for this job."

10

Cortland Baxter stood in the driveway, arms crossed over his chest, as Nena and Georgia pulled up to the Baxter home. The look on his face said it all. They were an hour late—partially Georgia's fault because she'd wanted to nail the training exercise they'd been working on all afternoon. Nena turned the ignition off, but neither got out of the car, both watching him watch them with what Nena had learned was Cort's disapproving-dad look.

"You did text your dad to tell him we were running late, right?" Nena asked, wincing.

"I did."

Georgia pulled out her phone to show Nena. The message was still in the text box, unsent. Nena's shoulders sagged. The one thing Nena had asked Georgia to do.

"Georgia." Nena let out a soft groan, swallowing down her prickly agitation like the bitter pill it was. She flipped the phone in Georgia's hand so the girl could see. "Come on."

Georgia leaned in, studying the screen. Nena watched her eyes widen when realization hit. Her mouth dropped, mouthing a silent "Oh shit."

Oh shit was right.

"Get out."

Georgia stared at her, open mouthed. "Please don't leave me with him when he's like this."

Nena gawked at her. "He's your father."

Georgia gave Nena side-eye. "You've seen him pissed before." She opened the passenger side of the Audi and climbed out.

Nena sighed. She was tired of peopling in these last couple of days, and now there would be nothing but people she'd need to interact with when she left for Tanzania. Having this new kind of mission dropped on her shoulders was proving to be much more angst provoking by the passing moment, and now she'd have to face Cort's annoyance at their disregard for his rules and schedule. It was bad enough they'd been training, something Cort had a tepid attitude about, but now lateness had added insult to injury.

She'd gone to Georgia's school to pick her up to take her straight to the gym. Nena had promised they could train, and Nena liked to keep her promises to Georgia. She liked to keep her promises to Cort too. And the promise was that the training would not impede homework time and the new soccer schedule Georgia would now have after making the team. According to the clock, it was 7:00 p.m., which meant Nena was on the hook for this one.

Cort met Georgia halfway down the drive, with Nena hesitating at her car door.

The scene was reminiscent of that first night when Nena had returned Georgia home after the attack by the Royal Flushes. It was the first night Nena and Cortland Baxter had met face to face, and the moment Nena realized she was scheduled to dispatch the unsuspecting district attorney the following day.

She pushed away the memory. Clearly, she'd not followed through with the mission as planned, instead killing Attah Walrus, one of the very bad men from her past, who had been set to begin trial. The Tribe had nearly had an innocent man executed in the place of a vile one. But Nena had set all that to rights. Didn't stop Nena from the occasional guilt that raked her over hot coals. But if she'd followed through as the loyal Tribe member she'd always been, Cort wouldn't be here, and Georgia would be one more child without a father.

Nena knew they were in trouble. She joined Georgia and Cort where Georgia was rapidly explaining what had been more important than her father's lasagna. Nena could have kicked herself. Tonight was lasagna and movie night, and Nena had forgotten the tradition she and the Baxters had established since the first time they'd invited her to dinner.

Georgia was saying, "I nearly had it, Dad, and we couldn't leave yet because if we waited until the next training, it'd be like going back ten steps. Like, it's a sick move."

Cort's gaze shifted from his child to Nena. Words weren't needed to explain how he was feeling. "Training again," he said, his voice deep and weighty, "for homework, I hope."

Georgia blanched. "Homework?" She made a sound, waving off what she thought was a joke, but Nena knew was not. Georgia didn't seem to notice the silent conversation occurring between her two favorite adults or how they fell in step behind her, following her into the house.

"Sorry we're late for lasagna and movies. It's only seven. We can eat now. And you can pick the movie, since it's our fault."

"Lucky me," Cort muttered, stepping to the side so Nena could file in the front door after Georgia. He followed and closed the door after them, locking it. "You know the best time to have lasagna is right when the cheese is all melted and stringy when you cut into it. Now, it's overcooked."

"I prefer crispy lasagna," Nena said helpfully.

Georgia snickered, dropping her rucksack on the floor. Her dad looked pointedly at it, at her, then back at the bag again. As graceful as a ballerina, Georgia bent down and scooped it back up.

Cort said, "Before you take your bag to your room, I gotta tell you, the training thing you're doing, it's becoming too much. You have soccer now if you're trying to get in shape."

Getting in shape wasn't it at all. Nena watched as Georgia's wall shot up. This was not the first time the discussion had been had about Georgia learning how to fight. She saw the hostility building behind Georgia's eyes as she prepared to once again tell her dad why training was the only thing she wanted to do. And, from what Nena had observed during their earlier training, needed to do. Georgia wanted to be like her.

Only Nena didn't need her to say that to Cort. They were late. She'd been in New Jersey for three days, and he had clearly planned dinner and a movie for the three of them, which both she and Georgia had disregarded. That was their bad . . . her bad, because apparently, she was supposed to be the responsible adult. For the hundredth time, Nena wondered where the rule book for relationships and teenagers was.

Nena touched Cort's arm lightly. "We were on our way here, and I had to make a run home. I had a sudden meeting." She ignored how his eyes darkened when he heard she'd had a sudden meeting. He knew what that meant. His jaw worked under his skin.

"I apologize. I should have contacted you directly."

"I told you what I had planned for tonight," he said to Georgia, who merely shrugged a response in the annoying way teenagers do. "You were supposed to get you both here on time."

"Sorry, Dad. I wrote the text." Georgia shrugged again, not getting Cort's point. "I just forgot to send it. It's not like I totally blew you off. I really tried to let you know." She went high and defensive on that last part. The high part was what always grated on Nena.

There wasn't a book on how to combat irritating teenage behaviors. Nena was learning the hard way and second-guessing whatever maternal inclinations she'd had when she met Georgia.

"Maybe we need to lay off the training?" Cort suggested, pushing past Georgia's gawking and moving toward the kitchen with the two of them following behind, sharing the *here we go again* look.

"I saw your interim grades. Not good, Peach. You could be spending the time after school hitting the books instead of the sandbags."

"This is what makes me happy, Dad. I'm good at this."

"She is," Nena said. "It's just training. Exercise, if you think about it."

"It helps me," Georgia added. "Knowing how to do that stuff."

"Helps how?" Cort dropped a dish towel he'd picked up and faced them. "Where do you intend to use it? When? I mean, Peach, when you asked to learn that Krav stuff, I wasn't entirely cool with it, but I went along anyway." He shot a look at Nena, his demeanor screaming accusation. "You both promised it wouldn't affect school."

"It's *not* affecting school," Georgia cut in, rolling her eyes. "What's the big freaking deal anyway? God." She drew out the last syllables, emphasizing her increasing emotions. How quickly she could go from calm and quiet to turbulent never ceased to make Nena's head spin.

When Cort finally spoke, his words came out stiff, a warning underlying them. "How about you go wash up for the dinner that's now cold," he countered.

And crispy. Nena could barely keep up with them. This was why she should have just dropped Georgia off and gone home. She was tired of peopling. Cort was picking at them, though maybe he had a point; Nena wasn't sure. She'd have to think about it some more. Now Georgia was upset, first glowering at her father, then turning on her heel to stomp away in the manner only a sixteen-year-old would to emphasize that her father was now her least favorite person in the world.

When they were alone in the kitchen, Nena waited a beat, deciding on the best course of action. Whether she agreed with Cort or not, she couldn't very well invalidate his feelings, could she?

"I won't let her be late again," Nena said softly, approaching Cort from behind. She laid her cheek against his back, her arms circling his waist. "I'll also make sure she's not shirking her schoolwork to train with me. Don't be upset with her. She just really enjoys it."

He was stiff beneath her touch, agitated by Georgia's behavior, likely confused about how everything had gone from zero to a hundred in seconds.

"What is it about this training?" he asked. "Why is it so important to her?"

What was her role here? Did she back Georgia, who she believed had the right to learn what she wanted when it came to defending herself? Or did she agree with Cort, who had every right as a dad to want his daughter to focus on school and not this?

With foreboding, she asked, "What is your real concern?"

Cort let out another sigh. Then he pulled Nena's arms away so he could twist around to face her. He wrapped his arms around her, bringing her close.

"I don't know. Just don't want her to lose focus, is all."

Nena took in a deep inhale of the faint scents left from Cort's aftershave and deodorant. She could use her mother's Olay and father's Hugo Boss right about now. When she left, those would be the things she sought out the moment she made it home. Nena let out a slow breath, hating the words tumbling through her mind, hating how vulnerable she had felt today, watching Femi on her dispatch, dealing with Billy's insolence and insinuations, now worried that Cort's real concern was that he didn't want Georgia to be anything like her.

11

With only a day before the big trip, Nena was feeling unsettled, and that was putting it lightly. She didn't like this feeling, the uncertainty of what was to come when she was in country and of what she was to do. She felt like she was making it all up as she went along, and that was on top of trying to figure out the role she had now assumed at Dispatch.

She thought taking some quiet time in one of the few places that gave her peace—the backyard oasis she'd spent substantial time creating to be as tropical as her Ghanaian home used to be but with the flair that living in Miami could bring—would alleviate her anxiety. Even there, sitting in one of her lounge chairs, sipping a chilled glass of sweet tea she'd grown to enjoy (but not nearly as sweet as southerners told her it was supposed to be), Nena could not find any respite.

She was a person who needed structure and a definitive plan. She was one who did not like to act unless she knew the intel of the whole mission better than the back of her hand: the players, their histories and motivations, the intended outcome for the Tribe, what was at stake if things didn't come to fruition.

Nena knew some, but not nearly enough to guarantee her success. Granted, there had never been guarantees in her past missions. There were no guarantees in life (a lesson Nena had learned when she was even younger than fourteen and lost her mother when she'd suddenly taken ill and died) or in dispatches, but this new venture was different and way out of Nena's lane.

Plus, the constant stream of "helpful" texts from Elin with ideas of how to woo the Tanzanian prime minister and the locals in Latema, the small town that sat atop the latest and biggest find in decades of the rare tanzanite gem found only in the Manyara Region of northern Tanzania.

Investment companies from all over were clamoring to get the miners to sign away their rights, enticing honest villagers with more money and promises than they'd ever imagined for their lives. And because so many people had a rightful mistrust of their government, they weren't inclined to believe that this time, their government meant to put a formal structure in place to protect the villagers from underselling the value of their mined gems, from being taken advantage of, and from turning on one another.

This was the tumultuously repeated history of mining precious gems and resources in Africa. It was something the African Tribal Council had sought to put a stop to when they'd first come together to prevent the historical rape and pillage of African resources by outside factors that gave all advantages to the big businesses and not to the common person.

On the table next to the sweating glass of amber liquid, Nena's phone buzzed. She was instantly stressed, wondering what Elin could possibly add to her to-do list that she would likely opt out of doing.

The phone switched from buzzing to an incoming call just as Nena's hands touched it to check the message. Her father's name and number popped up in white on the black backdrop. Nena's finger hovered over the icon to accept as she debated which was worse, the endless *one more thing*s from Elin or whatever bomb (because those were all Noble dropped these days) her dad was about to drop on her.

"What took you so long to answer?" Noble asked, annoyed. The phone had barely rung. The span of time had been only seconds.

"Hi, Dad."

"Open the door. We should talk."

It was an in-person bomb. Nena's throat dried because rarely, if ever, did Noble make house calls. He most certainly wasn't keen on taking the drive from his lush home in one of the canal neighborhoods in Miami, so this had to be important. Another thought popped into Nena's mind. *And bad.* This was going to be bad.

Only, Nena could have never prepared herself for how bad.

Noble was at her front door as she opened it, wearing his typical suit, even though the temperature was in the humid nineties with the sun beating mercilessly on their heads. Noble, however, remained cool in it all with not even a trickle of sweat on his brow. Beyond him, parallel parked on the street in front of her house, was his usual blacked-out Escalade. His driver and two other guards surrounded it like he was the president come to visit. The fourth, Noble's personal guard, was beside him on the small porch, his hands folded in front of him, eyes hidden behind dark sunglasses. Another dark SUV with four guards sat idling behind Noble's.

If Keigel was home, Nena could expect some *Coming to America* reference on the horizon.

Noble dipped down to give Nena a light hug before stepping in. "Hello, my girl." He seemed to remember his manners now, greeting her. Or maybe he was softening her up for what he was about to detonate. Yes, likely that. And the hug was the icing on the cake. Nena acknowledged the guard, not bothering to ask if he wanted to come in. He wouldn't accept. He nodded back his acknowledgment. She gave a slight wave to the others at the vehicle, and they also nodded back, looking severe. And hot. Nena closed the door behind her father.

"Would you care for anything?"

"A cuppa would be nice."

Nena made a face. "It's like a hundred degrees, Dad."

He looked around her living room and the hall as if he'd never been there. She thought about it again. It had been over a year since he'd been over. Maybe two. Nena usually came to him because every other time he had complained her home was too small and not safe enough for a child of his.

"Have you forgotten where I come from? Africa is hot!" Noble announced grandly, gesturing. "This weather is nothing."

Nena rolled her eyes. It was easy to move from an air-conditioned vehicle to an air-conditioned home and make light of the sometimes stifling Miami weather, especially when a rainstorm was right upon them, which it looked like it was, and in the not-too-distant future.

Nonetheless, Nena quickly got her father his cup of hot tea, which she normally had at the ready; she enjoyed a cup several times a day. She found him in the backyard, beneath the vine-covered lattice pergola, in the chair she'd recently occupied. He looked out of place in his suit, sitting in a lounge chair sprinkled with bright tropical flowers. At least he undid the button of his jacket and removed it.

He thanked her, assessing his daughter as he took an appreciative sip. "Your mother is with Asym while Elin is conducting business for the hotel. Everything is a go."

Nena nodded. She could have met her father wherever he was, as was their norm. She didn't know why he needed to come here to give her updates on the plan. She told him so.

"Yes, well. I wanted to speak to you privately."

Nena frowned. As in, away from Elin and their mum? Noble never did that. The countdown *tick, tick, ticked* to detonation. Nena could practically see the hands moving above Noble's head.

"Did I do something wrong?"

His look was at first confused, then eased into understanding. He put the cup down and looked at his youngest with care and the fatherly love Nena had enjoyed for nearly eighteen years.

"Of course not," he said. "But I fear I may have."

It was Nena's turn to be confused. She had no idea what Noble could be talking about. She waited for him to finally say what he had come here for.

"The only way is to show you," he began.

Nena didn't like the tension building around his brow or the worried look in his eyes as he prepped her, urging her to open her closed laptop.

"You recall Frances Dubin, the American from Montana that I said I've known for many years. We had some business dealings maybe twenty, twenty-five years ago that didn't fare well for him. The man is only out for self-gain, which is why he should not partner with the Latema miners or sway them from the new mining standards by offering them something better he will never follow through with."

Nena nodded that he should continue when he paused to check if she was tracking. This information was nothing new to her.

"I haven't kept close tabs on Dubin. I find him reprehensible, and when you encounter him, he will likely treat you as if you're less-than because you are a woman, an African woman, and most of all my child. He won't like that I'm not there for him to have a row with."

Nena was used to people disregarding her because of the color of her skin or her gender. That was the world. Nena took pleasure in showing any naysayer, misogynist, or racist who she really was. She didn't waste time with words, and she had nothing to prove to them. She still didn't understand what the big deal was. This behavior, as unfortunate as it was, was nothing new.

Noble played with the gold wedding band on his hand. "Look at the file I sent you on the secure network."

Nena did as instructed, logging on and scrolling through the various photos of Dubin—blond, broad shouldered, and wide, like two whole men put together side by side, but muscular. He was nothing but muscle: a dominating force even through the photos. Nena bet there were very few times when anyone told him no.

"Why do we need the okay of Americans or anyone else in the West? We said we'd do it all ourselves."

"And we are, dear," her father replied, leaning back in his chair. "But no one does everything by themselves. Even our greatest advocates had to work with governments or whoever could help them further their cause. We're not selling ourselves out here, if that's what you think. But we know to get—how do the Americans say it?—something about getting more flies with honey than vinegar."

Noble continued to talk about the optics of securing this deal and reinforcing the proper mining practices to provide safety and security for the miners who should be the ones who gained the most. It was nervous talk, Nena could tell, and it unnerved her because Noble was never nervous.

"Soon, we will have lasting partnerships with tech industries who use resources mined throughout Africa for phones, automobiles, and other technology used around the world. I am nearly comfortable with attending the highly private summer retreat the big business owners attend every year. Before, I wanted the Tribe to do everything by ourselves, and I still do, but we need partnerships outside of ourselves. It's imperative we are seen as equals in this world—to those who call themselves First Worlders. We need to be involved in those conversations in addition to creating our own so that we may guide the paths of our destinies."

This was not new to her. Her father didn't need to justify anything to her. She continued scrolling through the intel. Most she'd seen when her dad initially informed them of the job.

He continued, but his words fell away as Nena landed on the last photo in the file. She zoomed in on the image, posted in a French news outlet, of Dubin and his wife laughing at a garden luncheon. His wife, beautiful and delicate standing by his side, gazing at him adoringly with eyes that Nena had barely thought of since she had embarked on her solitary mission of revenge against the men who killed her birth family and burned N'nkakuwe to the ground, Nena's mission ending when she had landed her killing blow at Paul's neck. Nena had dispatched everyone who'd played a hand in the dissolution of her first life.

Except one. She could have saved Nena but instead delivered her into the hands of pure evil.

Time reversed for Nena, though she fought to remain in the present. Her father had become silent, knowing what he'd brought to Nena's doorstep. It had been seventeen long, hard rebuilding years since Nena had seen this woman. Since the taxi door closed with her on one side and Nena on the doorstep, Robach's heavy hand on her shoulder.

The last living nightmare from Nena's *before*.

Bridget.

12

Nena's eyes flew from the screen, left Bridget grinning back at her as if she had not a care in the world, and looked to her father. Noble looked back, waiting for Nena to speak first. She couldn't. She didn't know what she was to say or how she was supposed to react. She could understand why he'd opted to bring this intel to her without Elin or Delphine around. He meant for Nena to continue on the mission he'd assigned, even though Nena would be confronting one of the key members of her past. Nena didn't know which was worse: that Noble was too afraid to just tell her and instead gave her pictures or that he was asking her to do a thing that was too much of an ask.

He picked up his tea, sipped to find it was too cool, and made a face, putting it back. He focused on her. "What are you thinking?"

"That I should like to kill her."

"But you cannot."

Nena knew he'd say that, but it grated on her nerves just the same. "Why?"

"You know why."

The deal. The reform. The bloody deal. Always the Tribe. Always everyone else. What about Nena?

Noble's voice was measured. "She is not a killer."

"She is a groomer," Nena said coldly. "The same, in my book. She is a liar and the worst kind of person because she knowingly provided aid to Paul and the rest."

Noble nodded. "She is. She was. She has done nothing else after. I have searched and searched. All she did was marry Dubin and become his French trophy wife."

Nena snorted. As if that absolved Bridget of what she'd been a part of in the past.

"Does her husband know of her former career? That she'd prep children for delivery to the people who bought them like animals?" Nena closed her eyes, rubbing them. "Dad, please. Let Elin do this if you want this woman to remain alive and well."

He scoffed. "I don't care about the woman. I only care that we don't jeopardize the reform and subsequent deal. Her sudden death could cause blowback that could negatively affect the Tribe. I only wanted you to know what you'll be facing when there."

Nena reopened her eyes, focusing them on her father, a new feeling bubbling up in her. Something she'd never felt toward him before. Her rage simmered just below the surface, about to boil over. She felt contempt and resentment for Noble Knight. And the feelings were alarming.

"What am I supposed to do with her?" She couldn't even say the name.

He said, "Ignore her. She is insignificant."

Easy for him to say. It was all Nena could do to not laugh in his face, so she unmasked herself, allowing her father to see her true feelings.

"I know . . . ," Noble tried, "what I'm asking is difficult."

He had no idea. "I will attempt to ignore her," Nena finally said.

"Mission first."

She gritted her teeth, feeling like a shaken bottle of soda about to blow its top if she didn't get away from this scene. Most of all, from her father.

"Mission first."

Noble took measure of the hands she hadn't known she'd balled into fists at her side, and how she was sitting ramrod straight and refusing to look at him. In this moment, Nena was his soldier, and she would treat him as such.

"Are you not the head of Dispatch?"

A fissure opened, a bit of Georgia's haughtiness cutting through. "So you keep telling me." Perhaps the teen was onto something. The response was deliciously satisfying.

He eased back slowly. His lips drew to a point as he actively and wisely chose to leave her rare display of insolence alone.

"I am sorry for this," Noble said, changing course. "I beg you to understand, it is only because of my utmost faith in you that I ask you to put aside your instinct to remove the woman from this world and keep the Tribe's interest first and foremost."

Wasn't that what Nena had always done? Wasn't the Tribe always first for her? Hadn't he seen what had happened with Paul, when the Tribe bought into Paul's cover, initiating him onto the Council, mere seats away from Noble's High Council, where Paul could have and nearly did destroy everything about the Tribe? For once, Nena needed him to choose her. And yet she would never ask it of him. She wouldn't ask it of herself because Nena was a loyal member of the Tribe. Full stop.

She looked away from her father until she could squirrel away these warring emotions. She missed Witt terribly. He wouldn't have done it this way. He wouldn't have put Nena in a situation where Bridget would be in her face, churning up feelings from before . . . when Nena was fourteen-year-old Aninyeh. Unlike for Noble, the mission wouldn't be about optics or business or politics for Witt, and so he wouldn't have his operative be around potential disaster. He would have chosen another, like Noble should have done.

Conversations like this—the handing down of assignments— were what had happened between Witt and her. Down the chain of command. Then the two of them would brainstorm next steps, strategy, and how best to conduct the mission. Now, a link in that chain had been removed, leaving only Noble and Nena to bridge the gap.

"Will you see to it?" Noble asked. There was only one answer he would accept.

She'd have to let it go. Despite the anger she was feeling toward Noble, he had been there for her in more ways than not. And he had made the journey here to speak with her directly. Even if it was only to tell her to not kill Bridget. Nena wasn't going to betray him or the Tribe. She'd just have to deal with Bridget and all the emotions that would come with being in her presence.

Nena nodded.

He patted her knee. His indication that their time had drawn to an end. He got up to leave, and Nena followed him back through the house. She walked her father and his guard to his car and accepted the awkward hug Noble gave her, and the one last bit of advice. Her body stiffened as his words sank in. He pulled away quickly, noting her change in temperature. His face was a canvas of shame and unspoken apology. She relished her father's discomfort.

As she watched her father drive off, Keigel was at his chain-link fence, his boys flanking his sides. All of them gawking at Noble's vehicles exiting their busy neighborhood as if they were spiriting away the president himself. Although in many circles, Noble was considered one.

Keigel's arm perched atop the fence as he whistled, so she could hear him from her location up the street.

Her friend called out, "That's still some *Coming to America* type of shit. I don't care what you say!"

He was as giddy as if it had been Barack Obama or, better yet, Eddie Murphy in the car. Noble had that effect on people. Though he and President Obama had entirely different styles.

And, yes, career paths.

She left them to their chatter, sending a single wave to acknowledge she'd heard them. She didn't stop to chat as she might have normally done. At the moment, Nena had to take another look at the intel and convince herself not to commit murder.

Nena performed a mental check of her list, ticking off her to-do items to ensure she wasn't missing anything and would have everything she'd need while in Tanzania. She'd be going wheels up on the Tribe's private jet late the next night with none other than Keigel to drop her off, upon his insistence. She found it endearing that Keigel wanted to see her off. She wished she could take him with her.

He'd been the first person she'd seen when she awoke in hospital after being held captive by Mariam at the safehouse and then her harrowing escape through the jungles of Gabon. Then, at the Tribe's charity event, when Mariam launched her final assault to take Noble down, Keigel had taken a bullet for Nena. For that she'd be forever grateful. He'd always be her number one. However, this particular mission Nena would have to go on alone.

In this short span of a week, after she'd received her latest mission, Nena's world had become too small and claustrophobic. It was seeing the image of Bridget, older but still very much the same woman who had sat back among the plush limo seats as the two of them bumped along the roads on the way to Accra, Nena thinking all the while that this woman was too nice, too soft to be anything like the monsters from the Compound or at the market, where rich people perused the girls Paul kidnapped like merchandise, after he'd let his guards defile them.

Ever since Nena had seen those images, Aninyeh had been fighting hard to come out and seek her vengeance again. Noble had ordered Nena not to go off course like she had done in the past when she spied Attah Walrus through the high-velocity scope of her sniper rifle.

Noble had implied that Nena should think before she acted. Laughable. Noble telling *her* not to act from emotion when *he* was the king of such behavior. Nena recalled Noble's last words before he was whisked away.

"I know you want to hurt her as she hurt you, but now is when you must be a leader," he'd said. "For heavy is the head that wears the crown."

It was the first time Nena felt the true grip of anger toward her father. Had he considered that when he decreed Goon's retirement? Or accepted Paul into the Tribe to make him a member of the Council without thorough vetting because Noble wanted Paul's deep political connections in Gabon? Had her father considered the weight, even now, when the blowback of his choices these past couple of years was not on Noble's head but on hers alone?

The crown, Nena thought bitterly, was heavier for some than it would ever be for others.

13

The following day, Nena had just returned home after a long run to chase out the effects of her father's visit and of the weird place she and Cort seemed to be in. She'd gone through the logistics report and reconfirmed the time she was to be at the private airstrip late that night.

NENA: Any tech you think you need make sure you have.

EVERS: Already on it.

She placed the secure phone on the dresser and went to shower while running down her mental list. Her mind whirred with all the things, but this felt like home to Nena. The checking and rechecking and checking once more to make sure every plan and contingency was down pat. And things would come up, and that would be okay. This was Nena's element. Being in the field and physically working. Not watching monitors and barking out orders. Not thinking about ghosts from the past or the guilt of lives taken or teen angst or boyfriend troubles.

Nena stopped. Was that what Cort was? A boyfriend? She just . . . couldn't right now.

When she reentered her bedroom, cleaned, lotioned, and halfway dressed, she checked her phone. One message stood out above the others.

GEORGIA: Meet at hm 911

With nothing else.

All Nena's earlier worries seemed insignificant as Nena merged onto the interstate. Hopefully, luck would be on her side and traffic would flow, but for Florida near lunchtime, that was a tall order. She must have gotten in at a good moment because the lanes were clear, and Nena was able to get down the road in record time. She didn't care if she was overreacting.

Nena didn't like not knowing what was going on. She'd sent three messages and received no response. Then Nena had sent Cort a message.

Nothing.

Nena's mind ran rampant with images of Georgia or any of the other students and faculty at her school hurt from an attack, or worse. Nena's world was one with violence and bad people, and the outcomes were to be expected, but everyone else outside of that world . . . Georgia? No.

———

Nena was sitting idle at the curb of the Baxter home when Cort's blue Chevelle pulled into the driveway. Nena could see the tension between Georgia and Cort from the way Cort gripped the steering wheel so tightly she was surprised he hadn't ripped it off and Georgia stared out her window, her body practically smashed against the door, like she wanted to be as far away from him as possible.

Georgia was out of the car in an instant, her rucksack swinging uncontrollably against her shoulder. She made a move to slam the car door, remembered whose child she was, then thought better of it, closing it firmly instead. Enough to make her anger clear. Cort had exited, cupping both his and Georgia's phones in his hand. Explained why Georgia hadn't replied to Nena's texts.

Nena looked from Georgia to Cort and back again, trying to assess what was going on but finding there wasn't enough information.

"What's happened?"

Nena scrutinized Georgia for injuries, seeing nothing more than a little mussed-up hair. Georgia, who looked like her world was ending, walked right to Nena and buried her face in Nena's chest. Taken aback, Nena slowly raised her arms to circle around Georgia's trembling body. She was saying something, but her words were muffled. Nena's eyes flew to Cort's, but he only looked back, stony faced and defiant.

Nena had never seen him this angry or Georgia this upset. Not even when the Flushes had her. Or when Paul had put a gun to her head. Nena pulled Georgia away from her body. The dam broke, and Georgia's large brown eyes filled with tears, which then cascaded down her cheeks.

"It's not fair! He always believes everyone else!" Georgia said. She turned to her dad. "You always want me to just take whatever those rich, elitist kids dish at me. Sasha started with me like she always does."

Sasha had a long history of coming after Georgia. Gum in her hair. Racist comments masked in wide, blue-eyed innocence. Classist comments about Georgia attending the private school on voucher and Cort being a lowly public servant while her own father sat on the judge's bench.

Nena had never seen Cort this angry. He was usually so restrained and thoughtful. "And yet she's the one with the broken nose." Cort stepped in closer so his voice wouldn't carry. "She broke a girl's nose, Nena. That's serious. Peach could have done worse if the PE teacher hadn't stepped in. So tell me, where the hell did she get those moves from, huh, Nena?"

Nena regarded him with cool eyes, creating silence between them to let his words settle in and take root. He didn't need a response. Instead, Cort sidestepped her and moved around to his side of the car. The words he didn't say told Nena at whose feet Cort lay the blame for Georgia's fight and her possible expulsion.

Hers.

Her mind went over every lesson she had imparted to Georgia about hand to hand. They hadn't even scratched the surface of training, with Nena always holding back and Georgia aware she was. The lessons were all light work, even the ones with weapons. Though Nena had to concede any of them were enough to inflict the damage Georgia had caused, and more.

The one thing Nena had imparted to Georgia, one of the key rules of combat that Witt had taught her, was to remain on the defensive, not to engage unless engaged. And now . . .

"Do you know if the cops had been called, you'd be the one arrested for assault?"

"Oh, now you want me arrested?"

He planted his feet on the ground, throwing his hands up. "Are you serious right now? I never said that."

"Didn't have to! It's all over your face. Your disappointment is always all over your fucking face!"

"That will be enough, Georgia." Nena cut through Cort's surprised inability to reply. His hurt evident in the way his shoulders drooped. Nena had been quietly following them, the three walking as if in a funeral procession.

Both Baxters looked around guiltily, realizing they weren't alone and that their argument was very much on display for the neighborhood to see and hear. Georgia's mouth snapped closed, fury and betrayal flashing in her eyes. She shook her head, tears trickling out.

Georgia said, entering the house with Cort and Nena following, "I thought you of all people would understand why I fought her and that it wasn't my fault. You don't know what she did."

Cort looked from Nena back to his daughter. "What did she do, Peach, that made you attack her?"

Georgia reared on him, her bag falling off her shoulder so she had to catch it in the crook of her arm before it hit the ground. "What do you care? You'll just say it doesn't justify fighting, even if it was self-defense. The girls in the bathroom told Principal Daniels that Sasha started it."

"How can I justify self-defense if you won't tell me all the facts, Peach?"

"Sometimes there isn't a justification! Sometimes there is only doing what you have to do!" The force with which Georgia yelled reverberated, hitting Nena from all angles. It was a feeling Nena found too familiar, more than she cared for. A feeling from which Nena's life had been sculpted, and Nena couldn't—wouldn't—fault Georgia for that.

The words took all wind from Georgia's sails, depleting her entirely. She cast one sorrowful look Nena's way before spinning on her heels, head of curls bouncing, and running to her room. Nena nearly ran after her, but Cort zeroed in on her, a storm gathering in his light-brown eyes, usually so loving.

Nena hesitated, debating whether to go after Georgia, leave, or deal with Cort. They all needed a cooling-off period and time away from each other to process and come back without saying hurtful things to one another. The continuous buzzing from the phone in Nena's rucksack reminded her of her departure later that night, but the shift in the room told her there were things she and Cort needed to say.

He closed the door behind her, placing his and Georgia's phones on the kitchen counter.

She held out a cautious hand. "Be careful, okay? You know I have a lot of things on my plate, as do you. And I try the best I can with Georgia, as do you. I don't need you blaming me for her fighting."

She rushed it all out in a whisper. Georgia was just down the hall, and neither of them wanted to disagree in front of her.

"I'd never blame you for what Peach chooses to do." He put his hand on his hip, raising an eyebrow at her. "I'm saying you gave her the tools to do it."

Nena could feel the tension building in her chest. Cort was being obtuse on purpose. "By showing her a few moves to defend herself?" They didn't need to talk about training with blades or teaching Georgia gun safety. "That wretched girl's been after her for years! Do you want Georgia afraid and feeling as if she can't protect herself? Did you forget what nearly happened at Jake's?"

"I want her to just be a kid, Nena! I want her to be *my* kid."

14

Nena rocked back, her body reflexively creating distance from the source of its pain as Cort's words ricocheted in her head.

My kid.

The idea that had swung over Nena's head like a guillotine and that she was sure she would one day hear from Cort—or even Elin, now that she had Asym—was always in the back of Nena's mind, keeping her from fully believing there were no barriers between her and those kids she loved as if they were her own.

My kid. And the unspoken second half that he didn't say. *Not yours.* They were as razor sharp as a bone-cutting saw.

Nena was reminded of her place, that she didn't have a claim on Georgia. Her reaction seemed to shock Cort back to his senses, and he ratcheted down.

He softened and started to reach out toward her, but when she shrank back, the hurt she felt too hot to the touch, he thought better of his actions and pulled his arm back down to his side.

"I'm sorry, Nena. That's not what I meant."

Her chin lifted. "I think you were very clear."

"What I meant was that Georgia is not you. She hasn't been through what you have, and so what she needs is not to learn to resort to those things when faced with conflict."

"So, you're saying I resort to 'those things' when faced with conflict? As if I merely act out off the cuff? What exactly is someone supposed to do when someone else attacks them? Roll over and take it? Call the authorities?"

This wasn't her, wasn't them. Usually, she'd keep this to herself. Here she was defending who she was to someone she thought understood why she had to be that way. Maybe she'd been wrong all this time. Maybe she and Cort had been fooling themselves into thinking this would ever work. Maybe Noble had been right to think that if Cort wasn't in their way of living, he'd never understand.

"Course not! But breaking that girl's nose was not defensive fighting. It was offense. Georgia went at her."

"Stop with the black-and-white nonsense." Nena had had enough of it. It was a hamster-wheel argument they would never get off and needed to be a topic they didn't discuss. "Georgia said that witnesses corroborated her story that Sasha started everything. You can't fault Georgia for finishing it."

"And what if Peach had opted to do worse?"

"But she didn't. And Georgia knows better. She has control, which I teach her. Yes. She was angry and went a little overboard." Nena would give him that, but she didn't think Georgia had done anything wrong.

"Contrary to what you think, Cortland, when Georgia and I run through moves, it's me teaching her not only to protect herself and be reactive to situations, but responsibility also comes with those teachings. We talk, understand? Maybe try doing that yourself once in a while, instead of handing down edicts. And stop acting like when you were a DA, you didn't have a line of enemies banging at your door. Even as a defense attorney now, your job doesn't come without its own issues."

She continued, "I'm not sorry that she defended herself. I am not happy with the fighting, and I doubt it will happen again. Georgia's not my child—no, you made it perfectly clear." Nena held up a hand when Cort opened his mouth to speak. He only had to say it once, and she'd never forget it.

A lump was forming in her throat, but Nena was determined not to let it take over.

"She is not my child, but I love her no less than if she had come from me. And all I have now and have learned, I happily give her, as I would a child who came from me. You should know my character well enough by now to know that I share nothing with her lightly. And perhaps I am the square peg trying to fit into your perfectly round hole of a life.

"Perhaps there's no place here for a person like me. I am still proud Georgia stood up for herself and of the degree to which she chose to handle her conflict."

Nena lifted her chin. "Now, if you don't mind, at some point, I'd like to see Georgia. Yeah? With your permission, since Georgia's your kid and all." She couldn't help it. Another Georgia-ism spewing from her. "Before I head out on my next job?"

Cort's flinch and the pained clench of his jaw sent a sliver of satisfaction through her that she refused to feel guilty about.

Cort ran a hand over his head. "Nena, please."

She stopped him with a headshake. "Enough has been said between you and me for the moment."

She waited defiantly. Willing herself to not look away, to show him how proud of herself, and Georgia, she was. Cort looked like he had plenty more to say. Looked like he had an apology waiting on his lips and like he wanted to wrap Nena up in his arms. Nena wanted that very much as well. But, for now, enough had been said between them.

15

Nena knocked and called through Georgia's closed door, "May I come in?"

Nena took the muffled response she heard as an affirmative and opened the door, glad it wasn't locked. Meant Georgia was open to conversation. On her full-size bed, Georgia lay on her back. She was staring at the ceiling, where crisscrossing white lights twinkled down at her. Large posters of Broadway shows like *Hamilton* and *The Lion King* mixed with endless K-pop bands papered the walls.

Nena watched her, thinking she should take Georgia to a show in New York one day. Georgia would love that. That is, if Nena and Cort were able to sort things out in the end. Nena pushed the thought away and took a spot on the floor against Georgia's bed, where Georgia's head flopped lazily over the edge as she gazed up at her stars.

"Try not to be too upset with your father."

Should Nena even be saying this when she didn't feel it herself? She forged on.

"He means well. He's trying to protect you."

Georgia scoffed. "Control me is more like it. He's overreacting with this whole training thing. Dad thinks just because I know how to fight, and maybe more—"

Georgia cut her eyes at Nena, who pretended not to notice.

"He thinks I'm gonna become a killer or something. If I was a son instead of a daughter, it would be different. He'd be cool. He'd probably be proud I 'manned up' or something."

Nena had to agree, though she wasn't going to say it out loud. But what did she know? She wasn't a parent. She'd just been playing at being one ever since she'd met the Baxters, and Cort had made that perfectly clear.

Was the maternal urge to protect a child that wasn't hers biologically beyond her reach? If so, what did that say about Noble and Delphine? Nena hadn't come from them biologically, and yet . . . who she was now did come from them. She was their child in every way that counted. As Georgia was hers.

"Your dad and I care for your safety and your future. I don't want you fighting and getting expelled from your school. You have one more year and then whatever you choose afterward. University, maybe. Whatever it is that you want."

Georgia whispered, "What if I wanted to be exactly like you? What's wrong with that?"

Nena had suspected this was coming for a while now, and she'd been thinking of how best to respond. She wondered if Georgia was testing her, trying to see if Nena would take her seriously. But the lilt in Georgia's tone, inquisitive and open, felt more like she was laying her deepest desires bare.

Nena could never crush her outright and break the news that Georgia would not be on the Dispatch team, as she'd been. Georgia didn't have to be on it, didn't need Dispatch as Nena had. Georgia was whole, whereas Nena, after thirty-something-odd years, still remained atop the wall, spackling herself back together again, like Humpty-Dumpty.

While Nena did not regret her choices and was proud of and loyal to Dispatch, there were some things Nena didn't want for Georgia.

Like ever having to choose between taking a life or saving one.

"Georgia, I don't mean to sound cliché or like fighting is power, but you know when you have great power, what it comes with?"

Georgia turned to face her, raising an eyebrow. "We're quoting lines from *Spider-Man* now?"

Nena breathed. *Spider-Man* had been the last movie playing when she left the marketplace back in Ghana after having been sold to the Frenchman Robach.

"It's the same for me. And now you, too, since you've learned moves that can be harmful if you use them incorrectly."

"Except I didn't use it incorrectly."

Nena gestured that Georgia should humor her. "What I'm saying is I'm teaching you what I know so you never experience what I went through." She thought for a second. "Did I ever tell you how I started doing what I do for my family?"

Georgia shook her head.

It had been a long while since Nena had thought about her *before*, but ever since Witt died, Nena had found herself thinking about a lot of things that went on *before*, and what they meant for her present. She used to believe that thinking about her past brought nothing but pain, and while it still felt horrible to dredge up the past, Nena was finding that sometimes knowing the past was what one needed to move on in the present.

"When I went to live with my parents—when my mum found me—they saw I was dealing with pretty intense trauma. They didn't know what I needed from them. And I really didn't know myself. They asked me what I wanted and needed in that moment."

Georgia rolled onto her stomach, propping her chin on her arms. The room was quiet.

"I told them that I wanted the ability to make myself safe. I wanted to learn how to protect myself and to keep others safe." Nena bit her bottom lip, thinking back. "But most of all, I wanted to walk around without fear." She looked at Georgia. "Because I was afraid all the time, Georgia. All the time."

Nena stopped looking at Georgia because looking elsewhere was easier as she got through this part. "What I grew to realize was that you can never live your life totally unafraid. You will know fear. But if I could teach you how to give yourself a fighting chance to never know the fear I knew, then I succeeded at the thing I told my parents I wanted all those years ago. That's why I teach you these things. That's why you're privy to so much that I do. You understand?"

Round eyed, Georgia nodded.

"But in knowing those things comes immense responsibility. You need to think steps ahead of your opposition. You need to think of the outcome. And your motivation for doing it. For pride? Or for life? Because those two things are different, and you need to determine if you're right or wrong in what you're doing. Just because you know how to break someone's nose, does it mean you should?"

She looked at Georgia, and Georgia looked away.

"Is that person equally matched to your skill? Would it be a fair fight? Or does that now make you the bully?"

Georgia didn't answer. She drilled holes into the floor with her eyes. After some more time, Nena asked softly, "Are you ready to tell me what happened?"

Georgia pulled herself to a sitting position on the bed. She swung her feet off and slid down beside Nena, drawing her knees up to her chest. Her hair was out in full glory, a mane of twisted-out loose waves that hung past her shoulders, tickling Nena's bare arm. Georgia began pulling at the threads stretched across the crater-size hole at the knee of her jeans.

The ball was now in Georgia's court. She sat stewing for a long while, playing with the threads of her jeans until she was ready to explain what happened. "She just made me so angry, Nena, and I'd finally had enough. There was a party I went to a little while ago.

"She invited me, and I stupidly thought she was trying to change. Even my bestie, Kit, thought maybe Sasha was gonna let this grudge go. But nope."

There were tears pooling in Georgia's eyes now, and it was alarming. Nena's instincts were on alert and telling her that something more was going on, and Georgia had never spoken of it.

"What did she do?" Nena said, her voice low.

"She tried to get me drunk and high at her party so she could take pictures of me and show them around school, I guess."

Nena fought hard to keep her face free of expression and her feelings reined in. It was harder in this moment than when she was on a mission. With bated breath she waited for Georgia to continue.

"There's a guy I like, and she used him to get me comfortable. She called a truce and said she was sorry for always being a bitch to me but that she's realized that voucher kids were just as good as the ones who could afford to go to our school."

Nena's fist clenched, and she wanted more than anything to pay a visit to that horrid Sasha and the boy and whoever else had played a hand in trying to embarrass Georgia. Now she understood why Georgia had broken her nose. One never knew what mistreatment did to a person and how they'd react.

"I knew what she said was bullshit."

Nena bristled at the curse, but held her tongue.

"That voucher comment was her throwing shade, but I didn't care. I was finally invited to a party and could finally just be a kid." Georgia's voice lowered. "I got drunk . . . and took one Molly."

Nena was thinking about drug and alcohol rehab. Was it too soon? Did Georgia need an intervention?

"I was pretty messed up," Georgia admitted. "But the guy I like didn't try anything. He was so sweet, and he kissed me. I kissed him back too. That was it."

Forget about Nena killing anyone. Cort would have this boy's head. "Sasha burst in the room and started recording on her phone, laughing and telling us to do more. The guy told her to stop, get out. And I realized that it was a setup. That Sasha had invited me to humiliate me. She was yelling about why we weren't fu—having sex yet. She thought she'd get me in that moment."

The threads over the knees snapped. "I was yelling at her and at the guy—"

"His name?"

Georgia's eyes narrowed. "Why, so you can pay him a visit? No way. Because he wasn't in on this. He thought Sasha was just setting us up because we liked each other. And he didn't make me drink or take the Molly."

He didn't stop you either, Nena thought.

"Anyway, Sasha's college boyfriend came in and took her out. She was loaded. And I was pissed because even though she didn't catch us in anything, she could have. I felt stupid that I fell for her fake plot. And violated that she'd do that to me. And I was angry. I'd never been so angry. I went to find her, to give her a taste of her own medicine. Not really, because videoing anyone is gross. But she wouldn't know it. I found her and her boyfriend, and they weren't just kissing. They were all in. And they were doing coke too. I had my phone out, but it wasn't on. And I told her if she didn't delete whatever she had, I'd make sure my dad showed hers the video. You know our dads know each other. He's a circuit court judge, and my dad's been in his courtroom. She tried to bluff, but her boyfriend made her erase it because he's, like, a sophomore in college, and she's not eighteen. And then I left."

"Not with the drunk boy whose name you won't reveal!"

Georgia finally cracked a smile. "No. I took an Uber."

Good, not the bus, which Georgia had an affinity for. A bus was how Nena and Georgia had first met. That and a few gang members who weren't around anymore. But that was another story.

Nena's tumult of emotions began to ramp down. Okay, okay. It seemed like Georgia had handled it. She hadn't called Nena for help that night. She didn't seem anything more than mad. Okay.

"You should have called me, if not your father. Even Elin would have helped."

"With a baby strapped to her chest and all? It wasn't a big deal, and I handled it. Or at least I thought I did that night. But today, she cornered me in the bathroom with a couple of her friends, demanding I give up the video. I told her I don't have it. That I never recorded anything and was just bluffing. She didn't believe me. And she slapped me. And it triggered me. I got so angry I snapped. And I unleashed on her. I guess for all the years of her bullshit."

A scratch was swelling up on Georgia's cheek, with a tiny bead of blood as a remnant. It was the best Sasha had been able to get in, Nena surmised. She hadn't been much of a match for Georgia at all. And though Nena wouldn't say it outright, she was quite pleased with these results—not that Sasha had a broken nose but that she was clearly more bark than bite. Nena had never believed Sasha, who was more interested in being a social media influencer and shopping at Balenciaga, could be a physical match for Georgia, even without Nena's training.

However, Sasha was still a force Georgia had to reckon with in other equally damaging ways—as a proud Black girl in a predominantly White school. As a middle-class single parent's child who's had to work in an environment of inheritance and elite families with parents who traveled weekly to exotic islands just because. Georgia had fought to find her place somewhere in that system, and Sasha had decided to be Georgia's daily reminder of why there was no place for Georgia there.

Cort had enrolled Georgia at the school when he served as a district attorney fighting RICO crimes and other like offenses. He'd thought she would be safe in that school as the daughter of a cop turned lawyer for the local government. Except he hadn't thought about the fact that rich kids with nothing to gain from behavior like this, except to bolster their own stunted egos, would prove to be more devastating in emotional ways.

For the three years they'd been schoolmates at the prestigious private school, Sasha had been the source of Georgia's grief. "She started it, and I only ended it. Maybe breaking her nose was a bit much. But I had a point to make."

Georgia had made her point and a good plastic surgeon could get Sasha's nose back to perky perfection.

"I'll never tell you to not defend yourself. You always should," Nena said. "But the degree to which you defend. That's part of your training, the thinking ahead. That you can gauge how far to go. That you don't let your emotions take over your actions. That you calculate your next moves. A balance. That night you acted with thought and got the girl to delete the video. You didn't do to her what she did to you, though you caught her in a compromising situation. I am proud of you, make no mistake. However, today, you were not thinking, and you could have killed her. There are degrees to what we mete out that we know they deserve. That is the responsibility we bear."

While Nena was speaking, Georgia's head was down, as if she'd been ashamed Nena was scolding her. It was the last thing Nena wanted to do, either, but today what happened with Georgia had scared Nena. Today, she realized how serious the decision to be so open with Georgia could be and how she had a responsibility to Georgia not only to protect her from the ills of the world but to sometimes protect Georgia even from her.

"Can I tell you one of my deepest worries, Georgia?" Nena asked so softly Georgia had to look up.

Georgia nodded, her eyes wide and full of fat tears that would soon spill. She looked all of five in that moment, and the only thing Nena wanted to do was hold her and let nothing else happen to her. But there was no way for Nena to prevent harm.

"My greatest fear is that I am failing you or making things harder for you and your father. Perhaps your lives would have less conflict in them if I wasn't around. Perhaps I am being selfish by remaining here."

The tables turned, and it was Georgia who threw herself fiercely into Nena's arms, the tears flowing now. Georgia hiccuped as a small cry eased out of her while Nena held her tightly, inhaling the shea-butter-and-essential-oils smell of Georgia's hair as Nena stroked her back and closed her eyes to the stinging behind them.

"Don't you dare, Nena," Georgia managed, her voice muffled as her face crushed into Nena's chest and her tears wet Nena's T-shirt. "If it wasn't for you, both me and my dad wouldn't be here. Like, literally wouldn't be here."

The door creaked open, and Nena looked up, catching Cort's eye and the apology in it.

"It's true," Cort said, his voice gruff. He pushed the door open wider and leaned against the doorframe, his eyes moving from his child to Nena. "We wouldn't be here, and we wouldn't—I am not better off without you." He cracked a wry smile. "I probably shouldn't forget that again."

He watched them, the anger and accusation replaced with what comforted Nena the most. The love and tenderness that was Cort's true self. The attentiveness and thoughtfulness. Those were what had made Nena eventually fall for the guy who shouldn't have been in her orbit. The guy on the other side of justice and who had the right to deliver it.

There was more that still needed to be ironed out between Nena and Cort, but now, the time was for Georgia. Because she needed them. Her father . . . *and* Nena too.

16

The private plane would be wheels up in twenty. Nena was already in her seat of choice. The farthest row, right in front of the tiny restroom, where she could observe everyone who entered and their goings-on. In front of her was her Network-issued laptop; on the screen were two windows, one with the profiles for all the Dispatch members, courtesy of Billy, her second, unless he continued acting up, in which case she'd make him number one hundred. The other window loaded with intel Network compiled for her. She pushed the top of her computer lower as the plane began to fill with the rest of its travelers.

Her new Network team. Or Dispatch? Some blend of the two?

Femi whistled a tune, waving lightly at Nena but paying more attention to the decked-out interior. She stood in the middle as if trying to decide on which plush leather seat, as soft as butter, she wanted to spend the next fourteen hours plus. There were only a handful, distanced enough from one another to ensure privacy, but they could still facilitate discussion if necessary.

"Evening," Femi said as she chose the opposite side, two rows up. She plopped her rucksack on the floor and stretched her limbs before removing her cargo jacket and tossing it in the seat across from hers. Twenty-three, only child of parents who owned a successful chain of international markets in Arizona (markets stocked using Tribe shipping) and first-generation Eritrean American. Femi had been about to join the marines when Witt had had her recruited, seduced by a world in which she was not under the watchful, overly protective gaze of her parents.

Their dream for her was to marry and have "plentiful children" (their words exactly, Femi had told Nena—twice). But Femi always was a stubborn child. She went to military school instead of going to a conventional school to get a degree in medicine . . . or accounting . . . or business . . . or whatever degree would get Femi a tangible biweekly-paying job until she found a suitable husband to provide the "plentiful children."

Long story short, the ebony-hued powerhouse of a woman with almond-shaped eyes and a pair of deep dimples that seemed cavernous when she smiled (and she did often) had her own plans for her life and cared not what her parents thought.

As long as she wasn't asking for money, Nena supposed her parents no longer cared either. Then Nena rethought that. If Nena knew nothing else, she knew African parents always cared, even when they claimed they didn't, and that nothing their children did was ever good enough. They always had "well-meaning" input to interject. Noble and Delphine Knight were no different.

Not long behind Femi was Everlasting Nevermind Chinoba, preferred name Evers, stumbling past the slightly annoyed flight attendant who'd attempted to relieve Evers of his bags, tech, and all the accompanying accoutrements. Nena lifted a hand to wave her off. If Evers felt he needed to carry all these items aboard, so be it.

Evers was first-gen Nigerian Canadian, twenty-eight and a Harvard and Yale grad. He was very methodical, liked order and structure. Like Nena, he tended to be literal and very serious, and she saw a lot of herself in him in that regard.

His tech prowess had shot him up to chief systems engineer in Dispatch, and he was the one Witt used when he managed all operations in whatever control room they happened to be in. Though his name was mighty, Evers was slight, mostly arms and legs, and adorable behind his rather thick glasses.

Evers had been found teaching a high school computer science class in a small South Carolinian town. All that schooling to be a high school teacher. If asked, Evers's response would be because he liked computer science . . . and sometimes kids. Nena was still trying to figure that one out.

"Nena," Femi said, "listen to this." She had begun grilling Evers the moment he arrived on the plane. She found him devastatingly interesting, and Nena wasn't sure if it was because Femi *liked him* liked him or because he was so razor focused on work, he was an enigma she wanted to solve.

Nena tore her eyes from the last entry, William Thom, a.k.a. Billy, South African and thought he was God's gift to everyone, including God himself.

Femi waggled her eyebrows, playing with one of her honey-blonde braids. "Evers has a sister."

Of which Nena was aware, but she merely nodded for Femi to continue.

"Ask him what her name is." Femi grinned. If she thought about it, she'd realize Nena would know the name of Evers's sister. But Nena realized this was one of those moments when socialization was supposed to be happening, and people wanted to feel at ease.

Both Keigel and Elin had reminded her to follow people's lead and not be so one-track minded about work. Sierra had alluded to that once upon a time, too, but Nena didn't want to think about that. If Nena had to have one regret, her death would be it.

"Sometimes, things are meant to be funny, girl," Keigel had said on one particular occasion. "You can't *wah, wah, wah* folks all the time when they're trying to lighten the mood!"

Nena wanted this new team to be different from the last. And because they were relatively new to each other, and she was definitely new to them in this capacity, she wanted them all to get along and trust one another. And that meant not *wah, wah, wah*ing folks.

Nena trained her attention on Evers, who'd finally gotten himself situated in the row directly across from hers. She didn't mind Evers's intensity. His razor focus reminded her very much of her older brother, Josiah, the younger twin to Wisdom. She bit back the sharp pang from the memory of the last moments of his life and of his smile.

Nena asked, "Evers, what is your sister's name?"

Evers furrowed his eyebrows, knowing where this line of dialogue normally went. But rarely did he not indulge.

"Eternal Destiny Chinoba, though she'll be Marshall when she marries in three months. He's an American. He's blond and a professional surfer from Los Angeles. We shall see how that goes because Etee—that's what we call her—is not fond of too much salt water. She does hair for celebrities."

Femi smacked her hands together gleefully. "That's amazing! What were your parents thinking when they named you?"

Evers looked at her. "What were yours?"

Femi blinked twice, rapidly, processing that his was a serious question, and he was not trying to be cheeky with her.

"That will teach you to be nosy and talk about things you're unfamiliar with," Billy threw in from his seat at the front, farthest from Nena, but still able to see her and glare her down when he needed to.

"As first-gen, you should know that all cultural names have meaning, and many countries choose names that they believe fit the personality of the child," Billy finished. Two large diamond studs sparkled from his earlobes, like he was some musician about to head to a concert and the rest of them merely his entourage. The earrings were too big for his teeny-tiny ears and were probably why he always needed Nena to repeat her directives to him. He couldn't hear because they blocked the reception, like some bad tower signal. A bad tower signal with teeny-tiny ears.

Nena couldn't help the petty thought. Why did she always have to have someone like this as a member of the team?

"So why Nevermind?" Femi asked Evers, ignoring Billy. She knew who the real boss was, and Billy was a nonfactor to her.

He pushed his glasses up with an index finger. "My father says it was because after Etee, he couldn't think of more personalities for me, so he was like 'eh, forget it,'" Evers told them. "My mum tries to say he jests, but if you knew my father, you'd know he was serious."

Even Billy wasn't immune to the hilarity of Evers's response, letting out a snort. And Nena, despite her attempt to remain professional, tried to mask the laugh bubbling up her throat with a cough.

"Now that everyone's settled," Nena said, "time to talk business, yeah?"

She ignored the way Billy's mouth tightened into a disapproving line. He had questions, she was sure of it. She'd even entertain them for a moment because likely Femi and Evers wondered as well but weren't rude enough to question her authority.

After all that had transpired, she wouldn't put anything past anyone again. Anyone, Nena had learned in the hardest of ways (as if she hadn't had enough learning to last several lifetimes), could betray another. But she wouldn't let the errors of others be a hindrance to this new small team of four with room, one day, for more.

17

When the plane was in the air and well on its way, they accessed their electronics using the plane's Wi-Fi, and Nena instructed the team to open the file Evers had created and sent to them. He pulled it up on the big screen at the front wall of the plane as well. The flight attendant closed the door to their cabin for privacy as they conducted their meeting while she put together the in-flight refreshments.

Nena began, "On screen is Judah Wasira of Latema, a village in the Manyara Region of northern Tanzania and close to the Merelani Hills. He speaks for them, liaising between the people and the elders, the government and the people. He is their fiercest advocate and fighter. They love him. You can see all the specs on him in your files. He used to be involved in local smuggling, strong-arming, gambling, thefts, you name it. The one thing is, whatever illegal dealings he was involved in seemed to benefit Latema in some way."

"Like some sort of Robin Hood?" Femi asked. "That's pretty cool."

"Or pretty stupid." Billy snorted unhelpfully. "Because the government won't ever consider him a team player. They'll never trust him. He's a bloody wild card."

Nena gave him an unappreciative look. "But," she picked up, "Judah has begun to assume a more advisory role and one of activism on his town's behalf since his arrest years ago. Yes, he was at times a thorn in the officials' sides, but only because he was promoting the interests of the farmers and miners, the people most underrepresented in the government's decision-making. He and the Tanzanian government have a precarious understanding. If he doesn't get in their way or get too out of hand with what he does in Latema and the outlying villages, they let him do what he needs freely. However, now he's slowing down their progress and not eager to be a part of Tanzania's mining reform."

Nena knew his history by heart by now, having read the intel on him repeatedly since Noble said he needed to be watched.

"Judah has been convincing the miners, the ones who discovered the tanzanite on their lands, to hold off on agreeing to the mining reform with the government. DubiCorp is on hand as the representative for outside investors to ensure their interests are also considered when enacting this reform."

Billy surmised, "Western countries have always seen to their own interests in matters like this. What's the difference here?"

Nena shrugged. "Everyone's tiring of his stalling, and we will be on hand to help him to see reason and make sure everyone is on the up-and-up."

Evers asked, "Get him to see reason Dispatch-style?"

Femi's eyes grew with anticipation. "Oh, this is a *mission* mission?"

"No," Nena said quickly, trying to head Femi off before she got too excited. "No, this isn't a *mission* mission. This is not a dispatch. We are emissaries sent to assist Councilman Tegete. We are there to make sure Dubin doesn't get the deal without the proper measures put in place to protect the miners and their interests. The government wants to work with them on selling the mineral to interested Western parties. That's where the Tribe comes in. One of the Council members, Councilman Tegete, is a Tanzanian national and is serving on behalf of Tribe interests. He's negotiating between the miners, the government, and the outside factions to ensure the miners aren't taken advantage of, as has happened historically."

Femi pursed her lips. "How do you mean?"

Evers adjusted his glasses. "Historically, some corrupt government officials have made deals with outsiders to make themselves wealthy, cutting out or stealing from the miners, who have no way of fighting back. Or miners try to deal directly with these companies, who in turn lowball them. They put up mines with unsafe conditions, and it is the miners who ultimately suffer. The miners can't go up against the governments of their own countries, so they lose everything. Or, in even worse cases, are forced to continue to mine the very resources they should have rightfully owned and become wealthy from."

Femi's mouth dropped into an O. "Like the whole thing with conflict diamonds."

"Among others, but yes," Nena said. "Except in this instance the Tanzanian government, as well as other countries, has been working to reform the whole mining process and ensure the miners and villagers have fair trade at market value, safe mining conditions, and a say. That they retain the rights to their lands and what's found on them."

What Nena didn't say was that ensuring the success of this deal meant Tanzania would owe the Tribe for their part and would become an ally, and that the Tribe would be another pipeline that Western countries seeking African resources could use. Noble wanted seats at their tables, to broker deals between them and the Tribe, to be seen as a global contender. He'd get that and more if the Tribe was seen as a success in brokering this major deal.

"Okay." Billy finally spoke up, sounding annoyed. He rubbed a hand over the top of his low mohawk fade. "We're talking business negotiations. None of us work negotiations. Isn't that your sister's bag? And you don't need me, Evers, and Femi to take Judah out of the picture."

Femi and Evers waited expectantly. Billy's was a fair question. None of them worked business or politics. That was for Council members. Elin. Lawyers. Not field and tech operatives.

"Again, we're *not* taking Judah out."

Billy rubbed at his forehead as if dealing with a confusing child. Nena's fist balled at her side, the only indication that she was getting annoyed.

Billy said, "But you just said he's strong-arming the locals. Trying to cut in on their deal, right? Get it all for himself?"

"He's not strong-arming anyone," she corrected. Her frustration growing. This was why she was not the person for this job. "The Latemans love him, so the resistance he's giving is with their blessing. Judah doesn't trust the government and doesn't want them a part of the deal, and he doesn't trust Councilman Tegete or the Tribe. He wants to deal directly with whatever interested parties want to buy their gems."

Femi said, "They will eat him alive."

Nena agreed.

Billy continued with his line of questioning. "Are we then doing a retrieval? Interrogation? Are we confining him until the deal is brokered with the miners without his interference?"

Nena answered, "Surveillance."

Billy looked confused. "But we can do that from home, where we have all our resources at the ready."

"I know," Nena said simply. "But for this mission, we need to be in country and in the thick of it."

Evers was contemplative. "I've never been up close on a mission, providing Network support. This is intriguing."

"A new challenge I know you are up for."

Femi mused, "So no offing this dude?" It seemed a new concept for her.

"Nope."

Billy grumbled something inaudible. Nena thought she heard *bull-shit*, but she let it pass. She switched the screens, showing the photo that had flipped her world again. The Dubins . . . Bridget.

Femi said, "Who the hell are the White people?"

"The man is Frances Dubin. He is the head of DubiCorp, a global corporation that purchases rights to resources for their client corporations. He is also in Tanzania to provide the perspective of outside interested parties. From my research, he is a shark and has been known to be mired in conflict diamonds in the past. So the part he plays here is dubious."

"What, we're spies now? Top-flight security detail?" Billy asked. "We should be assigning a Dispatch team for that. No disrespect, but it looks like we're no more than glorified babysitters, and that's not what our department does."

"We are members of the Tribe and serve it when we're called to duty." She leveled a stare at him. "I have called you to duty, Billy, whether you like it or not. I have entertained your questions and your endless doubt, your disdain, your contempt, your exhausting whining."

The way his mouth dropped, the way all their mouths dropped, did not deter Nena. She'd reached her limit with Billy, and now, as they flew over water to parts unknown, she wasn't about to step foot in country with Billy not yet contained.

Slowly she put the remote clicker she'd been holding on the seat beside her. She took her time as she considered him, relishing the shift in his shoulders, a tell of his discomfort. He'd forgotten what she was capable of, that she could end him easily before he even knew what was happening.

Keeping herself measured, Nena said, "Witt is no longer here, understand? And you are not in his place. I am, whether you approve or not, which doesn't matter, if you think of it. If you take issue with it, Billy, you are free to leave the employment of the Tribe. But you will not remain here, under me, and be undermining me in front of other team members or at any moment. Never forget with whom you're dealing. I know you are very aware of my own profile and of the work I have done, so you know I make no empty promises. Continue this tantrum of yours, and you will lose your post with me and in the organization."

She was flexing. She was throwing her weight, reminding him that she could oust someone from the Tribe, though she'd never do that. She wouldn't have him retired, as Billy was undoubtedly thinking at the moment.

Only the sounds of rushing wind could be heard as the sleek plane cut through. It bounced a little when they hit a tiny pocket of turbulence. The temperature in the cabin had noticeably cooled. Nena did not avert her gaze from the weak-chinned man sitting diagonally from her. She waited for him to try her again. He tried to be stoic, to save face in front of their subordinates. But he knew exactly what Nena was laying down for him.

No one moved until Billy gave an imperceptible nod. He looked as petulant as a two-year-old, his swagger knocked down to the lowest peg.

After a moment, he shrugged, a slow smile spreading across his face. "It's not even that you slipped into the sweet spot of head of Dispatch and Network right out of fieldwork. No up the ladder one rung at a time for you, eh? Not like me or any other lead. It's not even that you're the daughter of High Council and can choose to do whatever you want, and no one will bat an eye," Billy drawled, using his feet to push off so his chair twisted lightly, left and right.

He pursed his lips as if in deep thought while Nena and the rest of them waited for his inevitable mic drop.

"It's that whenever people are around you, they all seem to end up dead."

18

"That is actually not factual, sir." Evers spoke up haltingly, to the surprise of the others.

"In other words," Femi chimed in, arching her eyebrow, "fake news."

Billy stopped his swinging to gawk at his subordinate, who had never said a peep out of turn. Had never said a disagreeable word to sow discord.

"Come again?" Billy challenged.

Evers pushed up his glasses with his right index finger. "While there have been some unsuccessful missions resulting in the deaths of multiple team members, the reports have shown that Nena—or Echo—was not at fault. The general's outpost was a Network system failure. Well, actually"—his eyebrows scrunched in thought as he course corrected—"there wasn't a system failure either. Network was compromised by the mercenary group the woman Mariam was using to sabotage the Tribe."

Femi said, "First of all, Everlasting—"

He coughed. "My preference is Evers."

She pointed to Billy. "Don't call him 'sir.' He is a prick." She raised her hand in a stop when Billy began his objections. "We're all a team here, right?" Femi looked at Nena.

Nena nodded, wondering where this was all going. She was still rocked by what Billy had said, which had hit much harder than she expected when said out loud and to her face. Imagining people saying it, hearing whispers that stopped when people thought she could hear was one thing. Having the words said directly to her was a whole other situation.

"So you don't get to reprimand me for calling you what you are. A fucking prick. She's too proper to say it, but I'll do it."

Keigel would really like Femi. Elin too.

"And that was a prick thing to say. 'Everyone around you seems to end up dead.'" She'd lowered her voice to mimic him, jiggling her head in mockery. "What do you think this is? *The Blacklist* or something? Please." She flicked her hand dismissively, turning back to Evers. "Don't call him 'sir,' because he doesn't deserve that honor."

"You can't speak to me like that!" Billy said, about to launch from his seat.

Femi faced him. "The hell I can't. Don't come up in here with all of that bullshit, okay? Grow up. We have a job to do."

"Our rightful lead, Witt, was killed on her watch!" Billy exploded. "Doesn't that mean anything to you?"

"Witt was killed by the op," Femi returned, rolling her eyes. "Everyone knows that."

Nena looked out the window into blackness.

"That is true." Evers spoke up. "Mariam killed Witt, and so it makes no sense to blame Nena for his death."

"It was my fault." As low as Nena's words were, they shouldn't have been heard above the team's bickering or the roar of the plane as it charged through an outside turbulence that was no match for what was happening inside. Memories of Witt's death always came in flashes and when she was least prepared.

"Never speak of how Witt died. No one needs to know except your mum and sister that it was by your hands. No one can know that Witt attempted

to take the Tribe for himself," *Noble had said after a long silence following Nena's recounting what had happened earlier that night at the foot of the cliff where she had had her final showdown with Mariam and had retired Witt for orchestrating the attempted coup against the Tribe.*

Noble sat beside Nena on her hotel room bed, his bandaged arm in a sling, his breathing labored. His reddened, hollowed eyes were proof of his grief. His pallor was ashen, and he hung his head down, like a man defeated. Day was breaking, and the two of them were extremely tired, having recently returned to their hotel in Accra after the mayhem at the charity event.

"All he had helped me build, he was willing to destroy?" Noble asked, dumbfounded. The news that his most trusted man had turned on him, had decreed his death, had rocked Noble to his very core.

"Tell me again." Noble wiped briskly at his eyes. "Tell me why he did this thing."

Nena didn't want to. She didn't want to relive that night, but like so many other horrors she'd witnessed, the memory of Witt waiting for her to retire him permanently was forever seared in her. She had done him a service, but she felt like what she had done was a disgrace.

"Tell me what he said."

"He lost faith in you." She wanted to lie so badly. The words were the worst a person could say to another, especially to her father, for whom faith and loyalty and belief were so intertwined. But her father had to know. He needed to know the domino effect Goon's death had had on Witt's faith in Noble and his loyalty to the Tribe.

"I thought he loved the Tribe as much as I."

"He did. He wanted the right things, Dad," she said. "He wanted to protect the lower members of the Tribe from the whims of the upper echelons. Goon's death was what broke him."

Nena's team heard her loud and clear in the plane's cabin, her words silencing them.

"I was the team lead. I gave chase after Mariam, and Witt was with me. What happened was on me."

Because I shot Witt, she finished silently. Words she was sworn not to repeat.

"If you admit to killing him, then that means we are admitting that Witt turned, my closest man. If the Tribe learns that someone of such high standing within the Tribe could turn like that, could kill his own people, then all the Tribe has worked for, all we seek to do in this world and for our people, will be destroyed. There will be no faith in the Tribe or its ability to protect everyone else."

She was cold and tried to tamp down an involuntary shudder. "I think about it every day."

Finally, she turned to them, regarding Evers, whose eyes were luminous behind his glasses. Femi remained uncharacteristically silent. Nena landed last on Billy, who tried to come across tough, tried to hold her gaze like he had somehow been vindicated. She held him hostage.

"But this is what we do." Nena clicked off the TV monitor and pressed the call button to inform the flight attendant she was free to enter.

———

The plane touched down by late afternoon at a small regional airport about forty-five minutes from Latema and the Merelani Hills, about a scenic seven-hour drive from the capital of Dodoma.

While they were still in the air, even the breathtaking view of the sprawling plains didn't distract Nena. The images were the stuff of *National Geographic*—beautiful, seemingly untouched stretches of wilderness where animals roamed—yet she couldn't enjoy it, her mind churning with logistics and contingency plans. She imagined everything that could go wrong on this trip and wondered what she hadn't thought of.

"There are several game reserves located throughout the country," Evers informed them when Femi commented about wanting to go on safari to see giraffes and zebras up close and personal and not confined by zoo walls.

"Game reserves mean people go in to shoot and kill them, right?" Femi surmised. "I don't want to do that!"

Billy, who seemed more relaxed, said, "And yet shooting and killing is literally your job."

Apparently, a long nap did Billy good, and not only had his mood lightened, much to Nena's relief, but he had good reflexes, dodging the ballpoint pen Femi threw at his head.

"Bad humans, not animals," Femi clarified, resuming her watch at the window.

They were told they'd be landing shortly, and Nena began her process of shutting down her equipment to ensure security of Network systems remained intact. Across from her, Evers was doing the same.

"Are we really landing in country without a solid plan of action?" Billy threw out to the group. "Witt would have never put us out there like that."

Just when she thought Billy had relaxed, there he was to remind Nena of who she was not. But he was right. Witt would have had a solid plan of action. Witt would have settled his issues with his job, and Bridget, and been able to give his team clear instructions rather than the bouts of second-guessing and attacks of impostor syndrome Nena was dealing with. Until she got a feel of the place and the people, the team would have to play it by ear. It wasn't like her, but it was all she had.

Witt was no longer there.

And they would all have to come to terms with the fact that this was her show—Nena most of all.

19

The team's lodgings were in a newly built resort that was there to promote tourism in the many preserves in the area and around the country. The climate was tropical, with a wet feel to it, but Nena and the team barely noticed.

They were glad to be off the plane after the long overnight flight and eager to get started. The drive in the open-topped Sprinter bus to the resort allowed Nena to take in the scene as it passed by her large window. She enjoyed being in Miami, but every time she traveled back to Africa, it didn't matter where, she was reminded of how beautiful the continent was, how full of life and light and beauty that was close enough to touch. The vegetation was lush, with mangroves and sprawling baobab trees that stretched into savanna and wooded areas with rivers cutting through, creating waterways that were similar enough to Ghana's to make Nena nostalgic for home.

They passed several smaller towns and villages along the way. Each chock full of vitality and happy people waving and going about their lives. Nena was happy to see it. They finally made it to the resort, a white four-level sprawling building.

Several vehicles, including those of the local police, lined the circular drive as the Sprinter pulled to a stop in front of the ornate double-doored front. Employees, clad in off-white airy uniforms that helped wick the stifling heat away from their bodies, stood at the curb, ready to receive their newest guests.

The grounds were beautiful and lush, with vivid green plants, baobab trees, and vibrantly colored flowers cascading from the hotel walls and along the walkways. Their fragrance permeated the air, and Nena took a deep inhale. Inside, the layout Nena and the team had familiarized themselves with prior to arrival did the actual place no justice. Her family would love it here, she thought. Cort and Georgia too. She wondered how they were doing and if Georgia was feeling better today than she had yesterday, when Nena had last seen her.

Hopefully Georgia wasn't letting the wait from the school about whether she'd be expelled weigh too heavily on her. Nena bet that liar Sasha was already back at school. Her father had probably thrown his weight around. Nena was tempted to fight fire with fire, but that wasn't her style. And she couldn't risk another argument with Cort about whose child Georgia was. The argument she and Cort had because of the fight was bad, but the makeup was much better.

Images of the makeup with Cort that had occurred after Georgia went to bed popped into Nena's mind. Georgia made it through the earlier version of Stephen King's *It* before crashing, the emotions of the day finally taking their toll on her. She left the adults to their own devices. Enjoyable devices. Nena's face warmed in spite of herself, and she ducked her head away so her team members wouldn't guess what kind of memories she'd been having about her and Cort.

She pulled out her luggage and the multiple go bags the team had assembled of mostly mission and surveillance items. Nena tucked all those thoughts away to save for later. It was time to get to work.

She heard her name and abandoned what she was doing to greet the reception team—wiry Councilman David Tegete with the shiny bald head and glasses that were too thick for his lean face and the eternal good mood. He wore a traditional printed cloth flung over one shoulder. He was flanked by a sour-faced, portly man in police uniform, another in a suit—the latter wearing the same jovial smile as Tegete—and an impeccably dressed and serious woman with her natural hair pineappled into a high bun.

The surly man, whom the team would soon be introduced to as the local police chief, wore his distaste like a badge of honor. Nena could tell from the way his eyes traveled the four of them and counted off their bags. Nena made note of his displeasure.

"Mr. Tegete," Nena said, channeling her inner Elin for these social situations.

She accepted his extended hand, allowing him to pump hers vigorously as he beamed at her. He was truly glad to see her and was one of the few Council members who'd been warm and welcoming to her from the beginning. He was one of Noble's closest confidants and staunchest supporters, always kind, always the same and without airs. Nena appreciated the slight man of five foot five wearing loose cream-colored linen pants, a matching button-down, and sandals she'd heard Keigel refer to as "Jesus shoes." At least he wasn't wearing any socks with his divinely designated footwear.

Nena sighed. She missed her friend, and it had been only a day.

Tegete peeped at her from behind thick wire glasses, giving her a toothy grin. Beside him, the taller, bearded, suited man Nena assumed to be Samwell Asogi—the prime minister, who was also from Latema—matched Tegete's excitement and took her hand. Nena found she liked him immediately. He didn't shake as if she were some delicate woman or as if he were trying to show her who was the boss.

"We are so thrilled you are here," Asogi said, releasing Nena's hand to greet the others. She appreciated that he gave the rest of the team the same amount of respect he'd given her. She filed that away too.

"Thank you," Nena said. "I am glad to be here."

Tegete gave her a sly look. "Are you, my dear? Truly?"

She lifted her shoulder and let it drop. "I am happy to be wherever I am needed, and especially when it's to assist you, sir." He squeezed her arm in response.

Asogi turned to the woman beside him. "This here is Ms. Farida Odemba. She is the minister of mining and has been working tirelessly on the mining reform. Usually, I leave these matters to her, but because this is Latema, I cannot stay away! These are literally my people, do you follow?"

His exuberance was both charming and overwhelming, and all Nena could do was nod in agreement and shake Ms. Odemba's firm hand.

The minister of mining, who had been taking Nena's measure, said, "A pleasure to meet you, Ms. Knight."

Tegete gestured toward Nena. "Nena Knight, my colleague on the Council."

Nena wasn't on the Council, and she masked her surprise. Rarely did they refer to the Tribe out in the open, especially not with government officials, because sometimes there were jobs politicians shouldn't know about. She noted the glint of interest in Odemba's eyes as the woman took her in.

"My schoolmate's already done all the legwork. We are nearly there!" Asogi boasted. "If we can make Judah agreeable to the terms and he relays his approval to the chieftains, all will be well. I would much rather all parties come to an accord than for the government to have to take over or for some black market deal to happen between individual miners and outside factors. I mean, right?"

Nena asked, "Like DubiCorp?"

"Or even bad parties in country." Asogi leaned conspiratorially toward her. Beside him, the last, unintroduced man coughed to remind them he was still there.

"Apologies, Pengo." Tegete clapped the pouting man on his back. "Chief Constable Pengo here has been serving Latema and the surrounding rural areas for years and has graciously given some of his police force to keep us secure while we are here. He is dedicated to ensuring everyone here stays safe and sound during your visit to our wonderful region."

Chief Constable Pengo raised a wily eyebrow at Nena. It reminded her of a caterpillar crawling along his face. His eyebrows seemed to make up a good portion of his forehead. "The key term is 'visit,' eh, Ms. Knight? You are all visitors, guests, here."

Nena's lips pursed as she took him, and the chip on his shoulder, in. Asogi said, "You are welcome here."

Pengo groused, "Nice of you to be so welcoming in *my* domain!" He muscled his way to the forefront. "Welcome to *my* town." Then he mumbled, "If you must be here."

Ms. Odemba's mouth dropped open and shut quickly, her eyes flickering to Nena to see her response. Nena was well aware the entire group had fallen silent as everyone waited for Nena to say something.

Nena gave him a tight smile. "We are honored to be and appreciate your hospitality."

The constable gnawed at his bottom lip, sizing her up. Finding her unworthy. "Good, then. Well, see you don't muck it up, eh? You are guests. Only me and the people in my employ dispense justice. I am the law here. You get to go back home to the West, eh? While we will have to still live here." He looked at Tegete, Asogi, and Odemba one at a time. "See you all remember, eh? I have work to do. Policing to conduct and such."

Nena could relate to the chief, wanting to return home with nothing more than signed paperwork and goodwill.

When he marched off, flanked by his accompanying officers, Tegete, Asogi, and Odemba guided Nena and her group into the cool foyer of the hotel.

Asogi said, "Excuse him. He takes his position very seriously, as he should, of course. He is proud of the work he's done here. Crime is low to nonexistent even with Judah's people and their protests and whatnot.

We have had an influx of outsiders with the discovery of the tanzanite. He is very protective, you see?"

"Of course," Nena agreed.

Asogi clapped his hands together as a little girl, about nine, with gorgeous rows of thick oiled braids that ended in big blue, brown, and white wooden beads skipped to him with a large piece of paper in her hand.

Asogi bent down to receive her. "Darling!"

"Uncle," she said, burrowing herself in his outstretched arms. He kissed her on the top of her head, then turned her around to face Nena. Billy, Femi, and Evers stood off to the side displaying an array of disinterest, boredom, and polite attention. In that order.

Asogi prodded his niece. "Go on, Abiola."

Shyly, Abiola flipped her large paper around. Nena read **WELCOME TO LATEMA** sketched on the paper in many colors surrounded by a shining sun, a rainbow, a giraffe that looked like a zebra with giraffe colors, and maybe a rhino.

"It's wonderful." Nena meant it. The drawing was wonderful and the perfect salve to the worries storming within her. "Beautifully done, Abiola. Thank you."

"I used colored pencils. Not crayons."

"I can tell." Nena took the welcome sign Abiola held out to her and raised it for the team to see. "My mates and I appreciate your thoughtfulness. Right?" She looked at the team, as did Abiola, both expectantly.

"Great symmetry," Evers said first, nodding.

Femi said, "Best picture I've ever seen. I bet Billy would love to have the welcome in his room to wake up to while we're here."

When Billy didn't answer, Femi elbowed him. He squinted at it from where he stood. "Is that a rhino?"

Abiola took the sign back from Nena, held it out so the team could still admire it, and scrutinized her masterpiece upside down. "It's an elephant."

Nena pursed her lips, taking a closer look at the animal.

"An abstract artist," Billy surmised. "Genius."

Abiola walked the sign over to Billy, holding it up for him to take because Femi had said so. "If you put it next to your bed, you can wake up to the sun every morning." She held a hand to her mouth as if they were sharing a secret. "Even when it's rainy."

If Nena didn't know better, she'd have thought Billy melted a little right in front of them. He couldn't answer, swallowing hard, temporarily at a loss for words. He bent to her eye level and took the sign from Asogi's niece.

"That's a good idea," he said softly. "Thank you."

Nena's phone buzzed and she tore herself away from them.

ELIN: How is it? Seen any cuties yet?

NENA: I wouldn't know. I'm working.

ELIN: ☺ Sometimes I can't stand u!

Nena's lips twitched at the message. She put her phone away, catching Billy's eye as he looked up from his new friend. So, children could crack through Billy's tough exterior. Maybe he wasn't as bad as Nena had been thinking since she'd been forced to work with him. Nena hoped that this was the first step toward a better working relationship between her and her second-in-command.

Nena indicated her team had had a long journey.

Under the watchful eye of Odemba, Asogi replied, "Of course! Let's get you to your rooms, yes? And then the soccer game occurs tonight. It will be big fun."

Wonderful, Nena silently cheered, thinking about the perimeter checks her team needed to run around the grounds and in the village, setting up their tech and their base of operations . . .

Big fun indeed.

20

The team freshened up and settled in their rooms before meeting in Nena's. Evers had come in a few minutes earlier to check her work—fitting the room with white noise machines so their words wouldn't carry and scramblers to disable any electronic signals or radio frequencies attempting to listen in on their conversation—while Billy and Femi conducted a preliminary perimeter search, with Evers's drones taking aerial maps. Nena planned to conduct a personal search when they returned from the soccer game. She wanted to know the layout of the land herself, and especially at night.

With her team assembled at the dining room table in the living quarters of her suite before they were to head to the game, Nena went through their objectives.

One: Watch all players.

Asogi, the constable, Odemba. And eventually Judah and Dubin and . . . his wife. Just when Nena thought everything would be fine, Bridget crept back into her thoughts. Haunting them. Poisoning them.

"Next?" Nena grounded herself in the present.

Two: Ensure the miners sign off on the deal the Tribe is brokering rather than allowing them to sign with DubiCorp directly.

Three: Handle Judah.

"Nonlethal," Nena added quickly, cutting Femi a look.

Femi twisted her lips and flipped her hand as if to say *if we must.*

"We're only letting the air out of his tires a little," Billy added with a smirk. He gave Nena's surprise a sidelong glance. "See, I can team play too."

Nena gave him an appreciative nod. She'd take it. "Next?"

Four: Provide backup and protection for Councilman Tegete.

Nena said, "We keep him safe so he can get this deal done and we can all go home. However, we need to keep a low profile. We are a delegation, not Dispatch, okay? Don't come in heavy on anything or look militaristic. That means don't scare anyone with talk of guns or killing . . . Femi."

Femi's sigh was heavy with disappointment. "If they're animals, then they have nothing to worry about."

"And the most important objective of all," Nena began. She waited for the team to give their suggestions, but when all they did was offer back blank stares, she stood.

"Is for *all* of us to make it back home."

She looked at Billy pointedly. "Alive."

———

The soccer game was supposed to be a welcoming event for the arrival of the rest of the visiting delegation. Clearly Asogi's and Odemba's appearances in Latema were to build trust and partnership between the government and the people. Nena only hoped the government would hold up its part of the deal and that the people wouldn't come up short in the end.

"A soccer game isn't going to make these people suddenly say, 'Here, take all my precious gems, please,'" Billy muttered as they took their seats alongside Tegete in the packed stands. The players were already assembled on the low patch of land that had been cut away into the ground to create the makeshift field.

Nena sat beside Tegete, who reminded her of a quiet scholar. With skin the color of toffee, he leaned over, chin in one hand, elbows on his knees, intently watching the crowd of villagers as they cheered the start of the game.

He came across as relatively safe and genuine, if not a little overly excited at the prospects of not only securing this deal but showing the world that Tanzania was serious about reforming their mining problem.

"You know, Tegete," Asogi said as they clinked two bottles of Heineken in commemoration of their partnership, "when the miners sign off on us selling their tanzanite and whatever else they find on their land, it will show the rest of Africa—ah, the world—that we are invested in our people. That we want them to succeed as we want to succeed. It is good, no?"

Tegete nodded. "Yes, brother, it is good." They clinked again. "That is all the Tribe wants, you know. To ensure everyone is honest and gets the fair deal. To make sure the people come out on top over it all."

Asogi slapped a hand on Tegete's tiny back, which Tegete absorbed silently with only the slightest twitch of his eye.

Asogi said, "With the Dubins and DubiCorp. They are one of the many investors interested in securing the mined resources. Their deal would be a hard one to pass up, but you are correct that we need to make sure whatever is agreed upon for the reform, and the deals that come from this reform, are what's best for the mining community in Tanzania. Now, enough business talk. We should have some fun now, yes?"

Asogi continued, "Nena, your father is well known here. I've had the pleasure of meeting him on several trips abroad. I've been to England, where he entertained me at his offices. Your mother is quite lovely too. Very dignified. Quite regal."

It was a good description of Delphine Knight . . . dignified. Quite regal. Nena would have to share it with her mother the next time they spoke.

"Thank you, sir."

"And your sister, Ellen, is it?"

"Eh-lean. Happens a lot," Nena said quickly when Asogi began to apologize. She surveyed the crowds, eyes scanning faces for her unofficial mark, Judah Wasira.

Nena looked for signs of him, wondering why he wasn't at the game that was supposed to be for him and his fellow townspeople. What did it mean that he wasn't here? Nena didn't like that Judah seemed to be a no-show to an event meant for the people he claimed to represent, and she hoped his absence wasn't a sign of what was to come.

"Most beautiful and very smart. I had the pleasure of meeting with her too. But you were not around, no. Perhaps in the States?"

Or elsewhere.

"It was likely that."

Nena shifted from the focal point when Asogi's name was called. The crowd was in a roar from a goal scored, the field and stands erupting in celebratory chaos that wreaked havoc on Nena's earpiece and on proper surveillance. Anyone could be up to anything in this, and the mayhem nearly drove Nena over the edge. Her team was on alert—well, Billy and Femi were. Evers was tapping away at his phone, earbuds in. He looked as if he weren't paying attention, but Nena knew his appearance was purposeful. Evers was more aware of what was happening in that moment than any of them were.

"Dubin's arrived." Evers's voice was coming through the tiny piece in her ear, proving she was right and that he was watching. "Odemba is guiding them in."

Asogi and Tegete stood from their chairs, a regular smiling welcome brigade. Nena supposed she should, too, though she was perfectly content remaining in her chair.

"I don't see any other detail around," Femi said, throwing her hands in the air in a cheer. She pounded Billy once on the shoulder. Hard. Probably on purpose.

Nena heard his "Ow!" both through her comm and in real time. He scowled at Femi, rubbing the abused shoulder.

"Sorry," Femi said in a manner that displayed how totally unsorry she was. "I am unaware of my own strength."

"Still no sign of Judah," Billy concluded. "He's gotta be somewhere watching all of this, right?"

Nena had to agree. If Judah was smart, and all evidence indicated he was—he had the government of Tanzania and a multimillion-dollar corporation held at an impasse, awaiting his word—he would be watching, checking out the new actors like her coming into the mix, watching the old players to see if they suddenly flipped the script. Nena might have never actively participated in the political checkers that her sister and parents were so heavily involved in, but she'd seen plenty. It was easy to observe a lot when one watched from the shadows. Still, Nena didn't like Judah having the upper hand, having first sights on them from wherever he was perched while she waited.

Evers continued his updates. "Dubin's wife's bringing up the rear."

21

Nena no longer paid attention to her team's chatter because her thoughts were now consumed by the announcement of Bridget's arrival. She felt herself being pulled down into that dark place and fought to remain in the present. She'd have to slip on a mask and pretend all was normal, for Tegete and Asogi and for her team.

Bridget had come after all, and in a moment, they would be face to face. Would Bridget recognize her immediately? Or would it take some time, as it had with Paul? Or never at all, like with Ofori? At least Nena was somewhat prepared for this. She wouldn't be caught unawares. Not like she'd been when Paul had entered Elin's condo in Miami for dinner, pretending to be Ofori's father and Elin's soon-to-be father-in-law.

Back then, when Nena had come face to face with Paul, posing under the assumed name of Lucien Douglas and about to be the next appointed Council member, she had run into the restroom and nearly vomited what little of the meal she'd eaten to keep herself from slicing Paul's throat over Elin's beef Wellington. Nena told herself she kept Paul's true identity from everyone to protect them.

No, she needed to be honest with herself. She hadn't kept his identity a secret for the others. It was for her own sake. Because she wanted him all to herself. To exact her revenge. For the family he'd murdered in front of her and the village he'd burned. And for the innocence Paul had cleaved from her.

Nena had learned from that mistake. She'd suffered too. Because she'd had to kill Ofori, who had changed so much—both of them had—that they hadn't even recognized one another. Maybe if she'd confronted Paul that night, Ofori would be alive. She didn't know how they'd have worked out because there was too much poisoned history between them. Paul had dug his clutches too deeply into her older brother. But at least Ofori might still have lived.

Nena stood up, stepping out a little past Tegete, who, along with Asogi, was between her and the approaching Dubins.

She hadn't been sure what she'd do if the moment came. She'd hoped Bridget would have opted to stay home, maybe in the Netherlands, in one of the several places they lived. She knew they had a home in England. Or the Alps, where they vacationed. It irritated her that Bridget had been so close all these years with nothing but easily traveled miles to separate them.

Without knowing it, Nena was holding her breath as she looked past the ruddy-complexioned, fair-haired, broad-shouldered giant of a man and to the woman traipsing behind him. There was Bridget beneath a wide-brimmed straw hat and wearing pastel-colored capri pants with a feathery-light top.

Nena's skin dampened as her body heat and stress level increased. She realized she was holding her breath and she needed to breathe or else she'd pass out in this bearable-until-this-moment heat. Instinctively, as they always did, Nena's fingers itched to take up one of her daggers. To reach for the push blades hidden inside the folds of her belt. Her blades were her security blanket, more than. They were extensions of her.

Bridget was as Nena remembered her except older. She still had her deep-red hair and those glittering eyes like jewels, as watchful as when the two of them had traveled to Accra. Bridget's image was seared in Nena's mind, like those of Paul and his right hands Bena and Attah Walrus, and of Robach—some sort of cruel **WANTED** lineup poster on Nena's mental wall with the faces of all who'd harmed her marked out, with only one remaining.

The couple joined them, Frances Dubin's voice arriving before they actually did.

"Asogi! How goes it, man? Thank you for setting up the expedition for us. I'd been wanting to go on safari since we landed."

Nena found the American abrasive and much too loud even if they were at a sports event. His voice carried above the roar of the crowd, causing some spectators to look curiously at the gigantic wrestler of a man currently squeezing the stuffing out of their prime minister's hand. Asogi, not a small man himself, looked diminutive next to Dubin, and Tegete was practically nonexistent. A tiny freckle against that much Dubin.

Nena stepped closer to Tegete when Dubin's bulk got too close, towering over the councilman as if meaning to devour him. Dubin noticed Nena moving toward the councilman, and his mouth firmed slightly. His clear blue eyes took stock of her as she did him. He was curious. And he was annoyed with her presence. Dubin took a half step back, breaking into a smile like the snake Nena smelled him out to be. No intel needed to tell her Dubin was bad news.

"Mr. Tegete, it's good to see you again," Dubin greeted him. His clear eyes shifted to Nena, interest alighting in them again. "And with new friends!" Dubin said. "Who might this divine, lovely lady be?" He considered Nena from head to toe. She could feel his judgment of her.

He winked conspiratorially. "Kind of young, huh, Tegete? And for all to see! You're brave. Do you still marry a harem of wives? That's the one thing I wouldn't mind adopting from you people." Dubin was loud enough to carry to the top of Mount Kilimanjaro.

"Only took him two minutes to go there. 'You people.' Racist bastard," Femi muttered through Nena's earpiece.

"You are a funny man." Tegete waggled his finger. His tight smile reflected he was unamused, but too much a gentleman and politician to tell Dubin his true thoughts.

"What people are you referring to?" The question came before Nena could stop herself. She was eager to see if Bridget recognized her as Paul initially had not, but Dubin made it hard to stay on task.

He attempted to blink away the surprise at her gall in speaking. This girl. This toy of Tegete's. Nena could read all that in the flash of annoyance in Dubin's nearly clear eyes.

"You people of the Tribe, of course. Isn't that who's here mucking up what should be a slam dunk deal in this beautiful country?"

He laughed, and after half a second, Asogi laughed, too, loud and bawdy with a tinge of nervousness mixed in. Tegete merely smiled. Nena bothered with neither.

Tegete gave Nena side-eye, asking her to be still. "If by 'mucking up' you mean we aim to ensure a fair deal for the miners, then yes, that is our goal. As I'm sure it is yours. You don't want these people cheated, am I right, Mr. Dubin?"

Tegete smiled wide, and now it was as if he was the one looming over the American.

"Course not. We are here to serve the people of Tanzania." Dubin's eyes were cold, his voice tight—a contrast to his earlier light tone and Hollywood smile, making him appear jovial to everyone except those trained to know otherwise.

"He's not happy," Evers observed.

"Major prick," Femi added.

Nena's attention switched to the woman who'd been silently watching the exchange from behind her black sunglasses. She began trading pleasantries, her attention shifting from one person to the next. She landed on Nena, then moved away to the next face. Her smile began to drop as realization began to hit. Shot back to Nena. Her fingers moved to the top of her glasses, and with them, she pulled her designer eyewear down enough to take a closer look.

Bridget stared at Nena.

And Nena stared back.

Bridget blinked. Her eyelids fluttered rapidly.

Nena remained unmoved.

Bridget's mouth dropped slightly, then snapped shut as if she'd remembered she was out in public.

Nena watched as Bridget's trembling fingers pushed her glasses back into position on her face and she was once again hiding behind their darkness, closed off to the world.

But she couldn't hide from Nena.

Bridget was the siren. She was the house of sweets used to entice and ensnare children for the evil witch who would devour them.

What was Bridget now? And did Nena really want to know?

Dubin's rumbling voice cut through, tearing Nena away from her thoughts.

"Won't you introduce your mystery companion?"

Asogi picked up the volley. "We are lucky! Nena Knight has joined us to assist Mr. Tegete, who you know well! You know—"

Dubin's lips pursed. "As in Noble Knight?"

"Her father. Yes." Asogi was highly pleased, likely thinking things were already running along smoothly. However, Nena knew otherwise. "We are quite lucky to have so many highly important people visiting our fine country and this even finer town."

Nena addressed him. "It is actually our honor, Mr. Asogi. Thank you for hosting us."

The prime minister beamed at her as Dubin looked on, as if he were trying to figure out the competition. Nena was doing the same, trying to sort out the dynamics of his and Asogi's relationship. Nena pretended all was well, keeping her feelings in check when Bridget was mere feet away, close enough to strangle. But the whole time, Nena could only think, How in the world had Bridget ended up back in her world? And how would Nena remove the woman from it?

BEFORE

Bridget's crime is worse than those of any of the men I have encountered. What she does is deceive and deliver.

Bridget says, her voice saccharine, "Consider this an adventure toward a brand-new life, Aninyeh. You can have whatever you'd like."

"My freedom?" I blurt before catching myself.

"Except that." She studies me through the darkness with a smile full of false sympathy.

Somehow, I fall asleep during the journey to Accra, though I fight hard to stay awake. I want to know where they are taking me. I am afraid that if I sleep, they will spirit me away into some nightmare place, and I will never be able to find my way home. Little do I know how true my fear will be.

The thing to which the woman eventually delivers me, the monster, the devil known as Robach, is indeed stuff made of nightmares. His dungeon, my prison for half a year of my life, is that nightmare place. And the things he makes me do to the dead American woman, the horrors I am forced to listen to on the other side of my cell door, the debasement he subjects me to . . . words cannot explain how each of those acts chips away at what little soul I have left after my death in the Compound.

As I reflect on it all, I have had many deaths. Just when I think things can't get any worse, they do. It wasn't just at the Compound where I died. Or in my village, when I was tied to the tree, *after* . . . or when I watched the last of my family struck down as if they were nothing. Or when the ink-black sky was illuminated by the raging fires consuming N'nkakuwe.

The worst is when Bridget, the deliverer, takes me from my homeland and puts me in the hands of something that I have no words to describe— there is no limit to how depraved Robach is. Bridget knows what is coming for me. She knows what he is capable of. And she lulls me, first with her gentle humming in that beautiful voice of hers. She sounds and looks like an angel, and even though she tells me she won't give me my freedom and that I'd better enjoy this little bit of time with her, I don't believe she'd really put me in harm's way.

I don't believe there are people like that. I think I can change her mind, that if I am the perfect little girl who listens, who does not fight, who is docile and perfect in every way, then Bridget will take pity. That she'll see what evil she is a part of and do the right thing, ending this cycle and Paul's system of trafficking. Ending this torture for me.

Bridget is nothing but a mirage. She makes my time with her seem like an adventure. She almost makes me forget how I've come to be, where I have ended up, and where I am going. Even when, down deep, I know she has to be pretending to be kind, allowing me last rites, so to speak. I glom on to the fantasy I have already created in my mind. I need the kindness. I need the smile.

The three days we spend in Accra, eating food of my country, touring the market, lounging lavishly in the hotel room while we wait for my falsified documents to be made so we can fly to France, Bridget acts like a big sister. I've never had one before, and even though she is White and friends with that evil man Paul, it is easier for me to pretend she is. She paints my nails and attempts to do my hair.

"It's okay," I say, gently pulling her slender fingers from my beautifully spongy curls. "I can do my hair." With deft fingers, ignoring her pretty pout, I braid my hair in two French braids and pin them.

"Maybe you can teach me," Bridget says, and I do.

And after three days in Accra of being drawn into a sense of safety and actually having fun—so much fun I nearly forget all that happened only weeks before, only three days before—the memories float from my mind as if on a balloon, carried away.

Three days is all it takes for me to forget the pain I've been suffering for too long. And on the fourth day, I am brought back to earth by the gingerbread house that is Bridget. Put there to lure me in and lull me into a sense of false safety.

Until she delivers me to the witch who is really a demon.

Until she delivers me to the nightmare house of the killer Robach.

22

"A gingerbread house."

"I'm sorry?"

Bridget's voice startled Nena back into reality. Disoriented, Nena looked around until her focus cleared. She recognized the dirt-packed restroom she had stumbled into in her attempt to distance herself from Bridget. Yet there Bridget was, staring at Nena in the dusty mirror. The woman had followed her here. She must have a death wish.

Bridget looked just as confused as Nena had been when she came to and realized that she'd spoken and couldn't remember what she'd said, or where she'd just been. What she did realize was that her blade was halfway drawn from its housing, and had a moment longer lapsed, the floor would have been red with Bridget's blood.

Nena swallowed. "What?"

Bridget stammered, "Ginger . . . you said something about 'a gingerbread house.'"

The soccer game was nearly over, and Nena had left the group to check out the growing number of Judah's people milling along the outskirts of the field. She'd instructed her team to fan out and get a feel for what was going on. Secretly, she'd also needed space away from Bridget.

She herself had needed a moment when eyes weren't on her. When she could breathe and bottle up the torrent of emotions threatening a geyser-size eruption. And Nena had been so deep into her past, she hadn't realized where she'd ended up, that she'd been followed into the restroom, or that she had spoken her thoughts out loud.

The last person Nena needed to be alone with was suddenly at her elbow, watching Nena's reflection with some sort of rapacious curiosity. Nena's body went rigid, instinctively shifting into fight mode as she glared at Bridget's slightly distorted image in the mirror.

Bridget was too close.

Outside, a chant began coming from a few male voices. Then joined by more. And more.

"Something's brewing" came Femi in Nena's ear. She made no indication she'd heard. Didn't want Bridget knowing.

Billy said, "J's people. They're amassing. Sounds like protesting."

There was too much noise, and Nena couldn't pick the protesters' words from the cacophony with her own ears or through the earpiece. Something like *the choice is ours*?

Nena couldn't ask for clarification because Bridget was in her face, smothering her, and she didn't need the woman in her business.

Nena spun around, making a move to leave. She should have just gone to her suite rather than stop here. She needed to be out there with her team, ensuring Judah wasn't making some foolhardy move against the visiting delegation.

"Where is she?" Billy asked, annoyed. Nena knew he was referring to her.

Evers now. "No sights on our One. You think she's compromised?"

"It's getting rowdy. J's people have stormed the field. Game's been stopped."

What was this woman doing? Confronting her? Bridget was half blocking Nena's way, and Nena surely wasn't going to touch her to get through the door.

Bridget slid farther into her path. "Aninyeh."

Nena saw red. "Don't. Call me that."

Noble had told her to leave Bridget alone. But he hadn't said what to do when Bridget came to her. Hearing her name from Bridget's lips wasn't something she could remain silent about.

"Bathroom," Nena finally said through clenched teeth, hoping it was loud enough for the team to hear.

"Seriously? Now?" Billy asked. "Well, clean up and come on. Shit could be hitting the fan. They're approaching the stands from the field. PM's security detail has their asset wrapped tight."

"See to our asset." Tegete. They needed to make sure he was safe.

Bridget frowned. "Who?"

Nena swept at her ear, so it looked like she was brushing hair. She palmed her piece, feeling for the tiny switch to turn it off.

Bridget said, "Could we speak a moment? This . . . seeing you here is unexpected to say the least. I thought you were—"

"Dead?" Nena's tone was flat. "Is that what you'd hoped? Well, you're right. Aninyeh is a ghost, thanks to you."

Bridget's hand fluttered at her throat, eyes widening. "No, of course I didn't mean dead. It's just, I had learned back then about Robach's—"

The room was growing too thick with the dirt, with the carbon dioxide poison Bridget was breathing out.

"—death, and I assumed you had also not survived."

"Reckon you all thought I wouldn't live to be this ripe old age, yeah? I wasn't supposed to live past your French friend, was I?"

Bridget flinched, wearing a wounded look that Nena wanted to use her blades to carve out. Her hand flexed over the handle of one of them.

"He was no friend of mine. I had no choice."

"You had every choice, while I was divested of them."

"Aninyeh, please."

Outside, the chants grew, a chorus of voices crying for choice, the constable bellowing over the megaphone for them to disperse or risk being arrested.

Nena seethed, releasing her knife from its holster. She turned on her heel and pushed Bridget up against the wall, the tip of the short and extremely sharp blade against the soft skin right beneath her chin. "I won't warn you again. You don't get to call me that. You don't get to *anything* with me."

Bridget's hands remained at her sides. Her eyes exposed her fear, and she blubbered in her native tongue. "I'm sorry. I'm sorry. I won't call you that. I am sorry!"

Nena breathed heavily, trying to regulate her rage, trying not to put her hands around Bridget's throat. Nena considered the woman she had thought would be her salvation rather than her damnation. Of them all, Bridget was the one who'd shown her empathy and kindness and then taken it back when she handed Nena over like a trussed-up doll to Monsieur Robach. And so, of all the trauma inflicted on Nena by Robach, the pain Bridget had caused was beyond the physical. She'd gotten Nena to trust her, made her believe Bridget was an ally when she had been the enemy.

Nena spilled out into the crush of fast-moving people exiting, trying to get away in case anything beyond protests happened.

She slipped her piece back in her ear.

"They're clearing. I think they've made their point," Evers commented.

Femi said, "Our asset is secure."

Nena searched for her team and their asset. *Always the enemy.*

23

How Nena made it out of that restroom without dispatching Bridget was a blur, but she'd managed. She'd hurried down the hall, trying to put distance between her and Bridget lest the woman attempt to come after her and shove more apologies down her throat. And Nena needed to widen the distance between them in case she couldn't hold herself back from unleashing all this anger on the woman's head.

Femi was in the car waiting when Nena threw herself in without a hello, a tornado of tension and negative energy surrounding her.

"You okay, Nena?" Femi asked, concern creeping in. They were going on a small recon to the village of the teams from the earlier soccer game, trying to suss out the lay of the land and get a feel for the villagers. Nena needed to focus on what they had to do, not be distracted by the restroom encounter with Bridget. Being off her game could blow the whole thing, and her team had only one shot to make a positive impression on the villagers.

Nena's forehead pressed to the backs of her fingers. "I'm fine." Then she added, "Slight headache."

Femi continued her side-eye appraisal as the driver started the car. The time was nearing eight in the evening, and the light was nearly gone.

"Ready, ma'am?" the driver asked after a quick peek in the rearview mirror.

"Are we?" Femi asked, and when Nena gave a single nod, she said louder, "We can go."

A slight lurch indicated they were off and running, and after several minutes, Femi leaned over and said, "You have twenty-seven minutes to get in this if we're gonna do it. Otherwise, we can turn around and try again another day."

"We're on limited time here," Nena answered, unmoved from her position.

"Then you need to get in gear," Femi said under her breath so the driver wouldn't hear her, "with all due respect . . . of course."

———

By the time they reached the outskirts of the town, Nena had done just what Femi had ordered and regained her focus. They had a job to do, and Nena couldn't let her feelings about Bridget get the better of her. Tomorrow the talks would begin, the serious ones in which all parties would be laying their cards on the table, which would guide the miners' decision.

"All is quiet on the home front." Billy updated the two through their comms. "Tegete is in his quarters. Asogi is visiting with his niece. Mrs. Dubin is in their quarters, and Mr. Dubin is walking the grounds and smoking a cigar." He paused. "Or a joint. A fat one."

"Billy's attempts at humor are an utter failure," Evers chimed in.

"Shut up and surveil something," Billy returned. "Anyway, Dubin's either texting or playing on his phone."

"Keep eyes on him. He may just be relaxing with a cigar. Or he may be on legitimate business calls. He is the liaison between the parties here and his investors," Nena murmured under her breath as Femi chatted up the driver about the town's history to distract him from Nena's secret conversation.

Nena asked, "Can we access his phone?"

"All my equipment for that isn't here." Evers sounded as if someone had stolen his toy. "So no for now. You said this was a scaled-back op. You want me to put a call into a satellite?"

No, she didn't, and if she wanted them to be as low key as possible, they would have to do the best they could without the full scope of Network's capabilities at their disposal.

Dusk had transitioned into night when their car pulled into the village lit by a grid of lighting fixtures and also torches, flames licking at the air. The village was alive with movement, and the air was heavy with humidity not yet evaporated since the sun went down. It would stay until the sun reappeared the next day. It was always horribly hot and much too sticky.

Nena stepped out of her side of the car, and her senses were immediately assaulted by the aroma of cooking spiced food. They'd eaten back at their lodgings, but that food had smelled (and probably tasted) nothing like whatever was being cooked here. Steam and smoke rose from the tops of the small houses as villagers made their meals.

Spurts of laughter rang through from kids chasing each other. From men as they hung out in groups after a hard day's work, chopping it up, as Keigel would say—or doing what Nena would just call gossiping. Women and girls wove in and out between the homes with tan baskets filled to the brim with wares they were selling or had purchased at market. They passed through the groups of social circles smoking cigarettes—or other things—and sharing bottles of malt beer, Guinness, Heineken, or the amber-colored hard liquor.

"It's like a party here," Femi observed, placing her hands on her curvy hips and taking in the scenery.

"I knew we shouldn't have come. How'd we end up on babysitting duty?" came Billy's reply. He was becoming more tolerable, having chosen to fall in line and become a team player, much to Nena's relief. One less thing to have to deal with.

It was the way the villagers gathered, the way the brightly lit village looked like a photo from a travel magazine—gorgeous, with lush green jungle surrounding a vibrant, bustling town of African people—that made Nena stop in her tracks, made her mind clear itself of her interaction with Bridget or the thought that she was there for work. That this wasn't home. N'nkakuwe.

Because that was exactly where Nena thought she was. Back home. She moved past Femi, ignoring the woman when she called out asking where she was going. Nena walked right into the village as if she knew exactly where she was going. She was going home. To her house where she lived with her father, Michael; brothers, Wisdom, Josiah, and Ofori; and her auntie. Auntie, who made the best bofrot, which Ofori would steal and cause war within the household. Where the deep cast-iron pan of bean stew sat bubbling next to a skillet of hot oil frying plantains.

She was vaguely aware of her name being called. Someone named Nena. But that wasn't her name. She was Aninyeh. And this was N'nkakuwe. And she was home and would find her father, who was right around the corner, where he'd be holding court, the chieftain with the other elders of the village, discussing the day's dealings, airing grievances, looking for his daughter—

Something bumped into her foot, jolting Nena out of her reverie. She looked down, seeing a black-and-white soccer ball there. She placed the toe of her foot atop it to prevent it from rolling farther. She stared down at it. A pair of dusty Crocs appeared in her line of vision, attached to two skinny and equally dusty legs.

"Sorry, Ma," a melodic voice said.

Not Aninyeh. Nena wasn't a girl, unlike the owner of the voice. Nena looked up slowly, from the legs to the red shorts with a wide blue stripe down each side, the green-and-blue striped T-shirt with a big blue six on the right side, and a head of fresh box braids, which ended just below a delicate chin.

The girl looked up at her, five other kids behind her all waiting for Nena to relinquish their ball.

"Do you play, Ma?" the girl asked, pointing at the ball under Nena's foot. "You play football—eh, soccer?" The girl had assumed Nena was American, flipping to the US term for Nena's benefit.

Nena hadn't played in years. Not since she'd been on a proper team in secondary school, during the start of her training for Dispatch. She'd been a fairly good winger. Was a bit rusty now.

Nena pulled herself out of it. She searched the area, nostalgia and loss bubbling within her. This wasn't N'nkakuwe. She wasn't Aninyeh . . . not anymore. And her father and family—she surveyed the area, the different people, the different buildings, the guards that belonged to Judah, wearing their gaiters around their noses and mouths because they'd seen her thunder through the village as if it were hers with Femi nervously following, no doubt wondering what was wrong with her boss.

Nena let out a low breath, pushing out that grief. Remembering that all of it—her village, her people—was no more. But these people were here. She mustered a tiny quirk of her mouth.

"I haven't played in a long time," she finally said, clearing her thoughts of *before*, rooting herself in her *after*. "Not since I was a little older than you." Nena frowned. "I'd say eleven?"

"I'm twelve!" The girl pointed at her chest, blown away that Nena had had the audacity to guess anything less than that ripe old age.

Nena's hands flew up in surrender. "Apologies, friend, twelve. Here you go."

She picked up her foot, then batted the ball between her feet, one to the other—the little move her father, Michael, had taught her—before passing it swiftly to the girl, who caught the ball with her foot, scooping it onto the top of her shoe and bouncing it twice, until it was up in the air, where she kicked it. It soared to her playmates, and one of them caught it, the game back in play.

"You are good," the girl said.

Nena held up two fingers, widening the space between them. "Rusty."

The girl suddenly grabbed Nena's fingers, pushing them closer together. "Only a little."

She smiled shyly at Nena, who could only return a dumbfounded stare in her general direction, blinking back a sudden spring of hot tears to clear her vision, entirely undone at this simplest display of kindness.

24

"Company's coming." Femi pulled up beside her when the girl had run off in a puff of dust, yelling and screaming, after her friends.

Nena straightened, recalibrating. *Get yourself together.*

The gaiter-wearing guards, foot soldiers, whatever they were supposed to be, approached, four of them, all with rifles or automatics slung over their backs. And Nena had blindly walked herself and her teammate into the heart of a location with a layout she hadn't memorized with potential ops approaching.

The men stopped short of her and Femi, who stood at the ready. Femi was armed, as was Nena. She didn't think they'd do anything, not with the deal looming, but what did Nena know?

For the second time that night, Nena held up her hands in surrender. This time with what she hoped was a disarming smile.

"We just came for sightseeing," she said. "All good."

"Yeah, man," Femi chimed in, her right hand tucked into the small of her back, where Nena knew her weapon rested. "It looked like a party, so we stopped."

It was hard to determine what they thought because the gaiters hid their expressions.

"Follow us," the one nearest Nena said. He beckoned with his hand for them to come. The other three parted, forming a pathway between them where Nena and Femi were expected to walk with the guards flanking them. Nena and Femi did as they were told.

"Do we send the authorities?" Billy asked through the comms.

"I'm using a drone satellite," Evers said. "I can give you a rough schematic of the village's makeup in case you need a way out."

"And what are we gonna do, huh?" Femi asked. "Run out into the jungle? I ain't Tarzan."

"It won't come to that," Nena said, assessing their surroundings now, something she should have done the moment she got out of the car. "Be at the ready just in case. But I think we're good."

Femi snorted. "Good? These guys don't look 'good.' Didn't look that way at the soccer game earlier either. While I love a good fight, we can't take them all."

"We won't have to."

Nena and Femi were led to a house at the edge of the village. It was in an area on the outskirts with the best vantage point into the village and the dense woods at its back. The guards were joined by two more on their walk through the bustling village. Nena tracked their way. The driver couldn't be seen; he was using his free time to socialize with the villagers, which meant no keys to the car in case she and Femi did have to make a getaway.

The front door opened, and Judah came out, stopping in the doorway. He watched them draw near. Average height and build, but sturdy and powerful beneath the tank that hugged his chest and camo pants cut off at the knees. His own gaiter was pulled down around his neck. Unlike his people, he had no fear of retribution from anyone on the outside, but he still wore it in solidarity.

He said, "Welcome, though your visit is unexpected." His voice was deeper than she'd thought.

"It was sudden, yes," Nena said, apologetically.

"Your visit is unexpected because I didn't expect it to happen so soon." Her eyebrow arched. "You knew we'd come?" she reiterated.

His gesture was coy. "Which one of you is the Knight?"

"Shouldn't you know already since you're telepathic?" Femi countered.

He laughed, clapping his hands once at her moxie. He nodded. "I'm not telepathic. I know strategy, and I know how rich people like you work to get the small guys to give you what you want. Everyone comes to my village ever since the gems were discovered. Everyone wants to own it. Wants to own us." He let the words sink in before offering, "Come in?"

"Stranger danger," Femi muttered from behind Nena where she'd angled to keep watch on the guards who'd brought them to Judah's.

"We enjoy the night air," Nena cut in.

She remained on alert, too, scanning the area for any hidden threats in the shadows. She had no doubt guns were trained on them, ready to cut either of them down the moment they stepped out of line.

"Knew you'd say that too." He snapped his fingers, his face brightening. "Maybe I *am* telepathic."

He gestured to the chairs that had seemingly materialized from his mind when another of his guys brought them out of the home without Judah having to say a word.

"At least honor me with a seat? Perhaps a beverage? Water? Beer?"

Femi sneaked Nena a hopeful peek.

"We're fine, thank you." Nena ignored the way Femi's face fell.

After a brief hesitation, Nena chose a chair, pulling it so hers was next to the one Judah had placed himself in. Femi followed Nena's lead, pulling her chair a little distance from Nena so she could keep watch over the areas in Nena's blind spot. Judah, aware of what they were doing, said nothing. The corner of his mouth twitched in a tiny, knowing smirk.

Nena told him, "Quite a show you and your—group—put on back at the soccer game. You could have at least let the game finish out."

"Free speech waits for no game." Judah chuckled, appraising Nena appreciatively. It reminded her of Elin's honeypot jokes. Nena closed the openings of her jacket. "We merely wanted your attention. Yours and the others', that is. This whole thing is our way of life, Ms. Knight."

"What is your claim to the tanzanite?" Nena asked when they were seated. "You have no claims to the lands where it was found."

"I do not," Judah acquiesced. "But this is my home. These are my people, and I don't want them taken advantage of."

"How do we know you're not the one taking advantage?" Nena asked. "You're holding them up from taking the deal that the Tribe is working to broker with the government and outside corporations on the miners' behalf." She leaned forward, placing an arm on her knees. "It's a deal of a lifetime for them. It gives them ownership for years to come. A legacy for their children and their children's children."

He scoffed. "I have heard that all before. If you think that will really happen, then you don't know big government."

Nena bottled her irritation, keeping her face blank.

Judah spread his hands as if to say *That's life*. "The government . . . is not always for the people."

"But you are." She eyed him skeptically.

He asked, "But why not deal directly with the Westerners, who are offering so much more cash money right now? Why not a huge cash payout that is a sure thing? Cut out the middleman?"

"You might get a large sum of money now. But it won't be for the long haul," Nena pointed out.

Femi tossed in, "Fast money isn't always the best money."

Judah threw an arm over the back of his chair. "Fast money will get my countrymen what they need right now. We need things right now." He pressed his finger onto his armrest, emphasizing the point.

She observed his people making patrols, weapons in hand, intermingling with the townspeople. "Your past techniques of hijacking and disrupting government business. Of inciting the public like you did at the soccer game. Has it all worked well for you?"

He watched the townspeople going through their nightly rituals, joking, preparing for the next day. Kids still kicking the soccer ball about and even his guards taking part in it. "I think I'm empowering my people to fight for what is rightfully theirs. And to be proud of who they are."

Noble would love this man. Judah's eyes shone with a ferocity Nena had seen only in her father, in Witt, in people who wholeheartedly believed in what they were doing.

Judah matched Nena's gaze with his own. "Absolutely."

"By any means necessary?"

He cracked an easy grin. "Malcolm X said it best, eh?"

Nena shrugged. "As long as you're not the one playing your people. Or the one being played."

He reared from the nerve she'd intentionally struck. She'd wobbled his pride a little, poked around in the brush to see what came out. Nena watched as anger rippled over him, and then how it seemed to melt away as quickly as it had appeared. "When you and your contingent visit our mine tomorrow, you will see all we simple farmers have achieved for ourselves."

Slowly, Judah Wasira straightened, and the handsome man of average height and build seemed much larger. His energy charged through the air.

"But do not think me a simple village farmer, Ms. Knight." Judah said this low and slow, his eyes steely as they bored into her. "Doing that would be a mistake."

She didn't back down. He'd probably expected that she'd cower because she was a woman, and most men underestimated women. They certainly didn't know what to make of a woman like her.

The tension between them was as thick as the humidity hanging in the air. During conflict, Nena always fought to the finish. But she also knew when it was time to retreat and recalibrate. This was one of those times. She'd poked and prodded the rebel leader enough.

She said, "I would never consider you simple. Your little stunt earlier at the game was proof that you are not simple or easily intimidated.

And neither am I." She watched his eyebrow twitch his surprise, and the smoldering fire in his eyes simmered down. "Have a good evening, Judah Wasira."

As Nena joined Femi in step, Femi said sagely, "I was right about his vibe. That old rob-the-rich-give-to-the-poor kind of energy. He might be all right."

Her comment traveled in the air and was like a switch, flipping the mood to a lighter note.

"Thank you, Nena Knight's friend," Judah said. His demeanor easing back to familiar smiles and cockiness.

Nena couldn't decide if it was endearing or not. She disliked not being able to put a finger on what made a man like him dangerous but one to be respected as well.

Nena hesitated, then decided to go for it. "You should rethink your strategy of how you're handling your government and your people," she said, working at the knot of frustration growing in her chest. "I don't sense they are against you, Judah."

"No disrespect," his words as sharp as a double-edged sword, "but you know nothing about my government, or about me."

A tell. He didn't like people assuming things about him or his country. But Judah's mistake was to show his hand and how he could be angered so quickly.

"Don't presume to know what I know and don't know." She matched him, refusing to concede even an inch. It was true: Nena didn't know Judah's government the way he knew it. But what Judah knew was a microcosm. Nena was disappointed that he was too thickheaded to understand help when it was being offered.

"At the rate you're going, you'll bring about nothing but problems for you and your people, in the end."

Judah stiffened. "Is that a threat, Ms. Knight? You are a guest here."

She shook her head ruefully. "Not a threat. What I fear is that it's a premonition."

25

The mine was on the outskirts of Latema, beyond where Nena and Femi had traveled to speak with Judah the night before. Nena and Evers were in the first Sprinter, a Mercedes truck ahead of them with a driver and local officers. Billy and Femi sat in the second Sprinter with Asogi, Tegete, Odemba, and Dubin and more of their entourage. Bridget had thankfully stayed behind.

The ride was bumpy, becoming more aggressively so as they coasted along, the vegetation becoming less dense as they neared the work area. The mud, a reddish brown, and there was no avoiding it clinging to clothes. The group had attempted to come out as early as possible to beat the worst of the unforgiving sun. But there was no beating the sun in Africa.

They passed a low-lying building. Nena guessed, and Evers confirmed, it was the base of the town's mining operations. An L-shaped one-level building of corrugated metal roofing of many rusted shades atop a sturdy-looking structure made of cinder blocks. Guards with rifles and long blades walked the perimeter, something Nena didn't like but had no authority over. But she and her team would make do if they had to. Hopefully they wouldn't.

They found Judah standing at the top of the spiral-curving mine, looking down at the people working in it. It went on several rows down. Everyone was mud and dirt caked, all becoming various hues of reddish brown. His guards milled around, not really engaging with anyone. But their weapons reminded the entourage piling out of the once-pristine black vans that they would go from relaxed to not relaxed in an instant if they had to. Nena counted as many guns as she could. Over a dozen up top. More down below. Too many scattered to properly gauge. She didn't like that at all.

But Judah was gregarious enough. With his own rifle strapped to the back of him, a bowie knife strapped to his right thigh, he threw his arms out in welcome with a huge smile on his face.

"Welcome!" he said, as if they were at his house for dinner.

Femi snorted, likely thinking the same thing Nena was thinking. He was bullshit.

Asogi replied with the same energy, only Nena suspected his was real. "We missed you at the game yesterday."

"Village matters required my attention," Judah replied without a hint of apology. "But it was a good game nonetheless, yes?"

"Until protestors spoiled the end," Dubin threw in. His eyes danced around as he took in the entire scene, processing the rhythmic strikes of pickax against hard-compacted dirt and rock.

The people—mostly men with some women mingled in, kids weaving throughout with jugs of water to give to the workers—chanted a traditional song as they threw their tools over their shoulders, then brought them down on the land with their mighty strength, breaking ground, revealing shimmering ridges of bronze-like glass beneath in the deeper parts of the mine. The *tink, tink, tink* of the axes on stone came every three or four words as the lead chanter sang in his baritone voice, accompanied by the rest, who chimed in, with the *tink, tink, tink* never breaking stride.

It was a mesmerizing sound. It was a proud sight to see these townspeople, working in one accord, mining resources that were theirs alone. There was a different vibe from what Nena had seen before in other countries where the mines were owned by thieving companies bent on pillaging the land and robbing the people. Conflict gems mined under duress and with horrible working conditions, or even mined by enslaved people with no say in when they wanted to stop.

Judah ignored Dubin. "So here we are. See how well things are going? We have a system in place. A rotation of townspeople in and out who sign up to take shifts."

Femi frowned. "I thought these gems were supposed to be blue."

Evers said, hands on hips, "They're trichroic."

"It's what?" Femi asked, annoyed.

Judah nodded. "It shows different colors depending on how you look at it. When it's in the ground, it's mostly bronze or brown, which is what you see here." His arm swept the expanse of the shaft. "It turns blue or violet when it's heated."

"Get the hell out," Femi breathed, mesmerized.

"What about the guns?" Odemba asked from behind her sunglasses, getting back to business. "If all is well here, why the guns?"

He looked at her as if she had two heads. "Because this is Tanzania, and shit happens."

Odemba's face went flat.

Tegete said softly, "Still, Judah, this is a huge undertaking, and you haven't even begun to scratch the surface of what is here."

"We are not imbeciles here, sir," Judah told him, wiping sweat from his brow with a mud-stained gaiter he wore around his neck to protect him from the sun. "We purposely mine in small increments so as not to overmine the area. We think long. We are in for the long stretch."

"I think it's 'in it for the long haul,'" Femi said helpfully. She gave Judah a doe-eyed look when he focused his attention on her, ignoring Nena's, which warned Femi to stay out of it.

Dubin had wandered away from the group and was conducting his own survey. His eyebrows bunched, and he craned his neck to see how far down the hole went. He watched carefully as the baskets holding rough-cut tanzanite were hauled up with the pulley systems or loaded into carts, and his eyes lit greedily when he saw the amount.

"What about safety measures?" Dubin called out from where he stood, his lips pursing. "How do you ensure the mine is stable? What of gas leaks? Structural supports?"

Judah frowned. His eyes narrowed at Dubin, and he hesitated before finally saying, "There's no gas here."

Dubin's eyes widened. "There's always gas trapped beneath the surface of the earth. In pockets just waiting for the unsuspecting shovel to strike a rock and make a spark. Then—" Dubin flashed his hands in the air and spread his arms apart wide. He mouthed an exaggerated *boom*.

Everyone watched Judah's reaction, which, to his credit, he tried to keep bland. However, Nena could see the zigzag vein pulsating in his temple and the way the corner of his lips firmed.

"You see, Mr. Asogi," Dubin said, approaching them with more swagger now that he had the rapt attention of the prime minister and minister of mining, "that's what DubiCorp can do—"

"And the other interested parties," Tegete interjected.

Dubin barely paused. "Of course. Them too. But what I'm getting at is that a professional team is what is needed to ensure the safety of the people here."

Judah took an angry step forward, and suddenly everyone was on alert, prepared to stop a potential altercation. "I protect our people. Their safety is of my utmost concern, always. What are you playing at, man?"

Dubin held up a hand as if in surrender. "I mean no disrespect, Judah. You've done a tremendous job here so far. For what you have."

They all knew a backhanded compliment when they heard one, and it was what Dubin had just delivered, though no one called him on it. It was a way for him to inform them the mine was below standards thanks to townspeople who knew nothing of regulations and gases and whatever else was needed to successfully mine in the earth.

Judah turned away from Dubin, to Nena's relief. Perhaps Dubin would get out of there with his head intact. The group followed Judah on the sloping path, heading into the heart of the mine. They rounded the first bend, picking their way over jutting rock.

"I did not invite your lot here to belittle what we've accomplished. You're here on good faith to see the wealth of the mine for yourselves so you know we can deliver."

"Of course not," Tegete cut in. At the same time, Mr. Asogi said, "No, no, brother. We commend what you all ha—"

Asogi didn't get to finish.

A boom, not from Dubin's pantomiming, erupted from within the depths of the mine. It ripped from below, shaking the ground they stood on, growing faster and harder until it exploded from an opening of a cave, spewing out rock, smoke, and fumes. The people in the mine closest to the eruption were screaming. Everything began shaking; a rumble, long, low, and violent, moved the earth beneath their feet. The people in the mine scrambled to climb out, their hands reaching, begging for someone to save them.

Nena and the others dropped to the ground, crouching low so they wouldn't lose their footing as the ground shook beneath them and nearly pitched them into the open maw of the mine.

"Take cover!" someone yelled over the screams.

The upper ridges of the mine cleaved off, crumbling like a cookie with not enough butter and pushing all the dirt and rock down into the mine and on top of those who were trapped in it. Nena threw her hands over her head, moving toward Tegete to ensure his safety as debris from the walls surrounding them rained down on their heads.

As quickly as the explosion and subsequent quake had come upon them, everything—movement, sound, breathing, life—ceased.

———

"Tegete, are you hurt?" Nena coughed, her lungs thick and burning with the dust that blanketed them. Her hand groped in the light, reddened from the dust that had blown up in the air. People screamed and moaned from everywhere. One by one, those in the delegation began to stir from their initial frozen state of horror and disbelief.

"I'm fine," the councilman said, blinking through the caked layers of dirt on his eyes. "Are you okay? Is everyone?"

Nena couldn't speak for everyone. She checked herself, finding nothing major, just minor scrapes and bruises. Everyone else in their group seemed to have fared the same. Nena checked for her team, finding them dazed but well. Luckily, none of them had made it too far down. They'd had to contend only with the top few feet coming down. But the people below, those on the side where the mine had crumbled, breaking off in large shards of sharp red rock with ribbons of glass-like bronze rock sparkling as they caught the sunlight . . . all Nena could see were dirt and mud and rock where people used to be.

And others, quicker thinking than she, were running to pull them out before it was too late. Nena didn't have to say a word to her team. They were already on the move, heading toward the disaster to help. She suggested Tegete and Asogi head back to the buses, but they refused, saying their place was with the people. Judah yelled at his scrambling men, trying to gain control and determine how many Latemans were unaccounted for.

Nena worked beside Billy, digging people out and pulling them to safety, but despite their efforts, three of the townspeople, the ones nearest to the site of the initial explosion, were dead.

Judah knelt at the edge of the mine, watching as the bodies were pulled from it and put on the flatbed truck. "There hasn't been one mishap since we began digging, until now. We check and double-check safety protocols. We are always so very careful."

His grief and confusion were apparent. Nena looked from him to the three side by side on the flatbed. She walked over to them, grabbing a tarp discarded on the ground. She shook it out, ensuring it was clean as could be, then draped it gently over the bodies.

Billy sidled up to her, giving the bodies a few seconds of silence before saying, "So what are you thinking?"

Nena squinted up at him, against the sun's glare. "I'm thinking it's tragic," she murmured.

Billy gave her a look that said he didn't believe that was all she had to say. It wasn't. But Nena was reserving her conclusion for later.

"Mines have incidents all the time." She played devil's advocate, casting a glance at Judah when she heard him going off on one of his people. Dubin sauntered toward Asogi, Tegete, and Odemba, their security surrounding them. He held them in a quiet huddle that, from the looks of Tegete, was not discussing something good.

Femi and Evers joined Nena and Billy where they'd moved a respectful distance from the bodies.

"How the hell does this happen?" Judah asked one of his people in a loud whisper, all evidence of his bravado from the night before, and his big-man attitude from earlier that morning, gone. "Today of all days. When they are here." The last part sounded both anguished and accusatory.

"Looks like everyone's been accounted for," Femi updated them.

Evers brushed dirt out of his hair. "The injuries aren't too bad. Other than these three, nothing else too severe. At the risk of sounding insensitive to the loss of life, the partial collapse wasn't that bad."

How convenient, Nena thought. The well-timed explosion was just enough to influence the course of the negotiations, but not enough to destroy the mine and its worth entirely.

"I can't believe this went down. Something doesn't seem right." Nena worked through her initial thoughts as Billy watched.

"It's possible," Billy threw in, coming to the same conclusion.

Evers, totally lost. "What's possible?"

"The risk is too great." Nena didn't want to go there. "We were in there. All of us."

Femi picked up the thread. "But we weren't that far in."

Evers bit at his bottom lip, working through the *Tetris* blocks of information dropping down until they began to take shape. He gawked at the three. "Are you suggesting . . ." He lowered his voice. "Sabotage? But the—the variables, the likelihood of failure, are too great. Anyone could have been killed, the prime minister and minister of mining were there, and the mine could have been completely lost."

"But it wasn't," Nena pointed out.

Her eyes went from person to person, trying to assess how each of them seemed to be handling the aftereffects of the collapse. It was a major blow to Judah's position as spokesperson for the miners and town chiefs. A collapse would undercut the trust the miners had in him to manage the mine and the deal on their behalf. They could feel pressure to sell, worried that investors would lose interest in a mine that was unsafe.

What would something like that drive someone like Judah, or any of the players, to do? It would all come down to optics for the government. Optics Asogi and Odemba would have to play by, no matter how much they might want the townspeople to win in this deal.

Dubin had kicked into "the expert" mode. His voice rising as if he were the ringleader of a circus. "I can tell you now, they don't have sturdy infrastructure, but that's expected because why would farmers have the tools and machinery for a proper mining setup? They would only have their shovels and buckets. The CO_2 level is likely off, and the gauges I saw are outdated. There's no telling the conditions they've been working under. The gases are combustible, and coupled with no sensors to alert anyone that levels are off, it's a powder keg." He made a *boom* sound. "Just like this. I'm betting that's what happened down there."

Odemba sighed with resignation. "This is a key reason why the reform is imperative. Why these people should sign on to it and have protection against collapses like these. We'll have to shut it down until it is deemed safe."

Nena found it difficult to gauge where Odemba was in this. Did she sympathize with the townspeople, or was she exactly what Judah claimed them all to be, only about politics and the bottom line? Nena just wasn't sure.

"You cannot do that," cried out one of the chieftains who'd come running when he'd heard word of the accident, approaching them. "This is our livelihood and will be our legacy. Any halt on production is food taken from our mouths."

"Papa, please. Let me handle it." Judah tried to stop him, but the older man pushed Judah off as if Judah weighed nothing.

"This is handling?" the man roared at Judah. "Three of our people are dead. We put these proceedings in your hands because you assured me and the other chiefs you were knowledgeable about these things and would deliver a good deal for us."

Judah told him through clenched teeth, "And I still will."

He was a rocket waiting to explode, and despite Nena's earlier feelings that Judah was too egotistical in believing he had a firm grip on any kind of power, she felt bad for him. He'd barely had time to understand how all he'd built had crashed on his head, quite literally. He hadn't had a chance to assess the damage and speak with those who'd been hurt. And now, one and now two more of the local chiefs who'd trusted Judah to handle the negotiations were converging on him and telling him he'd failed. And they were doing it right in front of the last people he'd want to be dressed down in front of.

"Three are dead, man. Do you not see? It is on your watch this tragedy has befallen us."

Judah reared on the man, seemed about to strike him down as the rage built to maximum capacity behind his eyes. His mouth opened for what Nena knew was going to be the worst possible thing to say.

She stepped in between them, placing a calming hand on his arm. She moved into his line of vision, blocking him from the direct view of the chief, now flanked by two of his kinsmen.

Nena cut in. "Perhaps a walk to assess the damage, see to the people. They come first, right, Judah? That's what you were telling me?"

Asogi offered, "We will provide recompense during this time."

"We can't afford it, Prime Minister." Odemba put a placating hand up when Asogi began to argue. "This is what the companies we plan to contract out would provide. And because we are still in negotiations for the reform, they don't have insurance for the dead, sir. And the government cannot accommodate their loss."

Dubin shifted on his feet, clearing his throat as if he wanted to say, "I'm here!" He remained smartly silent.

The chieftain pointed a shaky finger at Judah. "Eh heh, Judah, now you see?" His body vibrated beneath the traditional multicolored cloths wrapped around his upper body. "You said you knew what you were doing here."

Judah strained to look beyond Nena, likely to tell the old man where he could shove his reprimand, but when his head moved, she moved in sync, staying in his line of vision until Judah had no other option but to acknowledge her.

He blew out through his nostrils, his dark-brown eyes searching hers for answers she couldn't give. She didn't know what was going on. He couldn't understand how, in a matter of moments, he could effectively lose everything he'd been fighting so hard for.

Nena recognized the look of him, the pride he had in his people and what they'd accomplished on their own.

The vision and dreams he'd had for their future: that they'd be rich off their own supply and be beholden to no one ever again. She knew that look because it was the same one her birth father, Michael Asym, had had when he built N'nkakuwe into the bustling town it had become on Aburi Mountain. And she knew that look again in Noble Knight, her adoptive father, every time he talked about the vision for the African Tribal Council and the impact it would have on the African people.

Judah deflated in front of her, accepting that his fight could not be in that moment. He gave her a quick nod. He resettled his gaiter around his neck and shoulders, pulling it over his mouth, since he was going back down. Then he stalked off, back ramrod straight, with his fists balled at his sides, disappearing into the thick of his people, where he blended in and they were unable to tell him from anyone else.

"Horrible accidents happen, Uncles," Nena said, turning to the chief and his compatriots. "Judah is to be commended for his quick thinking, which saved many lives."

Another chief, short and squat, wearing a navy-colored Adidas tracksuit, said, "But still lost three."

Nena agreed with him. "Three too many." She looked away in a second of silence for them. "But all is not lost here, Uncles. Just give Judah a moment." She could feel prickly heat on her neck and turned to catch Dubin watching her. He'd let his facade slip, and his distaste and growing irritation were clear. When he saw that she was looking at him, his face mellowed into docility. He gave her a tiny smile that she didn't return.

She focused on the three chiefs again. "When all is clear here, Judah will return to you and discuss your next steps in more detail. Though you may be angry, do not address him here with us watching. He is still your kinsman."

Tegete slid up next to Nena, seconding her advice when he saw their misogyny was about to show at being addressed by a woman, especially one they did not know.

"Brothers," Tegete said softly. "Here and in front of strangers is not the place to air your grievances."

"Ah, but is there nothing we can do?" Asogi asked, dumbfounded. "These are our people! If we don't give recompense to the families for what has happened here . . ."

"We cannot. We have no deal yet, sir," Odemba said, always the diligent reminder of what they couldn't do per government policy.

Dubin stepped forward until he was next to Nena. Too close, in her opinion. "It's why they need companies like mine backing them up. Let me front the money to make the mine up to code and fully operational."

Nena watched the scene in front of her, unable to believe that just the day before, everyone here had been cheering and celebrating, with only a small protest to mar the end of their game. And today, grief and shock. She didn't even know where to begin. How to help. She looked to Tegete.

He had his sat phone to his ear. "Already on the line to put together relief."

"And a compensatory package for the families." She couldn't believe there would be nothing for them. That the lives lost were just that, lost, with no help for the families left behind.

Tegete confirmed, "We'll speak later." He moved away from the group when the line connected. "Noble?"

Asogi and Odemba melted away into the background, heading toward their vans to return to the hotel, their hands gesturing wildly as they held a heated conversation.

"Where's the fucking popcorn, right?"

"What?" she asked, startled. She'd forgotten Dubin was there, still beside her, his sweat making red and brown rivulets on his neck. His blond hair had taken on a coppery tint. She didn't like his ability to go around undetected or easily forgotten, especially by her. She couldn't make that mistake again.

Dubin's eyes shone brightly as he watched the chaos. Nena half expected him to rub his hands together in glee. He spat on the ground and ran his hand over his forehead, leaving a streak across it.

"It's a regular shit show, isn't it? I tried to tell them before there wasn't time to waste and get a contract signed right away. They're all in a predicament now. How do you think they'll manage?"

"I don't know what you mean." Her body told her to move. She didn't want to engage with this man, and being of assistance with the rest of her team was more important than being chatted up by Dubin.

He became serious, studying her. "You don't care for me much, do you, Ms. Knight?"

She shook her head, indicating she wasn't following.

"We haven't had a chance to talk much since you arrived."

She raised an eyebrow. "It's literally only been a day."

He lifted a shoulder. "Maybe we can reset and start off on better footing. We're on the same side, I hope."

She couldn't wait to hear this. "And what side is that, Mr. Dubin?"

"Asogi and Odemba represent the government, which refuses to help poor villagers when they've lost so much and have to start again. They look like uncaring assholes instead of the saviors they tried to be. A shame because it's not their fault. Their hands are tied. But business is business and rules are rules, right, Ms. Knight? You know it well since your father is such a big guy now, right? And your father knows optics. This here, bad optics. Dead farmers. A government that gives them the cold shoulder in their greatest time of need. Asogi will have to report to the president on this one, and she won't be pleased at all. Odemba could lose her job over this. Or maybe Asogi. Depends on who blames whom."

She hated to agree, but Dubin was right. This was business, and all the insurance and payouts for injuries or death would have been built into it. But now, there was nothing.

"Judah's knocked down a peg or two because he told his people to hold out. And now look what happened. Let's see how he talks himself out of this with the chieftains. Hard to stand on a soapbox, spewing ideals, when the mine's been shut down and three of these people are dead."

He smirked, causing an unease to build within her. His ice-blue eyes held a hunger. She stared into them, parsing out what it was that didn't sit right with her. While everyone else was in shock and despair, Dubin seemed to relish the devastation, like he was watching one of his American football games.

He luxuriated in this scene, fed upon it like the parasite he was. "Sounds like they need someone to get things in order."

He turned to follow the rest of their entourage, who had collected at the vans, tipping his imaginary hat to her. "Sounds like they now need . . ." He pretended to think about it while Nena fought to keep her face blank and not show her hand. "Well, me!"

The smile he cracked was an oil slick that left a lasting residue, clinging to her like a tacky adhesive. She felt her repulsion for him in her gut, felt that throughout all this, Dubin was too chipper, too eager to jump in and show Odemba, Asogi, and the chiefs that they were lucky to have him accessible, offering a ready-made deal with no red tape or bidding wars.

The town chieftains would be eager to sell, worried about another collapse. The government, under Odemba's guidance, would be relieved to get this messy situation handled before any negative news leaked. Which made the circumstances ideal for DubiCorp to make a deal quickly—and disproportionately in its favor. Nena had no way to prove the collapse was anything but accidental, not unless she called for a team to conduct some investigation. She made a note to bring that up to Tegete.

She had no proof that Odemba or Dubin was behind the collapse, either, and she wasn't one to make accusations without something concrete to back her up. Through the thick of people, in a dirty and torn jersey that notes from intel said was his signature, gaiter pressed against his nose and mouth to keep the dust from his lungs, Judah worked side by side to salvage what they could from the disintegrated portion of the mine.

As much as he had done and would do, as much as he had fought and tried to make the people as self-sufficient as possible, the makers of their own destiny, Judah would be labeled the bad guy here because, in Odemba's eyes, he was foolhardy in holding up progress on the reform—which in turn had denied the workers' families the insurance needed for the deaths and injuries of their loved ones—and for making everyone wait.

To his people, Judah's light had dimmed because he'd put himself, his pride, and his ideals above the needs of the people. To Asogi and Odemba, he'd shown himself to be in over his head. Like Icarus, Judah had flown too close to the sun, and he'd crashed hard and fast to the ground. Leaving Dubin—Nena watched him sauntering off, in his element as the big boss—to become the great White savior. And all she could think was, *God help them all.*

26

Nena was eight hours ahead, which put Miami at 5:00 p.m. Alone in her suite, Nena set up her computer at the table. She switched on the scrambler and proceeded to log on. She was only using WhatsApp, but the added layer of security made her feel that it was less likely anyone was hitchhiking on her line, finding their way to the people back home she fought desperately to protect at all times.

Her first video call was to her parents and sister to give a quick update to her father. As tense as her body was feeling from everything she'd encountered so far, she plastered a pleasant enough expression on her face so her family would be less likely to think anything was wrong.

"What's wrong?" Noble said immediately when his image flickered onto the screen, showing him with his forehead creased into several rows of worry lines. Delphine crowded in next to him. They lay in bed with Delphine's hair pulled into the head wrap she'd sleep in. Nena silently chastised herself. They were in London, which meant it was pretty late to be calling them.

"Hello, Mum, Dad," Nena said. "Had I known you'd returned back home, I wouldn't have rung you this late. You're supposed to keep me posted of your whereabouts."

Noble looked at his wife in faux disbelief. "Eh, but who is the child and who is the parent?"

Elin's video popped on, showing her against the background of the glass door that separated her balcony from the rest of the condo. From the looks of it, the day was very sunny and blue. She held a wiggly Asym in her hands as he peered seriously at his grandparents and aunt in the small box before him while holding his bottle with fisted hands. Nena felt a pang in her chest. She missed his pudgy segmented baby arms immensely.

"Hi, sweethearts," Delphine said with a wave, totally unbothered. She cooed at the baby, talking in the high-pitched baby language only she and Asym seemed to like. He broke out into a big gummy smile, drooling some of his milk.

Elin groaned. "Mum, don't get him all bothered. I just changed him."

"I can't help he loves his mimi," Delphine replied, still in her high for-Asym-only voice. Asym cackled, reaching for his second-favorite person in the world, because Elin was his first.

Noble waved his hands, dismissing the lot of them. "Don't mind the time. We came home for some business, but we'll return soon. Has something happened?"

His wife side-eyed him. "Nena, dear, how are you doing? Are you okay?"

Elin scrutinized the screen. "Yeah, sis, you look tired."

Nena said, "It's about one a.m."

"What's happened?" Noble barked.

"Nothing's wrong, Dad," Nena said. "Everything's still the same. I met the leader of that group in his village."

"For what? You shouldn't be going off to parts unknown," he said. "I want this deal, but I want you safe more."

"It was fine. I needed to see him in his element. There's so much . . . politics here with the PM and the councilman. Dubin is something else."

Delphine rolled her eyes. "Something else is right. And he has that insipid wife. The woman needs to grow a backbone and put him in his place! She makes wives look bad with all that mewling and deference to him like he's some king."

Nena tensed. She looked to her dad, wondering if he would break the news. Their family had promised to have no more secrets among them.

Elin was incredulous. "Mum! Taking the poor woman's plight a bit personal, yeah? Maybe she likes it old school. Docile wife. It's a thing, and people like it. No judgment."

If Nena hadn't been preoccupied wondering when her father would say something, she'd have commented on Elin's "no judgment." Elin had plenty of judgment to pass around when it came to women's empowerment and who she felt were empowering themselves.

"Maybe she'd like a friend," Delphine suggested to Nena's growing dread. "The wife, I mean. Maybe she can be a way into figuring out what her husband's up to. I don't think his investors will be good for the country or the miners." Noble became more uncomfortable as Delphine spoke, shifting around like he couldn't find a comfortable position. Nena imagined he was weighing his next words and whether he'd remain in that bed that night or have to sleep elsewhere.

"Nena's not befriending that man's wife," Noble finally said gruffly. "Absolutely not."

Perplexed at the sudden mood swing, Delphine turned to him. Elin cocked her head to the side. Even little Asym suddenly stilled, looking at the screen with concern, his mouth in the shape of a wet *O*.

"Dad," Nena started, not wanting to be the cause of any family strife. "It's fine." She didn't need her mother and sister worrying any more than they already were. And she certainly didn't want her parents arguing over her.

Noble put his fist to his mouth in deep thought. Or maybe he was psyching himself up for what was coming next. His fingers spread out to stop any more conversation. If anyone outside looked in, they'd never believe a big man like Noble Knight, High Council of the Tribe, could ever be concerned about what his wife and daughters thought about him.

Delphine knew her husband well after forty years. They'd built the African Tribal Council from the ground up and had created an empire. She could read him better than herself and knew his mannerisms—the way his shoulders hunched like they were currently doing. The way he held his face when in deep contemplation or when about to drop unfavorable news.

"Noble Knight," Delphine said in the warning voice the other three knew too well.

Someone was about to be in trouble. Definitely Noble. Probably Nena too. For once, Elin was in the clear, and her audible exhale showed it.

"Explain," Delphine said.

The man who'd passed down death decrees, who ruled the Tribe with an iron fist and terrified all who encountered him, quelled by the simple command from his wife.

"Dubin's wife is from Nena's past," Noble rushed out. "Nena's *past* past."

Nena couldn't see her sister's or mother's expressions. She was too busy staring at the wall beyond her screen.

Delphine said nothing, leaving Noble dangling on a string to continue on his own.

"Nena recognized the woman's picture and brought it to my attention."

"When?" was Delphine's question.

"Before she left."

"And you still had her go?" Delphine's voice rose a notch. "I can't believe you, Noble."

"Seriously, Dad?" Under normal circumstances, Elin would have never interjected herself into her parents' conversation. She valued her life. But Elin would brave their parents to protect her little sister, especially when it came to Nena's past.

Elin continued, "I would have gone instead. I can come and take over now. I'll bring the baby to you."

Nena finally looked at the screen. Her mother was glaring at her father. Her father looked as if he'd failed them miserably. And her sister struggled with Asym, trying to juggle him and type out a message on her cell that Nena knew was coming to her. They were a family in conflict. All because of her.

27

Nena's phone pinged.

ELIN: Wut the duck?

Nena jerked back, frowning.

"Damn spell-check," Elin muttered. Louder she said, "Dad, I can be in country by end of day tomorrow."

"That would look bad to the people here and to the Tribe. That would make it look like I can't handle this." Nena could barely believe she was saying her sister should stay when all she'd been wanting was for Elin to take over.

Delphine's glower had not let up. "What role did she play in Nena's past?"

Nena sighed, telling them in one line who Bridget was to her.

Delphine, whose voice never rose, as she thought it improper, abandoned that practice. She let out a litany of words in Twi that only Nena could understand and would not repeat. "Noble, how could you subject Nena to that woman again. After Paul and the other two resurfaced, how was this Bridget overlooked? How is she not dead?"

That was only the second time Nena could remember that Delphine had ever verbally said someone should die. Paul had been the first, after he'd made an attempt on Noble's life and had threatened their family and the Baxters.

"Well, it can't happen now, can it? Her death would look suspicious not only to the outside world, but within the Tribe, especially after Witt and all the upheaval within the Tribe." Noble chanced a look at his wife.

Delphine's face registered disgust. "Is that what only matters to you? What the Tribe thinks? What about what your daughter thinks or feels coming across that woman again?"

Nena's phone buzzed.

ELIN: Why didn't u tell me?

NENA: Bc I can handle it.

She needed to own her part, knowing her father would take the heat and say he'd forced her to come. They'd believe it, knowing Nena was the most loyal and wouldn't go against her father's wishes.

"Mum."

Her mother stopped, turning her attention to her daughter with eyes that swam with concern only a mother could have for her child.

"Don't be too upset. I agreed to go."

"Like you'd ever tell Dad no," Elin grumbled.

Probably true. "I said I could handle it. I know what's at stake. And I am dealing accordingly."

Hadn't Cort said not everyone deserved a death decree? Perhaps confronting this bit of her past could be what freed Nena from the prison of it.

"Darling . . ." But then Delphine trailed off. She hesitated as if she wanted to say more, but she knew her children, and she knew to support them how they needed, not how she wanted.

Nena continued, "It's not like before with Paul and how I kept his identity secret trying to protect you."

"Yeah, no more secrets. We agreed. Right, Dad?" Elin scoffed.

Noble's set jaw indicated he didn't appreciate Elin's tone, but he inclined his head. The most she was going to get.

"Right," Nena said, resetting the mood. "Now, if I can update you with what's happened . . ."

———

"And so, I'm figuring things out," Nena said after giving her family the rundown of the past day. "Like you said, Dad, there is more to Judah than meets the eye. But I'm not sure in what way. And Dubin is—"

"An arsehole," Elin added helpfully.

"Elin, your language!" Delphine chastised. "The boy—"

"Doesn't speak a bit of English yet," Elin finished. "And some language won't hurt him."

Delphine said no more, but her girls knew that didn't mean she'd given up. Elin would hear all Delphine's thoughts when she was back in the States with her grandson in her arms. Probably just like Noble would hear an earful once they logged off.

"You're doing well, sweetheart," Noble said, getting back to business. "Speak with Tegete about where we are with Asogi and how Dubin fits in. I don't want the miners thinking he's their only option just because he's there. They should have a choice of who they want to sell to. Make sure Tegete ensures Asogi also doesn't feel Dubin's the only option because of the mine incident."

Doubt began to creep in again. "This is more Elin's lane."

Elin held up her hand like a stop sign. "You got this, sis. But I'll be on the next flight out if you need me."

Delphine added, "You have always been more than you ever give yourself credit for."

Elin agreed. "You're not just the brawn of this fam. You're the brains too."

Nena was glad they were thousands of miles apart because if she'd been in their presence, she wouldn't have been able to handle their unshakable faith in her. Her family had always had more faith in Nena than she thought she deserved. It had been that way since the moment Delphine had invited young Aninyeh off the cold Paris street and made Nena a Knight.

"Thank you."

"Just don't piss off that bloody Judah anymore, yeah?" Elin moved on. "You don't need everyone against you. You need him, so channel a lil bit of me, yeah? Especially when you all have the big meet later."

The meeting . . . when Asogi and Odemba would officially talk terms for mining reform with Judah and hopefully get him to agree. Dubin was supposedly there as the representative for the outside private companies, but really for himself. Tegete would make sure everyone's interests were considered, with Nena rounding them out in whatever role was needed at the moment.

If Elin were here, she'd already have Judah eating out of the palm of her hand. And with either of her parents here, Nena bet the Dubins would have already been on the first plane back to Montana, the UK, or France—wherever it was that they lived. But Nena didn't have Elin's finesse or her parents' shrewdness for business. She didn't have their charisma or the eloquence to sway Judah to support the mining reform and urge his people to negotiate under those new terms. What Nena knew were her blades and how to dispatch.

Nena considered it all. Channeling Elin was more acting than Nena was capable of. She could do what she did best: use her knowledge from Dispatch and Network. She wasn't one for diplomacy or too much conversation.

Nena wasn't a quitter, either, so she was going to get this unusual mission successfully completed in the ways she knew best. Watch. Gather intel. And handle all the marks accordingly.

After all, she wasn't called Echo for nothing.

BEFORE

"Boss," Goon says to Witt, "YA's tagging on wet work with us from here on out?"

Goon has muscles on top of muscles. He's often found bench-pressing hundreds of pounds and admiring himself in the mirror with no shirt.

"Why do you call yourself Goon?" I ask—a rarity, because most of my questions are perfunctory, about training. But names and the stories behind them now interest me, especially since I've had so many already. Like the one Goon calls me, for instance, *YA*, because I am what they call a young adult. I like it, unlike what others have called me since I was taken from my home.

He shoots me a grin, crooked from a scar received from a job years ago. It makes him look menacing. Goon is like a grizzly, large and imposing, but inside sensitive and tender.

"That's what I am, YA, a goon. So that's what you'll call me."

Marla, another team member, pulls a face as she passes, carrying ammunition. "His name is Marcel," she says balefully.

Goon tosses a wadded-up paper towel at her face. She snaps her head to the side, and the ball misses. She did it without looking. All I wonder is when she will teach it to me.

Goon raises his eyebrow. "Marcel is no more and hasn't been since I was recruited from the rebel gangs back home. Goon is who I am."

I nod that I understand.

"But in your mind, call him Marcel," Marla sings from the other side of the room, closing the door behind her as she heads out to the warehouse, leaving me, Witt, and Goon alone.

Goon lets out a burst of annoyed breath. "Anyway, Boss, the wet work?"

Witt says, "You know I dislike the phrase 'wet work.'"

Goon groans. "Dispatch, jobs, missions, wet work . . . what does it matter? It's what we do: getting them bloody, wetting them up . . . why romanticize the fact that what we do is kill people?"

Witt fixes him with an annoyed stare. "We dispatch with cause. Why call it something vulgar?"

Goon purses his lips, pretending to think long and hard before saying, "Killing isn't vulgar?"

Witt is not sure how to respond. Goon has him there. "Regardless, refer to it as the Tribe specifies when on the job. You know how they are about rules. And yes, Nena will tag along, but only to observe." He looks at me. "She does not engage in the field."

Both Goon and I know he will let me engage in the field. He always says you can't learn if you're only watching. But he says that only when Witt cannot hear.

Goon rocks back in his chair until it's on two legs. "Okay, but we can't call her Nena. And only I can call her YA." He winks at me, and I avert my eyes, my face flushed. "What's her field name?"

Marla reenters, still working on her inventory. "She's always watching and mimicking what we say and do. She absorbs it all and projects it back. Like a parrot." She gives me a half smile, and I look away.

"Good thing she's not with me on dates." Goon laughs while Marla groans and Witt makes no attempt to mask his disgust.

I have actually seen him with a woman he met one night. I couldn't sleep, and we were to stay in our training domiciles. He sneaked her in because we were not supposed to have guests. I heard noises of pleasure or pain and went to investigate, spying them through a corner of the dirty window and leaving when I realized it was pleasure.

I cannot help but be embarrassed at my eagerness to consume everything each of them knows so I can prove myself worthy. I thought I was being discreet, but they have noticed I am a replication of them—not unique.

Goon says, "Then let's call her Parrot. Or better yet, Polly. We can walk around with little biscuits to give her when she does well." He breaks out in raucous laughter, pleased with himself, and he nearly falls from his chair. Around us, the team attempts to stifle their amusement while I try to figure out what crackers have to do with anything.

I can feel Witt's eyes on me as he studies me. Finally, I gather up what courage I have and stop sneaking looks from beneath my lashes to meet his inscrutable gaze. Any name he gives me, I will accept, as long as Witt does not fail me in my trainings, turn me away, and make the Knights regret allowing me into their home.

"Nena, you have an innocence that we have all once had. Yes, even Goon," he says when I side-eye the team member I could never imagine as innocent. Witt continues. "You are the echo of how we used to be." Witt's words are barely above a whisper but come through like a megaphone. "I hope you never lose it."

The room falls silent with all eyes on me, making it feel as if I will be crushed beneath their gazes.

Finally, Witt breaks the mood, returning to the notes he was transcribing. "Her name will be Echo."

Echo. I try the name on for size, finding I like it.

Goon reaches a closed fist out to me, and I bump it with mine. "Then, her name is Echo."

28

Nena knew when she answered Delphine's call that it came because Delphine was worried about her child after her husband's admission. She knew that Nena would follow instructions, no matter how she was struggling or feeling. Delphine needed to call her daughter, hear Nena's voice without Noble around, and check that her girl was okay.

"I'm fine, Mum. I'm doing my job." Nena tried to reassure her, hoping her mother would buy it. She should have known better.

Delphine called Nena on her lie. "I know. That's what worries me. I can hear it in your voice, Nena. Once this work is done, will you go after her like you did the others?"

Nena adjusted in the chair of her bedroom, saying nothing. How'd her mother guess Nena was toying with the idea of eliminating Bridget afterward? Elin would call it "psychic mum shit."

"I thought about it. After the family call," Delphine continued, correctly taking Nena's silence as confirmation. "I think this time, killing her is not right for you."

Nena sighed. Delphine had thrown the proverbial monkey wrench into her plan. Delphine was siding with Nena's father.

"Why?" Nena scoffed, uninhibited at being sidelined. "Because she's White and rich and people notice when they go missing more than if they are Black?"

"Of course not. Her husband and your father are old business rivals. Because your father plans to take some of the Tribe's enterprises public, we need to tread lightly. Believe me, I would strangle this woman with my bare hands if I could. But we must think of the fallout of our actions. Everything we do, my love, affects something else, and eyes are always on us, waiting for our slightest misstep."

Nena knew what she meant. Her mother was referring to the fallout from the deaths of Paul and his men and to Witt's death. She was saying without saying it that Nena had had her pass when she took out Paul and his men, and now it was time to think beyond that. Nena knew she was right. She'd been grieving the loss of her brother Ofori and then Witt, always worried about the impact her deeds had on the Tribe's ultimate mission.

But Nena couldn't yet let it go. Couldn't let the thought of Bridget continuing to live go.

"I don't know if I can let it go, let her go, Mum."

Delphine switched tactics. "Does Cort fulfill you? Make you happy?"

Heat flushed Nena's face. She didn't know where her mother was going.

"Mum, we really don't—"

"Humor me. We rarely get an opportunity to speak about your future, much less one with love in it."

Nena racked her brain for a response that would appease her mother and shut the topic down. "I don't know. I mean, yes, Cort does. Our world in the Tribe is very loud, and my life has been nothing but noise for a long time. But he and Georgia provide a bit of silence."

"Good," Delphine said. "It's what I wanted to hear. Despite Cort's misgivings about our family's work, he provides you comfort and happiness. It's all I ever would want for you. If you ever decided to walk away—"

"I'd never."

"—if you did, I would be happy for you that you found someone to be . . . silent with. What you do is hard work. It takes a toll. You were not meant to dispatch forever, and you should not feel as if you must."

"Mum—"

"As for this woman. Do not allow her to drag you back to that place, because that is what revenge against her will do to you. You have come so far. And if you kill her, you will only go right back to where you were, and you may lose the silence you have with Cort and Georgia."

Nena didn't want to admit her mother was making sense.

"Plus, her death will not bring what Paul, Attah Dolphin—"

Nena smiled in spite of herself. "Walrus."

"They both swim. Anyway, I don't want her on your conscience. The best revenge against her is for you to live well in spite of what she did to you."

Nena closed her eyes. She hated to admit that her mother might be right.

"Let it go. Her time will come, Nena, believe you me. And you will know what to do with her properly when it does. But until then, do as your father asked and only what he has asked. I will deal with the position your father put you in, but meanwhile I know you will make the proper decisions."

Nena wanted to believe her mother. Wholeheartedly. But she didn't entirely trust herself. Didn't know if she could continue to see Bridget and not want to send the woman where she'd sent the others. To hell.

When the conversation ended, Nena needed to relieve some of her pent-up energy. She went to her suite's balcony, peering through the glass doors at her view of room windows. It was dark, and the surrounding world was fast asleep. A slight shift in the corner of Nena's eye caught her attention, and she opened one of the french doors and stepped through. She focused on where she'd noticed the movement; nearly all the hotel windows were dark. There was a slight breeze, and it caught the gauzy, sheer curtains through a couple of the open windows, causing them to flutter.

She focused on one balcony. It was across from hers, up a level. The door was open and an interior light on. She watched a shadow pass and then pass back—the person, maybe a male, pacing back and forth. She could hear only snippets of an angry voice as she strained to make out what was being said. As parts of the conversation trickled down, cutting the serene Tanzanian savanna atmosphere, Nena recognized the voice was Frances Dubin's.

Nena folded herself back into the shadows, not wanting him to see her as he continued to pace and bark into his phone. She closed her eyes, focusing on her hearing, filtering everything else out. The snatches shaped themselves into discernible phrases. "Working on it" and "contingency plan." She replayed Dubin's conversation. Contingency plan. Then what was the original?

Dubin's last words left her mouth dry. "Don't worry about that either. I'll handle her."

Nena didn't doubt the "her" Dubin was referring to was Nena. She'd been a thorn in Dubin's side since he'd arrived, had made her disdain for him perfectly clear when everyone else couldn't get past their good African upbringing to be good Christians and welcome all into their homes, even those they didn't particularly like.

Dubin was aware by now that Nena wasn't bound by restrictions of politics and had no qualms about saying the ugly truth of the matter. But the ominous call was next level, and it meant that Dubin was worried he wouldn't be able to smoke and mirror Judah and the miners into submission. It meant he thought Nena was a legitimate threat.

Nena didn't know whether to be insulted or honored. Meant she was leveling up or something like that. Nena didn't know, but she'd take it. It had been some time since she'd had some action—not that she was angling for a fight—so maybe things would prove interesting.

29

Nena woke before the sun rose, dressed in her running gear, stretched in her suite as she looked out through the large sliding glass doors leading to the balcony.

When she was ready, she slipped one of her longer blades into its sheath at the back of the belt buckled around her waist. She took the stairs to the lobby level to stay warmed up.

A half mile into Nena's run, thoughts of Dubin's call and his plans still weighed on her, pushing her to run faster. The clock was ticking, and she had no idea what it was counting down to. She was coming around a bend when she spotted the very man who'd been on her mind. First thing in the morning? Just her luck.

Dubin wasn't alone, and as he moved to the side, revealing who he was engaging in an intense discussion, Nena's stomach twisted. Dubin was with the very man he shouldn't be speaking with alone. She made a quick pivot into the vegetation before either man caught a glimpse of her. Hunched low, she tried to inch closer to where they stood by the side of the empty road, a splinter from the main road that led from the hotel to the main parts of the town. The hotel was at her back and in perfect view, yet among the lush greenery. It was still early, and the road wouldn't be busy with people heading to and from the market. Nena had no gear, save the blade at her back. She wished there was a

Network satellite nearby so she could call for a drone to listen in or that she had her phone to ask Evers to perform some techie miracle. To inch closer would be to reveal herself. She had to stay among the trees in the brush, hoping that a word or two would come through and make this illicit meeting make sense.

Dubin's back was to her, his blond hair blowing in the warming wind. He gestured at the hotel, driving home a point. He had to be referring to them. That could mean any of them. Asogi, Tegete, her. This could be what Judah had said he wanted to do, cut out the middleman. Judah listened, but his expression was unreadable. He pulled out a cigarette and lit it. He took a long draw, then blew the smoke out as he listened, nodding occasionally. He took one final pull, the cigarette only a quarter smoked. He mashed it on the bottom of his shoe, then reached in through his open car window to put the extinguished butt in the car. Well, that wasn't in his intel. Judah could add environmentalist to his growing résumé.

He turned back to Dubin, who moved with impatience. Judah laughed. The sound of it carried all the way to Nena. Dubin recoiled, surprised, his hand going to his hip. He shook his head vehemently. Judah was facing her, and all she could make out from his lips was something like *we shall see*. Possibly. Or perhaps, *not for me*. Lip reading was not Nena's forte.

Dubin planted his palm flat against Judah's chest to stop Judah from rounding the front of his car and leaving. Judah looked at the hand until Dubin retracted it, doing nothing else to stop Judah's departure. Dubin watched him drive off, standing there for a long while, hands on his hips, staring at where the car had disappeared.

"Fucking little piece of shit," Dubin exploded. He kicked at a tiny mound of dirt. Reached down for a branch and flung it into the woods. "Fuck!" he yelled, his voice going high. He spun on his heels, charging back toward Nena as she stepped back into the thick of trees while pulling out his phone and punching his finger at it. She was glad her dark clothes camouflaged her as he passed.

"Change of plans," Dubin growled.

After the incident at the mine the day before, Judah had been justifiably busy. However, he'd sent word that he would attend the meeting to hear the terms to take them back to the chieftains and townspeople. The angry chieftains likely forced his hand. There weren't supposed to be conversations without everyone present, for transparency's sake. And yet, Dubin and Judah had done just that.

Judah was supposed to be a champion of his town, but after observing his secret meeting, Nena was beginning to question where Judah's allegiance truly rested, and if he'd go as far as to sabotage his own people.

30

Later, when Nena tried to catch Tegete just before the meeting, he said, "Judah will see how much Asogi and Odemba want the people as partners. Whatever Dubin tried to do, clearly Judah declined. That's a good thing, yes? Have faith, Nena."

Nena didn't deal in faith. It was about making sure this deal went through, and it wouldn't if Dubin was being unscrupulous. When the time came for the negotiations and Nena entered the conference room, she had no idea what to expect, and that morning's meeting ate away at her.

Nena still questioned how Dubin was allowed to be at the negotiations when none of the other potential buyers were. Who'd permitted his being there? He'd wormed his way in prior to her involvement, and there wasn't anything she could do now to cut him out.

"What's it looking like?" Elin asked. Nena had known Elin would be awake and tending to Asym, who loved to wake up as early as possible—much to Elin's dismay—and speak his baby language that no one could understand but everyone pretended to. Elin groused about it every morning but secretly loved the conversation, calling it enlightening.

"Asogi and Tegete are here. Ms. Odemba," Nena answered. "Judah and Dubin not yet." Nena didn't like that neither were here.

"Judah's not going to screw up this deal for his town."

Lowering her voice and turning into a windowed corner of the long room facing the back garden for some privacy, Nena asked, "Remind me again why Dubin is here when no other outside interest is?"

Asym cooed in the background. "Sounds like Asogi or Odemba were trying to be fair for all parties who'd be involved in the reform," Elin guessed, half-distracted. "They want input and representation from the miners, the government, and the outside businesses they would eventually have to deal with, so it's good to get their input. I guess they chose Dubin as the rep."

"Yes, but why him specifically?" Nena glanced at Asogi and Odemba. "Could you run a check and see who authorized Dubin's participation? If it was anyone from the government. Or from the town. He's got to have an in somewhere."

The door banged open. Dubin sauntered in, Judah coming in close behind him. She disconnected before Elin had a chance to say anything more.

What was Judah doing with Dubin? Nena wondered. Had they come together? Had they been talking in private again? Dubin was his usual boisterous self, while Judah more like an Instant Pot not sealed tightly enough and about to blow.

She moved to intercept Judah and make sure all was well before they got started. Asogi was already calling them to sit at the table and begin talking, touting a great meal being prepared for them that he wanted them done and ready for. He rubbed his stomach for emphasis and laughed at himself.

Nena walked briskly to Judah, who was wearing his usual: gaiter around his neck, a soccer jersey this time, and a pair of cargo shorts—his version of business attire.

"Judah," Nena whispered when she was close enough, just as he was about to take his seat.

He looked at her, his eyes cool and vibe different than it had been the night they met. Something was definitely off, and it made Nena uneasy.

"Is everything all right?" she asked under her breath as Asogi called for the servers and their refreshment service.

Judah gave her a hard look. "You tell me."

He selected his seat, a couple of chairs down from the head seat, which remained unoccupied. Nena assumed Asogi wanted everyone to feel like equals and not as if one of them ruled over the others.

Dubin smiled broadly at Nena, appearing on the other side of Judah. "Had a good run this morning, Ms. Knight?"

He'd seen her. Couldn't have been as he passed. Maybe upon her return? She wasn't about to show her hand to him.

She forced a smile. "Invigorating. A great workout."

Dubin's smile faltered. "Is that so? I've heard it isn't very safe, running alone in the wild."

Judah's jaw tightened. His eyes slid to Dubin and his hands balled into fists. Nena could read him easily. Dubin calling Judah's home "the wild" was akin to calling its people savages.

"Had to insist my lovely wife use the gym in here instead. I'm a big guy myself. I can take it if anything comes at me. But I still wouldn't hang beyond the gates by myself. So you just be careful there. We wouldn't want a little thing like you hurt or snatched up by some vicious lion, or worse."

Nena bit back her true retort, offering instead, "It's good that this little *thing* can take care of herself."

Dubin waved her away. "Ahhh, ma'am, you know what I mean. I know women these days like to be strong and equal. I'm not saying you aren't . . . equal, that is. Of course you are."

Nena rolled her eyes, not caring if he could see her doing so. Asogi asked for everyone to be seated so they could get started. To her dismay, Dubin quickly took a seat next to Judah, leaving Asogi and Tegete to sit across from him with Odemba at the head of the table, farther away from the action. The arrangement made the scene look like an us-against-them situation. It wasn't good. Nena knew exactly what Dubin was doing. Knew he'd waited for Judah to sit so he could claim the seat next to him, as if they were on the same side.

And whatever he'd said to Judah prior to the meeting, however he'd intercepted him, Judah was not the same as he'd been when Femi and Nena visited his village. Perhaps it was the stress from the mine accident that had made Judah look at them with furtive distrust in his eyes. The hope Nena had started off with dissolved into impending dread. Nena took her place next to Tegete, silently preparing herself for what was to come.

"Can I start off saying," Dubin began, working his way through a plate laden with fruit and slices of jam-topped cakes, "I am happy you've allowed me to be here, Mr. Asogi, Ms. Odemba, and Mr. Tegete. I mean, I never thought a guy like me, born in Montana raising horses, a little guy, you know, would be sitting here with people as prestigious as you, talking about the best way to get these gems to the public and to industry. Never had I imagined this honor. I thank you!"

Nena told herself to remain quiet, not give Dubin any energy, and keep her focus on Judah. But already, Dubin was making it about him. What were these people to him but another means of income? He was a millionaire several times over, with homes scattered all over the world and whose family owned a large cattle farm. He might have raised horses, but he had plenty of family money to help him get where he was today.

Asogi beamed at Dubin, making Nena wonder if the PM was really that gullible or if he could read Dubin and was pretending to buy into his antics. Nena hoped the latter.

Nena clamped her mouth shut. She pushed the colorful melons and strawberries around left and right on her plate while stealing occasional glances at Judah. She tried guessing his thoughts, but he gave nothing up. He kept his head down as he flipped through the portfolio placed at his seat. It held the draft of the reform paperwork, and Judah focused on reading every word.

Dubin continued, "I really appreciate that the Tanzanian government has been working so closely with Mr. Tegete and his organization. It's like I was telling you, Judah, the two of them have been thick as thieves, coming up with a solid plan for how mining will happen in this country and with you. I have faith we'll feel fully represented."

31

Asogi grew somber, leaning forward. "Judah, how are the families of the deceased? And the injured? How do they fare?"

Judah didn't answer immediately. He leveled his gaze at the prime minister. "They would be better off with help from your office." His tone was measured with a dash of accusation, as he knew well what the answer would be.

Asogi grimaced regretfully, drawing back. He looked quickly at Ms. Odemba, who replied with a quick shake of her head. Nothing had changed for them. Tegete had requested help from Nena's father, and that would be coming, but it was not for either of them to say just yet.

"I am sorry, Judah. We simply cannot right now. Not without the reform measures in place," Asogi finally said.

If looks could kill, Asogi would be with the ancestors. He knew it and withered beneath Judah's death stare.

Dubin let out a deep sigh, as if some miscarriage of justice had been done. He gave Judah a pointed look. "Of course. It's like I said."

Tegete cleared his throat. "Have faith, Judah, perhaps help will present itself." He moved on. "This is the first time we're officially meeting all together before Mr. Judah Wasira presents the reform provisions to the Lateman elders and townspeople for their approval. It will be the guide for all mining contracts going forward between the people of Tanzania, the government, and outside interests. There is full transparency here. We thank your village for being the voice of Tanzanians."

Judah said, "My village wants all rights to the land. We don't need the government to dictate who we sell to, how much, and what we retain. We want to deal with the companies directly. If the government is truly about transparency and giving the people what they deserve, then step aside."

Nena looked up. The idea was to form a partnership. There was no way private corporations would give up all that to miners without someone overseeing them.

Asogi looked at Tegete. "Cut us out entirely? But who will negotiate mining regulations on your behalf? The miners? Chieftains?" He almost said "you," but smartly refrained. "How do they know to do such things? And what to ask for?"

Judah jabbed his chest with a thumb. "I can do it."

Dubin suppressed a smile.

Nena said, "Judah, let's pause a minute."

Judah said no. "You think we don't know how to get what we want. We do."

"There's no doubt that you do," Tegete said. "But why not help create regulations that also work for all people? Use the help being offered."

Asogi interjected, "I don't know why you believe the government is out to steal from you or control what you own by right. Aside from the reasonable tax you'd pay."

Judah scoffed, pushing the portfolio of papers from him. "See, that's what I mean. Taxes. You will tax so high it will be like we are only mining to pay your tax. This is what government does. What rich people do. Become richer off the broken backs of the poor and lower class."

"The taxes would be nominal," Asogi debated. "That is the way of business."

"Says you. We're better off dealing with the companies directly."

"I think Judah has a point. You don't want to put limits on earnings the miners could negotiate without a middleman to pay. Too many cooks in the kitchen could do that," Dubin said. "I'd give them what they deserve, more than."

Asogi's face hardened as he directed his attention to Dubin. "Then you're offering for the outside parties to pay the taxes for the miners. Those are the provisions you're willing to put in the reform on behalf of all the other companies?"

Dubin said nothing, offering a tight smile. "It could be considered."

"Who would tell the miners the value of their goods?" Nena finally asked.

Dubin hemmed. "We'd guide them. Offer a more than fair deal."

"How, if they don't know market value? If the only people they would depend on to provide that information are the people who want to buy it from them, they will be underbid. That makes no sense," Nena returned.

Judah said, "Neither does paying taxes for something the government doesn't own."

Dubin banged his hand on the table. "Hear, hear." He leveled his cold eyes on Nena, then on Tegete. "What do you have to gain here? What would be your cut?"

"I am from this country, Mr. Dubin," Councilman Tegete said, anger threading his words.

Dubin threw his hands up in mock surrender.

"Judah," Nena tried again, hating the way Dubin barely kept the grin off his face as he stoked the embers of this blazing fire. "I don't know what you've been told, but the taxes are a fair price to pay to ensure everyone is following the same regulations set to protect the people."

Dubin snorted. "Government is always out for government, in my experience."

"I thought we were here to negotiate together. I don't understand your sudden shift, Judah." Nena's words were measured.

"Produce the list of other interested buyers. Why are they not here?" Judah jutted out his chin.

Ms. Odemba said, "You know we cannot disclose that list until we are all in one accord on the reform. And Dubin cannot be privy to who's on the list when the others don't have the same advantage."

"And yet here he is," Nena grumbled. She closed her eyes, silently chastising herself for her lack of restraint. When she reopened her eyes, Dubin was glaring his contempt for her palpably.

"Your logic makes no sense, Ms. Odemba. He already knows more by sitting in on our talks." Judah stood abruptly. "Which means you intend to hold the bidders as ransom for me to get the miners to sign. You will dangle their names over our heads until we submit. Well, we will not. If you are as transparent as you say you are, you'll show us all now who is interested so that I know you aren't making these 'interested parties' up to get us to vouch for your reform only to learn there are none and be forced to go with whomever you want. The only interested party I see is Dubin. He is here."

Dubin raised his hands innocently. "Now, I'm just here to make sure the new rules are something outside companies can work with. I can't put in an offer yet." He grinned. "That wouldn't be fair."

The color drained from Asogi's face. "Judah, be reasonable."

Dubin sighed as if he was spent after corralling unruly children. "Well now, I don't know what to make of all this. I am concerned that Judah feels you all"—he gestured to Asogi and Odemba, Tegete and Nena—"are in some sort of collusion in which his interests are not being considered. As a private entity, I feel you don't have faith in the outside buyers to be honest with the people and buy at market value. And it seems you don't think the people shrewd enough to broker deals that work for them. It looks"—Dubin paused for effect, his face falling as if sorrowful and disappointed—"as if you think Judah and his people are stupid."

Dubin landed with perfection, having said the word that would trigger Judah's wrath, and Judah did not disappoint. He shot up from his seat and, in one fluid motion, whipped a long curved hunting blade from beneath his shirt.

Judah ignored the chorus of yells as people at the table scrambled to get out of his path. He flipped the blade, slamming the point into the table, pinning the contract papers to the wood. The blade wobbled.

Nena was out of her seat, her sidearm unholstered from beneath her jacket, her gun drawn. She was faster than any of the guards, who'd swept in upon Odemba's scream with their weapons drawn and trained on Judah. "I won't vouch for this so-called reform."

Nena said, "Back away from the knife. You're acting like an idiot. A loud, obnoxious one. You don't know when you've been misled by the same person who claimed to be your ally." She looked at the guards. "Stand down, please. He's fine."

Judah glowered, assessing the number of guns trained on him. He let out a breath, relaxing his body. For the briefest second, she caught the hurt and confusion on his face before it hardened once again.

"Very well then. I'll remove my obnoxious, idiot, misled self. But don't think this is over." He dipped his head at the room in a curt goodbye before focusing on Nena. He waited a beat, his lips twitching like he wanted to say something more, then changed his mind.

"Ms. Knight."

He strode out, not waiting for her response, leaving the portfolio with his blade pinning it to the table. Guns lowered, the guards continued to watch Judah hawkishly. Tegete followed him out, attempting to talk him back to the table, but to no avail.

Nena holstered her gun, the gravity of her colossal screwup coming down on her. Dubin stared at the table, the only one who'd remained in his seat through the whole episode. He twisted his chair gently, a self-satisfied smile playing on his lips. He found Nena watching him, letting him know she knew he orchestrated the breakdown of the negotiations.

Dubin offered a light shrug, his smile stretching wide, enjoying the win of his masterful chess play.

This was his checkmate.

32

Nena's team probably wondered where she was. She wasn't wearing her comms. Her phone had been turned off since receiving Judah's text to meet in secret. Prior to that, she'd waited, sending him several messages after he'd stormed out of the negotiations. She tried to ignore the sickening dread growing in her that Judah stood on a precipice of something he, or Latema, wouldn't be able to walk back from.

Nena slid into the passenger seat of his car, having walked the same route she'd taken when she'd seen his morning meeting with Dubin. She wouldn't mention that yet. She'd see what Judah had to say, where he was at. She closed the door behind her. It was just the two of them, with Judah behind the steering wheel. The muscles of his jaw moved beneath the skin, and he looked through the windshield out into the darkness stretched in front of them. The tension was so thick in the vehicle, it was as if all the oxygen had been sucked out. Nena wanted to open her window to get a little air in with them.

"It's not what you think, Judah. They aren't trying to cut you all out of the deal."

It was best for her to start off by addressing the elephant in the room. She'd told Judah that the rest of them would listen and consider the needs of his village for them to allow access to their land that held the precious tanzanite. She'd promised him a fair deal. He was working off misinformation and emotion. Didn't know whom he could trust, and while she knew he could trust her and Tegete, she could understand why he wouldn't.

"I have it on good authority that the plan is to cut us out of the deal. That whatever it is we think doesn't matter. Asogi and Odemba will do what they want anyway," Judah said flatly.

"Who told you that?"

"Does not matter. It's the truth."

"But how do you know that? They could be lying."

He scoffed. "They probably are, and yet the meeting today proves them true. Everyone in that room thought me some lowly rural farmer. Because I didn't get a Western education, I am not smart. Because I do not have millions of dollars and cannot fly anywhere at a moment's notice, I am not First World." He poked himself in the chest. "But I am of *this* world, Nena. It is all that I know. I've seen what government, corruption, and big business have done in other countries with their mined and stolen resources. Conflict diamonds. Buying up land and making war profits off of it. Resources stripped until there is nothing left but useless earth for the people who rightfully own it to deal with. They are tricked into selling or giving up their claims and then forced to mine the exact resources they own by right to line someone else's pockets. To line the pockets of corrupt politicians and the greedy Western corporations, who never seem to have enough."

His voice, though remaining at a reasonable level, held so much conviction it gave Nena pause. Judah was so angry, so hurt and disenfranchised. And people who felt this way were apt to do the worst things for themselves and everyone around them. Nena knew this to be true because it had happened not so long ago to Witt.

"Judah."

He silenced her with a look. "No. No, Nena. You said you were here to help. My people drive our own destiny, not the government, not the West. Not the Tribe."

"We understand, Judah. The Tribe doesn't want to run anything. We only want to create opportunity for you to succeed. We have done it time and time again with many other countries."

"No, you want to sway me with promises of supply and opportunities for work and education. You want to trick us with sugared speeches when all you want is to bleed us dry and leave us to rot. Like Asogi. Like Dubin."

Judah's words hurt. It was so wrong, so unbelievable to her that anyone could think the Tribe was anything like that. Her mind churned. Why wouldn't he think the way he did, with Dubin whispering in his ear? What if it was too late and Judah had already made a deal with the devil?

"Don't be rash." She sensed the energy emitting from him was on the cusp of another explosion, a bigger one.

Judah stared out into the nothingness out there. His hands clenched and unclenched, punctuating his anger. But when he spoke, his voice was low, his tone soft and sad.

"Our African history has always been steeped in theft and betrayal," he began. "There have always been warring tribes, but when the European countries invaded and colonized us, bringing in their weapons and diseases we weren't immune to, speaking those honeyed words to convince the kings and chiefs here to turn on one another and delve into the slave trade, it was the beginning of the unrelenting assault against this continent and the people from it.

"As if they hadn't taken enough, taken enough resources, taken land, taken our religious beliefs and culture, taken our people to ship them off to other countries to slave away as if they were not kings and queens. All of that may be different, but their effects are forever lasting. And despite the fact they know of their atrocities, they have the audacity to return over and over.

"But this time it's for our resources, because nearly half the world's gold and a third of all minerals are in Africa, last I heard from the internet. When they realized it, do you think the Europeans let us be? Do you think they left us alone to heal from the trauma they inflicted earlier? Did they say, 'Oh please, this land and all it has is yours to do with as you will'?"

It was a rhetorical question. They both knew plainly what the answer was. Nena said nothing, waiting for him to make his point, waiting for him to vent so he could hopefully be reasoned with now to not make decisions out of anger and retribution.

"They came back to take more. To trick. To manipulate and steal. They were the reason why Africa is as divided as it is."

And why the Tribe wants to make it whole again, Nena thought.

Judah returned to her, studying her face, his eyes trailing down every detail of it. Nena felt too exposed. Words died in her throat. His argument was true, and she had no response for it.

"Did you know"—Judah asked, pulling out his iPhone; as he held it, he turned it this way and that, scrutinizing it—"that more than half of what makes up the mobile phones are mined and semiprocessed materials? And a great portion of those materials are mined here."

"You know a great deal about Africa's resources and mining."

Judah made a face that reminded Nena she shouldn't assume he wouldn't. Immediately she felt guilty for having made the comment.

"And yet those in that meeting thought me simpleminded. I know our country and other countries heavily depend on mining for their economic needs, especially if there are resources no one else has. I know our worth."

"They know it too."

"I am tired of the recursive cycle of outsiders getting rich off our backbreaking work. All we want—and I'm sure other countries who depend on a mining economy do as well—is a fair deal. That's why we have been forced to smuggle goods, you see? Because we have no seat. We have no voice. They do not see us."

Nena knew the rest without Judah having to say it. If they were not seen, then they did not matter.

33

Nena stared down at her hands clasped in her lap. She wanted to ignore the trepidation growing to boulder size in the pit of her stomach. She could hear the edge in his voice ramping up as he drew to a conclusion she knew couldn't be good.

"Whatever you're thinking to do, Judah, do not. You will only undermine your cause. You will prove Dubin right."

He cocked his head in confusion. "Dubin? What about him?"

Should she play her cards now? Ask him about their private meeting? Ask him outright if he had a hand in the mining incident and resulting death of three of his people?

"He has spoken against me?"

Perhaps she could play it another way. "I think he would prefer to deal with you without any of our. . . umm . . . interference."

"Hmm." Judah sank back in his seat.

"Judah." She wasn't ready to give up on him. She didn't know why, but something about Judah Wasira made her want to help him even though he just might be the opposition.

"You should head back, Ms. Knight. I appreciate your coming to speak with me. It means something."

"And you'll allow me to soothe things? Perhaps schedule another meeting for all of us after Mr. Asogi's speech tomorrow, where I'm sure we can all come to an agreement everyone is comfortable with."

Judah offered her a ghost of a smile, his expression opening as if he wanted to say more. Nena waited expectantly, hoping that he'd tell her his thoughts, tell her how she could help fix things. But as quickly as his face opened, it sealed back up, and Judah was once again closed off to her. Nena hoped not for good.

"I thought you were nothing more than some rich westernized woman." His gaze was warm as he studied her intently, as if he were memorizing her face. As if after this night, they would be on opposite sides.

God, she hoped not.

"In these few short days, I have been happily proved wrong. You came after me when you didn't have to."

"I did." She fought not to put her hand to her forehead. It was so hot.

"You said I knew nothing about you."

"You don't." Something, in this car, between them was shifting.

He flipped the switch, his voice deepening. "And you say you have a man at home?"

She hadn't said.

"I do," she answered, not knowing why she replied. She ignored the tiny tug of curiosity at what would happen if she said no.

Judah reached his hand out, making as if to touch her face. Nena did not move, wondering what he would do. It felt nice being here with him. She felt the heat from him as his hand hovered over her cheek, fingers just barely grazing her warming skin. She thought to maybe lean in, place her cheek against his hand, initiate the first move.

But that wouldn't be right. And it wouldn't be fair for her to be swept up in the moment. Not to Cort, who awaited her back home. Or to Judah, whom she didn't want to lead on and make promises to that she couldn't keep. But most of all, it wouldn't be fair to her. Nena didn't want to develop feelings for someone she might have to later kill.

So Nena slowly pulled away. A fraction of an inch. Enough to let her message be read clearly.

Judah's hands returned to his sides, then grasped the steering wheel of his white 2009 Chevy Cobalt while Nena climbed out.

"He is a lucky man," Judah said ruefully.

Nena's mouth quirked. "That he is."

Judah, taken by surprise, roared with laughter as his car also roared to life. "Be well, Ms. Knight, and stay safe."

———

As Nena stood on the dirt road that would lead back toward the conference room, watching the taillights of the Cobalt growing smaller, then disappearing as the dense trees and bushes swallowed it up, Femi's words from their first night in Tanzania came to mind.

He has that rob-the-rich-give-to-the-poor kind of energy.

Nena's foreboding intensified. When someone felt pushed up against the wall and felt they had no other recourse, they were capable of anything. Even if in the end, it would destroy them.

Witt had shared similar views. He'd felt the Tribe and Noble had lost their way and, in turn, Witt had betrayed them. Look what had happened to him.

Nena hoped Judah wouldn't make any rash decisions that would earn him a death decree. She didn't want to be the one to land the kill shot for someone she had come to respect, and like. But Nena would. If she had to.

34

When Nena returned, the group had reconvened after a dinner break. They were continuing the discussion, despite the fact Judah was gone. It felt wrong to do so, as if they'd already written him off just as he feared. Nena couldn't let that happen, no matter how "uncooperative" Judah was being. There were other forces at play here.

"Asogi, Ms. Odemba, really. Why this sudden push for mining reform?" Dubin asked. "What's wrong with what we've already been doing?"

Nena took her seat, ignoring Dubin's "oh, you again" eye roll. "What's wrong is there was no one regulating these deals. In the end, the miners were lowballed and taken advantage of. You wouldn't want that, right, Mr. Dubin?" Elin had said to channel Nena's inner Elin, and that's exactly what Nena intended to do now.

Dubin let out a laugh that Nena knew was fake. He was buying himself time.

"Of course not," Dubin finally replied. "I love the people, and I welcome this reform of yours."

Councilman Tegete waved away another round of whiskey Asogi offered. "Reform is needed to ensure all parties are safe and there is equity."

Dubin tore himself, reluctantly, from Nena. "All parties like the government, hmm, Asogi? No offense."

Dubin was nothing but offensive, and the slip in Asogi's affable demeanor reflected it.

"Not our government, Mr. Dubin," Ms. Odemba finally spoke up, her distaste for him evident.

"I believe what Mr. Tegete is saying is that without a formal system to get resources from the mine to the buyer, then it opens up the disadvantaged to being manipulated or worse," Nena said, leveling a firm look unabashedly at the man.

Dubin's response was not immediate. He narrowed his reddened eyes at her, the right one exhibiting a tiny twitch that Nena was sure only she had noticed.

"Ms. Knight, it almost sounds as if you think I would do such an atrocious thing." He bared a little bit of teeth, looking like he wanted to rip her head off.

She shrugged. Who knew what he'd do. That's what she was trying to figure out.

Tegete chuckled uncomfortably. "Of course not, Mr. Dubin."

"I mean, it is what history has shown," Nena continued. "So, it is appropriate for Judah and any villagers to be skeptical of the part you play in this."

Dubin leaned in. "And your part, Ms. Knight. What is the African Tribal Council's purpose here? You're a billion-dollar corporation, as is my investment firm and the parties I represent. I'm not even sure what you all do. Real estate? Construction? Feed the needy? And what would you all get out of this deal?"

"The Tribe is here in the interests of all parties," Nena said.

Dubin pointed to himself. "Including mine?" He smirked. "How very noble of you."

Nena's face twitched, and before she could recover, Dubin had caught her slip and held on tightly. He relished his small win. "Speaking of, where is your father? You'd think that for something as important as ensuring mining reform, as you call it, that the big man would be here to facilitate it rather than sending in his little girl."

"Mr. Dubin," Asogi began, nervousness saturating his entire being.

Councilman Tegete cleared his throat, saying sharply, "We're veering off track."

Inside, Nena was on fire. Her fingers itched to fling her blades across the oak table and into Dubin's face. Her feet throbbed to run across the newly buffed floors and show him just what kind of "little girl" she was.

"Perhaps your father doesn't think Tanzania and this whole deal is good enough for his grand presence."

Nena inclined her head. "Perhaps." She pursed her lips. "Or perhaps it's the company I'm currently keeping that is not much my father's flavor."

She waited a beat, unflinching in her stance as she watched Dubin process what she was saying. Suddenly, she broke out in a bright killer smile to deflect the mood. Better she kept him on his toes and not let him know how much she raged inside. Would Elin be proud of her? Of course. Elin was where Nena had learned the art of verbal warfare.

And war against Dubin it was. That he'd said her father was a "big man," as if that word was a joke and insult, when in her culture the term was as esteemed as "chief" or "king." That he'd referred to her as a "little girl," as if Nena didn't belong in this space with the menfolk. But the joke was on him because Nena was not the outsider here. That dishonor was all Frances Dubin's.

Dubin blinked long and slow and then let out a loud "Ha!" as he clapped his hands together thunderously. "Good show, Ms. Knight. Good show!" He pointed at her. "You can hold your own with the men. Well done!"

Dubin was still going on while Asogi and Tegete tried to change the subject. Tegete slid Nena a warning look, telling her to stop. Nena got up to leave. Dubin's bull filled the room like noxious gas, and she'd had all she could tolerate. She was just outside the door when she came upon Odemba, who Nena realized must have slipped out during her and Dubin's verbal sparring match, and Bridget approaching the room. She tried to avoid them completely, but Bridget told Odemba she'd catch up to her and veered off course, making a beeline toward Nena.

Nena considered running, but that would look odd, as they were still in the sights of the people in the room and Odemba. She shot Bridget a warning look. These past couple of days, Bridget had given Nena a wide berth.

It wasn't a surprise.

Bridget was likely afraid, as she should have been.

"If you know what's good for you," Nena began, her voice in a low growl. "If you value your life, you will stay out of my path while you are here."

Bridget stepped forward, and like it was a dance, Nena retreated a step.

"Can we not talk?"

Was the woman mad? Did she not hear Nena clearly enough?

"What is it you think we just did? I owe you nothing."

Bridget wrapped her arms around her sides. "I know. It's just. Of course not. It is I who owe you."

"What you owe, I do not think you'd be happy to give."

It took Bridget a moment to register Nena's meaning. She glanced toward the door, the bottom of her lip quivering.

"I only want to tell you how sorr—"

"Don't try to appease your guilt by forcing apologies on me. Your entitlement allows you to think that you should get your way in all things when it comes to people like me, even an apology that changes nothing. I think you have forced enough on me, don't you?"

When Bridget didn't reply, Nena continued, "This isn't going to happen, Bridget." She switched to French. "Tu ne peux pas discuter du passé avec moi. Tu n'as rien à dire du tout." *You don't get to discuss the past with me. You don't get to say anything at all.*

Nena's look warned Bridget to step aside, but Bridget either had a death wish or didn't notice. Nena was holding herself back by only a thread. Finally, she slid over. As Nena prepared to leave, Bridget whispered, "Be careful of Frances. You've put yourself in his path, and he . . . is not one to anger."

Nena hesitated for only a fraction of a second. She craned her neck, making eye contact with him as he chatted with the people inside, Odemba joining them. He caught her eye, seeing his wife was beside Nena. His eyes narrowed, and while he didn't miss a beat speaking with the trio, Nena knew his mind was working, calculating ways to take her down. She was the barrier between him and Tegete. And Tegete was the barrier to Asogi. He chatted them up but watched her with the look of a predator.

"Perhaps he should be careful of me." Then Nena added, "And you had better as well." Nena stepped around Bridget and walked away.

Nena wasn't the scared and gullible girl Bridget remembered from years past.

Nena recalled that night, and Bridget's sickeningly sweet warning— as the sedan carried them off from Paul's market house and into the darkness toward Accra—came back to Nena as if it danced on the wind. Beautiful words wrapped in darkness.

"Profites-en maintenant, chérie." *Live it up now, sweetheart.*

Back then, Bridget's words had shaken Aninyeh in her seat.

Nena was grown now. Those words took on an entirely different meaning.

It was Bridget's turn to shake where she stood. Her little husband too.

35

Mr. Asogi was scheduled to have a public meeting at the pavilion located in the center of Latema the next afternoon, and the whole town bustled as they prepared. Nena had been up since before sunrise, in Evers's quarters, pacing behind his now-empty chair as the team watched the three monitors he'd set up to observe the perimeters of the resort and the town hall where Asogi's meeting would be held.

Two hours in, Femi was complaining about her sudden weakness due to food deprivation. She claimed she couldn't think well and couldn't be mission ready if someone didn't feed her quickly. Nena had hoped to squeeze in a little more prep time before the world got too hectic, but Femi persisted.

"This is inhumane treatment," Femi whined, batting her extralong lashes lined with hot-pink eyeliner. There wasn't a moment when Femi wasn't camera ready, and Nena appreciated her ability to keep to the things she liked to do for herself even when working a job such as theirs.

Clearly, they weren't going to get any more work done, with Femi distracting them with her hunger pains and the ferocious growls from her stomach that backed up her claims. So Nena sent a silent plea to Evers for help.

"Let's go to the kitchen and see what we can find," Evers suggested, pushing his chair back from his ad hoc workstation.

"Yes!" Femi was already out of her seat, grabbing her light jacket from where she'd tossed it on the sofa before Evers could complete his sentence.

For a scaled-down job, Evers managed to create an impressive setup, complete with several monitors and charging stations for the nearly silent drones that he used to scan the perimeter of the village so they could get maps of the area and follow anyone Nena tasked them with watching. There were five: Councilman Tegete, Asogi, Odemba, Dubin, and, of course, Judah. On the side, Nena had asked Evers to keep an eye on Bridget as well, not to the same extent as the others, but just to see what she got up to when her husband was away.

The characteristic that Nena appreciated the most about Evers was his discretion. He'd agreed to keep tabs on Mrs. Dubin without asking Nena why, as Femi might have, or pushing back about wasted resources and time, as Billy would have. Evers just said okay. Nena liked that a lot.

Seemed Bridget Dubin got up to a lot when not skulking around Nena like a kid trying to make a friend. She spent her time luxuriating in the hotel spa, at the bar self-medicating with wine, or chatting it up with Ms. Odemba, with whom she'd become surprisingly close.

Currently, Bridget was still in bed while Dubin was up and dressing. Asogi was in his quarters with his niece, who was preparing to return to her mother near the capital, her visit to her uncle's hometown ending. Their relationship reminded Nena of Cort and Georgia, whom she missed tremendously. She longed for the simple life with them, where there were no politics beyond choosing whether they should watch a horror or an action movie and who was on dinner duty that night. Nena missed Cort's lasagna, the first meal the three of them had had together.

When the door closed, Nena scrutinized the image of town hall that Evers's drone had captured, and its entrances, for the hundredth time. She picked up one of the tiny fingertip-size black trackers sitting on Evers's workstation. They would be useful to better track Judah's movements, and she should have thought of it earlier and planted one when they had met in his car. She was losing her touch.

"What do you think?" she asked, palming the tiny location device. She put a hand under her chin and wrapped the other around her waist. She acknowledged Billy when he came to stand beside her, narrowing his eyes at the screen.

"Any blind spots that you can see?"

He shot her a dubious look. "In a place like this, there are blind spots everywhere."

"I was afraid you'd say that." Her eyes flickered over the image, locating all the points that weren't secure, which was all of them.

"We've walked the perimeter as much as we can without looking too obvious," Billy said in a tone that suggested he was attempting helpfulness. Nena wasn't sure she was buying it. While Billy seemed to have surrendered to his fate with her as his boss and their ragtag team, he'd still held firm to his superiority and suspicion when it came to her.

"There's not much more we can do without calling in reinforcements. And since this is not a Dispatch operation," he reminded her, correctly reading her mind, "we're only supposed to be watching Councilman Tegete's back. No ops, we're sidelined."

"We need operations to ensure his safety, though. Judah was angry after that meeting yesterday. There's no telling how he might lash out, especially in front of the whole town when Asogi and Tegete address the people."

Billy shrugged. "He'll get over it. They could use the money. You've done what you can, I think. The rest is up to Tegete and Asogi."

Surprise filled her as she gawked at the mohawked man. "Is this you giving me a pep talk?"

He snorted, moving away from her and toward the sofa Femi had vacated. "This is me thinking of self-preservation. I still think people around you drop like flies. But like you said on the plane here, I don't plan to be one of them."

———

Deep in thought, Nena walked down the sunny open halls with windowed ceilings draped with enormous leaves from tall palms and other trees and thick branches and vines of flowered foliage that filtered the burning rays of sun enough to allow the light but not so much the heat from it. It felt as if she were walking through an enclosed botanical garden, and Nena appreciated the beauty and serenity of it all.

The talk with Billy had distracted her from her ritual reviewing and re-reviewing all logistics. Then Femi and Evers returned with breakfast, and Nena figured it was wise to eat with them and build their new team beyond planning and executing missions. So now, before the public meeting where Asogi and Tegete would field questions from the villagers, Nena was feeling overwhelmed and underprepared. Would Judah show to the meeting as he was supposed to? Or did his storming out the night before mean he was done with the whole thing?

Nena still held the tiny tracker in hand but was too preoccupied to retrace her steps to return it to Evers, having decided against using it at all. The drones should be enough. Nena tucked it in her jeans pocket. She'd give it back to Evers when she saw him later. He'd be monitoring while she, Billy, and Femi traveled to the meeting place. A thought hitting her, Nena pivoted, deciding to do something her mother had told her she did too little of.

Stop whatever you're doing and breathe.

That was what Nena decided to do at that very moment. She exited the hall heading away from Evers's room and entered the inner courtyard, a botanical garden of the region's most noted flowers and foliage surrounding a small pond and cascading waterfall with several benches forming a circle around the centerpiece.

She chose a bench and sat, tilting her head back to feel the warming sun on her face. Her eyes closed, and she took a breath.

36

"What are you doing?"

Nena's head came back down, and one eye cracked open toward the owner of the breathy whisper. Asogi's niece, in denim shorts overalls, high socks, and sneakers. Her Mario Kart rucksack was slung over her shoulders.

"Breathing," Nena answered, reclosing her eye and returning to position. "Won't you be late for your trip home? You get to see your mum."

Nena felt the bench jostle as weight was added to it. So much for just breathing. It seemed she'd have to talk as well. When she opened her eyes, she found the little girl had hers closed, with her own head facing the sky. Nena smirked, finding the act endearing.

Nena asked, "What are you doing?"

"I'm breathing too," Abiola said, eyes still closed. "What's it supposed to do?"

Nena hadn't asked her mother that part, never planning to actually do it.

"I'm not entirely sure. It's something my mother told me to do sometimes."

"I like it." Abiola opened her eyes, focusing her attention on Nena. Her perfectly braided and beaded hair jangled from the movement.

"Anyway," Nena said, pushing herself until her back rested against the bench, "shouldn't you be on your way? Don't want to be late. I'm sure you miss your mum?"

"I'm waiting for Uncle. He's going to drop me off and then go to his important meeting. Mr. Dubin showed up at our room and wanted to talk."

"Did he?" Nena's interest was piqued.

"Yes." The girl nodded, her eyes luminous. She swung her legs, since she, too, was now sitting back against the bench, and her feet didn't yet reach the ground.

"Was your uncle happy to receive him?" Nena felt a pang of guilt for interrogating a nine-year-old, but Dubin approaching Asogi now without Tegete in sight was perplexing.

Abiola shook her head. "I don't think Uncle likes the American man much." She wrinkled her nose. "And he smells awful." She waved her little hand over her nose, the bright-pink nail polish she wore glistening in the sunlight.

"His cologne?" Nena controlled her expression. Whatever scent Dubin used *was* pretty bad. Way too strong in this weather and only encouraging the mosquitos and biting gnats he continuously complained about.

Abiola nodded. "It's really bad. His wife should tell him so he doesn't smell like that." She fanned her small hand over her nose again.

Nena's mouth twitched, but she didn't want them to lose focus. "Did you hear what they were talking about?"

The girl fiddled with her socks, pulling up one that had been slipping. It had a heart on it. "Uncle told me to wait in the car for him, but I had to pack my bag first. Mr. Dubin asked about the other offers on the table. Then he said, 'Gentleman's deal.' And then I left because I'd finished packing, and then I saw you . . . breathing."

Nena acknowledged the cute girl's joke, but her mind was whirring, computing Abiola's information. "Gentleman's deal"? Was Dubin trying to cut a side deal with Asogi? His company wouldn't have the only offer on the table, and Odemba made it clear Dubin couldn't know who else was on the list, as it would give him an upper hand. Dubin wanted this inside information no matter how he tried to play it off, and now he'd made an actual play to obtain it. The snake.

Dubin would have never asked in front of Tegete, which was why he'd approached Asogi before the town hall to discuss the village's options. And if her assessment of how Dubin did business was correct, he was probably very insistent. Probably to the point of browbeating the malleable prime minister. Nena thought about Evers's surveillance and how cozy Bridget was getting with Odemba. The Dubins were tag teaming, and Bridget was still grooming prey for the predator to devour, only the stakes were different now. She wasn't dealing in children. Bridget was dealing in politics. Nena only hoped that Asogi and Odemba were able to see through the Dubins' ruse.

Tegete was already on-site at the pavilion, and Nena tried to stay positive. However, her field-conditioned mind—forged from her Dispatch training and from all the evil she'd seen in her life—taught Nena to always expect the worst. It was that feeling of unease that gave Nena pause now.

"I am honored you took the time to breathe with me, Abiola. I know you're a busy young lady." Nena returned to the child waiting expectantly for a response. "But you should head to the car, yes? You don't want Uncle to be looking for you, and you don't want to miss the plane."

Nena rose, hooking her thumbs in her pockets as she waited for Asogi's niece to do the same. She did. The girl slipped her arms through the straps of her teal-colored rucksack and made to leave the garden, but Nena stopped her first. She pointed to the gaping opening of the bag.

"You're unzipped. May I?"

Abiola turned her back to Nena in a nonverbal reply. Nena quickly tucked in a protruding notebook, its edges curled in from being handled many times. Nena made sure nothing else was sticking out and pulled the zipper on its track until the bag was sealed and the all-important contents secured inside.

"You're all good to go." Nena put a hand on her hip.

"Thank you," Abiola said in Swahili, to which Nena replied she was welcome in the same manner. Nena had picked up some words here and there, using her refined ear and natural affinity for learning languages. Maybe next time she and Abiola met, she'd know enough to have a conversation.

37

The town hall was already filling when Nena and Femi's car pulled around front to let them out. Billy had come on his own already to get a feel for the security challenges in real time. Nena observed lines of people from all sides streaming in. They all seemed happy. Today was the day they were supposed to hear what the next steps would be in the mining, with Asogi detailing how the government was working transparently on behalf of the people—with no backdoor negotiations—and prioritizing two things: fair rates and decision-making power for the villagers, who would choose whom they wanted to sell to.

Nena stepped out, scanning the area, which of course looked different in real time than it did in the aerial drone scan. She looked for Judah, hoping he'd used the time to calm down from the previous day and had had a change of heart and would stand with Asogi, showing the rest of the villagers that this time would be different, and all the horror stories they'd heard about what mining companies and governments did wouldn't happen to them. If their Judah believed in this deal, then they could too.

But when Nena and Femi wove in and out of the snaking lines and through the growing crowd surrounding the raised center where the PM would make his assurances, she saw no sign of Judah, and her heart fell a little. If she were being honest with herself, it wasn't only because his absence meant more of an uphill battle for Asogi and Tegete, but because she'd been hoping to see him too.

"Do you read?" Billy's voice came through the comms, and if Nena and Femi hadn't been used to how sound came through, they'd have turned, thinking Billy was right behind them, whispering in their ears. He wasn't, though. Nena spied Billy way up front, near Tegete and Asogi, looking like one of the entourage without looking like what he really was: security.

It seemed everyone was in great spirits, laughing and eager for everything to get started. The weather was agreeable, and the humidity was kept at bay. There was even a breeze and, carried on it, the smell of cooking food and savory spices from the line of kiosks posted along the outside. A small band played music off to the side, making the whole event relaxed and merry.

"The Dubins have arrived," Evers announced, his tone bored.

Nena hadn't spotted them yet, so Evers must have noted their location from aerial surveillance back at the resort. Reluctantly he'd stayed behind but made them promise to return with food. The Dubins appeared a few moments later, smiling and waving like they were at a ticker tape parade. Nena couldn't help rolling her eyes. They were so false. Dubin acting like he had just won the lottery, and maybe he had, with his secret morning meeting with Asogi. Bridget the ever-present doting, supportive wife and saccharine charitable philanthropist, like she hadn't been a child peddler nearly twenty years ago. All lies that Nena would have loved to expose. Right before she drove her blade in.

But neither of them was Nena's priority.

"We'll split so we can cover more ground," Nena said to Femi. They parted so the people behind them could get to where they wanted to be.

"What are we looking for?"

"Anything or anyone out of place, maybe." Nena ran her hands over her waist, feeling the handle of the Glock nestled in the holster at her back. There was another in her ankle holster and, of course, her hidden blades. Femi was equally armed, just in case. In groups this big, when they weren't entirely sure of all the players and with loads of money at play, one's friend could easily become one's enemy.

The meeting had started, and the moderator, one of the village elders whose name Nena couldn't recall at the moment, began speaking. He wore his traditional cloths, an array of golds, greens, and reds, and introduced the panel behind him, likely in order from least to greatest, with Dubin coming up first. Nena suppressed a grin, hoping that was the case. Dubin's response from the audience was tepid. They were very dubious of the grandstanding man, wild stories of Americans abroad reaching town ears way before Dubin had.

Next up was Councilman Tegete. With each, the moderator listed their credentials and why they were there. Tegete's audience response was significantly better, as he'd spent a lot of time with the people in their homes, surveying them and trying to figure out what they needed so that when all this was over and everyone else went back home, the Tribe would be there to continue the support they had promised, as only the Tribe could.

Nena watched the councilman and how he easily joked with the moderator about the too-hot cassava soup he was fed at the elder man's home—"hot" meaning spicy. To Africans, spice was like salt, so if Tegete was complaining, the soup must have been nuclear. The ease with which he was able to make people feel comfortable was something Nena admired, a quality not needed in her line of work.

A vacant seat stood between Tegete and Asogi, its emptiness like a bullhorn to Nena. It amplified Judah's absence. She swallowed a knot of disappointment at not producing the village rebel like she had been tasked with doing. She'd tried texting him earlier that day but to no avail. His silence was disconcerting.

Last was PM Asogi, who was greeted with a strong round of applause but an undertone of grumbling. Out of all the politicians who'd visited Merelani Hills, Asogi was the one who rang true to them.

He was of the people, and it was easy to see how much they wanted to believe he was being true with this deal as well. They wanted this money. They wanted Asogi to deliver it to them, and they'd wanted Judah to make sure it was all well. His absence would mean he did not support the reform, and perhaps they shouldn't either.

Femi blended in with the crowd, their multitude of colors from their traditional or contemporary wear displayed brightly beneath the sun. It was hard to see her, but Nena, who was in full view of the raised platform, could pick her teammates out. They were the ones who looked serious among the easygoing people, their heads constantly on a swivel, checking for anything out of order. With each scan, the tightness in Nena's chest eased a little. She began to think that all was well.

"There's incoming." It was Billy, who Nena couldn't see but knew was in his position at the stage, gazing out over the masses. "Coming up on E's six."

Billy wasn't referring to Evers, knowing Evers wasn't on-site. Billy's reflex had him using Nena's code name, Echo, when they were in the field. She didn't mind it. Made her feel like the old days when she was just that. An echo.

Nena peered out beyond her, trying to spot what Billy was referring to.

Billy continued, "Could be Judah, maybe? His face is covered by those gaiters they're always wearing, but he's the same build. Moves like Judah. Seen the jersey before. But everyone wears jerseys."

It wasn't enough of a confirmation. Nena spotted a few other gaiter-wearing people dotted throughout the pavilion, some with jerseys, some without, all seemingly tense. She'd noticed a couple of them before and thought they were on duty, protecting the rest of the villagers, as they'd always been doing. She'd also hoped that seeing them there meant Judah was coming around and hadn't washed his hands entirely of the whole thing.

Nena located the man Billy had marked, and confirmed he did appear to be the village leader, weaving purposefully through the crowd, carving a curved path toward the platform, where Asogi was answering the moderator's question about mining reform and what it meant for Merelani Hills. Asogi twisted around, beckoning behind him, and Tegete rose from his seat to join him. Dubin perched at the edge of his chair, his expression practically begging to be called to speak.

Nena's feet were on the move before her brain registered that she was advancing on the quick-moving man. Her eyes flittered over the crowd, identifying, by the gaiters they wore around their necks, who she thought to be members of Judah's group, dotted among the joyous crowds of people.

"There are more gaiters in the crowd," Nena murmured, fixing her eyes on the lead, on Judah and his advance to the stage. "Could be more outside the pavilion, but they're all focused on the stage."

Billy said, "I see them."

"Could be watching out for their boss," Femi suggested.

Could be, Nena thought. She focused on their boss, too, trying to get closer to him, but the throng of people was nearly impenetrable, closing back in whatever gap he made as he cut through. The audience seemed to part for him, thinking they were making way for the late panel member and their golden boy.

"Guys," said Evers through the comms. He was back at the hotel, watching monitors as his drones provided aerial view. "I'm hearing a couple of reports coming in on the line from the local police feed. There's something happening at the airstrip."

Nena slowed, processing Evers's announcement. "Something like?"

"Not sure," Evers replied, louder now with the sudden infusion of energy.

Nena asked, "Is there a drone nearby? Can it get there to show images?"

"Already on it."

Meanwhile she was on the move again, trying to remain single minded, though she was fighting a losing battle, and her thoughts were splintered into many shards: Judah, Tegete, Asogi, the airstrip, Judah's people in the crowd, the tightness of everything, and her inability to easily get to either person she was tasked with protecting or tasked with watching.

Nena asked, "What is the chatter saying?"

"Not sure. It's hard to understand," Evers mumbled, his voice flooding with frustration. "They're speaking their language, and—wait!"

The mass of people between Nena and Judah was an unmovable wall. The villagers pushed toward the front to see better. They stood on tiptoes and held younger children atop their shoulders, clamoring to get a good view of their momentous occasion, the day they'd all become rich farmers.

"I'm hearing . . . something about a vehicle and people jumping out."

"Where's the drone, dude?" Femi asked. "I can't get through the crowd. B, is it better for you up there?"

"Negative," Billy said.

"They're approaching the plane, it sounds like. And I think I'm hearing gunfire. No, it's definitely shots. They're saying there are bodies down. They're begging for backup."

"But all of it's here," Nena muttered.

Realization hit her. The prime minister's niece was supposed to be flying out, back to her mother, home, at that time.

"Shit," Femi muttered. "This has gotta be a distraction."

Nena didn't reply, her thoughts running through possible scenarios, reasons why. "Yeah," she mumbled, more to herself than the others. "Which was the distraction? The airstrip? Or here? And who—or what—was the intended mark?"

38

Time was not on their side. And there was nothing to be done about what was going on at the airstrip. Nena could only focus on what was happening now and intercepting Judah before anything worse happened.

Nena was nearing Judah on his right as he cut swiftly through the crowd, not caring about the angry catcalls that indicated he was elbowing his way through them too roughly. He ignored them all, moving closer to the front with razor-sharp determination.

She called Judah's name, but he did not turn. He didn't even falter in recognition. He was zeroed in on the platform and on Asogi speaking and Tegete approaching to stand by him, wearing a wide smile. Tegete threw an arm over Asogi's shoulder in solidarity as they shared a joke between them, while Dubin glowered behind them, reddening like a child picked last to join a game.

Nena quickened her pace, bumping people out of her way and channeling Judah in not taking the time to ask their pardon.

Something appeared at Judah's hip. It hadn't been there before, but it was there now, and that meant either there had been a handoff with someone else in the crowd, or he'd had it up the sleeve of the jersey he wore and had managed to pull it down. She tried to analyze it as she pushed even harder to get through.

The something was now in his right hand as he began to raise it.

Now she shoved a man and his child—she'd make apologies later—to the side in her push to get to Judah and whatever he was holding.

Nena hesitated calling him out. She didn't want to start a panic with all these people packed in and cause a stampede. Her vision of what he held wasn't clear, but the way her senses were on alert, feeling as if lightning was about to strike, told her whatever he held was something lethal.

"Either of you have eyes on Judah? There's something in his hand at his side. Can you confirm what he's got?"

Could be a walkie-talkie or a sat phone. Could be something worse.

"The stage is blocking my line of vision," Billy said. "I'm getting in closer."

No one wanted to disrupt the crowd, to terrify them and cause a stampede if they didn't have to. They moved painfully and purposefully as fast as they could, but it felt like they were crawling at a snail's pace.

Evers kept them apprised of the situation at the airstrip. "Someone's carrying something small to one of the trucks . . ." He trailed off.

"Coming from the left," Femi reported, all-business, no jokes. "But I'm not close enough for a clean one."

Nena was already on it. Judah was raising his hand, the dark object in it. It was only a second before it cleared Nena's vision.

"He's got a weapon," Nena said. "Can you take him out? Are you clear? Get Asogi and the rest onstage down."

She tried to keep her voice low, but it was too late, and they were packed like sardines. And someone else had seen what Nina had seen because now Judah's arm was raising and pointing. Someone screamed what it was.

And then complete panic erupted.

The crowd closest to him—the ones who could see what he was doing, hear and understand what the person was screaming—tried

234

to scatter but to no avail. There were too many of them compacted together.

The people surrounding Nena saw the gun in her hand and tried to get away, unsure who was friend or foe. She couldn't appease them. She barely even took note of them as she tried to make haste to her target.

There was no clean shot.

She pushed through the surging crowd, her gun muzzle up in the air, but the ones who had been near the front, near Judah, pushed back against her, actually lifting Nena from the ground and carrying her back several precious inches before she could gain ground again and pummel through like thread shoved through the tiny eye of a needle.

Billy broke into a run across the platform, trying to get to the prime minister and the councilman.

Judah pulled the trigger, a tiny puff of smoke emitting in the air. And then another. And then another, his arm sweeping across the panel as he fired.

Left to right. Three. Four.

They were rapid fire. So fast. No time to even take a breath.

The space was pandemonium. People were everywhere, jostling Nena, moving her back and forth as if she were in rough water, swells making her at their mercy.

Nena fought against the riptide crowd, engulfed in them, her own gun in hand, aiming, then pulling up when an innocent ran into her line of vision.

Five. Six. Seven.

The moderator and panel ducking as Billy sprinted across the platform, weapon in hand and aiming at Judah.

PM Asogi freezing and then falling, not in slow motion, like in the movies. Fast, and hard.

Everything was too fast and hard.

Then Tegete spinning right as Billy tackled him down to the ground.

Judah turned to run with the dispersing crowd, shoving those in front of him toward the entryway. They cleared just enough space.

Nena fired.

Judah's left shoulder jerked back. His steps stuttered.

Another shot.

Judah's body arched forward. Femi firing her weapon at his back, coming in from the other side, where she had also finally broken through.

And a third shot.

A light pink misted the air, as a hole opened in Judah's head. His knees buckled, and Judah dropped to the ground like a bag of stones. Then Nena lowered her weapon.

39

Outside the pavilion, sounds of medics and police could be heard, the whirring a rattling cacophony.

"Whoever was with him is getting away," Femi said, meeting Nena at the body, where they both stood over it. Femi bounced back and forth on her toes. Her weapon down as she awaited orders. Her adrenaline pumped, whereas Nena wanted a hole to open up and swallow her. She knew the ramifications of this. But as she looked down at yet another man she had not wanted to take down, her mind drew a blank. Surveillance and security had escalated into a dispatch, and she didn't know what to do next.

What. Are. My. Orders?

"I can help them," Femi offered, her eyes pleading for her to be cut loose.

Nena waved her away. Femi nodded, like she knew Nena was not in the headspace to give any commands. She pivoted, and went off following the terrified, retreating crowds to help secure the area as best she could. If Judah's people were attacking, Nena's team was well outnumbered.

Through her earpiece, Nena could hear Femi telling Evers to look for the car with the kid using the drone. And then Evers informing them he'd lost it, the dense trees providing cover for the getaway. Nena ignored the rush of noise around her and the flurry of communication in her ear among her team.

There was only the body. Judah's.

The blood, darkening the ground. A blackened hole through the soccer jersey at the shoulder. Another at the back from Femi's shot. The last, the headshot, hidden from when he'd fallen on it. She squatted next to the still body, checking the pulse, confirming what she already knew. Nothing.

"Billy." Nena's senses were coming back to her. They were in the field. The mission had changed. She had team members unaccounted for. "Are you okay?" She looked up frantically at the stage, tried to see through the converged mass of medics and security on it.

The months melted away, and Nena was back at General Konate's outpost, taking on increasing fire after her team had been sabotaged and Network had gone dark from a sophisticated computer virus. She was watching as one by one, members of her team were taken out by Konate's men as she tried desperately to save them. Tried to reach Network. Tried to find a way out. The weight of her team's deaths— even of those who'd betrayed them and tried, in the end, to kill her— was the cross she bore every day.

It felt like eons as she waited for word from the pavilion stage, from Billy, who'd reminded her how everyone seemed to die around her. Had she lost him too?

"Billy." Had she spoken it? Had it come out as desperate as she was feeling? Her free hand fisted; the other—still holding the gun—nervously tapped against her leg while she waited for something, anything. She would not, could not look at the stage. She didn't want to.

Nena Knight, this fierce modern-day African warrior, the tip of the Tribe's spear, daughter of the Knights and Chieftain Michael Asym, could not force her eyes to gaze on another one of her fallen.

Nena just wasn't strong enough. Or brave.

Evers cut through her personal hell. "I can't locate the car. The girl is gone. Any of you read?"

It hadn't even occurred to their junior that any of them might be dead. He hadn't thought to ask. That was sweet, Nena thought. That fresh-faced team member had such confidence in his teammates' ability to stay alive.

The silence stretched an eternity. "I'm here" came Billy's breathless response. "The comm fell out of my ear. I'm here. I'm good."

Relief flooded her. She sucked in air. She finally saw Billy on the overcrowded stage, kneeling over a prone figure. Others were there; medics rushed in to help. A flood of officers and more medical personnel converged to either secure or triage the scene.

Dubin and the moderator, with some other officials whose names she couldn't currently recall, gathered around. Dubin gawked, his hand to his mouth as if he'd be ill. Bridget, tears flowing, practically quaked in the arms of security as they held her back from rushing the stage to her husband.

Nena asked, "What's the prognosis?" Billy looked up and at her. His face, long and drawn, gave the answer before his mouth formed the words.

"The prime minister is dead. Tegete is unresponsive but alive. It doesn't look good."

She unfurled her fist and brought her fingers to the bridge of her nose as she bowed her head, needing a moment to collect herself.

Nena's shoulders firmed in resolve. She had work to do. There would be fallout from the death. Fallout from the government because Judah had assassinated the prime minister. From the village because the Tribe had killed their golden boy and mouthpiece—murderer that he was and, Nena supposed, kidnapper of an innocent little girl. From the Tribe, which was most assuredly aware of the situation as she stood there, with the Council convening in an urgent meeting to discuss her complete and utter failure, at every level conceivable.

She holstered her gun and leaned over the body. With both hands, she rolled the body to its back. The blood was all over its front. She gazed down at Judah, a mix of emotions she'd have to unpack later. Why had he thought this was the path to choose? Why kill the PM and take the niece?

Nena pinched the bottom of the gaiter with her fingers, tugging it down.

Little jagged pieces that had been flickering in her mind from the moment she'd spotted Judah were syncing up now; things now jangled free that had given her pause from the first moment she saw him at the soccer game, standing among his people and the men who followed him. He'd never worn the covering as they did, with it wrapped around his nose and mouth. But when she'd seen him in the midst of the crowd, marching toward the platform like a man on a mission, all covered up as he'd never been before, something had scratched at her consciousness.

Judah always wanted the world to know who he was. He took pride in himself and where he was from, despite being labeled a thug or a problem. So why would he cover up today, especially here, when he was going to make his grand stand?

Nena pulled the gaiter free of his mouth. She leaned back as she confirmed what her subconscious had been trying to tell her, that the whole scene wasn't adding up.

This dead man, the one hidden behind the gaiter, who'd killed a good man while pretending to be another, was not Judah Wasira.

Question was, Where was the real Judah, and who had sent in this dead one?

40

When the medics had loaded Tegete onto a stretcher and Asogi into a body bag, Nena and Billy followed them out to the front of the pavilion. The place was still teeming with villagers, who were held back by a chain of police and security so there was a pathway to the awaiting ambulances. The moment Tegete, a native of Merelani Hills, and Asogi, one of the few "good ones" that they thought were in government, were wheeled out—one behind the other—a wail went up through the crowd.

It was as if they were in a sports stadium, and the crowd was taking turns at doing a uniform wave. The pain of loss and grief rippled through the onlookers in a sweeping crescendo from one side to another and back again. And back again. It was the most heart-wrenching moment Nena had ever experienced.

The women, some clad in airy blouses and colorful cloths wrapped around their waists, head wraps tied perfectly, began praying, falling on their knees to bless the body of Asogi as it was hoisted into the back of the vehicle. They chanted that his soul be calm and not angered by the way his life had ended.

They sent blessings over Tegete, who still had not awakened, praying that he would not leave this world, that his work here was not yet done. They lamented over the evil deed that had been done, for now they'd heard the whispers of Asogi's niece's kidnapping and worried that their homes would be cursed from all this evil and death. This was supposed to be a good day, and now it was a day that would be forever known in infamy.

The men stood stoically behind the praying women, their faces a sea of disbelief and mistrust. They called out, wanting to know if it was true. If their Judah had killed the PM and Mr. Tegete. The head of police confirmed the body in there was not Judah's but that he was wanted for questioning about the assassination, murder attempt, and kidnapping.

"If you know where he is," the head of police said loudly as the waiting crowd hushed, "tell him to turn himself in, or we will come for him and anyone who was working with him."

One of the men asked from within the crowd, "What does this mean? Will the military come to Latema?"

"Only if you make it so" was the angry response from the police, and the people began chattering anxiously, looking to one another in fear.

Chief Constable Pengo wouldn't want the military to come into Latema. No one did. The military meant their local authorities had no control. The military meant the government believed the Latemans had revolted and had conspired to assassinate the prime minister of Tanzania, a Lateman himself. They would have to give Judah up.

It was a hard call, suggesting the villagers turn their backs on a man who had, up until this point, championed for them, had been their Robin Hood, until he'd put them in the line of fire. The air was thick with their confusion and their concern. When the medical vehicles, the horns blaring, pulled off to the nearest medical facility to stabilize Tegete and then life flight him to a bigger hospital in the nearest city, only then did the crowd began to dissipate.

Talks of going back to their villages and planning next steps to prevent any escalation of police while the investigation continued. And, of course, ever present on their minds was the question, What would become of the tanzanite mine deal if the representatives negotiating were no longer there? Who would speak for the Latemans now?

"I'm still here," Dubin said, materializing from nowhere in front of the crowd. "I have been working closely with Mr. Asogi and Mr. Tegete. If you'll be patient, I will update whoever sits in their place, and we will keep our offer on the table during this time of mourning."

Nena and Billy met up with Femi, who'd had no luck in running down any of Judah's people who'd been spotted in the pavilion, one of them possibly handing off the weapon Judah's double used.

Nena's upper lip twisted as she listened to Dubin, showboating and using this moment to push his agenda as if he were the big man and would deliver what the people wanted. Of course, he wouldn't tell them that there were other deals on the table, that the choice beyond him was theirs, and that that was what Asogi and Tegete, with Judah by their side, had been going to tell them . . . until Dubin had driven Judah off, effectively halting negotiations and making it prime for him.

No, the people didn't know that, and there was no one here to tell them Dubin was a wolf in sheep's clothing. His wife hovered behind him, looking pale. A slight wind could have blown her over. Her eyes were red and swollen from her crying. They matched Dubin's everyday coloring perfectly. She kept casting furtive glances toward Nena, as if she wanted to speak, but Nena had nothing for her.

"Have I said lately how I cannot stand that prick?" Femi grumbled, toeing the dirt. "Can we push off? I can't take another moment of him."

Nena agreed, but she wanted Dubin in the car first. She didn't trust leaving him here alone with the people so he could say anything. "You can go. I'll follow when the Dubins leave."

What Nena needed was a moment to think. She needed to call her father. She needed to process what had happened. She needed to figure out how to find Judah. And she thought about Abiola, of how scared the little girl was and of the news she'd receive (if she made it out alive) that her uncle was dead.

Nena froze. Abiola.

In the midst of all the chaos, she'd let what Evers said about the airstrip slip through. "E, are you still on the line?"

"Always. What's up? I'm canvassing for Judah but not finding him."

Billy said, "If he's kidnapped the Asogis' niece, he needs to go underground. They'll bring in the military on this one."

"How the hell are we gonna find the girl?" Femi asked. "We don't have enough manpower. We need to call in reinforcements."

Nena watched as Dubin shook hands like he was running for office. His rebound after his harrowing ordeal onstage, where he'd barely made it out with his life, was nothing short of amazing. He lavished assurances on the scared and confused Latemans, promising that he'd take care of them the way Asogi and Tegete had intended. That their deaths wouldn't be in vain.

"He's not dead," Nena called out before she had a chance to check herself. Even Billy and Femi stared at her sudden outburst. Dubin's body tensed in midshake, and Bridget watched, her hands wringing and eyebrows furrowed as she looked from Nena to Dubin as if viewing a tennis match.

Slowly, Dubin turned his hard, nearly clear eyes on her. "What was that?" he snapped, though he'd heard her clearly. He was giving her a chance to correct herself.

Oh well, I'm all in now.

"You said their deaths wouldn't be in vain," Nena clarified, taking a couple of steps toward where he held his ground.

He dropped the villager's hand and turned to face her. His upper body bulked up as if to intimidate, and he planted his hands on either side of his hips as if he and Nena were now in some sort of standoff, about to draw on each other.

Nena thought, maybe they were.

Nena continued, "Mr. Tegete isn't dead."

Dubin was unable to hide his contempt. Even those around him appeared uneasy, as if suddenly sensing some evil vibe emanating from him.

He gestured to her. "He's unconscious. He's critical. Not much he can do," Dubin said patronizingly.

"But—" Nena raised her voice so it would carry. She wanted the people to know that not all was lost, and Dubin was not the only one left. "Tegete is not dead."

She wanted Dubin to know that as much as he might want to be the last one standing, there was still another person in play.

Dubin stared at her dumbly and then shook himself out of it. It was as if he were shaking off her childishness too. "Whatever you say." He turned away from her, stretching out his arm to his wife. Bridget hesitated. She looked over at Nena, her expression as if she didn't want to, as if apologizing to Nena for her husband's bad behavior. She'd been doing that since she first set eyes on Nena in Tanzania.

It didn't matter that Dubin thought Nena a child with pipe dream wishes that Tegete would be okay. What mattered was that the people here heard her, remembered that Tegete was not gone and that all was not lost. People weren't dead until they were dead.

Nena watched Dubin draw his wife into his arms, kissing her tenderly on the top of her head, whispering to her. She nodded at whatever he said, wiping at her eyes. They began walking toward their awaiting vehicle. Nena found the dynamics of their relationship perplexing. Dubin was abhorrent in every way possible. Callous and belligerent. Entitled and dismissive of everyone in this country whose skin was darker than his.

He thought them all savages, Nena was sure. He thought women were beneath him and needed "taking care of" from their big, strong menfolk. Every time he looked at any of them, Nena could see the shade of disgust in his eyes despite his every effort to hide it and play circus ringmaster, wearing a smile too big, welcoming everyone in his big tent of lies.

And yet with Bridget, Dubin was different. Soft. Protective. Attentive even. With her, he let his guard down. Nena reflected on the past few days. With Bridget, he was like putty in her hands. Bridget might know her husband's dealings, and so maybe . . . Nena sighed, unwilling to admit what she'd been avoiding since she arrived. She might have to go to the woman. Bridget had said she owed Nena, hadn't she? Nena swore she'd never collect, wanting no part of her. But Elin had once said, "Never say never."

Nena really hated when her sister was right.

Femi also watched the Dubins slide into their car. "He is going to be insufferable now."

Nena agreed. Insufferable wasn't the word for it. But that was the least of their problems. And now, dread regurgitated in her throat like acid reflux. Nena would have to force herself to talk to Bridget to see if she might reason with Dubin.

Nena waited until the Dubins were nothing but taillights.

"Run a trace," she said suddenly.

Billy and Femi gave her confused looks.

"On who? Using what?" Evers asked.

Nena began toward their vehicle, following behind the groups of leaving people.

She had work to do in a dispatch of Nena's own decree.

"Boss?" Femi prompted at Nena's right.

"Using the tracker I dropped in Abiola's rucksack."

41

Nena instructed Billy and Femi to head back to the resort without her when their car approached the Y-shaped intersection that would turn down to the airstrip or toward the resort. She wanted to take a look at the airstrip and what was going on there before heading back to the lion's den she knew the resort would be, teeming with police and reporters. Dubin was puffing his chest out and ingratiating himself everywhere now that Councilman Tegete wasn't there to keep him at bay. Nena wasn't ready to deal with it.

Her new team tried to go with her, said they'd just have the car take them there, assess the fallout, and catch up to Evers at the resort to regroup and make a plan. They shouldn't split up.

"You know what happens to people who split up in horror movies," Femi said sagely with a pointed look. "Especially Black people."

"We're on an entire continent of Black people," Nena reminded her.

Femi pointed at her. "Exactly." She twisted her lips and sat back in her chair like she'd dropped a bomb of knowledge.

Nena frowned, opening her mouth, about to voice her confusion, but Billy cut her off with a shake of his head. "Don't bother trying to figure that one out. That's a 'yes, dear' and drop it kind of moment."

Femi punched him in the arm. Hard. Billy yelped, edging away.

Nena asked the driver to pull to a stop by the side of the road and opened the door before the vehicle had a chance to roll to a complete stop.

"Get with Evers and see if that tracker can locate Abiola and maybe Judah too. We need to figure out what's going on."

"What's going on is Judah is a dead man walking," Billy said assuredly, his nostrils flaring in anger. "He may have put down a Council member. That's an automatic dispatch decree."

She was aware. If he was really behind the attack and the kidnapping, Nena would put him down, easily. It was just . . . she couldn't be sure. And she couldn't afford to put anything past him, no matter the gut feeling she had that Judah was not behind the kidnapping and the assassination. One thing she'd learned about him was that if Judah Wasira wanted to make an impact, he'd be there to do it himself, or he'd claim it immediately.

She looked down the road she was about to walk, then back inside the car. "I'll see you soon. Keep an ear out when you get there."

"Sure thing," Femi said.

Nena shut the rear door and made to leave, but Billy had rolled the window down and was calling her name. She turned to him.

"Stay alive?"

She gave a quick nod, accepting his thoughtful gesture. The tide had turned with them, and she was glad for it. At least that was one person who saw she wasn't the harbinger of death the whispers swirling around her for months had prophesied. And with this latest debacle (if it could even be called that—disaster), those whispers would be elevated to shouts and lamentations. The Council and Tribe members would be calling for Nena's head.

Those were the things she thought about as she walked through the scene at the airstrip. The police were there—thankfully not Chief Constable Pengo, who she thought was still back at the pavilion. Nena could see the tire marks from the kidnappers' auto as it had raced on scene and then off. She assessed the bodies spread out on the runway and by the small Cessna Citation that stood, door open ominously, with bullet holes splattered across its side. One side of the windshield had a crack in it that had spread out in a web of fractures. The officers on-site said the pilot was among the dead.

She indicated toward the open doorway of the plane. "May I go in? Look about?" she asked an officer standing guard.

He hesitated, scratching at the scruff on his chin as trickles of sweat rolled down the side of his face. "I shouldn't. Chief Constable said not to let anyone in."

"He's right. But I'd like to have a look just the same. I need to inform the Council of the Tribe." She was taking a chance that he knew anything about the Tribe, or cared. But the widening of his eyes and the quick way he straightened himself informed her he was very aware of their power. She supposed everyone in Africa knew the stories of the African Tribal Council.

"Truly?" Despite the grim surroundings, his eyes brightened, and his chest seemed to puff in pride. "You are from the Tribe? No lie?"

"No lie." If she'd had some sort of secret Tribe crest to prove it, she'd have shown it.

The officer said, "I hope the Tribe can assist. We need them in Latema." He looked around quickly before jerking his head toward the metal rollaway stairs. "Please be quick before the constable comes."

Nena nodded her thanks and made haste up the steps. She hadn't planned to be there long, only wanted to check for any clues or if anything had been left behind.

The plane was empty of Abiola's belongings. Nena breathed a sigh of relief for the tiny win. Hopefully this meant Abiola still had her rucksack with her and that the tracer could help them locate her.

It had been a last-minute act, and Nena couldn't explain why she'd slipped the small black disk in the bag and zipped it up, sending the girl on her way. But when Abiola mentioned Dubin's impromptu meeting with Asogi, it had triggered something in Nena. That it was better to be safe than sorry. Best case, they'd lose a piece of equipment if nothing happened and Abiola made it back to her mother safely. Worst case . . . there was this. At least they might have a lead, if the kidnappers let her keep the bag. At least they had a tiny bit of insurance. And with the clock timer now activated, there was only a small window to retrieve the girl before the kidnappers got what they wanted and either returned or killed her. Or didn't get what they wanted and killed her. Either way, Abiola's life was in imminent danger.

Nena couldn't let it come to that. One way or another, she had to get that child back to her mother alive.

Nena exited the plane, pieces of possible plans dropping like Tetris blocks, grimacing when she realized the car that had brought her was gone. She should have secured it. Heat radiated up at her from the hot earth. First things first, she needed to flag a ride.

42

Femi and Billy were standing at the entrance doors of the resort, waiting for Nena, when her vehicle pulled to a stop in the base of the U-shaped circular drive in front of the hotel. She got out and walked the rest of the way to her waiting team. Their visible relief made her feel a certain kind of warmth, and she brushed it away, not wanting to feel any kind of closeness to this team, to Billy. Nena had cared before, and it had cost her entire team.

The area was alive with activity. There were people everywhere, bustling about. Employees of the resort, police, security. She noted some of the village elders milling around looking very worried, including the moderator, who was wearing a white gauze bandage around his head from where a bullet had grazed his forehead. Nena was glad his wounds were not serious.

Nena's team slowed when they met up with her. Femi moved beside her and Billy walked backward as they updated her on what she had missed while she was at the airstrip.

"It's a madhouse here," Femi said under her breath. "Councilman Tegete was airlifted to Dodoma. Asogi's body remains here to be taken by his family. His sister . . . Glory Asogi, Abiola's mother, just arrived."

Nena thought the mother's arrival was quick until she remembered that it was a roughly 250-kilometer drive from Latema to Dodoma—a chartered flight even shorter. Abiola's mother would have been at the airstrip waiting for her daughter's arrival and, when she heard the news, got on the first flight out that they could secure for her.

"Who'd she come with?"

Femi told her, "Some military guy. Name's General Geofry apparently. Meanwhile, Ms. Odemba will be the acting PM until the president and other officials decide who will replace him. Now that she's in charge, you know Dubin's already stuck his head far up Odemba's a—"

"Any word from the kidnappers?" Nena cut in.

"They made a ransom demand while Ms. Asogi was in the air," Billy said as they neared the conference room where everyone was holed up to strategize.

Nena's steps slowed to a halt. "What do they want?"

"For the Tribe representatives and the government to be cut out entirely. To sell directly to corporations. They want a contracted promise that no one will intervene."

Nena's eyes narrowed. "Anything else?"

Billy was disgusted. "Two mil. American."

"Which Ms. Asogi doesn't have."

Nena pinched the space between her eyes. The kidnappers wasted no time. She might not have access to any money he might have. And two million American? Unlikely, even for Samwell Asogi.

"The kidnappers have to know she doesn't have that kind of money readily available," Nena said, looking around to ensure no one was close enough to hear them.

"They suggested she get the Tribe to foot the bill."

Nena was incredulous. "This is some elementary kidnapping. They're saying to cut the Tribe out of a deal the Tribe will not make money off of and then turn around and demand the Tribe pay a ransom when one of ours has been critically wounded?"

Femi whispered, quirking an eyebrow, "If you ask me, it sounds like the money was a last-minute add."

"Agreed," Billy said. "They're trying to milk a thing. That wasn't part of the original plan."

Nena agreed. Could Judah be a part of this? He wouldn't ask for money if the goal was to deal directly with the investors. What was two million when they had a land full of gems worth many millions?

Nena lowered her voice. "Has Evers located her?"

"He's tracking. They've been on the move. We should get upstairs and make a plan," Billy suggested. "We gotta short window, and it will be dark soon."

Nena nodded, thinking. "We will. But I have to get in there." She indicated toward the closed conference door. "And see what's what." She bit the inside of her upper lip. "Then, I have to call High Council."

Neither Billy nor Femi could hide the flash of unease that flitted across their faces at the mention of High Council Noble Knight.

"Can't we wait until we get back the kid?" Femi asked, bravado gone. "Nope."

Billy double pointed at Nena. "Then on that note, we'll meet you in Evers's room." The two of them began to back away from her.

"Oh, so no offer to be with me when I make that call?" Nena asked, amused despite the situation. "Thought we were a team?"

Femi shook her head while Billy coughed in his hand. They quickly turned from her and hustled away, leaving Nena staring forlornly behind them. That was one job they'd gladly let Nena do on her own.

Nena desperately wanted a shower. She wanted to wash away the grime and return to her team ready to move back into more familiar territory, planning a mission. She was wearing multiple hats, and she needed to first go into that room as the representative of the Tribe. She needed to be able to update her father on that part before she went to retrieve Abiola. She gave the man standing guard at the closed door her name and was grasping the door handle when she heard a halting voice calling her name from behind.

"Please, could I have a minute?" Nena looked around the open space to see where the woman could have been. Bridget had appeared from nowhere. Could she have been eavesdropping on Nena and her team when they were speaking?

Nena tensed, her mind warring. Earlier she'd toyed with the idea that she might have to call upon Bridget to learn what she could about Dubin. Now that Bridget was in her face, the thought of asking her anything was enough to make her violently ill. The only priority to Nena was getting Abiola Asogi back while there was still time. Still, Nena couldn't pass up an opportunity for potentially useful information.

Bridget pressed, "It'll only be a minute."

Nena continued to chew on her lip. Finally, she turned from the door.

"What is it?" Nena hissed. She stepped away from the guards at the door. Nena didn't need them gossiping.

"Now's not the time."

Bridget's hand fluttered as usual at her décolletage. She looked conflicted and like she'd better sit down before she passed out. Nena kept her distance and eyed the woman suspiciously.

"I wish you'd take a moment to listen. I can help." Her French accent thickened in her agitated state, and Nena had no time for this.

Nena impatiently spat back in French, "If you want to help, take your husband and go back where you came from."

Bridget's eyes lit up. "That you speak my language takes my breath away, chérie."

"Never call me that," Nena snapped, flipping back to English so fast Bridget stepped back.

"My apologies," Bridget said in English. She paused to collect herself, then in French said, "I only mean to be helpful. I may have information that could be useful to you."

Nena knew this was her chance to get the woman to handle her husband, but she couldn't get herself to do it. Her mind told her this was the strategic thing to do. But her heart and younger self wished to throttle the woman's swanlike neck.

Nena was skeptical. "What information?" This woman wanted to waste her time. She probably wanted to keep her out of the conference room so that Dubin could dig his claws deeper into Odemba and whomever else she was with before Nena could suggest anything. He'd already had too much time alone with them.

Nena's phone vibrated in her pocket. Casting a wary glance at Bridget, she pulled her phone out. Her eyes glanced over the notification, and her stomach tightened at the note from her father to call him. Immediately.

"Perhaps if we can go somewhere private."

"Are you trying to prevent me from entering that room?" Nena asked menacingly. She took a step closer, and Bridget shrank back, eyes widening, hand grazing over that neck of hers again.

"Is this some ploy to get your husband free rein on the deal now that Mr. Tegete is out of the way?" Nena continued. She shook her head, disgusted. "I'll never let that happen. Not while I'm alive. You can tell him that."

Nena turned to leave, but Bridget's hand was on her arm, tugging her back.

Nena lasered in on the bloodred-polished fingernails gripping her. Her eyes bore into them, and if she'd had pyrokinesis, the hand would have been on fire in an instant. Her head snatched up, meeting Bridget's imploring eyes, which stared into hers, desperate for her to listen.

Nena yanked her arm out of Bridget's grasp, the move making the pointed nails scratch marks into Nena's skin.

"Don't. You. Ever. Touch me." English. The words came out in a low growl, like some otherworldly thing. Not Nena. Didn't even sound like her. Her body trembled from trying to contain her emotions.

Bridget's mouth opened and closed. Opened again. Her throat moved from the constant swallowing. "I-I'm . . ." The rest of her words failed her.

Nena shot her one last withering glare and turned her back on her, marching to the door and opening it with such pent-up rage, it would have hit the guard standing on the outside of it had she not caught herself and the door in time, wrenching her arm in the process of stopping its momentum.

She gritted her teeth through the stab of pain. Nena would have to suck up the clumsy act. She needed to gather herself and assure everyone the Tribe was still very much a part of this entire thing, even without Tegete. Who they would deal with, now, was her.

43

All eyes turned to the newcomer. It felt like a war room, and in a sense, maybe it was. Only there was a woman sitting in a chair at the side of the conference table, dabbing at her eyes with something white balled in her hand. Her twists were tied into a large chignon at the back of her head, a few stray ones escaping out. She was the younger, much prettier version of her older brother. She stared down the oak table, her eyes going side to side as she listened to the chatter around her. No one paying attention to the fact that they were talking logistics about her dead brother and missing daughter as if she weren't there. Nena felt for her.

The chief constable conversed with his officers in a corner, trying to map out where Abiola could have been taken. They talked about how time was winding down and the longer they took, the less chance they'd have to get the girl back alive. Ms. Asogi flinched when she heard this, and Nena wanted to throw one of the thick crystal vases at their heads to remind them to be sensitive to who was around them.

Ms. Odemba had not been at the pavilion, had stayed behind to take meetings on other mining matters with other towns. Nena didn't know how Odemba had taken the news of Asogi, and her demeanor now was unreadable as she listened intently to Dubin, whose back was to Nena. He was gesturing wildly with his mammoth hands, driving home whatever point he was trying to make. Next to Odemba stood their newest member dressed in full military uniform, the high-ranking General Geofry, sent by the Tanzanian president after Asogi's assassination and whose presence could mean disaster for anyone associated with Judah, whether or not they were involved in what had happened that day.

"So I am clear, Mr. Dubin, you think we should do as the kidnappers demand and throw out the reform, plus give them that ridiculous sum of money?" Odemba asked, her hand to her chin. She glanced at Ms. Asogi and lowered her voice. "We do not negotiate with kidnappers and especially not assassins of government officials."

Nena had definitely assassinated a government official or two, but they had been corrupt. Asogi, it turned out, had been one of the good ones, and his niece didn't deserve to be left behind.

"Ms. Odemba is correct. We can't give them what they want. Call in the military and enact martial law, or let Pengo do what he needs to. We cordoned off the villages and will smoke the kidnappers out. But we have to go after the girl," the general suggested.

Dubin said, "You don't let it go unpunished. No one will want to touch this town after the accident that occurred at the mine and now this. The liability will be too great. People are getting killed and kidnapped. Novices are running complex mine logistics without proper equipment, training, or safety measures. Excuse my French, but what you have here is a clusterfuck!" He took a breath, holding out a hand to stop Odemba from interjecting.

"Let me have the contract and get that off your plate so you can concentrate on ridding this town of Judah and his rebels. This is a political nightmare for you, no doubt about it."

Nena had been listening quietly before she was ready to join the fray. "The town is grieving their losses from the mine collapse, reeling from the violence they witnessed today, and a little girl has been kidnapped. And all you can go on about is signing the mine over to you?

To help Odemba out, of course." Nena didn't bother hiding her disgust. She'd had enough of Dubin and his silver-tongued ways.

The room had become quiet when their conversation carried. Odemba smirked, an eyebrow raised. Nena hoped the normally astute Odemba wasn't buying into Dubin's lies.

"Oh, this one," Pengo grumbled. "Where have you been all this time? We have many questions for you and this mess of yours."

Nena pointed at herself. "My mess?" she asked. "Explain."

"Well, you were here to keep this safe for Mr. Tegete, yes?" Pengo said. "You were here to ensure things went smoothly. Worked with Judah to ensure the villagers signed off on the deal for the mining reform so they would work jointly with the government to deal with outside interests. Now Judah is a killer. The villagers are scared, and the military wants to come and take over my village. Weren't you sent here to prevent all of that?"

Nena focused her attention on Ms. Asogi. "Ms. Asogi, whatever is decided here, I will find your daughter."

Hope filled the woman's eyes, and she brought her hands slowly down to her lap. "You can do this?"

"She can't," Pengo cut in. "She isn't the authorities here. That is me. If the girl is to be found, it'll be by me and my men. No military. No Tribe."

Dubin's eyes glinted when he heard "the Tribe."

"Not if," Nena corrected firmly. She gave Pengo a warning glare, silencing whatever was coming next from him. "And remember who is in this room." She pulled her eyes from the portly man and leveled her gaze on Ms. Odemba, the general, and the conquistador over there. "Perhaps we all should when speaking about next steps in getting Abiola back."

"You know my girl's name?" Ms. Asogi asked. "A big lady like you?"

"Of course." Why would the woman think her daughter wouldn't be known? "And I'm no big lady. Abiola is the utmost priority here. The deal"—she directed these last words to Dubin—"is the last thing any of us are worried about."

Ms. Odemba assessed Nena again with a detached sharpness Nena recognized in herself. It was a look that said Ms. Odemba knew how to move in the world of men very well and, like Nena, could maneuver and treat it like the minefield it was.

Odemba's head tilted. "You can do this? Bring the girl home without further incident?"

Nena didn't know about "further incident." She was pretty sure there would be a lot of incidents in the recovery of Abiola Asogi.

"If the Tribe is so invested," Dubin asked, "then where is her father? Where is Noble Knight to make the decisions here, see to his man Tegete, who's currently got a bullet-size hole in him?"

Nena was not moved by Dubin's tantrum. "I am here in his stead, as I have been since the moment I arrived. I speak for my father."

"You're a wo—" He stopped beneath the acting prime minister's withering glare. He recovered. "This work needs a seasoned hand."

Nena couldn't help it. "There is more to seasoning than just salt and pepper, Mr. Dubin." She turned her head, giving him no more of her attention.

Pengo pulled his phone from his ear, approaching the group with renewed frustration. "Reports are coming in. The people are protesting. They are claiming this was a government conspiracy to cast Latema negatively and dishonor Judah and them in front of all of Tanzania. Who would want to deal with a town that murders the country's prime minister?" The chief constable dabbed at the sweat coating his face with a towel that was less than white at this point. "Judah is about to be a martyr."

General Geofry said, "This is why we need more than local village police. I can have boots on the ground quickly."

One of the top commanders of Tanzania's military, he had swept in, quickly assessing the scene, ready to take over with efficiency, the polar opposite of the chief constable, who bellowed orders that were unnecessary and wasted valuable time.

"And wage war?" Ms. Odemba asked, fear and surprise slicing through her normally cool and unreadable demeanor.

At the same time Constable Pengo blustered, "This is my jurisdiction! I will handle my own people. Military is not needed here! These are a peaceable people."

"And yet the peaceable people have assassinated our prime minister and nearly killed a diplomat and representative of the African Tribal Council," Ms. Odemba returned sharply, turning over every angle of the situation. "Seems they have moved beyond negotiations."

Dubin cut in, his expression full of a morose gravity that Nena was inclined to disbelieve. "I agree with the general. Maybe you need military force here. I am a military man myself, retired, and sometimes there is no reasoning with those kinds of people."

The room cooled noticeably the moment Dubin's words left his lips. Words any person of color was all too familiar with when dealing with people who weren't like them.

"Pray tell, Mr. Dubin, what kind of people are they, exactly?" Ms. Odemba asked.

Nena had been waiting for it, and it had finally come. The moment where Dubin's facade would slip, and he would reveal his contempt for the people he claimed so loudly to want to help. His innate sense of entitlement and privilege, like that of his ancestors, to invade, infiltrate, with the belief that anything and everything he wanted was for his taking, all to manipulate and bleed dry Africa and her people no matter where they called home, until she, and they, were nothing but dried-out husks.

44

They all waited for his response, not allowing him any reprieve or any excuses for another of his Freudian slips. They offered no rationale for what he could have meant about those people . . . their people . . . them, in that very room with him.

When he realized who he was surrounded by, Dubin's face became so red it neared purple, making his eyebrows stand out against his reddening skin.

"With angry people, of course. What else would I mean? With people who have lost their leader." Dubin pulled at the neckline of his button-down, undoing the second button to give himself air. He made his face conciliatory, checking himself. It was about time.

General Geofry scoffed. "The elders are their leaders. No one cares about some farm boy."

"The elders defer to that farm boy," Pengo corrected. "Until these past few days, Judah Wasira has never steered"—he considered Dubin—"these people wrong. He has fought for many advancements and opportunities for the people of Latema and has gotten them for the people. We cannot deny him that. Until the mine collapse and all this bad business here with the killings, he's been their golden child."

Ms. Odemba paced the floor before turning back to Nena. "And you think you can bring back the girl?"

Nena nodded. "I can."

"She can't promise that!" Dubin blustered while Pengo said, "That is my job, and my officers are already on it!"

"Just give me the night. Recovering her quickly will allay some discontent. I can get answers about what happened and if Judah was involved."

Dubin said, "Of course he was involved. Those were his people out there at the pavilion."

"Doesn't mean it was Judah," Nena said.

"Murder and kidnapping is not his style, truly. To be fair," Pengo conceded. "I grew up with his father; then we served together both in the military and back here in the village before he went home to the Maker, God rest his soul." The chief made the sign of the cross. "Judah's fight has been political, never terrorism, never a means to fatten his pockets."

"Ridiculous! He blew up the deal the other day! Flounced out like a brat throwing a temper tantrum. And then he staged the assassination!"

Nena rounded on Dubin. "You made Asogi and Tegete think he wasn't fit to speak for the villagers because the collapse happened under his watch. You've practically convinced everyone to just sell to you and your investors to save the mine."

Dubin fumbled with the right response to make, surprise overtaking him. He thought she hadn't known what he'd been up to, how he'd played on Judah's suspicions, purposely diminished the others' confidence in his leadership after the mining accident, and quietly introduced doubt and discord among them all. Dubin thought there would be no one here to speak against him, with a near riot in front of Odemba and an angry Tanzanian president at her back. But Nena was there. He'd forgotten, so quick to dismiss a woman.

"I do have it on good authority that no one will be here in enough time to set up operations at the mine. All you have is me if you want to get this whole shit show under control before your president steps in and takes the reins from you, Minister Odemba, or blames you, Chief Constable Pengo, or even thinks your military inept, General Geofry," Dubin said, recovering. "Any interested parties won't want to touch this deal with a ten-foot pole after what's transpired today. My own people are thinking of pulling out if I don't assuage their fears."

"Only you can save the day," Nena deadpanned. Her phone was buzzing, and she needed to go, having spent more time than she intended here. "Can the rest of you not see what he's doing here? It's blatant gaslighting."

"I still believe in this deal and the good that can be done here despite what you think," Dubin shot back emphatically, his voice rising.

Nena slow blinked, delivering no reaction. If she hadn't known the vulture, she'd almost believe he was being for real.

She sighed deeply, preparing her last stand. "Ms. Odemba, General Geofry, Chief Constable Pengo." Nena turned to each, giving them their individual respect.

"Before you make any decisions on the reform or the deal, please allow me tonight to see what I can do. Let me try to bring the girl back, and then we can see about everything else. You will have the full support of the Tribe with the people of Latema." She gave an extra look to the constable, and she hoped he could see that she was genuine. "We won't leave you all in this state. We committed to helping, and we mean to see it through. Permit me only a few hours."

The room fell into silence as Nena observed each of them, trying to gauge their thoughts. Odemba was thinking politically, how to keep ahold of this derailed train without the government looking bad. The general wasn't entirely sure anything could happen without military force. Everyone needed to get a handle on themselves, and he thought only through military action could it happen. And the constable wanted them all out of Latema and to take back the ability to protect his own people. He didn't want to be divested of his responsibility to the people he served. Nena felt the same way, and the Latemans had become the people she, too, served. She didn't even bother with Dubin because . . . well . . . Dubin.

Dubin guffawed. "Well, if you're going, I'm going too."

"You're cracked," Nena told him. If he thought she'd let him anywhere near her operation, he was crazy.

He appealed to the others, to Geofry. "I'm former military, you know. I could show you across-the-ponders a few things." His chest puffed with pride. He kicked a foot up onto a chair, and all of them zeroed in on his placing his shoe on the upholstery.

They didn't put their shoes on furniture. Shoes were worn outside, and to put a dirty shoe on another's furniture was bad form, bad manners, an insult, and disrespectful of their belongings. Just like visitors were supposed to leave their shoes at the door before entering a house. It was a custom that neared superstition—that wearing shoes from outside around the house or putting them on furniture tracked in not only dirt but bad juju, omens, ill will, bad luck. Whatever you wanted to call it.

Dubin wouldn't think of it that way. He'd just dismiss their customs as superstitious and laugh, thinking the villagers simple "bush people."

"Besides," he prattled on, either unaware or uncaring about how disrespectful he was being, "Don't forget that I have prior military experience."

Apparently, Dubin was never going to let them.

"You think *you* can talk wild kidnappers down? Takes more than your pretty little face." He pantomimed holding a long rifle, put the imaginary weapon to his face as if he were looking through sights, and pulled the trigger.

Nena didn't know if Dubin realized how ridiculous he looked. She marveled at his entitlement. Dubin truly believed his obscene display was enough to have them label him the fifth member of their team.

"At least let me come along for the ride too," Dubin tried in one last-ditch effort. Nena shot him a crazed look at his gall. He would try anything to get what he wanted. "I know how to handle myself out there. Which is more than I can say for Ms. Knight, who has lived her life in a gilded cage and knows nothing about doing this kind of man's work."

The chief constable, not totally clear about Nena's exact role in the Tribe—though he had some guesses—whispered, "Father, Jesus."

Odemba tsked, and General Geofry remained stoically silent. Whatever they knew or didn't know, they'd never say. But what they did know was that Dubin had no clue to whom he was referring and what the Tribe and the people who ran it were capable of. It was an underestimation Dubin would do well to devoid himself of.

Nena remained inscrutable. Gilded cage. For sure Nena had been in a cage or two. Had been in a sweltering metal oven called the Hot Box for those who broke the rules of the Compound. This was twice that evening that Dubin had overstepped. No, his whole being was one big overstep.

"Mr. Dubin." Her voice was low and thick with warning, so much so that everyone in the room snapped to attention, sensing danger in her tone. "You do not know my life. Do not speak on it."

She watched him intently until he blinked in unease, becoming unsure and likely trying to figure out where he'd made a misstep. "Respectfully."

Ms. Odemba cut in. "I think it would be wise if you remained here, Mr. Dubin. We wouldn't want the US Embassy or the French or English ones to be upset that we allowed one of their citizens to be in harm's way. Wouldn't you agree, General? Constable?"

They replied with a chorus of agreement.

Nena eyed Dubin a little longer, and for a second time that day, Nena wished she possessed the power of pyrokinesis to set his head alight.

She refocused, making a point to respectfully acknowledge the other three. The only goodbye Dubin received as she swept past him and left the room was the long withering look warning him to stay out of her way.

45

After her shower, Nena felt almost like she could tackle the task she had ahead. Not the rescue operation she'd promised Ms. Asogi and Odemba that she'd deliver on—no pressure there. Ops were second nature to her and where Nena felt in her element. The task she had been delaying was returning her father's call. She should have answered when he'd first called. She should have called him as soon as Tegete and the PM were shot, but she couldn't bring herself to relay the bad news to her father that she had failed, and another person had died on her watch.

She couldn't delay any longer.

Lotioned and dressed in a pair of black cargo pants and a black sports bra, she sat half-dressed on the edge of her made bed, next to the soft terry robe the resort had gifted her. Nena's fingers dialed the number she'd been hesitant to call.

The line connected way too fast for Nena's taste, as if he was sitting by his sat phone willing her to ring him.

"What the bloody hell is going on?" Noble asked brusquely. There was no greeting, no terms of endearment, no loving father to tell her all would be well and excuse away her failure as the fault of someone else. He was High Council.

Nena forced herself to ignore how his tone struck a nerve. She reminded herself that this was business, and it was not her father talking.

Noble Knight would be dealing with her like any other member of the Tribe who'd made errors.

"Why am I preparing to visit one of my Council members in a Tanzanian hospital who was shot and the prime minister murdered under your watch? And why did I not hear it first from you? Are you not the head of Network and Dispatch?"

"I am, sir, but I needed to fully assess the situation and stabilize things around here first so I could give you a complete and accurate report. Well," she corrected, "as complete a report as I can provide at the moment." She thought of her sudden mission. "Things are still moving."

"How could this have happened? The last we spoke, you said you had things under control and that the reform may be a go. You were supposed to be watching Judah to ensure he'd get the villagers on board with Asogi. You were supposed to protect Tegete."

She nodded, though he couldn't see her. "I was."

"So, what happened?"

Nena rubbed at a kink nipping at the base of her neck. She was much too tense. Finally, she decided that the plain truth was the best route. She sighed. "Honestly, I don't know. I don't know how things went from Judah storming out of the meeting yesterday to what happened at the pavilion and the airstrip today. It all happened so quickly." Her head was still spinning. There was no time to sit and recalibrate. She studied the carpeted floor in frustration. Nothing was coming to her. "It was very well coordinated."

Still, Noble wasn't giving her any allowances. "Meaning?"

"Meaning I think the incidents were planned to happen no matter what, if Judah stayed on board or if he walked. But this plan isn't one from someone who was just angered and wanted revenge. That would be an act of emotion. What happened today was preplanned and methodic." Her voice became concerned. "How is the councilman?"

"Upgraded to serious but stable condition," her father groused. "But they think they got to him in time. There is a contingent en route to hospital in the capital." He took a measured breath. "And I will be in the city by tomorrow evening."

She started. "You can't."

"I can and I will, Nena."

She flinched at his unbridled anger. The Tribe was Noble's firstborn. It was his life's work, and everything hinged on its good name with the people of Africa. To them, the Tribe had to be above reproach, because if it wasn't, then how was it to help lead the advancement of African people? It could not.

"Perhaps it was my error in judgment when I tasked you to take all of this on . . . perhaps it was too soon after Witt's death and when you were taken last year. Perhaps you weren't ready, and I should not have pushed you."

It was too late for him to think of that now that she was in the thick of it. She tried not to feel resentful, but it was proving difficult to not be.

"I can do it, Dad," she said in a tight voice, feeling both childish and weak. Should the next thing she do be to throw herself on the floor and beat her arms and legs against it in a proper temper tantrum for not getting her way?

She searched for the word to describe how her father sounded speaking with her. Disappointed. And like his faith in her had been dimmed a tad. She'd never heard either from him before, and it ate at her because never before had Nena given Noble reason to think she couldn't produce results.

The only thing more devastating than the disappointment lacing her father's every word was if Delphine felt the same . . . and Elin, whom Nena would never be able to look in the eye again. Nena would not only be just the adopted daughter; she'd be the abject failure and embarrassment of the Knight family.

"Clearly, I need to rectify this business with Ms. Odemba and the villagers before the bloody bastard Dubin scares them into selling to him."

It would be too late by then. And who knows, perhaps the plan was to get her father there to eliminate him too. Nena couldn't chance him being hurt again. "It's not safe for you to come." She added, "Sir."

"Nena, I am coming," Noble said firmly. "I don't care if it's a trap or if they will throw a parade good enough for the queen herself. The integrity of the Tribe is on the line. I cannot have anyone thinking in the slightest that the Tribe might be involved or is inept. That cannot be the Tribe's legacy there. So, I will fix it."

Her hands balled into fists. She willed her father to cool his hot head. She said, "It is not secure, Dad. Your safety is not guaranteed here."

"My security is not a concern."

"Your safety is my *only* concern," she said hotly, surprising them both.

She mentally counted to five, listening to her father breathe. "You cannot come here. There is no time to prep another team to protect you or aid us. Bringing more people will only incense an already uneasy crowd, and the acting prime minister and Tanzanian military might think we're overstepping. If you feel you must come, then go to Tegete in Dodoma. Let me sort it out here."

Nena watched the clock as the minutes screamed that time was running out for Abiola. For Latema. And for her.

46

Nena was at a crossroads again. If she did not make the choice now to step fully into her role as head of Dispatch and claim her position as a true part and heir of her Knight family, then she would forever be thought of as the adopted daughter, the worker, not the leader. Most of all, she would always be questioning where she stood as a Knight.

Her image in the mirror floated on the opposite wall. It didn't look like her. It looked more like how she used to be. Scared and unsure if anything she was doing was the right thing. And Noble was unbearably quiet.

"Dad?" She hoped her voice would not betray her emotions. She was taking a huge gamble. She was scared . . . well, shitless.

The other end of the line was silent, and Nena braced herself. "There is too much at stake," he said regretfully.

She cleared her throat, remembering it wasn't the first time she'd taken a stand when she knew the right thing to do. "I know what's at stake, and I will fix it."

Noble cursed to himself in his native tongue. Something about *this child.*

"If you come here, you won't just be undermining all I have already established; you will feed the distrust the villagers and the government already have. You'll make us look like we're trying to take over."

And you'll strengthen their distrust in me, Nena did not add.

"You will make me look weak. I cannot have that . . . sir."

He sucked in air. "Girl—"

She plowed on before her courage failed her.

"You made me head of Dispatch and Network. You assigned me this job, so what I am doing as head is to tell you, High Council, that you are advised not to come here. I will report back to you when all is said and done and successful. If you want to send a team to watch over Councilman Tegete so that he is safe in hospital, then that is fine. But that is all. Let me do my job, Dad."

She stopped talking, waiting for the blowup Noble was known to have in the presence of insolence. But he didn't, the silence between them stretching further than the literal thousands of miles between them.

Nena used her pent-up energy to rummage through one of her bags for her mission gear, then pulled out a pair of black tactical pants and a T-shirt. The temperature in the room was increasing by the moment as her adrenaline shot up from both her father's wrath and the plan running through her mind.

His sigh came out deep and heavy and resigned. Nena imagined him running a hand over his face and then bending into the same pose as Rodin's *The Thinker* in frustration and defeat.

He had to be going over all her mistakes. Of how he'd brought her into the African Tribal Council to Dispatch. Placing her in a position of such high regard. And fought for her over and over, backing her when she disobeyed her mission objective and put a bullet in Attah Walrus's head instead of Cortland Baxter's.

Noble had stood against the Council countless times, like when she'd killed Paul, who'd become the newest member on the Council, and his son, Oliver, who'd turned out to be her brother Ofori she thought was killed back in their Ghanaian village, but was instead poisoned against her. And when she was forced to take Witt's life, Noble had announced her as Witt's replacement at Dispatch and Network despite the obvious misgivings and lack of confidence the other Council members and Tribe members had in her after all those deaths.

No doubt a slew of disappointed thoughts about his daughter was running roughshod through Noble's mind, just as they were Nena's. She couldn't stop them from doing so for either of them, but Nena could make one more attempt at salvaging what little faith her father might have left in her. She only needed him to allow her one more chance to see this whole mess through.

But the question was, would he?

"Dad, when you instructed me to come here, you did so because you believed in me," she began, softening her tone. "I was concerned I wasn't capable of handling the business side. I didn't believe in myself until I got here and realized how much of an impact we could make here. We help to provide seats at tables we Africans aren't typically invited to. I didn't understand that before as I do now." She took a steadying breath. "Please allow me to see it through. I have a plan to recover the girl. And then will sort out everything else."

Finally Noble asked, "And the ones behind the incidents? The ones who've been conspiring this whole time?"

Her jaw tightened. "I will deal with them too."

"Then be careful. We have suffered war both within the Tribe and without for too long. The Tribe is at a precipice to do real good for our people in Africa, to have the One Africa we've talked about for so long. We have opportunities with the West, with big tech in America, Europe, and Asia. We cannot blow this and make them doubt us. You understand, Nena?" Noble asked, his voice so soft she strained to hear him.

"Because, unfortunately, in this world, people who look like us, who come from where we come from, have to do more, be more, and live above reproach for anyone to take us seriously. One mistake, and that is all the excuse they need to never give us a seat at their table."

Nena understood far more than she could articulate. It was why she followed his lead without question, because Nena had lived without. She'd survived things no child, no person, should have had to. She'd been underestimated because she was a girl, or a woman, or Black, or from a tiny Ghanaian village. She refused to be underestimated ever again. And that meant finishing what she'd started right here.

Another agonizing moment passed while her father thought. Regardless of his decision, Nena knew what she must do. She'd gone against orders before. She could do it again, and she'd take the consequences. But she wanted her father on her side.

"Okay," Noble finally said. "Do what you need to do, however you need to do it." He said it with a finality that reflected why he was the High Council of the Tribe. "Sort this bloody mess out once and for all. Or I will."

47

Nena had failed. This was supposed to be a nonengagement trip. Schmoozing and learning how to make deals before they went bad and Dispatch was called in to clean up. But now, Nena wished she'd thought ahead more. She worried that they didn't have enough ammo, though they'd packed a small arsenal—she'd never let Dispatch go entirely— and Evers had given them a solid guess on how many adversaries they'd encounter.

Nena would have felt more secure with Network's eye in the sky, having their backs from a satellite office quickly erected in one of the nearby cities as soon as the mission was a go, with a fortified transport vehicle and a B team in case things went bad. She should have better surveilled the town center and the people filtering in and out of it. But she'd had to play nice. Had to allow the local authorities under Chief Constable Pengo's leadership to take the helm on security. So, was the colossal screwup and subsequent death of the country's prime minister on the police? Or was it on Nena because she'd known better? She'd smelled blood in the water, churning everyone up for a feeding frenzy that had resulted in Abiola's kidnapping and ransom.

Was that on her? She'd have preferred more time to recon the area undercover and learn the routines of the ops. She would have preferred to have hunted Judah down and extracted from him what he knew about the assassination of Asogi and the attempt on Tegete that had nearly succeeded. But she'd had none of that. She was going in with a skeleton crew and by-the-minute surveillance with on-the-go tech Evers had pulled together on a whim.

Nena and her three other team members would serve as both Dispatch and Network, with Nena both director and team lead.

The team had each brought two black go bags, one heavy canvas, the other a hard, durable case that housed their assault rifles and sidearms. They'd suit up out there, not wanting to risk anyone in the hotel spotting them.

Evers had a handheld device that monitored their whereabouts and where Abiola was being held. According to it, the girl hadn't moved for the past several hours. Hopefully this meant the kidnappers were settled for the night, waiting for their money to drop so there could be the exchange. Ms. Asogi allowed Evers to clone her mobile so they could listen in on any calls or messages she received from the kidnappers.

They had the banking information to wire the money, which Noble provided with ease, even going as far as to mutter "Only that?" when Nena gave him the amount of the ransom. If Nena's mind hadn't been preoccupied with getting mission ready, she might have commented that he sounded like the same elitist 1 percent he'd scoffed at all the time she'd known him. However, Nena knew how to pick her battles and kept her thoughts to herself.

Nena secured one of the dark-colored all-terrain vehicles that had been serving as their transportation while in country. They had made it their urban assault vehicle, stocking it with the team's bulging black go bags of tech equipment and the mission weaponry, ammo, and supplies like flash grenades, an extra set of blades, and retractable batons—items Nena made them pack "just in case," despite the argument from Billy that this particular mission was not a dispatch but that they were business emissaries for the Tribe. Billy's next argument had been to tell Nena where her place should be.

"You're not supposed to be conducting field operations," he'd mans-plained. "Your place is providing overwatch for them."

Nena's long silent stare had given Billy all the answer he needed. Nena's *place* was wherever she decided it was going to be.

Turned out, there happened to be a "just in case," and Billy would end up appreciating Nena's meticulous contingency planning and her inability to totally detach herself from dispatches.

The vehicles were the same they'd arrived to Latema in, open topped and not fortified. It wouldn't protect them from a hail of bullets, should the kidnappers get the drop on them, but it was all the team had available. If the plan played out successfully, as it had in Nena's mind when she ran through the scenario and contingencies as she showered, the team would be on the offensive and wouldn't have to worry about taking fire because of the element of surprise.

If the plan played out successfully—a big *if.*

———

"We can pull over here. Right in the thicket of trees, off the road," Evers said, peering at the small screen of his handheld device. The blue light from the computer on his lap illuminated his face and reflected off the lenses of his glasses.

From the driver's seat, Billy grumbled, "Some road. It's barely a dirt path." But he did as Evers instructed.

Evers continued, "The location is right up ahead. Only less than two kilometers from the start of the dig."

"I'm not trying to get my steps in with gear and a Kevlar vest on. It's like soup out there. And not the good kind, the kind with okra that's snotty and slimy and sticks to you," Femi added from the first row of seats in the back, already checking her sniper rifle. "Where do I post up?"

Evers pointed to an area on his screen that showed elevation higher than the central location where Abiola's tracer had her registered. "Your vantage point is here. Should be able to look right down at the building where they're keeping her. Should be able to see the whole layout fairly unobstructed."

Femi leaned between the front seats, touching his laptop screen with her index finger.

"There?" she asked, a wicked smile playing at the corners of her lips.

Evers cleared his throat, low and long, pushing his glasses up his nose. "Please. Um, don't touch the screen."

He used two fingers to gingerly pluck Femi's offending digit from his property, then began swiping away at the infinitesimal smudge on his screen with the cuff of his sleeve.

Nena completed her gear check, finding all accounted for. A long serrated hunting knife snuggled in its housing at the middle of her back hip. Her sidearm strapped in a velcroed belt on her upper thigh. Extra rounds attached to the other. Two smaller blades, cushioned into either thigh holster, and one tiny knife, attached right above her left ankle. A couple of flash-bangs hung clipped from her vest. Nena leaned the barrel of her assault rifle against a seat, allowing the butt of it to rest on the floor of the vehicle while she tightened the straps of her black gloves.

Beside her, Femi threatened the screen again with a hovering pointy finger like a buzzing gnat, which Evers batted away with bare-toothed aggression. The sounds of the light slaps of his hand on her finger filled the automobile.

"Knock it off," Nena finally said. She studied the scanned ground image on the monitor obtained from the drone crisscrossing the sky, counting multiple heat signatures in the domicile. Four more outside on watch. Two inside the building a room apart.

"Those two," Nena pointed out. "What do you make of them? There used to be two in that room from an earlier image. They've been moved now."

Evers rubbed a finger over his lips, deep in thought. "Could be Abiola."

"And the other?"

He shrugged. "A guard?"

"But why's he no longer in the room with her? Why have they left her alone?"

Nena watched the prone blob of yellow, green, and red. "Neither are moving."

The other three said nothing, having read the Konate mission report if they were good Network team members. They'd know the details about what had happened there. Nena didn't need to read the reports. She'd lived it.

Nena blinked, her mind traveling back to Konate's outpost, where her last team had been ambushed, and how Konate had used heat imaging to trick her team while he and his soldiers lay in wait. How six Dispatch members had gone in and only two had made it out. She swallowed, forcing herself back to the present. This was not Kenya. And now was not the time to dwell on it.

"Maybe they're asleep," Evers offered.

Nena pushed down the bubbling anxiety the memory triggered. She pressed her earpiece in like it would stop up all her thoughts, ran her final check.

"Count off."

Each of them did, confirming the comms worked.

"Let's go to work," Femi said, opening the door on her side.

Evers counted out the rest of the combatants in and surrounding the building. He'd stay with the vehicle, monitor for anyone else approaching while they went in. He'd come when signaled to get them out. Femi would take high ground and provide cover, watching for anyone coming in hot around the perimeter. Billy and Nena would be going in to extract Abiola.

It was a basic plan—no trimmings—and the only one they had without Network's extensive research, gathered intel, and government-level tech and weapons at their disposal. Evers's roving drones, a couple of computers, a handheld tracker, and the arsenal they'd brought with them would just have to do, and they'd hope for a bit of good luck.

As the distance grew between them and the vehicle where they'd left Evers, Femi split off from Billy and Nena to take her post on higher ground, where she could see the open area at the front and in between the main building and a smaller trailer, where two two-door pickup trucks, red and white, were parked. A couple of the men filtered out of the trailer, congregating in front of it with dark long-necked bottles. One of them had a rifle slung over his shoulder, while the other appeared weapon-free but likely had a Glock or long knife hidden on his person somewhere.

Femi would provide cover for Nena and Billy as they went in through the side door they were currently studying and attempted to funnel whoever was in the one-level building toward the front door. There were only the two exit points, unless one counted the couple of windows too small to fit an adult.

Nena and Billy continued a little farther, pausing at the crudely built makeshift fence of wire and wood. The two of them sheltered behind a patch of trees just beyond the fence that half surrounded the back of the 1,200-square-foot building with cement walls and roofing made of corrugated tin. The building was just at the beginning of the stretch leading to the areas that would be designated mining grounds once the deal went through.

If the deal went through.

48

Billy peered through his night vision binoculars and indicated he didn't see anyone. Femi counted two toward the front, armed but not really doing much of anything but hanging around. Ahead of Nena and Billy was the side door they wanted to enter through. According to Evers, it was closest to the room they believed held Abiola.

"What are you thinking?" Billy asked in a whisper, eyes sweeping from the door to the surrounding area for anyone to pop up. "Going in hard or soft?"

Nena was making her own assessments. "I don't want bodies if we can help it. Likely they're just scared locals who thought to make a quick buck. They may run."

"They left bodies when they snatched the little girl, though," Femi reminded her.

But Nena still wasn't of the mind to kill anyone unless absolutely necessary. She wasn't just following orders anymore. As head of Dispatch (or not, depending on how this all shook out) she had to think about the weight of loss of life.

"Just a casual reminder that there are more of them and two of us," Billy said offhandedly, as if making a casual observation and reading her mind. "They can afford to lose some bodies. Us, not so much. We don't even have a full team."

That was because they weren't supposed to be doing this. They were supposed to be schmoozing with the politicians, playing life's board game of chess, not *Halo*. According to Noble. Yet here they were.

She pondered, wondering if his cavalier attitude to killing was serious or not. She decided it was neither. "I don't want you to not stay alive."

He finally looked at her. "If only one of us is walking out of here, it sure as hell is going to be me." His mouth quirked, the only indication that he was half-serious.

"What an ass," Femi grumbled over comms.

Evers piped in, "Happen to agree. Comments like that do nothing for team camaraderie."

Billy snorted, resuming his surveillance of the area as Nena followed suit. The one-level L-shaped building lying just ahead.

Nena and Billy ducked behind a row of brush as guards walking the perimeter passed them, laughing softly from a joke they shared. Snippets from a TV blaring from within the building could be heard from where they were, a laugh track from whatever show was on. A radio trickled out some Afro beats. More guards talking and bouncing the soccer ball around. Nena's team needed to be quick in and quick out.

Femi piped in. "Any day now."

Billy looked expectantly at his team lead.

"Go," Nena murmured, readying her firearm.

"Charges set," Femi said.

A *boom* coming from the front, followed by a bright light that lit up the night, sent a shuddering sound throughout the vicinity. Then the guards became alive with fear and chaos as they tried to get bearings on where the attack was coming from.

It was Nena and Billy's cue to move. They broke out in a run, crouched low as they covered ground across the small stretch between the trees, advancing toward the building as muted sniper rounds sizzled past them, courtesy of Femi, providing them cover. Evers informed them the mine's operations building was not too far ahead. Nena made it first to the wooden-planked side door, which was warped from the heat and humidity. Since the mine had been closed due to the collapse of a couple of days prior, the building was a good place to hole up undiscovered for a little while, hiding in plain view, because no one would think they'd have the audacity to hide there. Until Nena and her team had found them.

One of the men thundered around the corner in a run. Nena was ready for him, one of her blades drawn and ready, glinting in the moonlight. Somewhere in the brush, a hyena sent out its eerie laugh as blade met with human. Nena sank her knife in deep, just below the rib cage. Her other hand caught the man. She twisted the knife, then released him. He went down with a muffled cry of surprise, then a thud when his body hit the dirt, sending up a tiny plume of it. They could hear shouts from the men up front, calling for water to douse the fire.

Nena straightened, turning to find Billy staring at her, his earlier cockiness replaced with disbelief.

Nena gestured with her blade tip. "Carry on."

Billy led first with Nena behind, watching their rear. She'd switched her blade for her Glock, readied it, as did Billy with his assault rifle. She adjusted her rifle on her back, ensuring she wasn't hindered by it. Billy counted off before trying for the handle. Better to go in soft rather than blow their element of surprise by using one of their small explosives to blast through the door. The door pushed in with a creak.

Nena stepped through into the black hole of a tunnel-like hallway, nearly colliding with another kidnapper on his way out. He saw them, and his eyes grew big. He fumbled with the gun he'd tucked in his belt, making a frantic call to his friends, and Nena shot him in the chest. He fell, and Billy was coming in right behind as Nena stepped to the fallen man, leveled her gun at his head, and pulled the trigger.

The report in the building meant their element of surprise was gone. The area would flood with hostiles. Billy had moved in front of her, preparing to clear the first doorway into a room. They were familiar with the layout from Evers's quick recon, and they needed to make their way down to the farthest door on the right, where they guessed Abiola was being held. The building came alive with sounds of sporadic gunfire and shouts, a door banging open, and the faint high-pitched screams of a little girl.

They heard several commands to check rooms, to get to the fire, to run, or to take Nena's team out. But they didn't know how many were out there. They were inexperienced, and their fear was evident in the pitch of their voices.

Nena processed it all, zeroing in when she heard, "I have the girl. I will kill her if you do not leave!"

A clear message for them.

"Be careful," Evers warned. "They are all over."

Nena ducked as a bullet sheared off a sharp piece of wood from a beam above her head as she tried to peer down the darkened hall, quickly filling with thick, gray smoke. The shard whipped past, leaving a streak of fire across her neck where it had grazed her.

Nena dropped to a knee, shielding herself with an overturned table. A pair of legs came into view and she fired, hitting an exposed kneecap. When he fell to the ground howling, Nena put another round in his head.

More shouts, and more of the men detached themselves from the dark. They blocked Nena and Billy from the room at the end of the hall. The assault weapons pummeled everything around Nena and Billy, especially the walls behind which they'd taken cover.

Nena said, "We need to clear the hall to get to her."

"Movement at the door," Evers announced through comms. "Looks like they have her. There are three together in that room now. Looks like she's on the move."

Billy said, "Whatever you do, don't let them leave with her."

"Got it covered," said Femi, and one explosion came through the comms, illuminating the dark hall and showing four bodies moving through the smoke like some horror flick. "Lovely game of Whac-a-Mole."

Another explosion rocked the structure, sending pieces of ceiling down on their heads.

"They can now only leave by foot or by Uber," Femi announced.

Billy chanced a look at Nena, ducking, then firing back at one of the men posted in the hall.

"Let's clear this."

Nena and Billy ran and ducked into the smoking doorway as another of the men rounded the corner, gun drawn and firing.

49

Billy's rifle swung in his direction, firing back. A hole opened in the man's chest, and he went down hard. Femi called out that three were approaching from the courtyard. Nena fired rounds, forcing the men back, taking another down in the process, pushing them into the long, dark hall that was more like a cave tunnel.

There was nothing but commotion around her as the men yelled at one another, trying to formulate a plan, but they were too confused, didn't know what was happening and who was attacking them.

Nena approached a room to her right, tugged one of her flash-bangs from its clip, and tossed it in. It burst in a dust storm of white smoke. She tugged her second and tossed it down the hall. It did as the first had. Out front, the men struggled to find ground against Femi's rapid fire, leaving them dazed and disoriented enough to believe there was an army out there for them. If they took a moment they didn't have, the kidnappers would have realized Femi's shots were coming from only one place at a time, wherever she posted up to fire. But again, Nena thought grimly, these kidnappers weren't the professionals. Her team was. And this was a fair fight.

She heard Abiola screech, fighting against her captor, and decided the fight was more than fair.

"One down out here," Femi updated. "Other two fleeing on foot. Take them out?"

Nena said, "Let them go."

Billy broke away, entering another room. Through the smoke, a body came at Nena, barreling into her from the right like a linebacker in American football. He slammed her into the opposite wall, sending a blanket of pain throughout her back. Nena took in a loud inhale of smoke and gunpowder and man stench.

She smashed her elbow into the back of his neck, where the tips of his vertebrae were located. His knees buckled, and he crashed down on one knee as if bowing before her. She gave him an overhand punch to the side of his face and staggered to the left. Nena abandoned her Glock. Sounds of a high-pitched rake of metal against hard plastic as she pulled her blades from her side belts accentuated her movements. She flipped them, grasping the handles so the blades pointed down. She lifted her arms at an angle. Below her the kidnapper retched, one hand clawing at the back of his neck, the other seeking purchase. His vision filled with her twin blades as they came down on him, burying themselves into either side of his neck to their hilts.

She pulled them out as quickly as she'd inserted them, and a warm spurt of blood gurgled out from the severed artery. He wavered slightly, his body not yet knowing that he was dead. Then he fell, Nena picked up her Glock, and she followed Billy down the hall.

50

Nena heard Abiola's screaming ahead of her and a man yelling. A door slammed open, and rapid reports of fire spurted off. A chip of cement wall shearing off right above Nena's head where a bullet struck. Nena pointed and shot. *One.* She paused. Twice more. *Two. Three.*

Outside, another explosion. If it was according to plan, that would be the barrels of gasoline they'd scoped out, out front. Femi had set them off as a distraction, lighting the night sky with the fireball. It shook the already spatchcocked structure they were in. Another of the adversaries, this one in a tracksuit, was heading straight toward Nena with a rifle in hand aimed at her.

Nena dropped to both knees in a half slide, aiming, then firing into his chest. He half-twisted, the force of the bullet driving him back and over haphazardly stacked crates behind him. He settled down between them, leaving a smear of blood to mark his path. Nena began to continue past him, making a quick assessment on her way. She stopped, her blood going cold. And stared down into the lifeless eyes of a young woman, her body splayed between the crates. Couldn't have been older than eighteen, if that. Nena's chest tightened as she lingered against the background concert of bullets. Instinct made her want to check for vitals, just in case there was hope. But she knew the girl was gone.

Nena tightened up, a calm settling over her as she once again became mission centered. Perhaps later she'd think about the girl, the kid, that could have been. But for now, there was no room here for remorse, and this kid had known the stakes before she'd participated in kidnapping an innocent child. Besides, when she was at work, Nena's gun or blade knew no gender. She was an equal opportunity provider.

Nena let the coldness of her job slide over her again like full-body armor. She aimed, squeezed, and put one more in the girl's chest for good measure.

Billy proceeded with his course of action, clearing the area as he advanced farther. Nena could hear the staccato sounds of his fire and the return fire of some combatants through her comms. Through the few windows, the sky lit up in flares of orangey light as Femi distracted and disoriented the fleeing or firing men with flash-bangs or small explosives, picking off any firing at her. There weren't any more left, the men either killed or having run away.

Nena hesitated when the door to their targeted room, where they thought Abiola was being held, opened and a man emerged through the doorway holding a child-size person against him. Nena aimed, commanding him to stop.

"No! No!" He punctuated his words by jabbing the muzzle of his gun in Nena's direction. He crouched so he was covered by the girl he was using as a shield.

He put the muzzle flush against Abiola's temple. "Put your gun down, lady, or I swear to God I will kill the child."

Nena doubted he wanted to do that. The way his voice quivered told her so. But fear and limited options made him unpredictable. She eased back from her position so he'd see she wasn't ready to take him down. She only hoped Billy would be able to secure him from the front when the man . . . boy, maybe, with a baby face, from what she could tell, and the makings of a scruffy beard . . . made it through the door and realized he was the last man left.

He inched his way backward, away from her and toward the front door.

Nena called to Billy and Femi that Abiola was being taken out. They needed to hold fire.

"He's too jumpy. I don't want him to hurt her," she said. "No sudden moves. No heroes."

The words reverberated in her mind, echoes of her past. No heroes. Because there were none.

51

The kidnapper inched back as Nena advanced, her gun pointed. He shifted his head behind Abiola's as they continued down, checking over his shoulder to make sure no one was behind him.

Nena took a quick beat as she approached the doorway of the room Abiola and her abductor had come from. Nena didn't know if there was anyone just behind the door, lying in wait to spring an attack. She debated rushing past and risking getting shot or worse, or clearing the room quickly so she'd keep Abiola in her sights.

She and the kidnapper danced. His couple of steps back to her one forward, while he demanded Nena and whoever was with her stay back or the girl would die. Nena didn't doubt that he'd kill her if he had to, but if he wanted to, Abiola would be dead. And that meant something. That meant they had a chance.

Nena's mind ran through the measures. There were many ways to take him out. But the girl was there. And the lighting was too dim. And Nena realized she needed information from the last man standing.

"He stays breathing," Nena told her team as he rounded the corner, pulling the small girl with him, her feet dragging on the ground. "Copy?"

Nena advanced so they wouldn't move out of her sight. She made it to the edge of the doorway where Abiola once had been. She was about to pass the door after a quick check that there was no one hiding just within the room when Abiola's kidnapper shot at her in an effort to shake her off him.

Nena dove through the doorway into the room as the bullet hit the wall, pieces of dirt and plaster raining down. Abiola screamed as Nena crashed to the floor, grunting as her momentum made her roll. She came to a stop when she came up against something soft and unmoving.

"What was that?" Billy demanded through her earpiece. "E? Echo!"

She coughed; her lungs filled with smoke. Her shoulder smarted from its impact with the dirt floor. "I'm okay. Don't lose them. Should be coming to you."

Nena performed a quick self-check. She was fine. Then she focused on what had stopped her roll. Nena did a double take. There was someone there. Not lying in wait, gun ready to finish the job Abiola's kidnapper had started, but on the ground. The body was in a heap on the floor and, from her cursory assessment, was not moving. A blood- and dirt-caked pillowcase covered the head.

She needed to keep going, get Abiola, who was her objective. But the body on the floor . . .

Nena said, "Who has eyes on them?"

"I do. They're coming through."

"Don't you move, man," Billy said. He had to have looped around and caught them up front, joining Femi to secure the area. "Let her go."

That gave Nena a few precious seconds. She got up, eyes trained on the body. The room was lit only by a single dim lamp. The high, tiny dirt-crusted window barely let in any light. She moved closer, until she was upon it. She trained her gun on the person.

"Hey. Hello," she hissed. She let out a sound from between clenched teeth. "Are you awake? Alive?"

No movement or answer. She nudged the person in the side with the toe of her boot. Nothing.

She dropped her right hand to her side, her fingers flexing as she considered her options and that she'd have to make contact. Nena shot a glance at the open door, always keeping it in her peripheral in case somehow someone was still around.

Nena squatted quickly, bending over to place her gloved fingers gingerly under the stained pillowcase, finding the neck. She felt its pulse throb, weak but there. She stretched some more, taking the edge of the pillowcase between her fingers to slide it off the face.

She braced herself, leaning over some more, pulling the fabric as she moved closer, then finally tugging it all the way free.

She sat back on her haunches, bottling up her surprise so she wouldn't cause her team concern. Nena was looking at Judah—a bloody, pulpy mess. The kidnappers had worked him over well. He seemed to rouse at her nearness, but that's all he could muster, and from what Nena could determine in the poor light, he needed immediate medical attention.

"What's the plan?" Billy asked. "We have eyes. Take him out? Hold?"

She glanced at the open doorway again, giving the noise in her comms enough attention to say, "I'm coming. We need him. Hold."

She set her gun on the ground, needing both hands to roll Judah onto his back. A low groan escaped him, and a hitch of pain. His face screwed up in a wince. He whispered Abiola's name, and in a shock of strength and adrenaline, his arm flailed out in the air, searching. It reached toward the empty bedroll Nena assumed had been Abiola's.

Clearly, there was some care in his delirious actions for the girl. How had he come to be here? Why was he in this state? There were more questions, Nena feared, and only a very select few had the answers . . . two, as it stood at the moment, who were in Nena's possession. One out there with a gun to an innocent girl's head and threatening her demise if they didn't let him go. The other in no position to talk: Judah had slipped back into his unconscious state right as Nena dawdled there, weighing her options.

She dipped down to his ear, saying, "We will return for you." Nena gathered her gun and rushed out of the room, updating her team on her find. Billy cursed under his breath as the kidnapper and Abiola moved across the threshold of the doorway and into the vegetable-soup humidity, pinned down by Femi and Billy, their guns trained on the man as he trained his own on Abiola. There was no way for them to get him without injuring her. It was too risky, and she wiggled and writhed in his hands, increasing the difficulty.

Nena came up behind them, and the lanky man half turned so his back was to the blazing vehicles that were supposed to be his getaway, destroyed thanks to Femi. He yanked Abiola up closer to his face, attempting to shield his critical areas despite her screaming and kicking.

"Stay back," he said frantically. "Let me go from here." He inched away from the doorway, toward the center, caught in between Nena's team and her.

"Be still, Abiola." Nena slowly closed the gap between her and them so he could hear her over the roar of fire without her having to yell. The light of the burning fuel illuminated the whole scene. Up ahead, the lights from their vehicle approached. Evers was at the helm. With Nena blocking the entrance of the building and her team eliminating any escape, the kidnapper had nothing to lose, and that ratcheted up his level of danger to Abiola even more.

"Be still," Nena repeated, but this time to the kidnapper, whose head snapped from side to side, looking at her, then her team, wild eyed. He was jittery. Terrified with nothing to lose—a terrible combination. Nena needed to give him something. And from him, she needed something in return. His mates had run or had been killed. There was only him. She told him that.

"We don't want to kill you. And you can leave with everything," Nena concluded, crossing over to move between him and her team to block their line of fire.

Billy released a string of curses. "What are you doing?" he seethed. Nena saw movement behind her and knew Billy was advancing to the side to clear her for a better shot. The kidnapper's eyes trailed Billy's movements and confirmed Nena's guess was correct. He would talk. She only needed to calm him and separate him from the girl.

"I can take him." Billy crept closer.

"No shot," she said under her breath and into her comms. "No one else has to die tonight."

52

"Put your guns down!" the kidnapper screamed in Swahili, switching to English as he mashed the muzzle of his gun against the side of Abiola's head. He didn't need to translate his words. They all knew full well what he was telling them to do.

"You don't want this." Nena's gun moved in tandem with his head as he bobbed and wove erratically to scrunch and hide behind the terrified little girl.

Nena fought the urge to try and take him out for using a child as a shield like that. He had no honor, but then again, there was no honor among thieves, and he surely was one. First priority, the girl. Second, intel.

"Let her go," Nena repeated. She held up her right fist, signaling to her team not to take a shot. They needed him alive. He might be able to tell them who had hired him and his friends, who had ordered the hit on Asogi and Tegete.

"Put your gun down," he said. "Now!" He pushed the muzzle in harder until Abiola cried out. He tightened his grip around her shoulders, straightening himself and lifting her off the ground, his head behind hers.

"Now, or I will kill her."

Nena tensed, her finger flexing against the trigger. She blinked away the sweat trickling into her eyes. She gritted her teeth, silently admonishing herself for going against her entire nature.

"Okay, okay," she said, her voice softening. "Okay. Look." She pulled her hand away from the gun.

"Don't do it," Billy said through the comms. "There's a clear one."

A clear shot, but he wouldn't say that aloud in case the kidnapper could hear him on the wind. Neither Femi nor Evers could move around back, either, since they were in his direct line of vision. Any attempt they made to move and find another way to get him, he'd see, and then he'd kill the girl. Nena couldn't take that chance.

She sliced the air downward with her open hand out. *No.*

"Stand down." She explained, "We need him."

Eyes remaining planted on the man's body, Nena bent down slowly, keeping her free arm out so he could see it, and placed the gun gently on the ground. Her left hand joined the right in the air, fingers splayed as a sign she had nothing to hide and was no threat.

She watched his every movement, his eyes, his body, checking he wouldn't make moves she wouldn't anticipate.

"Your friends are all gone," Nena said, taking a tentative step toward him. She waited a beat when she saw his grip tightening again. She licked her lips, continuing. "You are the only one left." She spoke softly, as if they were merely conversing and the life of an innocent girl wasn't literally between them.

"You want to go home? Or you want this to be your last stand?"

The muzzle pulled away slightly from Abiola's head. It was shaking in his hand. Nena watched the gun. The trembling was making her nervous. It was still too close, and he was way too jittery for Nena's liking.

In a small voice, he said, "I want to go home."

He wasn't more than twenty, if that, and Nena wanted to grant him a reprieve. He was scared. He likely didn't understand what he'd gotten himself into. He'd been swayed and enticed by the thought of quick money to help his people. But he was not a child. He was a killer.

Nena looked at Abiola and the wild, terrified eyes that looked back at her. So terrified, they couldn't produce tears. Nena knew that fear. Too well.

"Let her go and you can go home."

He watched Nena, trying to decide if she was telling the truth. Then he looked behind her at the rest of her team with their guns aimed directly at him.

"They won't let me go."

"They will."

Nena gestured for them to lower their weapons.

"Come on," Billy groaned in her ear. "Don't do this."

She gestured again, snapping her hand once downward, then making a fist. *Down. Hold.*

She heard Billy grunt his disapproval, adding more expletives in the mix, but he did as she asked. Femi and Evers tracked and kept their disapproval smartly to themselves.

Nena refocused on the kidnapper, appealing to him. She spoke slowly, soothingly. It seemed to work on TV, so why not?

"Let her go and you can go."

And her tone seemed to be working. Either that or the girl was getting heavy, because he released Abiola a little so the tips of her toes fought to gain purchase on the ground.

He said, "The money."

"What?" Though Nena knew exactly what he was referring to.

"The two million American. I want it, and I let her go."

"It's already in the account your lead gave us. You have that info, you have the money. It's there for you, and it's all yours," Nena told him. "Let her go, huh?"

His face showed deliberation and inexperience: he wasn't a professional at this. Just a kid who had seen an opportunity and made the wrong choice. Nena hoped he'd make the right one now.

"Let me see."

"What?" she snapped.

"The money in Najib's account. Let me see it is there, and I let her go."

Nena released short, measured breaths to let the frustration seep out so he wouldn't see her patience with him had run its course and she was apt to kill him even if he knew the secrets to the fountain of youth.

"Do you mind?" Nena pointed somewhere at her back. "My guy has the computer."

The kidnapper waved his gun to do it, and Nena turned toward her team. Evers was already on it, stepping toward her and tossing the handheld, the screen glowing white, in the air. Nena caught it in one hand, flipped it around, and brandished it in front of her.

"It's all there. Can you see? My people sent that money hours ago. All there. All yours," she told him. He could take the money and run. He could live until karma took care of him. He just had to let Abiola go. And answer her one question.

He deliberated again. Each minute after agonizing minute, Abiola gradually found more footing on the ground, as if her freedom was on time release.

Suddenly, he shoved the girl forward. Her foot caught on a protruding stone, and she stumbled, but Nena was there to catch her before she fell. Abiola broke into tears then, wrapping her arms around Nena's neck so tight she was cutting off Nena's oxygen. Nena gently placed a hand on the girl's arm to loosen it, whispering to her, "You're all right. You're all right."

Nena stood to her full height. She nodded at the kidnapper, who had stepped back, his gun at his side, watching them warily.

Nena put the girl behind her. "Can you tell me one last thing?"

He cursed, stepping back farther away from them. "I just want to go home."

"And you will," Nena told him. "Just tell me this. Who was it?"

"Who was what?"

"Who ordered the hit? Who told you to take the prime minister's niece?"

The kidnapper blinked in confusion. "What hit? We didn't have anything to do with killing anyone."

It was Nena's turn to be confused. But. How?

She recovered. "Then who ordered the kidnapping? Because they will put that and the assassination on your head. Don't have allegiance to them. They don't care about you. They may not even pay you. *I* paid you."

He nodded, realizing there had been a higher-up who had put them in this situation, who had signed their death warrants when all they'd wanted was to take care of their families and believed in the lies they were told.

"I don't give a shit about—" He stopped, distracted by something behind Nena. He craned his neck to see around her, broke into a smile of relief. His sudden excitement so evident that he forgot himself, lifting his gun hand as if pointing at what had pulled his attention.

"Eh heh," he said, suddenly emboldened. "Now, you will kno—"

But he couldn't finish. A loud crack pierced the air, splitting the silence, and silencing him. His head exploded in a burst of gore that immobilized Nena as the thick, warm spray hit her in the face.

53

Time stood still as Nena slowly turned, the blood trailing down her face. The kidnapper would have given up. If she'd only had another minute. He would have confessed everything and lived.

"Put it down!" Billy commanded; she wasn't sure who he was directing it at. Did he think she'd been the one to fire the shot?

"Down, man. Don't play with me." The seriousness in Billy's tone was deadly. And since Nena was not a man, that meant it wasn't directed at her.

She faced Dubin in full safari regalia complete with a top-of-the-line hunting rifle trained in her direction. Or in the direction of where the kidnapper had been before recognizing someone behind her and being about to say who it was.

Dubin seemed to hesitate a second longer than he should. Even in the dark, she saw how the adrenaline pumped him up and he could barely stand still. He was bursting at the seams, like he'd hit some sort of hole in one and wanted his buddies to join in celebration of his perfect shot.

But this wasn't a golf course, and he wasn't holding a club and wearing plaid shorts and a crisp shirt with the alligator logo. Instead, Dubin was sporting khaki attire and brandishing a massive hunting rifle that he'd brought to use on a safari excursion of the type Tanzania was known for during his trip.

Nena felt a tiny ball of force crash into her from behind, and she quickly kept Abiola there, shielding the girl with her body in case Dubin got trigger happy again. His gun was now trained, not in the direction of where the dead man once stood, but on her. It remained as her team shouted at Dubin to lower it, his finger lightly caressing the trigger. Nena could have sworn she saw the smallest flicker of hesitation before Dubin finally pulled himself out of his dark temptation and began to lower it. Billy and Femi's weapons were trained on him. Even Evers, who'd materialized from their vehicle, had his weapon drawn and leveled at Dubin's back.

Dubin delayed even longer, his muzzle wavering in her general direction. No, on her, before he finally pointed it to the sky. He raised his free hand up at them.

"Whoa, whoa, whoa," he said. "Now wait. I just saved her life there, bud," he said to Billy. "Just ease up on those triggers a little bit." The Western accent bubbled to the surface. "I saved her life."

"Saved my life? He didn't have a gun on me," Nena managed to say, coming down from the initial shock of someone's head practically exploding in her face. "He was talking."

Billy marched to Dubin, divesting him of his rifle to Dubin's minor objections. Billy patted him down for anything hidden, then pronounced Dubin clean.

Dubin eyed his rifle. "Careful with that. It's expensive, and I don't think you can afford the replacement."

Billy stared Dubin down as he proceeded to dismantle the rifle, popping out the second round, which had been chambered; detaching the extra mag; flipping the safety, rendering it an expensive piece of useless metal.

Femi's weapon followed every move Dubin made. She said to Evers, "I've got him, fam. You're good." She cracked a wry smile. "Pretty quick draw, my guy! I'm impressed." She slapped his back. Hard.

Evers stumbled, pushing his glasses up the bridge of his nose with the back of his hand.

"But you'll need to get contacts or something if you're gonna be in the field. Can't have Coke bottles screwing up the mission."

"That's the oldest joke in the book," Evers returned, holstering his weapon. "And there's nothing wrong with wearing thick glasses."

Nena made a mental note to ask what a Coke bottle had to do with their missions.

Not as easily distracted as his compatriots, Billy reared on Dubin. "What the bloody hell are you doing here? How'd you get here?"

"Followed you when she ditched me," Dubin said, directing the accusation Nena's way. "I told you I wanted to come along and help get the girl."

Some help. Nena looked back at the dead body and the rearrangement Dubin's gun had made to the kidnapper's face. Dubin had eliminated their potential lead in figuring out who was behind the kidnapping and the assassination. No one else was alive, and she wasn't sure Judah, in the state he was in, would be able to talk and that she could protect him long enough to do so.

"This isn't some police ride-along," Femi groused, no longer masking her contempt. She stood down, pointing her muzzle at the ground but remaining at the ready. She looked as if she were praying for Dubin to even try it.

Dubin watched them with wide-eyed curiosity. "Yes," he said softly. Nena could tell the wheels were churning in his mind over all he'd seen, and if he'd been trailing them from the resort, then he had surely seen everything from start to finish.

Nena rubbed at the goose bumps on Abiola's arm. As the girl clung to her, trembling, Nena went over it all in her own mind. Their weapons. The precision and efficiency with which the team had executed their plan going in. The way Femi had stayed out of sight to watch their backs and take out any opposition coming from the outside in, picking them off cleanly.

Nena and Billy had entered the operations building heavily armed, engaged in enemy fire, and eliminated them with military precision. If Dubin had observed even a fraction of that, he'd have questions she wouldn't be able to answer.

Dubin landed his gaze on each one of them. "What is it you all do again?"

"Business. Corporations. Investments. Good Samaritans," Nena returned. She approached him, Abiola hanging on her like a new appendage. She lightly prodded Abiola forward, gently cleaving the girl from her body.

"Femi, Evers, help Abiola into the car, please? And let's load up to head out." She turned to Billy. "Run a final check of inside the dwelling? Grab the equipment we left inside while I get Dubin on his way."

Billy narrowed his eyes. "You mean—"

"Yes, the extra go bag," she said slowly, giving her second a pointed look and sending him a telepathic message. With Dubin all in her face, she couldn't say more. "Think I dropped it when we took on fire and went after the guy holding Abiola."

Billy pursed his lips as he worked through her instructions, trying to remember when she'd entered the building with a nearly twenty-pound bag.

Femi, with her back to them as she assisted Abiola into the vehicle, whispered in their comms. Billy still hesitated, not wanting to leave Dubin, but he nodded and turned heel, heading back inside.

"Wowww." Dubin blew out a gush of air. "Leaving valuable equipment lying around like that. Kind of irresponsible."

Nena hit her forehead lightly, rolling her eyes. "Silly me."

Her mocking going over his head, Dubin offered Nena a sympathetic look. "Need to be more careful. What if there had been another one of them left in there? They'd have had all your gear and used it against you. That's the epitome of fucking yourself in the ass."

Nena frowned at his crassness.

"Luckily I had my big game hunting rifle to assist you."

"Yeah, real convenient," Femi mumbled. "Shooting people about to give up is very heroic."

"But for business folk, your artillery is pretty advanced. It's not for big game. Nothing I've seen when on safari," Dubin observed, pretending not to hear Femi. He stayed in step with Nena as they approached the team's vehicle. He seemed oblivious to the fact that they were trying to usher him out of there. Nena did not want him around when Billy returned with Judah.

"Seemed pretty covert. Militaristic." He scrutinized her. "You've been in?"

She shrugged as if it were no big deal. "Some minor training, yes. My father likes me to be able to defend myself."

Dubin let out a derisive laugh. "Leave it to Noble Knight. When most fathers give their little girls a tiny pink pistol or maybe some pepper spray, that guy pays some hard-up military guys to train up his little girl like some kind of G. I. Jane."

She'd let the "little girl" comment pass, but now his braying laughter cut through, grating on Nena's nerves to the point where she nearly rounded on him until Femi came in clutch. Sidling beside her swiftly and laying a calming hand on her arm without Dubin noticing anything was off.

"I always knew your father was trying to overcompensate for his"— Dubin continued chuckling—"inadequacies."

He was taking too much enjoyment in his unchallenged swipes at Noble Knight. Would he have said these things in her father's presence? Absolutely not. Nena knew that for a fact. There was one person overcompensating here, and it was not Noble Knight.

"My father overcompensates for nothing, Mr. Dubin. But I will share your concern with him, and perhaps he will get in touch to discuss it with you." She looked at her watch. "It's not too late. We can call him now, and you may speak with him if you'd like. Evers, do you have the sat?"

She gave him her widest, most innocent look, complete with long blinks and everything. Femi snickered in the background. She might have also made mention of a dumbass and a little-dicked prick. But Nena wasn't entirely sure. Whatever it was, Dubin heard it, and he straightened quickly, glaring at Femi and clearing his throat.

"No need to bother him at this late hour."

Nena pushed. "It's not late at all. Only a quarter till."

"Never mind it," Dubin snapped.

Nena had had her fun, and that was over. She sobered and asked, "Mr. Dubin?" It came out as if she'd just thought of it. "You say you were saving me?"

Dubin nodded, pointing back at his handiwork. "He looked like he was about to draw on you."

"But he gave up the girl. He wasn't even pointing at anyone." She pursed her lips.

He shrugged. "Looked like he was about to."

"Seemed like something distracted him. Or like he recognized someone."

He placed a hand on his hip, barking out a laugh. "I don't know if you've noticed, dear, but I'm the only White guy who's been hanging around for the past several days. I was on that stage at the pavilion. I guess I have that kind of face."

Dubin's attempt at an endearing smile won no one over. He looked more like his grin had been electrocuted onto his face.

Femi started, "Dude's lame as fu—"

"You could have hit the girl. Or me." Nena dropped all pretense. Her words came out directly, her meaning deadly.

"Next time, Mr. Dubin, you should be more careful."

54

His frozen smile dropped, and his eyes narrowed in the light of the fires, turning hard. His lips curled into a snarl, baring just a bit of teeth. He couldn't hide his contempt, his rage at not being in charge. Here, he'd let his mask slip. Nena recognized this look, and she knew she'd struck a nerve. Dubin didn't like anyone criticizing his accuracy or chastising his choices, least of all a woman, and especially not the daughter of a man he despised.

The corner of his eye twitched, and Dubin said coolly, "I could say the same for you, Ms. Knight."

They took measure of one another, sizing up the enemy in a silent exchange. The tension between the two of them was heavier than the air around them, so thick they'd need the knife nestled at Nena's back to chisel a small hole in it.

Nena spoke up, breaking their internal tête-à-tête. "You should head back now, Mr. Dubin. We've notified the authorities, and they'll be here shortly."

His mood flipped, and he waved her off as he switched back to an overly jazzed tourist or like he was some action hero who'd swooped in to save the day and still had some saving to do. He turned, walked backward, and looked over her shoulder at the man he'd put down.

His mouth parted as if he wanted to say something more. Nena wouldn't have been surprised if it was to ask if he could snap a picture with his trophy kill, because that's all it was to him. Dubin hadn't cared about saving Abiola and certainly not Nena. He had just wanted bragging rights.

"I'm sure they'd understand the circumstances in which the kidnapper's death occurred."

Nena inclined her head. "Understand the optics of the 'White guy,' as you put it earlier, killing a Black man?"

Her words held a heavily weighted meaning—centuries, decades, months, weeks, even days behind them—and even Dubin, in all his pomp and circumstance, false bravado, and intentional obtuseness, couldn't deny what Nena had said.

Dubin stammered, "He was part of an assassination and a kidnapper."

She inclined her head again. "And you are a guest of this country, of this place."

"As are you, and look what you did!" He waved his hand in a flourish, gesturing grandly to the scene before him.

Nena humored the man, twisting around to see the scene. She slowly nodded her agreement.

She returned to him. "Yes, well . . . you and I are not the same."

She held her rifle out to Evers as he approached, holding his hand out. The message she'd had Evers send to the three officials—informing them all had been handled and Constable Pengo could come process the area—meant her team had better clear out and let the local police do what they were going to do, including take all the accolades, which Nena was happy to give.

She tried it another way. "Constable Pengo and Ms. Odemba asked you to remain on the premises, so if you're found to have not followed their instructions . . ."

She let her words hang in the air, and when Dubin's face dropped its insolence and his body shifted so he could shoot a quick look in the direction from which they'd come, Nena knew her warning had finally taken root.

Dubin reminded her of a petulant child on the verge of a tantrum who refused to go to bed for fear their parents were going to have fun while they slept. He made it a couple of steps and then stopped in front of the open door of the SUV where Abiola sat in the second row, watching them with worried eyes. Nena reached in to give her a reassuring squeeze on her leg.

He spied his weapon at Evers's feet under the front passenger seat. Dubin pointed at it and made a move to grab it.

"No, sir," Evers said firmly, giving Dubin a stiff arm, which said a lot, since he was half the size of the hulk of a man. Evers pushed his glasses up the bridge of his nose with his index finger looking fiercer than Nena had ever seen him.

Dubin huffed, "But that belongs to me!"

Nena moved behind him, prepared to usher him along by force if she had to, clapping Dubin on the back good naturedly.

"We'll run it back for you," she offered. "You can retrieve it back at the resort."

Dubin considered her for a long while, an argument building behind his glinting eyes. He took measure of them as if trying to calculate whether he could make them give him his gun back.

Reason seemed to get the better of Frances Dubin, and he realized he wouldn't be able to impose his will on this unusually highly trained trio of Good Samaritans.

"All right, then, Ms. Knight . . . and pals," he acquiesced. "Have it your way."

Dubin's parting goodbye was a knowing smirk, one that promised his business with her was far from complete.

When he was out of sight, exhaustion hit Nena like a Mack truck, but her work was not yet done.

"Is he still moving?" Nena asked, bending her head from side to side. If she could, she would have lain down where she stood and slept for days. She turned around to face Evers, who was peering down at the handheld.

"He is. No stopping or doubling back. He's moving pretty quickly actually."

"Keep monitoring," Nena said, her attention drawn to the darkened doorway of the building, where she could hear labored breathing and spurts of curses as Billy emerged with an unconscious Judah slung over one shoulder, the strap of his gun on the other, and a rucksack swinging from the crook of his arm.

"Femi, please." Nena's head made a quick jerk in their direction.

Femi nodded, jogging over to assist Billy in getting Judah to the SUV.

Nena walked a circle around the vehicle, looking out into the darkness, surveying the area as Femi climbed into the third row and helped Billy secure Judah in behind her, where she could monitor him.

"His breathing is thready," Femi announced, assessing him. "They've really done a number on him."

Leaning over the back of the second row, Abiola watched on, her concern for a man she'd spent these last harrowing hours in captivity with evident in the tremble of her lips and the way her brows templed.

"Will he be okay?"

Nena couldn't have been happier to hear Abiola's breathy voice.

Femi answered with softness Nena hadn't heard from her. "We're going to do everything we can to help him."

Abiola and Judah had been confined together in that room. She'd seen or heard the kidnappers beat him within an inch of his life, and she had been able to do nothing. It was an ordeal she wouldn't soon forget.

None of them would.

Nena had been keeping watch as Billy and Femi put Judah in the vehicle. Before Billy pulled himself out, he paused by Abiola, who had been watching Judah intently. He held up her rucksack. "Think this belongs to you?"

He studied the front of the bag. "Used to play Mario Kart with my stepdad all the time after school." It was the most about his personal life that Billy had ever shared with anyone, and he chose to do it with Abiola.

"Thank you," Abiola said. She looked at the decal on her bag, then offered Billy a ghost of a smile as she took it. She clutched the bag tightly to her as if it were her lifeline. "I play it on my Switch. I'll show you sometime."

Billy seemed transfixed for a moment, and they let him have it. Then he coughed, breaking the mood, and got out. He faced Nena, his expression first embarrassed and then hardening, daring her to say something. She did not. Then he went over to the driver's side while she climbed in, closing the door behind her.

"Shall we go get him that help?" Nena asked. "Yeah?"

Abiola nodded, nestling back into her seat with the seat belt securely around her and the rucksack held tightly in her lap. She was knocked out before they had been driving five minutes.

Nena gazed at the girl's peaceful sleep, noticing the way her eyelids fluttered. She was dreaming. Nena hoped whatever it was wasn't too scary. She envied Abiola the ability to sleep and cast her worries to the side. To know that in the end, her mother, and the adults around her, would fix the problems in her world. Nena believed that being able to fix what had happened to Abiola today was one of her greatest achievements.

That was one problem solved.

But Nena's job was far from done.

55

Abiola's excited yelps for her mother reverberated in the hall of the resort as she ran into the outstretched arms of the deceased prime minister's sister, Glory Asogi. A stretcher with a still-unconscious Judah beneath a thin sheet came next, on his way to the temporary medical room they were creating for him. He wasn't going to any medical facility or hospital. Judah could hold the answers to all their questions, but until he awoke, they'd be in a holding pattern.

Bringing up the rear of the entourage were Nena and the rest of the team, each toting their go bags. They stopped out of respect, though they were fatigued and wanted to rest for a little while before reconvening for the next steps. Nena had toweled off some of the last kidnapper's blood in the SUV, but couldn't wait to get properly cleaned up.

Acting Prime Minister Odemba, General Geofry, and Chief Constable Pengo stood to the side, a somber welcoming committee, as the whole group observed the reunion of the mother and daughter, while Nena's attention was drawn to the four medics maneuvering Judah's stretcher up the steps on their way to the third level, where he'd be cared for under guard supervision.

"I was so scared, Mama," Abiola said, her voice muffled because her face was buried in her mother's neck.

Tears continued to stream down the petite woman's delicate face. "Me, too, my love." And she hugged her daughter tighter.

Nena watched, relieved for the good outcome for Abiola and her mother and that she was able to deliver on the promise she'd made to Ms. Asogi and Ms. Odemba. She didn't think that Ms. Asogi would ever let Abiola out of her sight again, and Nena didn't blame her. The two of them, though in politics for most of their lives because of the work of Ms. Asogi's older brother, had never experienced this kind of trauma in rapid succession.

Nena ached for them because, while the little girl and her mother had found their way back to one another, they still had a long road ahead of them, beginning with mourning the death of their loved one. Asogi was government to the people, but to Abiola and her mother, he was family. And he had been ripped from them in one of the most brutal of ways. Now they'd have to go on living without him. Nena felt all that more than she cared to.

"Mama," Abiola said, her voice teeny through the folds of her mother's clothing.

"Yes, love?"

"I can't breathe."

A ripple of relieved laughter moved through the lobby, and Ms. Odemba gestured to the standing guards and resort employees waiting for instruction.

"Take them to their rooms, please. Get Abiola what she needs," Ms. Odemba said, stepping to the still-hugging duo. She bent so she was at eye level with Abiola. "I know it is rather late, and you are tired, but is it okay if I come speak with you a little later?" She pointed at the constable behind her. "And perhaps Constable Pengo as well? To hear what happened?"

Abiola peeked at the stylish woman with rounded, guarded eyes. She knew Ms. Odemba, but after all she'd been through, she was cautious of everyone—new or old. She nodded her consent.

Ms. Odemba straightened, running her hands down the length of her hunter-green suit, giving the general and the constable a grim look. What was that all about? Nena frowned. This was supposed to be a moment of joy and not discontent. Yet discontented was exactly what Odemba looked like. Like she wasn't looking forward to what was coming next. Nena fought back the quiver of unease. She was tired and overthinking, sure that whatever look she thought Odemba had shared with the other two men was about her hesitation to interview a nine-year-old so late in the evening.

Nena's dark thoughts were interrupted when she was attacked, a pair of small arms wrapping around her thighs and squeezing her. She staggered back slightly, looking down to see the top of Abiola's head, with its intricate braids, as the girl hugged her. Her mother watched them as she beamed at Nena with joy and relief. Nena tentatively patted the girl's back while Abiola continued to hang on. Ms. Asogi approached them.

She took Evers's hands from where they hung at his sides and grasped them in hers. "Thank you," she said, first in her native tongue and then in English. "Thank you for my daughter."

She stepped up to him, wrapping her arms around his back, not allowing him to take the unsure step backward that he'd started. She gave him a peck, first on one cheek and then on the other.

"God bless you," she said. It was as if she were trying to memorize his face, and she released his hands as he stood stock still and in shock. She did the exact same with Femi, calling her sister, kissing her twice on each cheek. And then with Billy, doing as she had done with Evers. The three of them were left speechless, fighting back emotion they were unused to displaying, if they were anything like Nena. It was too much in this moment, too unexpected, not a part of any plan they could ever conceive. Being thanked for what they'd done, for the risks they'd taken.

Being thanked period.

Ms. Asogi appeared behind Abiola, who Nena didn't think would ever detach herself from her legs. Sandwiching her daughter between their bodies as she leaned in for a long hug, Ms. Asogi squeezed on top while Abiola squeezed down below.

It was a display they were unused to as Dispatch and Network members, who always had to work under the cloak of night or in a mission room. They never got to see the successful results of their hard work, of lives they had saved. Nena had never either.

"You are very honorable, dear lady." Ms. Asogi whispered because her words were only for Nena's ears. "Thank you, and praise be to the Tribe, which does the will most high."

She feathered Nena with a kiss on either side, holding Nena's face in her hands. She dropped her voice lower, her breath tickling Nena's ear. "Be careful, my sister."

Nena's gut constricted, but she maintained her composure. She remained placid, accepting Ms. Asogi's praise and thanks as the rest of the team had done. She pretended the dead PM's sister hadn't just issued a secret, ominous, and vague warning in front of everyone.

The woman pulled away, and Nena wiggled out of Abiola's viselike grip to drop to her knees and return Abiola's hug. "Watch out for your mum, yeah?"

Abiola nodded. "'Kay."

The two were ushered out of the lobby within a circle of their attendants to their room as the Dubins glided down the stairwell Judah had been taken up. Ms. Asogi stiffly accepted a pat on the arm by Bridget and quietly thanked Mr. Dubin when he let out boisterous exclamations on Abiola's safe return. Abiola wouldn't even look at him, clutching her mother's side as they walked past. Nena ticked off her checklist. One item completed.

Nena approached Ms. Odemba. "My colleagues are tired, as am I. We'll go freshen up and then can return to debrief if you'd like."

Ms. Odemba shot that look again to the general, and then the chief constable. She set her lips in a firm line and fixed her steely gaze on Nena.

"Ms. Knight, we need to talk."

56

The conference room quickly came alive, tension and a weird electricity permeating the air—Nena's team, Odemba, Geofry, and Pengo the only names on the guest list, though Dubin had apparently provided "key information" upon his return from his own efforts to find Abiola Asogi. Nena highly doubted Dubin offered an accurate description of his so-called efforts.

Nena's team was equally suspicious, but they remained silent, observing the situation. Better to know what they were up against than to react prematurely.

As Nena filed into the room behind her team, Dubin was engaged in a heated whispered conversation with Geofry and Pengo. Bridget lingered, forcing eye contact. She offered a meek congratulations on finding Abiola. Nena managed a curt acknowledgment.

Bridget always looked like she wanted to say more and might have, but she shut down when Dubin broke away from Geofry and Pengo and appeared behind her at the doorway, placing his hands on her shoulders. Bridget stiffened at his touch, but he didn't seem to notice as he bent down to whisper in her ear. Nena watched as they left the room, her thoughts on the Dubins roaming the hotel freely as she was stuck in here while Judah was left vulnerable upstairs.

Nena and the team sat along the table, across from the others. She noted the Tanzanians looked grim rather than relieved to have Abiola safely recovered and Judah Wasira in their possession. Nena didn't like her team being called in like this was the headmaster's office.

"What is the issue?" Nena finally asked, opting to get right to the point.

Ms. Odemba's hands were folded on the table before her. She waited a beat, considering her words first. She began with the thanks she should have offered when they'd arrived.

"I want to thank you first for bringing Abiola Asogi back. And for recovering Judah Wasira. We hope to speak to him soon to get this whole matter sorted out."

Nena's eyes narrowed. "Then, we're good." She made a move to get up, and her team followed suit.

"You left a massacre at the operations building," Pengo interjected, wagging a finger at them. "Rather convenient, eh?"

Nena's shoulders sagged slightly. She sat back down. Her team did the same.

"Chief Constable," Ms. Odemba warned.

Nena leveled a stare at the man. If he'd gone out there, he'd have made a mess of everything. The girl would not have returned. Nor Judah. Nena didn't say that.

"Convenient how?" Nena asked. "Speak plainly with whatever accusations you are about to make."

"You left no witnesses." Pengo's body vibrated with anger, his eyes so red and his face so sweaty Nena thought he'd bring on a heart attack.

Ms. Odemba, ever the politician, put her hands up to calm the rising tensions. "We're not accusing any of you of anything." She kept her tone even.

"Sure sounds like it to me," Femi threw in.

Odemba ignored her. "We are very thankful for your recovering Abiola. And your aid at the mine collapse and your thoughts about

Mr. Dubin." She hesitated, sliding a look at the general. All he did was quirk an eyebrow and remain silent, not wanting a part of whatever she was about to dish out.

"But?" Nena prompted. She tried to read the room. Odemba seemed unwilling to accuse them directly. The chief constable was just playing a pissing game, resentful of anyone he felt was trespassing on his turf. And the general . . . well, he was a man who'd been in combat, understood what happened in battle, and respected those who came back from it.

"But perhaps we were too hasty in allowing you and your mates to go after the kidnappers," Odemba said.

Pengo practically shot up from his seat. "Hell yes, too hasty. A good investigator will wonder why you were so enthusiastic to go after them and get rid of them so that they can't be witness to you orchestrating the kidnapping and assassination!" His bloodshot eyes nearly popped out of his head as his anger grew. He pointed as he berated them. "You thought we're just simple farming people in Latema, but our crime rate isn't one of the lowest for no reason."

Nena had thought the Tanzanians might resent her being there, but she hadn't seen this coming. Nena listened, digesting Pengo's words. She was well aware of the way Odemba observed her, watching for any indication that Pengo's accusations were hitting their mark. Had they planned this while she and her team were out there risking their lives? Nena's mind raced. Some kind of "good cop, bad cop" narrative they thought would work on her? Nena had become familiar with being under scrutiny. It seemed to be the story of her life these days. But this, whatever they were trying to do, was not about to happen.

Nena had initially thought Odemba was shrewd and wouldn't be swept up so easily in hysteria and wild mistruths. By allowing Pengo to go off, Odemba revealed she had an inkling of doubt about Nena and her team.

"So I am clear," Nena said when Pengo had exhausted himself and quieted. "You believe my team and I risked our lives to bring back the girl and Judah, either of whom could confirm our involvement in any plot against you and Latema? Did I get that right?"

Odemba played devil's advocate. "If your plan went bad, you could have tried to clean up your mistake."

"By bringing Abiola and Judah back?" Nena was incredulous. She sent a look to her team, telling them with her eyes to be cool and let her be the heavy. They didn't know how to read that particular look.

"Where is this coming from?" Billy cut in indignantly. The team wasn't supposed to speak out of turn if they weren't team leads, and any other time, Nena might have not appreciated his interjection. However, tonight, it was different.

Femi said, "Yeah, you all were too ready for us to do your dirty work and risk our necks to save the girl. Now you flip the script. That's hella ungrateful."

General Geofry said, "I never approved of allowing mercenaries to do what the military or even the local police, small as they may be"—he ignored the glower from Pengo—"might have done. But I am familiar with the Tribe and its dealings. And I want that on record. I do not trust that Dubin. He is an outsider, a modern-day colonizer."

He was more than that. Nena thought of the man Dubin had killed back at the operations building.

This was probably what Dubin had planned to do the moment he'd arrived. Turn them all against each other. Sow seeds of doubt. Make them see the Tribe as an enemy instead of an ally. He probably got rid of Tegete and Asogi so he could swoop in at the last minute to save the day, as he'd done at the mine collapse, making Odemba and the government feel so indebted to him they'd let his company purchase the mine straight out. Could Frances Dubin really have planned all that?

She should have stayed close and returned with him after they'd gotten Abiola to ensure he wouldn't run back and spin a false narrative she now had to undo. His words had no merit, and with Asogi dead and Tegete incapacitated, the people in this room had no way of knowing who believed Dubin's claims or not. If there was one thing Dubin did well, it was sowing seeds of doubt.

Femi boiled, like she was about to skyrocket from her chair. "Dubin? That asshole?" Her brown eyes flashed, and she gestured wildly with her bracelet-laden arm. "Did he tell you how he blew a guy's head off just when the guy had given up and was about to spill about who'd hired him?"

Odemba and Pengo shared an uneasy look. Geofry snorted, shaking his head. Odemba replied, "He did mention the kidnapper had Abiola and was about to kill you, Ms. Knight."

The scoff came out of Nena's mouth before she had a chance to put a lid on it. Dubin had dubbed himself her savior.

"And then you stripped him of his weapon," Pengo finished accusingly.

"Why wouldn't we have killed the man straight out and eliminated anyone who could confirm we hired them? He was going to talk."

Ms. Odemba sat back in her chair, focusing her attention on Nena. "He claims you paid off the kidnapper and offered him freedom."

"To let Abiola go unharmed, yes. It's called negotiating."

Pengo said, "We don't negotiate with kidnappers and murderers."

"Then you would have had one dead child," Nena returned.

Nena absorbed the new information. So Dubin had seen and heard more than he let on. His perfectly timed kill shot had slain the kidnapper as if he were some exotic animal on safari, felled by the American big game hunter. Odemba's words all but confirmed what Nena had suspected. Dubin had shot the kidnapper in cold blood, not to aid in Abiola's rescue or save Nena's life as he'd proclaimed, but to shut him up. And if they spent any more time spinning wheels here, he wouldn't be the last one Dubin would shut up that night.

57

The realization was a sledgehammer.

Nena's voice rose above the clamor, silencing her team. "What will you do now?" She directed her attention to Odemba. It was her show. Everyone would follow her lead until they were told to follow someone else's.

Pengo bellowed, "Investigate the claims. Investigate this entire thing, and see if you have been double-dealing behind our backs with all intentions to double-cross us."

Evers, who'd remained silent all this time, squawked, "Us? Double-dealing? Double-cross?" He looked imploringly at Nena, as if asking whether they were going to stand for this.

Nena was better than this. *They*—the team, the Tribe, and this government—were better than to be so easily pitted against one another by a disrespectful, smooth-talking outsider's lies.

"Enough, Mr. Pengo." Odemba was tired of his blustering accusations. They all were. He was struck by wounded pride because he had been benched in his own home. "You are being most unhelpful, Chief Constable. We're not accusing you. Please, let us be clear, and do not relay *that* to your father or the Tribe. We only ask you allow yourselves to be escorted to your rooms and that you remain there for the remainder of the night while we wait for Judah to wake, hopefully in the morning, and we sort it all out. Once we speak to him, we will reconvene. And by then, prayerfully, tempers have"—she shot Pengo a derisive glare. He wasn't happy at being sidelined, crossing his arms over his pumpkin-size belly and stewing—"have cooled. We mean you no disrespect."

Femi snorted "Too late for that shit" under her breath.

Nena asked, "While Dubin roams free?"

"He is being escorted to his room as we speak and will also be confined to his room."

No doubt after his whiskey neat.

If Nena was going to get her team in the clear, she'd have to do more than play politics or run missions. She'd have to be both Nena Knight and Echo.

"We'll do as you ask, but I request we stay in Ms. Black's room." Nena gestured at Femi. "My team is understandably upset after the events of this evening and this meeting. As normal protocol for our employer, we need to debrief about the recovery while it's still fresh in our minds."

Chief Constable was about to speak when Odemba silenced him as Nena had done Femi.

"Agreed," Odemba answered. "Though it is not our intent to upset you and your team. We are very thankful you returned Abiola Asogi home."

"Funny way of showing it," Femi groused. Nena held out a hand to silence her.

Odemba waited a beat. "Anything else?"

A plan was already taking form. "To ensure Judah's safety and the integrity of his testimony, I strongly suggest keeping visitors to Judah's room to a minimum, only medical personnel entering if they must, until he wakes in the morning and can be questioned by the appropriate authorities."

Pengo thumped the table with his hand. "This is my jurisdiction. Who is this small, small girl to tell us how to do our jobs? I know how to protect the people under my watch."

His insult meant nothing. It wasn't the first time an insecure man resorted to calling her names. Besides, the day's events spoke volumes for the chief constable's protection, and everyone knew it, including him.

Nena barely gave him a glance. "You're in over your head, Chief Constable Pengo. It's not your fault."

He bristled that she had the nerve to try to mollify him.

"Aren't you worried about what Judah Wasira will say when he wakes?" Odemba asked, trying to figure Nena out.

Nena returned Odemba's arctic appraisal. "Why? I have nothing to hide."

58

"What is the plan?" Billy spun on Nena when the suite doors locked behind them as instructed.

Nena ran her finger across what had used to be a peephole in the door but had since been covered over, after an American journalist had sued the hotel when it was found out some Peeping Tom had been watching her. So no peephole. She tried the next best thing.

Nena pressed her ear to the door, listening as the guards settled out front. Two of them.

"Do you hear me? Why'd you agree to us being held like some damn prisoners?"

"Because anything else would look like guilt."

Evers plopped down on the sofa, much to Femi's chagrin. "They already think we're guilty."

"Their hands are tied." Nena played devil's advocate. "Too much has happened today. They can't trust anyone who's not from here. Understandable."

Not really, but Nena didn't want her team to stage a coup. Anything that happened next would be on her.

"What's the plan?" Billy continued, following Nena as she looked around the not-so-neat room. Femi's clothes had been dropped in various locations.

Femi bent to scoop up a pair of jeans and cut her eyes at Nena. "Didn't know I'd have company after our thing."

Billy said, "Nena."

Nena's lips quirked. "It's not that bad."

She tried not to make a habit out of telling lies, but she made an exception here. Nena continued to survey the room as she made her way to the balcony.

"Nena."

The force in Billy's voice made Nena turn heel and look at him, incredulous that he'd address her in that tone, with bass behind it, like he wasn't her number two.

Even Femi paused midscoop, her eyebrows nearing her braided hairline. Evers sat stock still with an open Toblerone halfway to his mouth.

Finally having her attention and with an exasperated expression that was hauntingly familiar, Billy asked, "Is. There. A plan?"

"It's coming." She gave him one more lingering look before returning to her assessment.

With both hands, she peered through the slivered opening she'd made through the curtains covering the balcony doors. Femi's room was on the interior of the hotel, with a glorious view overlooking the garden where Nena and Abiola had conversed just that morning. Seemed like a millennium ago.

Nena pushed open the glass-paned door. She stepped out onto the small semicircular balcony with its curved wrought iron railing, making her assessments. Her eyes scanned from where she was, along the building, moving up as her brain made its calculations. All she needed was a chalkboard and she'd look like one of those frazzled professors writing formulaic measurements to break the speed of sound.

She gazed up at the half-mooned sky, taking it in, enjoying the slight cooling breeze, glad for it. Then her eyes shifted over, where satisfaction settled in nice and tight. Her memory had served her correctly.

She studied the balcony of the room one floor up, where Judah had been taken. Nena had watched them carry him up and made note of the room they'd secured him in, having already known which rooms in the hotel were occupied or not from her intel.

There was no light on in the suite that Nena could see, and the room seemed undisturbed; however, it wouldn't remain that way for long, if her suspicions proved true.

When she returned to the room, closing the door and fixing the curtain as she'd found it, Nena outlined her plan to the team, then stopped talking and took a deep drink of bottled water. She wiped the residue from her lips as she waited for the team to process and argue.

Evers, the first to speak, shook his head. "I don't like it. Too many unknown variables. There may be a guard already in there." He pushed his glasses up and sat back in the cushions.

"Our entire line of work is nothing but unknown variables," Nena answered. "And I prefer to keep my own watch on him."

Seated in an armchair across from her, Femi said, "I happen to agree with Evers. You're no rock climber. Or wall scaler, or whatever they call them."

Nena made a face. "Doesn't look that hard."

"Until you slip and fall and break your back," Femi prophesized. "This isn't *Mission: Impossible*, you know."

Evers said, "We should sit and wait. Minister Odemba, Pengo, they'll realize the idea of us having anything to do with what happened to Mr. Asogi, Councilman Tegete, and Abiola is ridiculous. And no one's stupid enough to go after Judah after so much heat."

"Again, I agree." Femi snapped her head toward Evers, holding up a finger. "Don't get too comfy with us being on the same side, okay?"

Evers raised his hands in protest, confused at how he had become the target of Femi's contempt.

"I'm just pissed that they would even insult us like this with these accusations. I say we sit our asses right here and let them figure out their own problems."

"Their problem is Dubin."

Femi crossed her arms over her chest. "Let them deal with him, then. If they can't see that he's the most corrupt motherfucker in this country, then they deserve his ass."

Evers said, "At least Judah will be able to corroborate our story and tell them what happened to him."

Femi scoffed. "If he makes it the night. I don't know. Maybe Dubin *would* be stupid enough to try and get in there to finish him off."

"And that's why I need to get to Judah's room and make sure Dubin doesn't. After what he pulled tonight, there's no telling how far he'll go to save himself. I saw where they took Judah. I think I can get to it." If Nena's calculations were correct.

"He could cut and run," Evers said. "Who hires a hit and stays around still trying to squeeze out one more thing?"

"A greedy-ass motherfucker," Billy grumbled. "That's who."

"No, a man who thinks he's better than us and has the audacity to shit in our hand and call it chocolate." Femi looked around when silence greeted her. "Tell me I'm wrong."

Billy threw a balled-up sock at her. "No, you're just disgusting, is all. That's the best you could come up with?"

Nena didn't disagree. She rotated in her seat. "Billy, what do you think is wrong with the plan?"

Billy had been quiet during the back-and-forth among the other three. As they spoke, he'd gotten up from his chair and made his way to the balcony doors, where he parted the curtain just a little to peer through. He was still peering when Nena spoke to him. He turned away from his scrutiny, appraising the rest of the team, who waited expectantly for his response.

He slipped his hands into the pockets of his pants. "Everything."

Nena sank into the soft cushions, deflated. Disappointment settled around her shoulders along with the fatigue. She didn't have it in her to debate with the rest of them. It was already past midnight, and who knew what was going on with Judah?

"You could get hurt," Evers said softly, his voice thick. "And maybe it's not worth it. Maybe we wait it out until tomorrow and cut our losses. Leave them to whatever they decide to do with each other."

Femi said, "Amen, brother."

Evers's tone made Nena pause. There was something more in it, beyond business, as had been the case between them since she took over Network command. It sounded like Evers was worried about her well-being, and Nena was touched.

She couldn't give it further thought because it was time to be Echo and pull off a successful mission. She was likely about to break her neck climbing up the building like she was in some sort of superhero movie.

Nena gave Evers a quick nod on her way out to the balcony. It unnerved her, but as she sat on the edge, she sneaked a look at Billy, Evers, and Femi, all standing there to send her off. She could see it in the way one's eyes squinted in deep concentration. How another's forehead crinkled into lines stretching across it. And how the last's lips twisted tightly. All of them with concern for her.

Billy scanned the exterior of the building up and down. "If you're going to go through with this stupid-ass plan, then let's get it over and done with."

Nena felt a geyser of warmth mingled with a knot of frustration at them. They weren't making it easy. In their line of work, there was no room to care beyond ensuring the mission was a success and your mate made it back okay for the next mission. There wasn't any place for feelings. And their ragtag quartet had been thrown together out of a desperate need to fill a huge void and not because of a well-researched and logical plan of execution.

But Nena had to be real with herself. Of the teams she'd been on, this was the one she'd genuinely grown to care about in these few days. Even Billy, who'd been the bane of her existence since she took over as head of Dispatch and Network: she'd grown to respect him and care whether he lived or died—though he'd still always be a big-headed tool, in her book. But that's why protecting Judah long enough for him to clear them was her number one priority.

Because she was going to get this team home safe.

And alive.

59

Scaling the side of a building, even with railings and jutting stones within reasonable enough distances to climb, was difficult work even for a person as athletic and conditioned as Nena. Femi's premonition of broken bones hung around her like a thick chain, and when Nena sneaked a look down below, the world went sideways for a couple of seconds, making her tightly grip the balcony she was currently hanging on to.

The fall might not kill her, if she didn't land in a way that hit her head or impaled her, but she could be severely hurt. Nena had an epiphany as she hung like Spider-Man on the parapet of the hotel. Maybe she wasn't a fan of heights. At least not when there wasn't solid ground directly beneath her feet. She took another quick look, closed her eyes, and counted to five, tricking herself into thinking the looming, treacherous ground thirteen meters below was no big deal.

She made it to Judah's balcony without any incident and climbed over the railing—one leg, then the other—before she sank to the floor. She didn't want to think about her way back down.

With the tiny screwdriver she'd borrowed from Evers's computer tool kit, Nena jimmied the lock to the french doors. They opened with no problem. She guessed when they had designed the four-story resort, the architects hadn't anticipated a balcony break-in on the third floor.

Nena cautiously stepped into the empty living room, wishing again for Network's overwatch, which could tell her how many bodies were in the suite and right outside the door. She closed the door softly behind her, scanning the dark room, which was identical to hers, only flipped in reverse. The kitchen was there. Two bedrooms right down the short hall, and in one of them, the one with a dull bluish hue shining from beneath the closed door, Judah.

Nena went through the suite on high alert, knowing anyone could come in at any moment. She went to the front door, pressing her ear to it to see if she could hear anything from the hallway. From below, yellowish light glimmered, with the occasional shadow cast when someone walked past. She couldn't hear anyone lingering by the door, but she knew the Dubins were also staying on this floor. From her memory, they were at the end of the hall, in the largest suite. She listened for the American's brash voice cutting through the quiet, respectful silence of the locals. He was always so loud, so she figured wherever he was, she'd hear him coming and prepare.

Faraway voices filtered in and out, but none, as far as she could tell, were right at the door, though Nena doubted a guard could be too far off. They'd want to make sure Judah didn't try to sneak out.

But there wasn't any other security around, and that bothered her.

She'd hoped Odemba and the others had gotten her hint and taken all precautions to ensure Judah's safety—not just locked her and her team up under the guise of "sorting things out" but really and truly made an effort to ensure no one else would be hurt tonight. Nena also hoped that Abiola and her mother, Glory, would soon be far away from here. They'd been through enough. But Nena didn't sense they were in any danger. Her self-appointed mark was now Judah.

Satisfied she was in the clear, for the moment at least, Nena made her way to the bedrooms, checking the half-opened one she knew was empty and clean. No personal effects, because the suite had not been occupied before they put Judah in it. Quietly, so as not to startle him if he happened to be awake, she opened the door to the bigger room. The king-size bed was in the center of the room, jutting from the farthest wall. She saw the lone figure in the bed, beneath the white sheets. She scanned the room: no medical equipment, save whatever first aid the doctor had used to temporarily patch him up before they shipped him out to a proper medical facility the next day.

Her footsteps faltered as she walked through the door, second-guessing herself—not for the first time since she'd arrived in Latema. Maybe the idea wasn't a good one. Maybe she hadn't thought things all the way through, like her team had made painstakingly clear when she'd told them the plan and they'd pummeled her with questions: What was she going to do, stay up there all night? And then what? If she was caught in Judah's room, Odemba and the rest would have no doubt she was behind everything, no matter what she said. The Tanzanians would think she went up there to silence Judah or pay him off, and Dubin would be in the clear. She'd create a colossal problem for the Tribe of epic proportions. And with Nena caught in this trap, she would be clearing the way for Dubin.

After Nena recovered from her team's combined efforts, she explained that Dubin was likely doing that as she stood there wasting time, either eliminating Judah or planting evidence to frame him as having orchestrated the mine collapse, the pavilion, and the kidnapping. Maybe that had been the contingency plan Dubin mentioned in the phone call she'd overheard.

But if she wasn't there, Judah would be exposed and vulnerable. He was unable to defend himself. As she cautiously approached him on the bed, she heard how his breathing was labored. How hard his body pulled for air and how it rattled when he did. Internal injuries, a broken bone, hopefully not a punctured lung. If that was the case, the in-house medic would have had him evacuated. Maybe. If Odemba permitted it.

She got close enough to see Judah's face and the tops of his shoulders, mottled with black and purplish bruising under crisscrossed bandages that seeped dark from the oozing blood. In the dim blue hue of the nightstand clock, she allowed herself one second to feel something for what had been done to him.

Judah was . . . nearly unrecognizable. His face had been battered in, with deep lacerations carved in his cheeks and neck. And that was just what Nena could see. One arm rested above the sheets, beside his body, the exposed areas covered in deep cuts and angry bruises. He was bandaged from the shoulder to the elbow, a possible dislocation or break. Nena wasn't sure.

Beneath the sheets, Nena knew it had to be worse—from the kidnappers' anger toward him or them attempting to make an example of him, she didn't know. And it didn't matter. For all the good Judah had done to give the people of Latema a fighting chance against a system typically set up to keep them down, this was his payment. Betrayal and a frame-up.

Nena reached out before she was aware of her actions. She hovered over Judah's pulverized face, flinching involuntarily as she remembered the pain and hoped he was in a deep enough sleep to not feel it as much. But she'd been in this very position not too long ago. He was battered, beaten, bruised by people he'd trusted, who'd been in his inner circle, with whom he'd shared everything. Nena knew of that betrayal all too well.

Her thoughts went to the last time she and Judah had been together in his small car. Of how close in proximity they were, and how she'd wanted him to kiss her. She could feel the energy of him, his passion for his people and his cause, and it had turned on things in her in a way she thought only Cort could. And before Cort, she had thought no one alive would ever be able to do that, because that kind of feeling had been cut from her in ways Nena would never truly get over. In the short time she'd spent arguing with Judah, trying to get him to see reason, she'd begun to care for him beyond his being her mark.

"Hey," she whispered to his sleeping form. She lightly touched the side of his cheek, the area that looked least painful. He hadn't deserved to be put here, no matter how hardheaded he had been.

"Sorry about all of this."

She snatched her fingers back when Judah's eyes creaked open, first out of focus, then zeroing in on her once he realized where he was. Judah blinked slowly. His lips moved as he tried to pull them into a smile. He winced at the effort, reopening the cuts on them. He looked at her. Then beyond her. Judah's eyes widened at a new sound. A muffled cry made its way to Nena's ears.

"A fucking tender moment if I've ever seen one." Dubin's brash voice came from behind her.

Nena whirled around to see Bridget's terrified eyes staring back at her as she clung to the doorframe behind her bear of a husband, who had his gun trained on Nena. Nena had let her guard down. Had let the moment of seeing Judah preoccupy her so much she hadn't registered the background noises she heard as potential danger. She hadn't heard the Dubins enter the suite until it was too late. A rookie move.

Dubin looked from Judah to Nena, a deadly calm descending over him. "One for the books, I'd say, huh, sport?"

60

His gun still trained on her, Dubin moved swiftly to the table holding medical supplies. He made his selection, tossing white medical tape at Bridget. She wasn't ready, and she fumbled with the tape as she fought to grab it. She held it up to him, confusion written all over her face.

"Come on out of there, Florence Nightingale," Dubin said, gesturing with his gun for Nena to step away from the bed and come toward him. With the gun still on Nena, Dubin traded places, sidling to Judah's bedside, where he looked down on him like one would an irritating rodent they couldn't get rid of.

"They fucking had one job," he muttered to himself. He redirected to Judah, fighting through the haze of painkillers that were barely killing any pain. "And you should have listened to me. Better to be my friend than my enemy."

Dubin reached for the phone by the bedside and wrenched it away from the wall, rendering it useless. All Judah could do was watch, the cocktail of drugs and his injuries making him incapable of much more than a feeble cry for help. Dubin held the gun higher on Nena. "Eh, eh. Don't move until I tell you."

Nena froze.

"Use the tape to tie up her hands. Don't want her getting any ideas."

Bridget's mouth dropped. "What, no! Tie her up? I can't . . . what?"

Dubin looked to the ceiling as if his patience was at its end. "Now, Bridget. Quickly. She's dangerous."

Bridget moved in front of Nena, her fingers pulling at the tape, stretching it out. "What is going on here?" she muttered to herself in French as she clumsily wrapped tape around Nena's wrists. Nena flexed them, trying to create space as Bridget wrapped.

"This makes no sense."

"Why not?" Nena said under her breath, her eyes remaining on Dubin as he inspected Judah's condition. Judah struggled to keep his eyes on him, but his swelling made tracking Dubin too hard.

Nena said, "You should be used to assisting bad men."

She winced as Bridget tightened the tape, not even close to being a pro at securing people.

"I have nothing to do with this, Aninyeh," Bridget whispered in Nena's ear. Her breath smelled like old wine. "I don't even know why he's here. I just followed him."

"Let's go," Dubin commanded, using the muzzle to urge Nena on. "In the living room. He's not going anywhere for the moment. He can barely stay awake."

Bridget drifted to the space between them, like she wasn't sure which side she should be on. Her words tripped over themselves. Her hand played with the roll of tape.

"I'm so sorry. He—so very sorry."

Was she? Nena recalled the times Bridget had tried to speak to her. How much of her history and her choices in bad men did Dubin know? Nena moved her wrists around.

"What is your deal with her?" Dubin snapped, his face contorted into a mask of incredulity. "Ever since we got here, you've been tiptoe-ing around this bitch like she was Mary, mother of God, about to walk on water or some shit."

Bridget flinched as she and Nena considered one another. Dubin didn't know. Bridget hadn't told him of her past as a groomer for traffickers. Dubin nudged them out of Judah's room, pulling the door mostly closed behind him and standing sentry in front of it as the two women walked into the open space.

Bridget said in a low voice, "Why did you have me bind her hands, darling? What is it she has done?" Her eyes held a different question, begging Nena not to say anything of their past.

"She's here to take care of her loose end. I happened to pass by and noticed the door was ajar."

Nena's lips pursed.

Dubin continued, "No security guard . . . she took him out! A renegade mercenary on the grounds. Oh yes, Ms. Knight, I know what you and your so-called Tribe do. I've heard the stories from my contacts."

So, this was the story Dubin was working on to explain why Odemba and Pengo would find her and Judah's dead bodies in this room in the morning. The wheels rotated right before Nena's eyes.

Bridget asked, "But what about the gun? Why would you bring a gun in here?"

"Protection. Baby, you got yourself a Montana man. We stay locked and loaded there. You know this." He moved into the living room, closer to Nena. She braced herself. "Do you realize she was coming for us next?"

Bewildered and unsure of the truth, Bridget shifted her eyes from Dubin to Nena, then to Judah's partially closed door.

Nena said, "How about you tell your wife that you came in here to kill Judah yourself?"

"Shut the fuck up!"

Dubin obscured her view of the door, hitting her hard across the mouth with the butt of his gun. Her knees buckled, and stars swam in all directions of Nena's vision as she staggered against the couch.

Dubin kicked out his foot, swiping Nena's legs from under her. She crashed to the floor on her bound hands and knees, falling harder because her hands weren't free to break her fall. She smacked the side of her cheek on the corner of the hard couch. Dubin was one of those, the type to kick people while they were still down, and he delivered one deep kick into Nena's stomach that felt like he had put the force of all Montana in it. She sucked in air like a Hoover with an object stuck inside the hose, each impact stealing her little bit of oxygen as he kicked her over and over. Nena felt her insides rearranging in ways she knew they shouldn't.

"This is absurd, and I'm calling security," Bridget said. "They will sort this out."

She strode to the phone on one of the side tables. Dubin moved away from Nena. He ripped the phone from Bridget's hand. His rage spewed at her insolence, and he backhanded her with the handpiece, the force flinging Bridget back like she weighed nothing. She stumbled, crashing into the wooden center table. The sound of it would have brought attention from whoever was in the room below if someone had been there.

Bridget was sprawled over the table and dazed. The only things that indicated she was conscious were the guttural moans coming from her as she moved awkwardly.

"Goddamn it, Bridget, why didn't you stay in our room? I asked you to do one thing, Bridget, and that was to stay in the goddamn room! Jesus!"

Bridget held the side of her bleeding lip. "You said you were going for a walk. You'd had too much to drink, and I didn't want you getting in trouble. They said we were supposed to stay in our quarters."

Dubin paced, the gun going back and forth while Nena calculated her chances of grabbing him without him firing and an errant bullet hitting her or Judah. "I told you I needed some air."

Nena said, "Apparently this room is the only place with air."

Dubin panted, heaving like the bear that he was as he glowered at Nena.

"See what you made me do? I love her and have never hurt my wife ever. Until you."

Nena looked up at him, tasting blood in her mouth, pushing herself to a better position. "Don't blame me because you're abusive."

Her comment garnered Nena another massive kick that confirmed to Nena that Dubin must have been the star kicker of his college football team with grand delusions of making it pro. His kicks were perfectly aimed and delivered maximum anguish. If she was a football, she would have soared through the goalposts for a perfect score.

Bridget said, "You're hurting her. Ms. Odemba—the chief constable and general—how will you explain to her?"

Dubin didn't answer, his original plan in flames. He kept the gun half aimed in Nena's general direction as he worked on yet another contingency. He glanced at the bedroom.

Nena sucked in deep gulps of painful air, using the table to shield her wrists as she continued to work at the tape. The one thing she could thank Bridget for was her horrible work at tying people up. She looked up at the ceiling and willed the galaxy swarming in circles above her like a crib mobile to dissipate.

She couldn't hold out any longer. Any more time with Dubin would be a disaster for her. He was unpredictable. He planned to kill Judah, and he'd kill Nena, too, and claim she'd tried to attack him.

What Nena needed was information first because when morning came, she'd need something solid on Dubin to bring him down. She didn't want to admit it, but she might need Bridget. The thought of needing anything from that woman was something she couldn't fathom.

She could take him hand to hand, she thought. But even she wasn't going to take a chance with an irate man with a gun on her at point-blank range. It wasn't yet time to strike.

Nena looked around the room, taking stock of what she could use. "I knew you'd come to finish your work."

He ignored her, coming around to face her. "On your knees," he commanded.

Nena stared up at him, refusing to do his bidding.

He didn't use a gun this time but his closed fist, which he barreled into her right temple. The pain sent white heat through her eyes, and blood rushed. The impact made her neck twist, reopening the cut she'd suffered from the flying debris at the operations building. Above the roar in her ears, Nena heard Bridget cry out.

Nena braced herself on the floor to stop her body from toppling over. She groaned the pain out as she fought to remain cognizant of what was going on.

Bridget looked from Nena, who'd managed to scoot herself up against the couch to a semiupright position, holding her pulverized stomach, to her husband, his gun pointed at Nena's chest as he glared at her with his blazing, reddened eyes.

"Stay back, Bridget. She's dangerous," he said.

Laughable, considering he was the one holding the gun and tossing her and his wife around. Any slight movement, any startle could make him put one in her. Bridget reasoned with him. Needed to distract him enough that Nena could get out of the line of fire. The gun, precariously pointed at Nena's chest, punctuated his words. She watched his hand and the finger on the trigger. It made her nervous. The tape loose enough, she inched her hand down her body toward her ankle, grazing her fingers over the handle of her hidden blade to get a good grasp on it.

"Did you tell her?" Nena said. "Tell her how you put a hit out on Mr. Asogi and Mr. Tegete so you were free to coerce the miners to sign exclusively with you and your firm. And you paid for the child to be kidnapped, ensuring everyone would be too terrified to do anything else but sign with you."

"I don't know what the hell you're talking about, putting hits out. I'm from freaking Montana!"

He pointed the barrel at her head, cocking the gun. Her body tensed, a silver ball of fear bouncing through her like in a pinball machine. He glanced at Judah's heavily sedated body.

Didn't matter how many times Nena had been on either side of a gun's muzzle, there was always fear when one was at the wrong end. And anyone who acted otherwise was full of crap. His clear blue eyes darkened. His voice was deep and promised he played no games. "On your knees. Hands where I can see them."

"You killed the last kidnapper to prevent him from outing you. Tell your wife."

"I was saving your life," Dubin deadpanned. "You're welcome, by the way."

"No, you killed him in cold blood." Nena tensed for another kick, but it didn't come.

Bridget said weakly, "What did you do, Frances?"

"Yes, Frances," Nena taunted. "What did you do?"

Painstakingly slow, Nena pulled the push dagger from its sheath.

"Anything I did was for us, Bridget. For the company and our future."

"He had Asogi's niece kidnapped," Nena called out.

Nena watched Bridget's delicate little fluttery hands going to her perfectly porcelain doll face in horror.

"Frances." Bridget's accent grew heavier the more upset she became.

"It was only to scare them into signing with us. We needed this deal. You know that."

"People died." Nena labored, hitching herself up farther.

If she could get in proper position. If she could keep distracting him so she could reach her blades, she might have a chance to make it out of here alive.

"No one was supposed to die," he explained, his gun hand dipping a few inches so it pointed at her stomach. Stomach wounds were horrible. Slow deaths. Nena eyed it cautiously. "They were only supposed to take her to force Asogi out of the deal. And make Tegete look unreliable, the righteous bastard. That was all. But . . ."

"But what? The kidnappers got greedy and changed the plan? Called her mother for ransom without your knowing, wanted money on top of whatever fee you paid?"

Dubin's face flushed beet red, and his mouth dropped, confirming Nena was on the right track.

Bridget crept to his side. "Why don't we just go?" She looked back at the door to Judah's room. "What are we even doing here?"

He blinked at her, unseeing. "What?"

Bridget gestured. "Just go, cut our losses? We don't need it. You have so many other ventures. So many other countries where you can get what you want. We don't need this place or their tanzanite. Let's just go, Frances."

In one giant step, he reared on her. Bridget quailed beneath his towering presence. The sound of his backhand across her face cracked like lightning splitting a midnight-black sky.

"Are you fucking demented, woman? This is the only place that has this gem, and I fucking want it! I rule supply and demand."

Dubin loomed over the body of his wife, glaring at her, breathing hard, totally lost in his rage. Nena heard a muffled thud behind him and hoped Dubin hadn't heard. She imagined Judah forcing himself to roll his broken body onto the floor. She bet the pain had knocked him out.

"And I can't leave him . . . alive. He can ID me. Some of his own people kidnapped him, so who knows what they told him or showed him."

Nena added, "You killed the last one."

"God, Frances." Bridget let out a strangled sound, a cross between a whimper and a cry. Her hand cupping where he'd hit her like she was trying to soothe away the pain he'd inflicted.

Bridget shook her head vigorously, her voice muffled from the hand at her mouth. "We can't. I can't do this anymore."

"Be silent, Bridget! I need to think."

So do I. Nena wiggled her hand from the tape. Gripped the handle of the blade tightly. Started sliding it out.

"I was just going to deal with Judah, and all would have been fine in the morning."

Nena's blade was nearly free.

"Like you did away with Asogi and Mr. Tegete?"

It was as if Dubin hadn't heard this accusation before. Dubin balked as if jolted by electricity. His face melted into confusion, and he looked down at her as if she'd grown two heads.

He started, "What are you talking about? I didn't do tha—"

His words died at what he saw.

The glint of her knife gripped in Nena's hand.

61

Dubin's eyes grew round and flicked back to Nena's, reading the murder in them. Dubin stepped back and aimed and shot at the same time as Nena ducked, already on the move. Her left hand lashed out, striking at his gun hand, pushing the muzzle away when a shot went off. Her right hand arched in the air and slammed her fist down on the top of his shoe with the blade protruding from it, driving it through the boot and into his foot.

Dubin howled at the ceiling, his long arms swinging wildly, swiping at her, but Nena was out of their reach. He staggered backward, his arms flailing in the air like propellers. He steadied himself just as Nena pulled another blade—one of the daggers she'd hid in her belt—from its sheath, arched in a half circle, and buried it into the calf of his other leg. He growled, bending to grab her by the hair.

Dubin wrenched her up, but she held on to the knife handle, letting it slice upward as he yanked her to him, tearing through tendon and muscle. He screamed, tossing her like a rag doll. Nena crashed into the table, where a lamp toppled on her. She tried to pivot away, but Dubin recovered too quickly, snatching her up again as easily as he'd done his wife.

Nena felt Dubin's brute strength and the rage feeding him through his rippling muscles. She had to make sure he didn't get on top of her, overpower her. She had to match his brawn with her wits and her experience in hand-to-hand combat. She needed something—anything—that she could use to bring him down. They spun in some sort of grotesque dance, the two of them crashing into an armchair. Nena ended up on top, and she fought to keep the upper hand. She couldn't find the gun. And the blades were in his leg or at his feet; she wasn't sure. She couldn't find them.

She beat at his hand, trying to break free of his grip on her shirt. He pulled her close to his face, too close. His breath rank, like sour alcohol and rancid meat.

"Let's see how you like it," he seethed as he drove one of her own cherished push daggers into her upper thigh.

Nena let out a long groan, shocked at the amount of pain. It didn't matter how many times she'd been on the bad end of a fight; the pain was always an unwelcome surprise. She wanted to howl, but doing that would have taken too much energy, and she needed to keep it together for as long as she could.

Dubin yanked out the dagger and raised it, probably to plunge it somewhere higher and lethal. Nena gripped Dubin's wrist, trying to keep the dagger from piercing the side of her neck. He was beneath her, half in the chair, half out, weakening.

But he wasn't too weak to win this backward match of arm wrestling. She pushed with one hand, trying to keep it away from her, trying to keep him from taking hold of her. She was losing the fight with the knife hand. The bloodied tip of Nena's own blade, like some sort of ridiculous hypocrisy, kept inching closer and closer to her carotid artery.

A shadow eclipsed the ceiling light over them. Nena couldn't see what was behind her, only sensing a presence, could focus only on taking out the man in front. Nena braced herself, preparing to go down fighting. She fought against her own weapon, now turned against her. The tip of the blade scraped her skin, then began to pierce it. If Dubin didn't go down soon . . . Nena couldn't afford to think about that.

Dubin tore his attention from Nena, looking past her. His clear blue eyes widened, fear in them, then horrific understanding. In them she could see the dark shape behind her. He shook his head, gurgled, "No." His grip loosened on her right hand, and his left arm struck out as if to stop what was happening behind her.

Nena jettisoned his body with one big push, still holding on to his hand, which held her knife, just as a sharp report cracked throughout the room, the noise so close it muted sound for Nena.

The bullet struck Dubin in the chest and he lost all control of his limbs, the dagger clattering to the floor. The force of the impact, of his surprise, pushed his body farther into the chair, its back legs scraping the carpet, catching in the plush and nearly toppling backward.

Nena staggered to her feet. She faced Bridget, whose cheek was inflamed from where he'd struck her. Bridget held the gun she'd retrieved during the struggle and was still pointing it, not at Nena but at her husband. Dubin watched her in complete befuddlement, pain not registering in his mind, only the betrayal and confusion at what his wife had done to him, and for whom.

Nena straightened, standing in Bridget's vicinity. They watched as Dubin's eyes shifted in and out of focus. When they focused, they homed in on Bridget, his eye contact never breaking from hers.

Bridget gaped at her dying husband. Nena looked to him, the dagger that had been in his hand now at his feet. His eyes lolled toward Nena.

The words fought with him, but eventually he succeeded only to say, "I did-n't ki-kil."

The last word ended in a slow exhale. His wound siphoning the little strength he had left, Dubin's body visibly deflated, slouching farther down in the chair. His eyes returned to his wife. She stepped closer to him, eyebrows furrowed and looking as if she'd go to pieces any moment now. Her hands shook. Shock would soon come for her. Nena bent to pick up her blades.

It was easier going down than coming back up, and with hesitation, Nena pushed herself to her feet. She breathed out through the pain. She looked at Dubin, considering what to do. The death that came for him was deserved. But he'd deserved prison, too, and Nena would have preferred him there, rotting for the rest of his pitiful life.

Nena put some distance between her and the Dubins. She went to the master bedroom and pushed the door open wider. Judah was on the floor, as she'd thought. He'd attempted to crawl toward the door. He was passed out on the floor. She considered helping him back into the bed but knew there was no time.

Two shots had been fired, and soon there would be people breaking down the door. Judah would be fine where he was until help came. Nena gazed at the dagger in her hand and the streaks of blood on it. She wiped one side of the blade on her dark pant leg. And then the other.

She regarded Bridget as the woman hovered over her husband, watching the life trickle from his body like the blood coming from his wounds.

Nena didn't know what to make of any of it. For once in her life, Nena's mind failed her. She had no explanation for what had just happened and what it meant for her that Bridget had saved her life now when Bridget hadn't lifted a finger before.

Over her shoulder, Bridget said, "You had nothing to do with this." She finally turned to face Nena, who had remained in the hall. She took Nena in, how she gingerly held her side where Dubin had pummeled it with his foot. Bridget's expression hooded and unreadable. Nena didn't know what she was really thinking.

"You had nothing to do with him," Bridget said in a hollow voice.

Nena hesitated. She and Bridget had been here before, on the precipice of a life change, with Bridget asking for Nena's trust. The last time Bridget had had the chance to save a life, she'd handed Nena over like a trussed-up doll and assisted in taking that life.

What if Nena left, only for Bridget to go with Dubin's original story, telling them that Nena attacked them and killed Dubin? Nena's experience with Bridget was riddled with deceit and betrayal. *Before*, when Nena was fourteen, she'd had no resources, no one behind her, no one to protect her. But now, *after*, there was an entire Tribe behind her.

Bridget lifted a shoulder, sensing Nena's suspicion. "It's not the first time he's hit me. This time he went too far, and I was afraid for my life. He was drunk and high. There is a baggie of coke in his bags." The ease with which Bridget created her story from air made Nena uncomfortable. It meant Bridget could do that to anyone, to her.

"Go, Nena. Getting you out of here is the least I can do for you."

Well, that part was true.

Nena considered Bridget a long while. Someone had to have called for help. Someone would be coming soon. She moved toward the doors leading to the balcony.

She watched Bridget and the gun hanging limply in her hand the entire time. Bridget looked down at her hand, seemed to notice what was in it, and dropped the gun with a dull thud on the carpeted floor.

Nena said, "You need to give them his phone showing his communication with the kidnappers."

"And the assassins," Bridget said quickly, sneaking a quick look at the dead body.

Nena had many questions and no time to ask. So much to still figure out about the woman before her, the first being if Bridget was for real or if she was a wolf in sheep's clothing.

62

Nena hesitated, consumed by her questions, like why Bridget had groomed all those children and proffered them like candy to the monsters of the world.

"You should leave now, Aninyeh. Before they come."

Nena pointed with her blade. "I told you not to call me that. That girl died for you the moment you handed me off to that monster."

Bridget was confused. "Robach?" She fluttered a hand when it dawned on her. "Yes, well . . ."

"You knew what type of man you were delivering me to."

"Those years were not my finest, A—Nena. I am not proud of what I was."

Nena shrugged.

"You are correct. There are no words to excuse the role I played in Paul's operation."

"As a groomer," Nena emphasized.

Bridget studied Nena, a spark of something in her eyes that Nena couldn't quite figure out. "Paul is gone. If I share the same fate, will you be satisfied?"

"You are the very last one on a very short list." Nena held up her thumb and index finger only an inch apart.

"But I didn't harm you."

Nena gawked. The audacity. "Your inaction was the most harmful. By looking the other way. By lulling us into a sense of security while in your care, making us feel like maybe things weren't the way we thought it would be." Nena's eyes stung, but she refused to let the tears fall. Not over Bridget, not so the woman could see just how devastated Nena was because of her.

Nena said, "You were the worst out of all of them."

All Bridget's hard years, years heavy with guilt and this burden, showed in every wrinkle that appeared. "I am very sorry, Nena."

"Screw your sorry."

It felt so good to say. It felt as good as the bullet Nena wanted to use on this woman. Nena raised her bladed hand again, the urge to drive it into one of Bridget's eyes intensifying.

The woman raised her hands slowly, as if in surrender. "Then do what you must." She waited a beat. "But think of your family. I have spent many years shedding those days of working with Paul. I have tried to atone for my part. No one knows about it. Except you. Not even Frances." She gestured to her dead husband. "You are the only one with my secret and can ruin me if you choose. Is that not enough? To wield the guillotine over my head? Go now and wield it. I will tell them I killed him. And they will believe me."

"Why, because you're a White woman, and they're always believed?" Nena snapped, her eyes narrowing as she dared Bridget to contradict what they both knew was a tale as old as time.

"Because I am his wife," Bridget shot back. "And I can prove he was a bad man. I'll tell them everything they need to know about his intentions to manipulate both the government and the miners and tank the reformation," Bridget said in a rush, looking nervously at the front door. At any moment the guards would be at the door. "I'll show them the explosives that were used in the mine collapse. Frances supplied them. He has the receipts, and I know where they are."

She took a breath. "And you keep my secret. Don't tell anyone what I did, and I'll just walk away. You'll never see me again."

Nena gritted her teeth, Bridget's truth rubbing her raw. Slowly, she shook her head, not wanting to play this game, not believing this is what all this had come to.

"I am not double-crossing you," Bridget said.

Nena lowered her blade. Even when she begged forgiveness, Bridget was always thinking of number one. Herself.

"If you kill me, you risk bringing down your family and the organization they built. Am I worth that?"

She was good. So good. Nena let out a dry laugh, shaking her head. Too good. And too right.

"You have not changed."

Bridget looked sad, truly sad. "Oh, but I have, Nena. I owe you for the rest of my life. There is nothing I can do to make up for what I did. But I can start now." She pointed at her dead husband. "I've already begun to start."

Outside the room, they heard security at the door.

They listened.

"It's not just you anymore to think about."

It wasn't just Nena anymore. It was her father and mother. Her sister. Her nephew and Georgia. It was Cort and Keigel and the Tribe. There was more at stake now than ever before, much more to risk than her own life and her desire to exact revenge.

Nena felt Bridget had been the worst of them all, but she was not a killer. Not until now. And when she finally killed, it was for Nena.

She thought of Cort's question. When was enough, enough?

The increase of noise on the other side of the door drew their attention. More hotel security, Nena guessed. Or Pengo's police force.

"Hurry," Bridget said urgently, waffling between where they stood and going to the door where security pounded. "They come."

Nena and Bridget stood on a precipice. Everything melted away around them. Nena weighed her options, thinking about her conversation with her mother only days ago.

You have come so far. And if you kill her, you will only go right back to where you were . . .

Nena's eyes glanced at Dubin, to the hall leading to Judah, and back to Bridget again. The pounding on the door intensified. Calls for someone with the passkey became more frantic.

. . . live well in spite of what she did to you. Let it go . . .

"Make sure they see to him immediately." Nena inclined her head toward the bedroom. Bridget nodded her understanding. Her cheeks flushed and eyes alert.

"And you'll keep it quiet? About the whole ordeal with Paul?"

Nena nearly laughed. Ordeal. Is that all what had been done to her and many other children was?

Bridget hesitated a second, her mouth forming a tight line of dismay when she didn't get her answer. Nena's eyes glossed over Dubin. The man was good and dead.

Bridget followed Nena to the balcony, keeping her distance as security scanned the key.

Nena opened the balcony door and stepped through, the sheer curtains billowing. Her breath came with the wind.

At the railing, she looked down and saw Billy down below, on the wrong side of the railing, and his relief when he saw her. Evers paced the small platform, his hands on his head until he saw her and pumped a fist in the air, then put his hands on his hips, feigning cool. Nena's mouth quirked.

She threw a leg over, and Bridget's final words tethered her in place.

"I can never make up for what I did. But I can do now what I should have before, and that was to save you."

Nena's heart triple-timed. Her vision swam with a hot mix of enraged tears that she swallowed. She refused to let Bridget get any emotion from her.

"Understand that you did not save me. Not then. Not now."

Bridget stilled, immobilized by the weight of Nena's words.

"I saved myself."

It had taken every ounce of energy she had for Nena to make a different choice in the face of her past. Nena hoped Aninyeh would be at peace with it. Nena surveyed the looming ground below, which looked more ominous as she peered down.

Security burst through the suite doors, greeted by a fresh flood of Bridget's crocodile tears and her devolvement into utter panic. She sank to the floor, blubbering that she'd been forced in there by her husband. Nena kicked her other leg over the railing, hopping off into the void before she could be spotted, with only Billy's outstretched hand as he leaned precariously over Femi's balcony railing to catch Nena when she leaped.

63

"Nena, you really said that shit? You really said"—Keigel cleared his throat, giving Nena some expression, a cross between sultry and googly eyed—"'I saved myself'? You really said that to the French lady? No bullshit?"

Nena shook her head. "Why would I lie?"

Keigel was dubious. "I'm just saying that was pretty badass. Everything sounds right out of a damn movie, a cross between a 007 and Lifetime, not that I watch that shit." He suddenly found his sneaker interesting and began brushing the invisible dust off of it.

Nena side-eyed him. "Lifetime?" She raised an eyebrow. "Really?"

He shrugged, refusing to answer, and continued to dust.

"I'm not suave nor sophisticated enough to be 007 level." Nena appreciated Keigel's excitement. He lived for these adventures-of-Nena stories, and she figured her time in Tanzania was no different.

He shook his head ruefully. "Man, I wish I'd been there. You should have let me come along. I'd have schooled Judah right. He seemed like an up-and-down dude. I feel what he was trying to do."

Nena knew Keigel would. Despite all the drama Judah had brought, his ultimate agenda was to make sure his people were taken care of. But he had allowed his anger and prejudice to cloud his judgment.

"It's hard to trust again after there's been history of abuse," Keigel said. "I can't blame him for that. It's like here in America. Sure, some shit's changed from when Black folks were enslaved, but not everything. We're still treated like second class sometimes. I can go to the shops at the beach and walk down the street about to jump into Louis V with stacks, ready to buy up the whole shop. There can be drunk-ass White folk sprawled on the street, and police will still trail me, or White ladies will hold their purses tighter, thinking I'm about to snatch 'em up. Makes it hard to remember all the progress that *has* happened because when we dip into their spaces, we're always reminded of our place."

Keigel spoke the truth. Change wasn't words or papers alone. The change would have to become the norm.

"They're gonna have to show homeboy that things have changed. And then, even then, he'll never forget how shit used to be. That's the curse of trauma."

Nena knew how trauma could cling like tar. Despite all the strides one could make after surviving one's darkest moments, the curse of the trauma always remained in the shadows, lingering there for a moment when recall occurred, and it could all come rushing back like a Mack truck.

"They just have to give Judah time until he feels comfortable that no one is going to screw them over," Keigel said.

"They can't. It's all signed and sealed between the Latemans and the Tanzanian government. Couple weeks ago, according to my dad."

Keigel gave her a dubious look. "The Emancipation Proclamation freed Black folk, but some remained enslaved until months later. So, sometimes a piece of signed paper don't mean shit. It's actions that count."

Nena promised to share Keigel's thoughts with Tegete. She hadn't thought of it that way. She knew Tegete wouldn't let his fellow Tanzanians fall to the wayside now that the reformation was finalized. He'd make sure there was action behind the talk. And hopefully Odemba, as the acting minister, would continue all Asogi had started, though Nena suspected that Asogi's sister would run for his office and win. At least, Nena hoped so.

Keigel remained serious a moment longer; then his true nature broke through, and he broke out into a lascivious grin. "How about the women?" His eyebrows waggled up and down like some villain in a black-and-white movie. "They looked good as shit, right?"

Nena reeled from the sudden topic change, her thoughts still on the assassination. "Shit never looks good."

"You know what I mean! They had some baaaad ones?" Keigel smirked. "I know it."

Why did she even entertain this conversation. "If appearance is all that matters to you."

"The first thing people see is not someone's brain, know what I mean?" He acted as if he were dropping serious knowledge. "Real talk, it's the looks that draw you in, and then the rest of the package that keeps you there." He pointed at her. "Remember that. Write it down. It's gonna be in my memoir that Obama will narrate."

Nena's eyebrows furrowed. "The former president?"

"Yeah, and then it's gonna be on Oprah's Book Club," he snapped. "Mark that shit, Nena."

She nodded, humoring him, then became serious when he seemed to be settling back down.

"Real talk." Keigel leveled a sober expression at her. "Leaving that lady untouched in that hotel room must have been tough. How you didn't off her is beyond me. But—" he drawled out when Nena looked like she was about to interject. "I get that she killed old boy instead of you." He inclined his head. "That means something."

"It doesn't mean I forgive her or that I forget," Nena said grimly. "Or that I'm done with her. It just meant she got a temporary reprieve until I sorted everything out. Bridget had to wait because there were more pressing issues I was dealing with."

Keigel nodded sagely. "Yeah, like not breaking your damn neck leaping off balconies and shit like some damn spy." His head nod switched to shaking his head at Nena disapprovingly. "Anyway, what happened when homeboy caught you and pulled you back in the hotel room?"

Nena played a mental game of name match with Keigel's creative nicknames. If "old boy" was Dubin, then "homeboy" had to be Billy, Nena surmised. As Nena sat in her backyard among her flourishing plants and the skinny lemon tree she had planted when she'd first moved to her neighborhood of Citrus Grove because it had reminded her of home, she regaled her closer-than-best friend with stories of her time in Tanzania.

Keigel had known just the thing she'd want as soon as she landed back in Miami at the private airstrip. Her American comfort food. Two empty white Styrofoam containers filled with the bones of lemon-pepper wings and balled-up bacon cheeseburger wrappers from Jake's lay on the glass-and-black-wrought-iron table between them as they each kicked back in matching plush chaise lounges after devouring the food.

"I jumped off the edge of the closest balcony, and Billy caught my hand."

It had been a pretty good catch too. Nena had been impressed once her racing heart petered down to a respectable rate.

"He pulled me up with the help of Evers."

Keigel sneaked her a sly look. "One too many wings?"

She cut her eyes at him. "You shouldn't make jokes about people's weight. It's insensitive."

Keigel snorted loudly. "Says the woman who kills people for a living. But I bet those folks think you taking 'em out was a little insensitive too."

He howled, thinking he was so smart, while Nena contemplated adding Keigel to the number of folks on her kill list, especially with the smug look on his face.

"Femi was trying to stall the guards at our door who were trying to get in and check on us after the alert went out about the Dubins upstairs. And we got inside the suite just in time for the constable's officers to come in and ensure we were all there and accounted for."

"Hold up, hold up. What about the fresh blood? They didn't ask you about that?"

She nodded. "I wear all black for a reason." Her mouth quirked. "And Femi might have thrown me a towel for a quick wipe. But truthfully, they were so out of sorts they weren't looking hard."

"I asked after Judah, if he'd awakened, and the constable was not forthcoming. But he permitted Billy, Evers, and me to go to our rooms for the remainder of the night."

"What about Judah? How'd he even get snatched up and end up with the little girl?"

That was a whole story in itself, and when Judah finally woke up under guard in the hotel room, he hadn't been able to remember how he'd gotten there. When the guards allowed Nena and the team out of their rooms the following morning, she'd been escorted to Judah's room, where he'd explained how he'd returned to his home after the meeting with her in his car and began to hear rumbles of a splinter group of villagers preparing for some big job. They'd tried to enlist him, promised huge money to kidnap the prime minister's niece. Said a man named Montana was paying them big money to take her and force the mining deal to be abandoned.

"Montana, as in old boy?" Keigel asked.

Nena nodded. "Dubin."

Judah had demanded they not go through with it. He'd known Dubin was up to no good after the negotiations, especially when he realized it was Dubin who'd planted those seeds that Asogi was going to double-cross them. When the group didn't seem to believe him, Judah went to confront Dubin. Dubin had refused to stop his plans, and when Judah threatened to reveal everything to Asogi and Tegete, Dubin had him taken and held in the operations building, where he was beaten and told he'd be blamed for everything.

Nena had figured as much when she'd seen Judah's look-alike at the town hall. Dubin had done it all to ensure the deal went his way, that the relationship among the parties had deteriorated so much that there was no way they'd work together, leaving the miners vulnerable and prime for the picking. A vulture, just as Nena had called him.

"But what about the assassination?" Keigel asked. "Judah didn't know about that?"

That was where Nena was unsure. Dubin had to be behind the assassination. That was the conclusion they'd all come to in the end, and with him dead by Bridget's hand, they couldn't well confirm with him. However, the paperwork Bridget released to them, as she had promised, reflected that Dubin intended to deal with the miners directly and that if they didn't fall in line, he had planned to use force to make them sign over their rights and property. The cell Bridget also produced showed a direct connection between him and the kidnappers, with text messages when she was kidnapped confirming they'd gotten the girl.

"He killed the kidnapper so he couldn't identify him." Keigel shook his head. "Of course he did. I tell you, these people . . ." He scratched the back of his head in disbelief. "What about Asogi and Tegete?"

Nena shrugged. "I guess Dubin took that one to his grave."

Something still bothered her about it. In Dubin's hotel suite, he'd seemed genuinely surprised about the assassination. He'd said he wasn't involved in it, and as much as Nena didn't want to, a small part of her believed him.

"That's some fucked-up shit," Keigel opined, "but I guess that's what people do, huh? Fucked-up shit to one another."

"Doesn't make it right," she said, thinking about the unnecessary loss of life, all for money and power. Always for money and power. Luckily Tegete was recovering and would be there to help Latema and the Asogis pick up the pieces.

Keigel was solemn. "Naw, it don't. Just means we gotta work harder to unfuck the shit people do. That's why what you and the Tribe do is what folks need, even if they don't think they need it." He pointed a long finger at her. "And don't ever doubt the Tribe or your dad. But most of all, Nena girl, don't ever doubt what *you're* about."

64

"You missed my first game," Georgia said. It wasn't an accusation but a simple statement of fact.

Nena bumped Georgia's knee with her own. "I'm sorry. You know. Work."

"I get it. It's okay. You're here now. That's what matters." Georgia sneaked a side peek at Nena sitting next to her as she gazed out onto the field. "Did you really save a little girl? Like, for real, for real? She was kidnapped, and you like went in like Liam Neeson and legit saved her?"

Georgia was on a roll, with a sly grin stretching across her face. "Did you tell the bad guys you had"—Georgia's voice lowered to a raspy tenor—"a 'certain set of skills'?" She covered her mouth with her hand, giggling.

"That's a movie, Georgia. And he's an actor." Nena had to add, "I'm the real thing."

Georgia flashed her side-eye, raising her hands in concession. "Okayyyy, I see you. Funny thing is you're being for real, you're not flexing."

Nena peeked down at the inside of her upper right arm. Her eyebrows furrowed. "What do my muscles have to do with anything?"

Georgia grimaced. "Wow, Nena, you really are way too literal for your own good. I've got major work to do."

Nena let that one roll, unsure what she had said or done wrong, but Georgia broke out into a soft chuckle, dismissing the whole thing. "It's cool, and what you did was cool. I'm glad she's safe. It's scary when someone takes you like that." Her head dropped, and Nena knew Georgia was remembering when she had been snatched right out of Cort's hands by Ofori and held with a gun to her head by Paul. Nena knew that fear all too well. It was a horrible experience that she, Georgia, and now Abiola shared. One that was lasting. But they'd survived it.

Georgia took a deep breath, straightening her long legs out in front of her. This time when she spoke, she was introspective. "So, it's not *only* killing for you."

"No, it's not only killing, if that's how you must think about it," Nena answered. "Sometimes it's saving a life, not just taking one. Most times, it's trying to make lives better."

"Yeah, I think I like that."

"And you know who taught me that lesson? About sometimes choosing life?"

Georgia eyed her suspiciously, lips pursed because she knew where Nena was going, and she wasn't thrilled.

"Your dad."

Georgia groaned, rolling her eyes in that annoying way only teenagers could when they didn't want to admit their parent was right or halfway cool. But Georgia didn't need to say anything. Nena could tell by the way Georgia turned back to the peewee football game that Cort was assisting Keigel coach, watching her father with a renewed appreciation.

Georgia spoke. Nena had to strain because it was hard to hear her over the roar of the watching crowd. "Can I tell you something?"

"Always."

"When I realized I broke Sasha's nose—" Georgia hesitated, took a breath, then forced herself to press on. "When I saw all that blood gushing and the way she screamed. The feel of the bone when it crunched . . ."

Georgia wiped quickly at one eye. And then the other. Nena waited patiently for her to continue when she was ready.

"It wasn't like I thought it would be. It wasn't like when we train. It was . . ." She dropped off, unable to verbalize her thoughts.

Nena helped her. "It was real."

Georgia nodded thankfully. "Too real. And I realized something else."

"You don't like hurting people."

Georgia shrugged, ducking her head. "Not like that. I mean . . ."

"You don't have to explain."

She looked over at Nena, worried that maybe Nena would think less of her. Would be disappointed. Her question sat on her lips, but she was too scared to speak it.

Nena helped her again. "I'm glad it was too real for you, and you don't like hurting people. I don't either." Nena sighed. "It's not for everybody. And it was never meant for you."

"It wasn't meant for you either."

Nena said nothing to that because she really believed that it was. She couldn't imagine being anything else, and she realized she was fine with it.

"I like knowing that I can," Georgia continued, feeling the need to explain anyway. "But I like knowing I don't have to much more. And I know you had to but that you only do what you have to do. I love you, Nena."

The backs of Nena's eyes stung something fierce. Her chest swelled to near explosive proportions. She looked down at her lap, then after a moment was able to look into Georgia's luminous brown eyes, at all the hope and future excellence that resided in them. The same look she saw when she looked into Asym's. And Nena knew she'd do anything in this world to ensure the two of them would soar above her and everyone else. And Nena would do it not because she had to but because she wanted to, ten times over.

Nena watched Keigel and Cort on the sideline. She was at peace. She didn't think about work or whatever was going on in some part of the world. She didn't think about the next issue that would arise the following day or what her next mission would be. She didn't even think about Bridget.

Nena chose life over death. To be clear, Nena still wanted retribution. Only this time, hers would be to live well and happily, with no ghosts from the past haunting her.

It was finally something Nena could live with.

65

The next night, Nena tried not to let her exasperation come through. "Mum, I don't need anything more in my room. I am only in here to sleep."

Delphine appraised her daughter. "It doesn't look like you're getting enough of that, dear. Perhaps you need to go on holiday."

"I was just in a tropical country."

Delphine twisted her lips in response. Her eyes swept over the dark-gray comforter and the minimalist furniture that served dual purposes. The dresser and armoire held her clothes and doubled as her weapons vaults. Delphine pulled a drawer out, riffling through and coming across a hidden compartment. Her look was guarded as she peeked inside, spying some of Nena's blades.

"Darling, come on. I don't think you need to distribute your things everywhere. What would Cort think if he came across this? Bras and a . . . knife."

"Not just any knife." Nena scowled, closing the drawer for her. "Cort doesn't go through my things. He's respectful."

"I'm your mum. I don't need to be respectful." Delphine waited a beat. "He's been back here, yes?"

Nena wasn't doing this, especially not with her mother. "How about I put a kettle on before I run you back to the house?"

"Don't bother, the car will retrieve me when I call. I don't like you out late at night." Delphine paused, a ghost of a smile playing on her lips when she noticed Nena's confusion. "I know being out late is the least of the worries I should have about your safety. But humor your dear old mum, yes?"

"Sure, Mum." Nena didn't wait longer, opting to be gone before Delphine could organize her underwear drawer next.

She was in her kitchen, waiting for the shrill of the kettle, when she noticed her TV screen showing white in her backyard. She thought she'd turned it off before her mother's unannounced visit. She must have clicked off too fast without pointing the remote properly at the sensor. She rounded the island counter, approaching the double french doors, and unlocked one. She pressed her thumb to the pad, deactivating the door sensors, and opened the door, greeted by the after-rain-showers smell.

Nena first noticed the remote wasn't in the exact position she'd left it on the table at the same time she heard the high-pitched multiclicking of a chambering gun as she reached for the remote. She froze, her fingers splayed out and hovering over the remote. Her ears strained to hear who was there, heavy or light. Male or female. She noticed a faint scent of perfume. She straightened.

"Isn't this poetic, chérie? It all started with little Aninyeh and now? Now, it ends with Knight."

The voice came from behind. Nena turned slowly, expecting a bullet to hit at any moment. Her eyes scanned the layout of the backyard before finally settling on Bridget.

"Did you think that was it in Tanzania between us?" Bridget cocked her head. "Truly?"

How had she gotten in? Scaled the high back fence? Had Nena forgotten to arm the backyard because of her mother's sudden arrival? Yes. Yes, she had. She'd switched off the TV, run inside to answer the door, and totally neglected to follow her normal routine due to the disruption.

Still, Nena was normally so good about arming security even during changes in routine. Not tonight, though. She was gutted. The one night she slipped and an unwanted came calling was the night that one of the most precious people in the world to her was there. Nena hoped her mother remained out of sight.

Bridget stood luminescent in the moonlight. Her teeth shone as she spoke. She indicated with her gun that they should step inside.

Nena thought quickly. Whatever they needed to do should be done out here and far away from her mother.

Bridget jerked her head toward the door. "In." Gone was her breathless damsel-in-distress tone from Tanzania.

Nena obliged with Bridget right at her heels. She'd been taken by surprise. Bridget had found where she lived and infiltrated her home, proving she had always been more than met the eye. Bridget was, after all, the woman behind the most reprehensible men. And Nena was realizing, too late, that maybe Bridget choosing them was entirely by design.

Bridget followed Nena into the living room, as far away from the open-doored bedroom as possible. Bridget barely glanced at the room, assuming Nena was all alone. Nena hoped Delphine heard them and would know to stay put.

"You see, I considered letting you go, bygones be bygones. But then I thought I don't fancy a guillotine looming over my head. And I don't fancy Paul's killer wielding it." She said the last part with an anger Nena recognized because she'd held the same kind. The vengeful kind.

Nena said nothing. Her eyes watched Bridget's every move, memorizing them.

Biding her time.

"Thank you for providing the perfect opportunity to rid myself of Frances. He'd become too much a liability. He was a—what do

Americans say—a blockhead. Too obnoxious and always underestimating everyone else while overestimating himself. Just like a man. You agree, oui?"

Nena didn't answer.

Nena focused on the pattern of her wood floor. She should have taken care of Bridget when she'd had the chance. This was what she got for granting reprieves to people she knew didn't deserve them.

"Paul and I . . . were partners in everything. I knew everything. About his hatred for your father—the father who had his head—" She ran her finger across her neck and then twirled it in the air, smiling.

Anger rocketed through Nena, and she tensed her body so she would not move. Her mother was in the house. She had to think about her mother.

Bridget continued, "I know about their history. Did you know Paul revered him, even though Paul was loath to admit it. It's quite interesting the depth in which people hold grudges and seek revenge. Not just on that person. But on toute leur lignée." *Their whole lineage.*

"Which is why he sent you to the worst possible client, Robach. Les péchés du père." *The sins of the father.*

"And all that sort." Bridget flipped her free hand, a mere inconvenience.

Her mother was in the house. Nena had to remember. She regulated her breathing. She wouldn't give this woman anything more. Not an ounce of emotion. Not a speck of anything.

The words wanted to tumble out, making Nena feel ill that she had gone there when she was trying to not give the woman an inch. Every moment depended on Nena keeping herself calm and Bridget not.

"If you haven't realized it by now, I like the control. And you knowing of my past, having the ability to tell the world about me when I have worked tirelessly to scrub it clean, is not an option for me."

"So what you're saying is you didn't kill Dubin for me after all?" Nena asked. She put a hand to her heart. Made a sad face.

Bridget laughed. "I couldn't care less what he did with you. But I know when the deal's gone bad. My unfortunate husband did not, and I had to decide which was my biggest threat. I didn't need anyone knowing who was truly behind Asogi's death and my attempt to seat that insipid Odemba in his place."

"Odemba?"

"She's untouchable now as acting prime minister. But she wants nothing to do with me, either, now that DubiCorp has gone under because of Frances's death." She rolled her eyes. "Well, you know. You were there."

Odemba had been hard to figure out. Nena hadn't thought she'd conspire against Asogi. And with her now in his seat, there was no way to get to her.

Yet.

Nena bided her time excruciating moment by excruciating moment.

"If you think your partner Paul was thinking of you in the end, you're wrong. Or that he was going to have you by his side if he took over the Tribe, you're wrong there too." Nena's hand slowly inched south.

Bridget's face flushed, transforming into fury and hatred and jealousy with a tiny speck of doubt that Nena might be right, and Paul had never intended for her to be in his plans.

"Once he took High Council and the Tribe, he was going to desert you." Nena looked defiantly at Bridget and into the barrel of the gun pointed at her chest.

"Fucking bitch," Bridget fumed, letting loose a string of barely coherent sentences in her native tongue. The grip on her gun loosened slightly.

Bridget was nearly at her tipping point. She'd lose control, and then it would be Nena's turn.

"I think it bothers you that the little African girl you thought you destroyed survived while you just prepared things for everyone else, groomer that you are." Nena shrugged. "But *I* remain the chieftains' daughter." Nena raised two fingers in the air. "Twice over."

66

Where those words came from—who those words came from—Nena didn't know. But there was power behind them. The story of Aninyeh Asym. Of Nena Knight. And Echo and everything she'd been through and had survived. Bridget could shoot her dead right now and never take from Nena who she was, who she'd become.

But Nena didn't plan on dying that night. Bridget had handed Nena off to Robach and driven away with a smile. She wouldn't be doing that tonight.

"I did you a favor," Nena told her. "With Paul."

Nena raised her finger, ran it across her neck, and then twirled it in the air in perfect imitation. "You're welcome."

Bridget screamed, rushing at Nena, Bridget's anger clouding her judgment. Clouding was good. Closer was good and just what Nena wanted. Nena feinted right, lashing her arm out, her hand flipping upward and out and open.

The gun went off next to Nena's left ear, the deafening explosion nearly rendering Nena senseless and muting sound. Her throw was good. Bridget gasped, as if she'd sucked a nut into her windpipe.

Bridget's hand flew to her neck, feeling around the short handle of the push blade embedded into the side of her neck. She took a stunned, staggering step back, her eyes round and rolling. Like her husband.

The wound was superficial, intended to stun Bridget and get Nena out of the gun's crosshairs. But not entirely.

Bridget let off a wild shot, the bullet glancing off the corner of the chrome-edged ottoman and hitting Nena in the side as she rolled away from the gun's direct line of fire.

Nena barely felt the hit. She would later.

There was no time to react, to think about the gun in her other hand still pointed in Nena's general direction.

She kicked one of her decorative vases at Bridget. Another wild shot to the ceiling as Bridget fumbled, cursing in French. In English. And something incoherent. Nena shot her arm out, using the distraction to push at the base of the ottoman.

Bridget pulled the blade out. It clattered to the floor when she flung it. Her fingers pressed at the wound in her neck. She glared at Nena.

Nena groped around the hidden compartment beneath the ottoman, one of several throughout the house for occasions such as this. Nena whipped a gun out, swinging her arm around just as Bridget pulled her own up, putting Nena in her crosshairs.

They fired.

The gunshots echoed in the room, reverberating in the small, once immaculate home that, up until that night, no one had ever breached.

One looked at the other, neither moving. They remained. Nena's left ear throbbed, the ringing pulsing to a frenzy within her head that made the immediate headache pounding. Sound just buzzing back after the first gunshot had gone off beside it. She held her breath, her mind going to the source of the blossoming pain, spreading wide like the petals of a lilac.

The wildness in the pupils of Bridget's eyes began to fade as her hand slid from her neck. Nena saw the small hole in her expensive white button-down blouse. And then the dot of blood growing behind and around it. Bridget fell forward, a growing red stain around a blackened bullet hole to her chest. Her body made a hard thud as she hit the wood-paneled floor, her head nearly falling into Nena's lap.

Nena was frozen in position, her mind trying to compute how Bridget had fallen forward instead of the opposite way. Then her wits returned. Nena looked up into the eyes of her mother.

67

Delphine Knight was still, gun pointed down at the ground as she watched Bridget's corpse. Her face, first expressionless, faded to an untroubled resolve. She had a preternatural calm to her that grounded Nena in a way only a child could get from their parent, knowing that they'd handle it.

Nena remembered this look. It was the same one she'd seen the first night they met. When Delphine had crawled from beneath the bodies of the would-be muggers who attacked her in the alleyway on a Parisian street. Right after Aninyeh killed them. Delphine had assessed them as if they were ugly pieces of furniture. Had opened her phone. And called the Tribe's Cleaners for a double order.

Delphine's and Nena's eyes met. In them Nena read no fear, no breakdown at the realization there was a dead woman lying on the floor. The dispatch of Bridget Dubin was merely a scene that now needed to be cleaned. Delphine, the grandmother, mother, the horrible cook who made their house a home, had taken a life and had not batted an eye.

She flicked a look down at the body, then back up at her child, and gave a little twist of her shoulders as if to say *And what?* Nena could only remain wide eyed. Words failing her. All she could think was that Delphine Knight was a complete badass.

"I told you her time would come," Delphine said. She was so cold, Nena shivered. "I'm glad it was on my watch."

Nena took a beat. "Shit," Nena breathed, the only thing she could think to say.

Delphine gave her daughter a look that said *What? This?* "Don't act all surprised, dear girl." She scoffed. "Do you know who I am?"

Then, Delphine Knight turned her back on the dead.

68

This wasn't some off-site mission monitored by Network. Nena and her mother were in a neighborhood full of people who would have heard the multiple shots. They were in Nena's home. There was no time to waste before the authorities were possibly called. Or if Bridget came with people, how long would it be before they came looking? Did anyone know she was here? Or did Bridget come under the cloak of darkness to tie up loose ends with no witnesses? Nena bet on the second. Still, just in case, Nena needed to protect her mother.

The ringing in Nena's ear reduced to a teeth-setting buzz, and Nena caught her breath at the pain when she rolled to her hands and knees. The acrid smell of gunpowder permeated the air. She used the ottoman to help her to her feet, casting a wary eye toward the prone body, and then another at her mother.

She hissed as she tried to stanch the blood flow at her side, where Bridget's second bullet had hit its mark, intended or not. She made her way to the body, wincing at each movement her body was forced to make. She checked Bridget for any signs of life, finding none. Not a beat or a flicker. Bridget Dubin was good and dead and hopefully in hell with Paul and Dubin and Robach.

Nena had tried to choose differently, to be a little Cort-like in moving on. To not let death be the only way she dealt with the devils of her past. But Bridget had refused to allow it. Bridget had chosen to end things between them differently, with one of them alive and the other not.

Now Nena would have to get new flooring. And reassess her security because how could someone like Bridget infiltrate her home?

Nena startled at the barrage of banging at her front door. The movement sent pain jolting through her. Company had come too quickly. Multiple gunshots were hard to ignore. But there was no way the authorities were here that fast. Nena stood up and began hitching her way toward the door, gesturing for Delphine to get in the back room quickly. Whoever was at the door, there was no way she was going to let them get to her mother or know she'd been the one to pull the trigger. They'd have nothing on Delphine Knight.

Her mother tried to say no. She wanted to stay, wanted to make sure there weren't more out there trying to get her daughter. But Nena was trained for this, not Delphine. Nena jerked her head toward the bedroom.

"In my room, in the closet. Stay there until I say otherwise."

The door rattled from the banging.

"Come with me," Delphine said, unafraid. Ready to fight. Nena had never been prouder. This was one of the many reasons why Noble was utterly in awe of this woman. And why everyone else was, for that matter.

"Please," Nena begged. "For me."

Her mother finally acquiesced and left, taking the gun—was it Nena's or one Delphine had? Nena wasn't sure—with her.

Nena opened the door, finding Keigel there. There was relief in both their eyes. Him to see her alive and well. Her to see it wasn't Bridget's backup or the authorities nearly breaking down her reinforced door.

Keigel's eyes searched her from head to toe to confirm she was okay. His thick eyebrows were creased and his forehead held rows of worry lines Nena had never seen before. In the several years they'd been neighbors, there had never been a stir at her house. The neighborhood was relatively safe and quiet, despite having residents like Nena and Keigel, but tonight there had been a violation.

Nena looked around his tall frame. Someone so slender managed to nearly take up the doorway as if a rescue made him hulk up. In a minute, he might turn green. Behind Keigel, his crew stood guard, locked and loaded like some neighborhood watch on steroids descending on her home to save the day.

"What the hell is going on, Nena? You good?" Keigel asked. Gone was the jokester, his easygoing smile that wiped away any disconcertion. He looked beyond her as if someone were there holding a gun to her head.

Half-right. And not anymore.

Nena pulled the door to her back to shield Bridget's body, though she didn't think they could see Bridget. She didn't want Keigel's men to catch a glimpse. To remember anything of the dead White lady if anyone inquired. Nena didn't know if Bridget had told anyone where she was or what she was going to do. Bridget should have been long gone, hiding in a country that didn't have extradition laws for her past crimes. But Bridget just couldn't let Nena live with the power to destroy her.

"I'm okay." Nena's eyes went toward Keigel's waiting crew.

He looked down where her arm was held to her side. He saw the wetness seeping through her white shirt.

"Not okay," he corrected, his eyes going to her side. Without speaking, they had an entire conversation. "You alone?"

"Not quite." Her look was pointed.

Keigel thought a minute. She wouldn't give that answer if whoever was in there had a gun to her head. Still skeptical, he called out behind him to the crew he'd led for nearly seven years. His eyes didn't leave her face.

"We're good."

Two on the lawn, on either side of the walkway. She thought about her grass, didn't like that. Another at the opening of her front gate. Likely another two around back in case they needed to get in. The gunshots had put them on high alert, and Keigel's people weren't too keen on leaving their leader and his mysterious neighbor friend without some kind of explanation. Plus, they'd never been this close to her home in all the years she'd owned, renovated, and lived at the house. Now they were up close and personal and eager to get in on the action. And crack the Rubik's Cube woman.

"Keig," Keigel's second, Carlos, spoke up. "For real, man?"

"Yeah. She good. Target practice."

"In the backyard," Nena said helpfully, as if that add-in would help sell the lie that, from the looks on their faces, they were not buying.

Carlos was on the circuit to becoming a professional lightweight boxer. He trained at the new boxing gym that Keigel had purchased a couple of months back . . . working his way to becoming legit and all, Keigel would say with a smile that said he'd never be legit . . . at least not in the eyes of the long arm of the law.

"Boss," Carlos said, approaching. "Three shots at the same exact time?"

Twisting so her bloody side wouldn't show, Nena raised her hands— hoping Carlos wouldn't notice the blood on her palms—making gun signs and shooting them at the same time as if she were some gunslinger on a western.

She mouthed, "Pow."

Carlos blinked at her incredulously. Good thing she didn't blow the imaginary smoke. That might have been too much.

Carlos put a hand on a hip like some father who'd had enough of these two. "What if the police come calling? Or some nosy-ass neighbor?"

Keigel said, "All good, 'Los. She'll tell them it was—"

"Target practice." She was being helpful again.

"Target practice," he repeated. "I'll catch you back at the spot. But keep an ear out."

Carlos still didn't want to leave, but he followed orders. With one last disapproving look, he motioned to the other two to head out. He put two fingers to his mouth and whistled their signal to the two watch-outs in the back, or wherever they were.

"Many thanks," Nena called after them with an appreciative nod. She meant it but was glad to see the backs of them.

When his five were beyond her gates and at the next house, making their way back to his, Keigel turned back to Nena.

"Now what the hell mess did you get yourself into this time, Nena?"

Nena looked up at him, tapping the bottom of the door with her back heel. It swung open to reveal burgundy heels and a little stretch of leg on the floor.

"Oh shit."

Nena looked back at Bridget's body, unaffected, then back at Keigel, who was shooting nervous looks up and down the street.

He leaned in, whispering, "You got a dead White lady in your house. Dead!"

Nena nodded thoughtfully.

"What. The fuck?" asked Keigel, his nostrils flared, all his cool deserting him. His body twitched, and the men who'd accompanied him watched from Keigel's porch, their discomfort growing because they couldn't tell what was going on.

"What the fuck indeed," Nena agreed affably.

Keigel put his hands out in a silent question that asked what was going on.

Time ticked, and each moment wasted was one where they could be discovered, and taking care of Bridget would prove more difficult.

Nena asked, "Up for a drive?"

69

"How the hell did you find this place?" Keigel asked, looking up and around the windshield as he followed Nena's careful directions deep into the Florida Everglades. "I mean, I'm Florida born and raised and ain't been in some shit like this."

Nena wasn't feeling all Keigel's energy, couldn't until their job was done.

"Real talk, are we about to be eaten or some shit? Because I need to know."

"If you're about to be eaten?"

Keigel took his eyes from the road, glaring at her in the dark. "Hell the fuck YES!"

They'd been driving for nearly two hours in a car secured from somewhere Nena didn't know. For a change, she'd allowed Keigel to handle all the logistics for their midnight adventure.

The only thing she'd supplied was the body and the location where they'd dump it. Nena didn't want to call on Network. Word would get to Noble, and even though Bridget's death was in self-defense, Nena didn't need anything jeopardizing her family or the Tribe.

Carlos's services ended up being needed after all. He had only been given instructions to take the Mercedes coupe Bridget had parked nearby to people he knew who ran a shop where they could strip the car clean, sell the parts, and make whatever was left disappear. All that was done after Nena and Keigel carefully wiped down the car and removed any materials identifying Bianca Collins, the alias Bridget had been traveling under.

Nena instructed Keigel to pull into the little space among the overgrown bushes in one of her few previously selected spots in the wild that she used to get rid of evidence of her wet work, though she hadn't used any of her locations in a long time. Nena's last visit had been several months ago, when she'd dumped Trek's body after he threatened Keigel and his plans to partner with neighboring local gangs to form a business co-op. It was the one time Nena had inserted herself into Keigel's business, something she was careful not to step a toe into until that night. Sometimes things just had to be done, obstacles removed. Kind of like the business with Bridget at that moment.

"You know Black people don't come out here. There are things that eat humans all over." If Keigel was attempting to whisper, he was doing a poor job of it.

"That is the point."

He rounded the back of the strange car, where she tried masking the grimace of pain from her wounded side.

He touched her shoulder. "Hey," he said softly, "why don't you hang back. Rest. I got this. I'll take it out."

Out was into the swamp, where Bridget would likely never be found again. And if she were, there would be much less of her after she had served as a meal for the local wildlife. They heard a splash ahead of them and a low shuffle to the side.

"I'm fine." Nena paused to listen, then reached in to pull at the bottom half of the black-plastic-wrapped cargo. Keigel did the same with the top. "Let's be quick."

"You don't gotta tell me twice." Keigel's voice cracked a bit. Nena had grown up with wildlife around her. Though N'nkakuwe had been nestled deep in the woods of Aburi Mountain, it didn't mean she wanted to have a reckoning with anything out here.

Together Nena and Keigel lugged the body to the waterline, as close as they cared to get. Gators were notorious for hanging around the edge. Snakes. And maybe even a Florida panther. Yes, the Everglades even had some of those. Keigel didn't want to meet them either.

"If I wanted to go on safari, I would have asked when we were in Ghana," he grumbled. "On three."

Third count, they lobbed Bridget's body into the water. Nena had torn the bag a little so the water would get in and nature would get to business faster . . . by means of either animals or the weather. They were closing the trunk when they heard one splash. Then another.

Then the night, which had been eerily silent, too silent, when they were traipsing around in the tall, reedy grass with deadweight between them, came alive with churning water and snapping teeth.

Keigel turned the car on and shifted to reverse, slowly pulling them out of the cove. "I don't ever need to come here again," he said, shaking his head. "I'm good." He turned the wheel. Shifted to drive. Pulled off along the thick, bumpy grass.

Nena didn't answer. She was staring intently into the side mirror at the blackness that swallowed the space they left behind them. There wasn't a star in the sky to light their path. Nena turned away from it and settled in her seat. For the first time in a long while, she allowed herself to relax, her body melding into the plush seat. She closed her eyes, feeling the heavy blanket of sleep overcoming her.

One eye slid open, and she sneaked a peek at her partner in crime. Again, Keigel had shown how down for her he was. Every time she'd needed him, without fail. Without question. He'd taken a bullet for her. And now he had a body dump added to the list of ways he had had Nena's back. The first day they'd met, Keigel had said, "I ain't no Superman, understand? You come across trouble here, I can't save you."

But he had done just that back in Ghana. Took a bullet meant for her. And he was about to do it again now. Keigel indeed was Nena's Superman.

Nena no longer had to keep her guard up when she was with him. Keigel was her little brother, and because of that trust they'd built in life and now in death, Nena could close her eyes again and sleep for real.

Because Bridget was gone forever now, with no more comebacks. They all were.

Nena whispered, "Au revoir . . . chérie."

She didn't wake again until they pulled up into her driveway and into her garage, where Keigel gleefully informed Nena that she snored.

"Little miss perfect assassin sounds like a damn Hoover with hair clogging the rotors and a car with a choked ignition," Keigel teased Nena later, to her horror. "With a drowning cat."

Nena was finally at peace, with her past demons dead and buried, ready to take on new challenges and a fresh start, whatever came next for her.

Beginning with the contents of Witt's letter.

EPILOGUE

Nena conducted surveillance on the garden-style apartment for a couple of days before she decided to make her move. She'd watched his routine. Followed him to the Kroger grocery store. Observed how he bought two boxes of Frosted Flakes and other junk food dotted with the occasional fruit and vegetable. He lived alone but had a lady or two. He worked late and often.

Briefly, she wondered why he'd chosen the quaint South Carolina city of Columbia when he could live in a bigger city. But then how different was she, living in a modest neighborhood when she could be living in places much bigger. She didn't need all that. And she guessed he didn't either.

The night she broke into his home, she was surprised and not a little dismayed that his security wasn't as it should be. The city might be small, but he should know better, she thought. A chain door and low-level turn lock weren't nearly enough.

Nena let herself in, her eyes sweeping the neat living room and adjusting to the light. She listened for noise, if he'd somehow heard her. There was nothing.

She moved in the dark, slipping her gun from its holster. It was good to stay ready, though she hoped it wouldn't come to this. His bedroom door was closed. She put her ear to it, listening for sound. His light had gone off a while ago, and Nena waited an additional hour to ensure he was in such a deep sleep he wouldn't hear her coming.

She'd thought long and hard about how best to approach him. Wondered if this was the right way. How her visit would be received. What she would say and what would happen as a result. Turns out it didn't matter. Because Nena had finally opened the crumpled letter that she'd nestled between her father's cologne and mother's night cream, and she had read the contents and Witt's final request.

I ask that you find my son.

She had known before she'd figured out a plan that she would do just as Witt asked. And when she read further, going over the name once, twice, three times, Nena had paused, wondering how in the world she would be able to pull this mission off. She had even mentioned it to Keigel, giving him the end to this particular story.

"Are you sure?" Keigel wasn't sold on the idea. "If you tell him, it changes everything. You'll have so many questions to answer."

As she should. Keigel was the only person who knew she was here and what she was doing. She couldn't tell her father about Witt's son. She didn't know what that would mean for him, not yet. She didn't know what that would mean for Noble either. Or, most of all, for her.

She opened the bedroom door. She'd been in the apartment earlier, when he was out, tested the door to see if it squeaked. It didn't.

She slipped inside, the fan whipping overhead masking any noise she might have made to alert him. She stood in her spot, listening to his deep breathing. Watching the lumpy form of him as he lay on his side, beneath the sheets of his bed, his back turned to her. He was so trusting of his space. Nena wondered what that felt like. To sleep so freely, to not be on constant high alert. Nena was amazed by it.

Nena walked softly to the chair at his desk and sat in it. She waited to see if he'd sense he was no longer alone. He did not. Was that stupid or a man's privilege to always feel he was safe and sound wherever he thought to lay his head?

She couldn't wait all night. She'd have to prompt him. Announce her presence and get this party—or funeral—started and tell him about her.

I ask that you find my son.

Nena readjusted herself in the chair, the gun resting loosely against her knee, pointed to the floor. This time he heard her.

The once prone form shot up and in a graceful fluidity that impressed how very much like his father this man was, he leveled his gun at her. But he did not shoot. No, he knew better than to shoot before assessing the threat first. Slowly, she placed her gun on the floor beside her foot, covered in black-and-white Converse All Star high-tops.

She raised her hands in the air in a halfhearted gesture, indicating she meant no harm.

His blinks came slow and delayed at first as they wiped the sleep away, like they were trying to play catch-up to his brain. He focused on her form in the dark, staring, disbelieving that someone, anyone, had made it into his home, into his room, without his invitation.

Find my son.

He spoke in a voice choked with sleep, surprise, and not a little bit of curiosity. "Nena, what are you doing in my room?"

She considered him, truly seeing for the first time how very much like Witt he looked. How some of his mannerisms were like her mentor's. She wondered what he'd say when he realized he'd worked side by side with his father for over a year, had trained under and worked with him for three years prior.

He wouldn't be pleased. Seemed Witt had major family issues, just as she had. She and his son were more alike than she had ever thought. She watched his gun lower until it rested on the rumpled covers. His finger still rested on the trigger as he stayed on alert due to this unannounced night visit.

I ask that you find my son.

"Hello, Billy," Nena said.

She'd found him.

She expelled all the breath in her body as she thought about what she'd say next. How'd she explain why she was there. She'd take whatever decision he made. To kill her. To listen. To continue to work alongside her. To leave. Whatever it was, she'd accept it.

This was the most terrifying thing Nena had ever had to do.

Billy's expression prompted her to get on with it. "Sooo, what are you doing here?" he asked. "And in the middle of the night." He let out a shaky laugh. "Kinda weird, don't you think?"

All of this was weird. Weird, for her, happened when she opened Witt's letter.

And tell him—

It was now or never. Nena felt her body heat rising. For the first time, her nerves clashed with her objective, and she wanted to run. She stood on the precipice. Her world had once been light, had gone dark, and then she had found the Knights. And in the world of Knight, Nena had found light once again. With her family. With the Baxters. With Keigel. With herself.

—about me.

She released another breath to ground herself.

"I am here to tell you about your father, Witt." She watched the cloud of confusion and disbelief descend on Billy's head. She held up a hand, silencing him. If she didn't get it out now, she'd lose her courage, and she'd fail Witt.

She started over.

"I'm here to tell you about your father, Witt . . . and why I had to kill him."

ACKNOWLEDGMENTS

Writing acknowledgments is hard. There are many people who have been on this ride with me, helping me, giving me grace, counseling me while I wrote the Nena Knight trilogy. If I miss your name here, charge my head, not my heart. I will learn (like the smarter writers) to keep a list as I go so that I won't forget when it comes time to fill up this page.

For anyone who's played a part in the creation of this book with suggestions, inspiration, or feedback; offered a shoulder to cry on; or provided some much-needed laughs and distraction, I appreciate you.

Melissa Edwards, my fabulous agent at Stonesong Press, is a wonderful person and friend. You are everything a person and client wants in their life. I am lucky to have you in mine.

Megha Parekh, my editor, has remained a huge support to me and believed in my storytelling from the beginning. You're always willing to jump on a call and talk things through, and I really appreciate you for that. The book covers you all love so much? That's Megha!

We've all heard the saying about how it takes a village. Well, that proverb definitely extends to publishing books and cultivating authors. Thomas & Mercer has been the village that rallied around me and my books. Thank you for your professionalism, your great eye, your kind words, your suggestions, and your encouragement to put out books about people who look like me doing remarkable things.

My husband, kids, mom, and mother- and father-in-law hopefully all know how much I love and cherish them. Thank you for the sacrifices you make and for lifting me up whenever the self-doubt rears its ugly head. You all inspire me and push me to keep going.

My family by birth and by marriage are the greatest people in the world, hands down. You make my heart full. I couldn't have asked for a better family!

My friends understood the endless writing hours and gave me grace. You were always there to say when I needed to stop watching all my streaming channels and get to writing. When you text those reminders, I get annoyed . . . but when the manuscript is finally finished, my appreciation for how you stayed on me is limitless.

The community of writers I have met and interact with is phenomenal. I am blessed to have made writer friends who fight through these writing trenches with me and understand the absolute struggle it is to create worlds and characters the readers can dive into. I don't know where I would be without your support and your teachings. I am in awe of all of you and am your forever fan. I feel like I've said this to you before, and if I have, then you know it's the truth!

And to the dedicated readers and the booksellers, libraries, reviewers, podcasters, and outlets who have boosted the series. Thank you for welcoming Nena Knight and her story into your hearts and giving her your time. Your time is one of the most important things you can give and so, that you gave yours to me and my books means the world. Thank you for the emails and messages on social and for singing Nena's praises. This won't be the last we hear of Nena and all the other characters we've come to love. Their stories will continue, if not on the page, then in our imaginations.

Meda w'ase.

Thank you.

ABOUT THE AUTHOR

Photo © 2021 Rodney Williams, Creative Images Photography

Yasmin Angoe is the author of *Her Name Is Knight* and a first-generation Ghanaian American currently residing in South Carolina with her family. She's served in education for nearly twenty years and works as a developmental editor. Yasmin received the 2020 Eleanor Taylor Bland Crime Fiction Writers of Color Award from Sisters in Crime and is a member of numerous crime, mystery, and thriller organizations like Sisters in Crime, Crime Writers of Color, and International Thriller Writers. You can find her at www.yasminangoe.com, on Twitter at @yasawriter, and on Instagram at @author_yas.